Sweet Raptor Jesus!

CRYSTAL WHISPERER

SPOTLESS SERIES, BOOK 3

CAMILLA MONK

This is a work of fiction.

Names, characters, organizations, places, events, and incidents are either products of the author's imagination or are used fictitiously.

Text copyright © 2016 Camilla Monk

All rights reserved.

No part of this book may be reproduced, or stored in a retrieval system, or transmitted in any form or by any means, electronic, mechanical, photocopying, recording, or otherwise, without express written permission of the publisher.

Published by Camilla Monk AKA "Yaypub"

Cover design by Camilla Monk

ISBN: 9781519064158

*This book is dedicated to Benoît and my dear readers,
who believed in me when I no longer could.*

TABLE OF CONTENTS

Local is Lekker 1

The Biltong 10

The Batcave 19

Viva Polo...................................... 33

The Legend 43

The Mother City 51

Staatssicherheit 70

Her 75

A Battle of Wills.......................... 83

Dead Ball......................................94

The Lady-Killer 101

The Golden Mountain............. 110

The Grain Collectors 117

L'Autre.. 124

GTA.. 131

Relationships 101 142

The Cannoli 149

The Mountain Dew................. 160

The Ritual 167

The Emperor's Wife 171

Jus in Bello................................. 176

The Invitation 189

The Bait 197

The Little Princess................... 207

Bone-Deep 217

The Osmeterium....................226

The Whitlow 231

Declaration of War 240

Da Boss......................................248

The Magic Flutes....................255

The Plan 261

The Elevator 266

The Life Aquatic 274

Parental Guidance 284

Der Hölle Rache 291

The Good Suit.......................... 301

Acknowledgements................ 313

About the Author 315

AUTHOR'S NOTE:

A handful of legitimate quotes appear to have found their way among otherwise fictional ones. I apologize for this; we're working around the clock to catch them.

ONE
LOCAL IS LEKKER

I'll tell you what, if this was a romantic suspense, I'd throw my tablet through the window and ask for a refund.

The plot goes like this: Island Chaptal is a beautiful computer engineer living in New York, and she's been waiting all her life for Mr. Right, reading romance books and saving herself for his expert touch—that's twenty-five years, six months, and twenty-eight days of saving, for anyone who cares. One night, she comes home to find a dangerous and sexy professional killer searching her apartment: a mysterious man with a dark past, known by the code name March. Also, he does the dishes and he knows how to change a vacuum cleaner bag, because it turns out he's a bit of a neat freak.

I won't go into all the details, but tons of exciting adventures ensue. Island learns her mom was in fact a spy and her biological father a supervillain; March takes her on a chase for a long-stolen diamond; she falls in love with him in Paris; he dumps her in Tokyo, comes back a reformed man a few months later, and they make up. But danger always lurks; she kind of becomes a spy too, and they embark on another perilous investigation in Europe, where they fight off killer platypuses and a shady CIA agent who seduces Island—love triangles always sell.

And, of course, in the end, March takes her to his tiny cubicle house facing the Atlantic Ocean in Cape Saint Francis—he's actually OCD *and* South African—where he makes passionate love to her until dawn.

Or not.

Because his condoms are expired, so they have to wait until the following morning for him to go buy some in town. And once there, they pass a surf shop, and he says "We have great weather today. Would you like me to teach you surfing after lunch?" Of course, she doesn't want to sound pathetic, so instead of saying, "I'm a twenty-five-year-old virgin. Surfing is not what's missing in my life right now," she says, "Sure. Cool."

Like I said, I'd slam that book with a one-star rating and return it!

Except Jeff Bezos won't let you return your own life. So here I was, stuck at third base, body still tingling from head to toe at the memory of a delicious, torturous night spent curled against the silkiest chest hair in the universe. March had been tender and thorough in his exploration of unmentionable places, which were now desperate to receive the *coup de grâce*. And—forgive me, Raptor Jesus—I had touched *Area 51*! Not for long though, because there's only so much clumsy teasing a man can take when he's been single for four years. Still, how incredibly torrid and forbidden is that?

"Island. *Island.* Focus! Watch your feet, or you'll—"

Slip and fall from the board again.

March caught me at the same time that I hit the water with a splash. I blinked the salt away from my eyes, took a big gulp of air, and looked up at him. Water dripped from his short chestnut hair, and I could read an equal measure of concern and amusement in my favorite dark-blue eyes. His lips curved, allowing a rare grin to light up the rest of his face.

I loved that. March was nothing but control and order, polished exterior and goddamn wrinkle-free shirts, but I was in fact drawn by his asperities—by the faint crow's feet betraying that he had recently turned thirty-three, the two dimples creasing his cheeks when he smiled, or even the slightest bump on his aquiline nose. I had never really paid attention before, but the shimmering droplets running down his face outlined it. I gathered that said nose must have been broken at some point over the course of his career. I guess you don't spend fifteen years killing people without earning more than a few scrapes of your own.

After several seconds of studying the aforementioned bump, I realized I was secured in a rather awkward position. My legs still rested on the surfboard, while in the water, his arms held the rest of me firmly against his chest. I gripped his hands, shaking off a delicious flashback of those same knuckles grazing my stomach a few hours prior.

"I'm good. I think we hit a particularly vicious roll!" I said with a laugh.

I didn't miss the beat of silence as March took in our surroundings: The quiet, sapphire-blue sea, the five-inch "rolls" lapping at his waist, and the long stretch of sand and rocks a few yards away from us, beyond which I could make out his little brick house standing on a patch of grass. On the shore, a couple of otters lay sprawled, warming their asses under the afternoon sun and observing my surfing efforts with absolute disdain.

"Yes. The sea is rough today," he conceded.

I freed myself from his embrace to readjust the black rash guard and bikini bottoms I had bought in Saint Francis Bay this morning. "But we've made some good progress. I'm really starting to feel that my body is centered on the board like you said."

"Absolutely. Your balance is remarkable, biscuit."

Modern feminism would have dictated that I took offense at this abject bout of patronizing flattery and the underlying assumption that I would never accomplish much on a surfboard. But, well, he had combed back damp locks from my forehead as he said so, and I found it difficult to resist him when he called me biscuit. I gave him a pass.

He jerked his head in the direction of the cubicle house. "How about we take a break from surfing?"

I willed my gaze away from the only real-life six-pack I had ever seen up close and the tempting line of wet hair trailing all the way down to the waistband of his swimming shorts. "That could be nice."

Back in New York, I shared a little apartment with Joy, my best friend since she had rescued me from a locked bathroom stall in college. As neither of us really cared about housekeeping, I had seen my fair share of underwear forgotten between the couch cushions or hair in the tub. Yet it had never struck me how intimate it was to share a house with someone until now.

Here, in March's narrow bathroom, with the steam from our respective showers hanging in the air, I couldn't quite shake that odd sense of intrusion. Maybe because the towel wrapped around my body was his, as were the toothbrush and the old-fashioned safety razor and shaving brush hanging from a chromed stand. I gingerly poked the soap resting in his shaving bowl. I had never seen one of those; not even my dad used that. I rinsed the foam from my finger, suddenly feeling a little guilty at the sight of the telltale fingerprint on the once-smooth surface.

In a bid to ease my remorse, I grabbed a smaller towel I had used to dry my hair earlier and carefully dabbed at the droplets running down the walls of the shower stall. March hadn't asked, but I had caught him doing it earlier, and I was pretty sure it'd upset him if I left drops—and therefore potentially *lime*—in his bathroom. Satisfied with my efforts, I folded the towel and hung it back on its chrome rack with great care before I slipped into one of my favorite hoodies and a pair of yoga pants. I quickly checked my gap teeth in the mirror for any trace of lunch's spinach, and combed my fingers through the tangle of auburn locks framing my face. No point in working too hard on that bob of mine: by the time it was dry, I'd be back to looking like Pepé the King Prawn . . .

I opened the bathroom door to find March standing on the other side, in the bedroom, wearing his usual "uniform": a pair of dark jeans and a perfectly pressed white shirt—I had discovered he ordered those from a London tailor boasting to possess some sort of super advanced "crease-free technology." Scanning him all the way down, I couldn't stop the quirk of my lips when I noted the way he had rolled his sleeves in flat, even folds and put on a pair of hotel slippers, grandpa-style. Bristol Paris: a little souvenir from our adventures, I figured.

It was the flashy chamois cloth in his hand—or more exactly the "Chamwow," according to the label printed on the yellow fabric—that betrayed the reason he had been waiting for me to come out.

I motioned to the shower stall with a prideful grin. "Already took care of it. Wiped everything."

"You didn't have to," he said, a hint of embarrassment in his voice. His gaze flitted to my attire and lit up with a devilish glint. "Lovely tail, by the way."

I didn't blush; I held my head up high. I regarded that gray raccoon hoodie and the furry tail dangling from its back as one of the most essential pieces of my garde-robe, but not everyone understood the proper etiquette to follow when dealing with high fashion. My eyes slanted in warning. "Do *not* pull the tail."

March raised his palms in a pacifying gesture. "I would never."

He didn't. Well, not until we were back in his living room, and my guard was down. As I went to check a mysterious white box sitting on his kitchenette's countertop, a sharp tug stopped me. I whirled around to face him.

"We need *trust* and *respect* in this relationship," I muttered, readjusting my tail.

"We do," March agreed. "Why don't you check your surprise while I make us some tea?"

My attention shifted back to what looked in fact like a cake box. "You have a surprise for me?"

He nodded while filling a kettle. It was all I needed to get my greedy hands on that tempting box. I made quick work of the flashy green plastic ribbon and pristine cardboard. Swirls of cream appeared. And chocolate. Things were looking up. Further examination of the cake made me hesitate though.

I frowned at the mixture of milk chocolate chips and unidentified transparent green shards scattered all over the fluffy cream. "Is that . . . some sort of crushed-glass and chocolate topping?"

March set two cups on the table, into which he poured a fragrant and carmine-colored tea. His nostrils flared in mild outrage. "It's Peppermint Crisp! It's a Peppermint Crisp tart."

Oh. I had almost forgotten about those. A popular South African delicacy made of layers of caramel-flavored whipped cream, mixed with crushed industrial mint chocolate, on top of Tennis coconut biscuits. I remembered having tasted it once, at the age of fifteen, back when my mom and I had been staying in Pretoria. It speaks of her parenting skills that, although she had been there to steal a two-billion-dollar diamond—aptly named the Ghost Cullinan—she took the time to try her hand at a local recipe for me. The result had been disastrous, nothing like the perfectly round and masterfully decorated confection March had bought. Yet the memory of my mother standing in the ruins of our kitchen and splattering cream all over a pile of crushed biscuits was a sweet one.

I watched March as he cut two equal slices and placed them on our respective plates with near reverence. All those years ago, sitting on a barstool and tasting my mother's Peppermint Crisp Smudge, I'd had no idea that he was out there, somewhere, and that I would meet him for the first time a few months later. No idea that my mom would be shot at the wheel of her car in Tokyo and that March would be the one to save my life.

The first bite was sweet, minty, and a little too rich. March was looking at me expectantly, no doubt waiting for a compliment. I thought of Proust ranting about his madeleine. I had none of the guy's talent—or single-mindedness, for that matter—and I didn't know how to tell March how I felt. How to tell him that it wasn't that the

Peppermint Crisp tart tasted bad or anything, but there was an ache in my chest, and I was filled by too many memories, too many emotions I wasn't sure I could name.

I looked down at the creamy mess in my plate and dropped my spoon.

March walked around the table to check on me. "Is it that bad?"

"No. It tastes great. It's just . . . I was thinking about stuff. Sorry."

The way his brow creased told me he wasn't convinced, but he didn't press the matter, choosing to pull me to him instead. Those were the times I was glad that he had a foot on me and my five feet three inches: there's no solace like that which comes from being tucked under someone else's chin and held tight.

The slow glide of his hand in my hair almost made me purr. "Peppermint Crisp is excellent for you." I squeezed him harder as he went on, his voice a little uncertain. "It's the eighth South African food group, according to the department of health. Should represent five percent of your daily caloric intake."

"You're lying," I said with a reluctant smile.

"No, I'm not. Müstlé lobbied hard for that. The police never found the health deputy minister's body."

I pulled away to look up at him. "Are you *serious*?"

"Absolutely. Peppermint Crisp *is* a very serious business here."

Catching the look of scandal on my face, he shrugged. "I had nothing to do with it. Now finish your five percent."

I complied with a chuckle, and he did the same before he rinsed our plates and spoons three times, placed them in the dishwasher, and meticulously wiped the sink clean afterward.

Once he was done, he combed back a curl that would never stay in place behind my ear. "You know," he began, "when something troubles you, you can tell me." He paused, his gaze settling on a fascinating point somewhere near my shoulder. "I won't always know what to say, but—"

"Being here reminds me of my mother. Not in a bad way, but in a way that puts everything in perspective, like it was all a puzzle from the start, and we're pieces, and no matter how long we waited on the table, we would have ended in the puzzle anyway; we just didn't know it." I took a breath and soldiered on before he could interrupt. "Also, I suck at surfing, and I'm thinking about how intimate it is to be in your place, and maybe that's why you're postponing . . . what it is that you're postponing. Because maybe it's awkward for you too, or maybe I sent the wrong signals—"

My rant was silenced by the brush of his lips against my neck. "What am I postponing, biscuit?"

What, indeed? I struggled to collect my thoughts and gave up with a gasp when the light kisses raining on my throat turned to a gentle sucking. A single nip caused my knees to wobble, and, yup, he was playing with my tail again. I felt his voice more than I heard it, a hoarse vibration against my skin. "So, tell me, what is it that I'm *postponing?*"

I gripped his shirt while he soothed the area he had just bit with slow, deliberate licks. "I don't know. I . . ."

His hands found their way under my hoodie, grazing my waist. "You seem distracted."

I was. Mostly because the trail of goose bumps his fingertips left in their wake felt like fireworks. His touch set me on autopilot; I started unbuttoning his shirt, slowly working my way down. When my fingers met hot skin and soft hair, felt the muscles twitch under my touch, I thought of those romance books about starchy men getting unstarched and unleashing their irresistible passion on the heroine until she lay limp on the sheets like overcooked chard. So be it. I was ready for March to turn me into a sizzling casserole. Plus, Peppermint Crisp was the perfect topping for this particular recipe: who wouldn't want a man who tasted of mint and chocolate?

I did register the faint buzz in his pocket, but I knew that trick already, and wouldn't let a phone call stand in the way of my first time. I unzipped my hoodie, barely allowing our lips to part. "Don't take it." I sighed. "Turn the damn phone off."

By then, March's starch had started to seriously peel off: to my amazement, he took out his phone and shut it down at the same time that he guided me toward his bedroom. I performed a mental fist pump.

Until my own phone started to ring.

Public service announcement: *Silence* your phone when you plan on getting your chard on all night long. Also, choose your ringtone better than I did. I doubt I'll ever forget March's face. The way he was blinking down at me, his shirt half unbuttoned and pants open to reveal visibly strained boxer briefs. And there I stood, in my bra, with my phone blaring the Minions' "Copacabana" cover from somewhere in the bedroom—yes, the one where they sing "bella banana" instead. My life is a tragedy.

He cleared his throat. "Would you like to take it?"

"No. *Nononono!*"

As I said this, March glanced down at his watch. There too, a single buzz announced a new message. *Harassment tactic, huh?* I could think of only one person who would know I was here with March and might need to reach him badly enough to try my phone.

"Phyllis?" I ventured.

I liked March's PA; I really did. But at the moment I wished for her to find raisins instead of chocolate chips in her cookies. Every day. For the rest of her life.

March confirmed my suspicions with a nod, and the black chronograph's glass went dark, turning into a small LCD screen—I needed to find out where he had bought that toy. I didn't get a good look at the words flashing on the screen, but he did. With an expression of utter apology, he moved away from me to open his laptop, which sat on a small desk near his bed.

I watched him connect to a news website and open the live streaming. We both stood still, tight lipped, as the anchors started reporting breaking news of what they called "the worst terrorist attack targeting the United States since 9/11": the bombing of a jumbo jet over Long Island. The aircraft had disintegrated before even touching the ground, killing all 613 passengers and crew.

If that background video of people breaking into tears in front of the cameras hadn't ruined the mood already, seeing the face of my biological father appear on the screen did.

TWO
THE BILTONG

"Let her go, Bin Salhad!"
"Ha ha! Do you think I'm afraid of a decorated SEAL? Destiny is mine!"

—Natasha Onyx, *Muscled Passion of the SEAL #1: Desert Heat*

—Hi, I'm Karen Mills, and you're watching ABN Live News. I'm here with Professor Emmett Stevens, director of the National Center for Terrorism Studies, and author of seven best-selling books on national security. So, Emmett, the first thing our viewers really want to know is: Who is Dries Kovius, the man suspected of having engineered the bombing of flight DL504?

—Good question, Karen, and the answer is that we don't know much at this point. What strikes me is how quickly his name filtered out after the crash was announced: we can assume he's been under surveillance for a long time.

—Wouldn't that mean a spectacular failure of our homeland-security efforts?

—I can't be the judge of that. But profiles like his . . . they're the toughest to assess, because he's been off the grid for almost thirty years. I honestly believe no one could have predicted what happened this morning.

—I have to ask. Are we looking at the new Osama Bin Laden?

—Hard to tell. To me, he sounds more like a professional anarchist, a man who'd embrace others' causes for the sake of creating destabilization.

—What do we know about him, about his life?

—Well, according to the FBI, he's fifty-two years old, born in Johannesburg. Our South African colleagues confirm the existence of a death certificate with his name, dated from January 1986.

—He was thought to have been killed in a helicopter crash, right?

—Yes, with his elder brother. It's very likely that he used his brother's death to stage his own disappearance. I think you're right to compare him to Bin Laden, Karen, in the sense that . . . here, we have the owner of an industrial group, someone wealthy, someone who grew up on the lucky side of the apartheid. And this man, he, um, went rogue, rebelled against the system that engendered him, but also used that system.

—But how do you go from selling beef sticks to bombing a plane and killing six hundred innocents?

—That's what I mean when I say he used the system. This is a man who spiraled into some kind of nihilistic, ultra-violent ideology, who faked his own death so he could train in Afghanistan in the eighties. But he needed funds just like anyone else, and that's why he invested in legit businesses and siphoned cash from them. Kovius built his empire of death on beef sticks.

—And ostrich sticks.

—Yes, and ostrich sticks, Karen.

—But why strike now? Why this particular flight?

—There's a combination of factors. First, this was a Venice–New York flight, operated by Delta Air Lines, and the majority of the victims were American citizens. Then we have the plane itself. The AirBW 850 is largely perceived as a symbol of American industrial superiority. We're talking about the largest commercial aircraft ever built and the first to feature a full-length sky roof. Additionally, as you know, contact was lost around 11:00 a.m., above the Hampton Bays—

—On US soil. So, Emmett, you agree that this is clearly an attack against

US interests?

—*Obviously, but I think Kovius is just an instrument here. There's a video recording, which I'm certain you've seen . . .*

—*Taken by security cameras in Venice Airport? Our teams are making some verifications as we speak. I know our viewers expect nothing but the entire truth from ABN, and we're working nonstop to authenticate this footage and share it with you. So stay tuned, we'll be back shortly for this special report on the bombing of flight DL504.*

I sat still on March's bed for a good minute after he had paused the live streaming. On the screen, a black-and-white picture of Dries stared at us. It must have been taken a decade ago, at a time when he was still March's mentor. He looked younger, with the same harsh yet elegant features. No trace of gray in his dark hair and, even back then, that razor-sharp gaze under somewhat bushy eyebrows. A million questions raced in my mind. Chief among these: "What the hell?" and "Of all the guys to conceive me with, did my mom really *have to* pick the vice commander of a secret society of South African assassins?"

Technically, Dries wasn't even the man I called dad—never had been. He and I had met for the first time six months prior during the hunt for the Ghost Cullinan. Long story short: when my mother got hired to steal the diamond by a tentacular crime syndicate called the Board, Dries convinced her to screw them and hand it to him instead. Or so he thought. She figured that it'd be unwise to help the Lions develop their business any further and vanished with me and the stone. Dries found us, but my mom was shot by one of his men before he had a chance to get his precious Cullinan back.

Nobody wins; fast roll the credits.

Except those Board guys—and especially their boss, a nice lady people called the Queen—never quite got over the loss. They kept looking for the next decade, until one day, at last, they found a single bread crumb. That led straight to me. The Queen, who was getting a little impatient, sent an OCD hitman to my apartment and, well, you know the rest: March and I followed the trail of bread crumbs all the way to the Cullinan . . . and Dries. It didn't go well, and there wasn't much left of Dries's Tokyo penthouse after March was done reuniting with his master. Yet, uncharacteristically, Dries initiated a reconciliation of sorts after losing the diamond and two dozen henchmen in the process.

But still, we weren't what I would call close.

I turned to March, who stood with his arms crossed, his shuttered expression betraying nothing of his thoughts.

"How much of it is true?" I asked.

"I have no idea."

"I don't mean the bombing. I mean"—I made an all-encompassing gesture—"everything else. All that stuff about his life."

"The biltong, it's a side business." March sighed. "The rest was more or less accurate, but he didn't go to Afghanistan for training, he—"

"I don't think I want to know what he did there."

"I understand."

"So that's his real name, *Kovius*?" I asked doubtfully.

I read the hesitation in March's eyes. Even after all this time, he couldn't bring himself to betray the man who had picked him from the streets at the age of eighteen, freshly out of juvie, to teach him a "better" way: contract killing. Dries had shattered an empty shell, reshaped it into a man, and given his creature a purpose and a brotherhood. A place in the world.

It had been ten years since March had left the Lions, but he could no more escape that past than he could his own skin: each new recruit received a large scarification on his back, in the shape of a fearsome lion head. I had seen March's own carving, traced its torturously detailed African pattern. I knew the code number it concealed. His pledge of loyalty to Dries was forever etched in his skin. It was an integral part of him.

March's lips moved, and in the twitch of his brow, I guessed what he was going to say. "Yes, that is his name."

A lie.

It wasn't as if we were married or anything; he didn't owe it to me to unveil every last one of Dries's secrets. But it still stung to have those cobalt eyes look straight into mine as he lied. Wasn't he the one who had declared a few days ago that now that we were together, we'd be honest with each other?

Unwilling to start a battle I had no idea how to fight anyway, I let myself fall onto the bed's comforter. "At least that expert didn't mention the Lions. It's good . . . right?"

March sat next to me. "I doubt whoever leaked Dries's name to the press would dare to bring them up. There are specific penalties for that."

I was tempted to ask what, but after a second of reflection, I decided that I didn't want to investigate the matter. We were probably talking about nasty stuff here. A chiming sound drew my attention to March's laptop on the desk; a call window had just opened, and Phyllis's face appeared on-screen. There was no trace of the usual sly cheerfulness in her gray gaze, and her wild red curls had been tamed into a loose bun.

I knew she didn't like Dries much—to be fair, I had once witnessed him call her a bitch and threaten to eviscerate her son—but her tense features softened into friendly understanding when she caught sight of me behind March. Her lips pursed before she spoke in a steady voice. "I tried to gather as much intel as possible, but this doesn't look good."

"Who's leaking his name?" March asked.

"Technically, the FBI, but they're being spoon-fed by—"

"The CIA?"

She gave a faint shrug. "Business as usual, boss."

I moved closer to the desk. "But why are they doing that? That doesn't sound like something Dries would do. Are they trying to frame him or something? I thought the Lions minded their own business, and no one minded theirs."

"Well," Phyllis began, leaning back in a black leather armchair, "based on the intel circulating right now—"

"ABN mentioned a video," March said.

"Yes. Just a second."

She typed something, and another window popped up, this time with some grainy footage playing. I recognized Dries as one of three men wearing sunglasses and standing near a private jet on a sunny airport tarmac. He was chatting with some heavy guy wearing what appeared to be traditional Saudi attire: a long, white tunic and a white-and-red checkered *ghutra*. After a few seconds, Dries handed his interlocutor a small suitcase. The fat guy could be seen opening the case and checking its contents before giving it to a third man. That one wore a dark suit and looked like some kind of assistant. He immediately left after a courtesy bow to the Saudi guy.

"What's in the case?" I asked.

"No idea." Phyllis began. "But what you see here is security footage recorded at Venice Airport ten hours ago. The guy taking a delivery from our favorite bedside rug is the lovely Sheikh Abdul Latif Ibn Muhammad Ibn Bashir, former minister of defense and aviation of the Kingdom of Saudi Arabia. He's in exile after some half-baked coup blew up in his face a few years ago, and he's now a strong supporter of the rise of a global Sunni caliphate that would spread from Turkey to Oman."

"The world belongs to dreamers," March commented somberly.

We watched as, on screen, the third man walked away and into one of the airport's terminals. "So we have no idea what his business with Dries is?"

"Oh, we *do* have an idea." Phyllis winced. "The one carrying the case is Dondedieu Saïd, better known as Abu Saïd. French jihadist. Small fry. He did the typical trip from Spain to Turkey, crossed the border to Syria to join Al-Nusra, until he got a higher calling and became some kind of low-grade errand boy for Bashir."

"Where did he take the case?" March asked.

"Onto flight DL504. He made it through security, embarked with the rest of the passengers, and now he's on both the victims and the suspects list."

I ran my palm across my face. "Dries gave him something to bomb the plane?"

Phyllis rapped impeccable red nails against her glass desk. "Sure looks like it."

I lay sprawled on March's bed in front of my laptop, combing conspiracy forums for unofficial news regarding the bombing. Already, the Internet was working its magic: Dries was a confirmed reptilian shapeshifter, the secret leader of Boko Haram, and many users also recognized him standing among the wreckage of the Silver Bridge on a picture dating back to 1967 . . . Never mind that he'd have been a toddler at the time: mothmen, as one guy clarified, only possess an external human appearance and do not experience any stage of growth.

March, for his part, had been sitting at his desk for almost an hour, hunched over his laptop, gobbling mint after mint from the precious tube that never left him. The video-call window kept popping up as Phyllis forwarded him bits of intel slowly trickling from the deep web. I could tell that, beneath his cool façade, the news had hit him hard too. Possibly even harder than me, because of the tangle of awe, disappointment, gratitude, and resentment weaved into March and Dries's bond.

I looked up from my screen, watching his fingers tap the touchpad every now and then as he went through yet another file about Abu Saïd. I was reminded of those Saturday nights, during my teenage years, when my dad would be working in his study, similarly hunched and silent. I'd creep down the hallway to watch him, waiting for him to be done. I wanted him to drop those damn financial reports, look up, and talk to me. He sometimes did, if I hovered around his desk long enough. He would groan that I was worse than a mosquito, get up from his chair, and take me to dinner at the Russian Tea Room.

In case you're wondering, I'm not talking about Dries here. I know it's gonna sound a bit opportunistic, but when my mom found out she was pregnant with the spawn of a professional killer, she chose to give the news to the nice American banker she had just met instead. And so, Simon Halder, one-week London fling, Olympic-level curmudgeon, became my dad. The kind of dad you spend two weeks in summer with, the one who sends you stuffed bears and postcards for your birthday . . . until my mom was killed, and I went to live with him.

I guess it's true that life's trials reveal a person's true colors: He rolled up his proverbial sleeves and grumbled his way through the challenge of socializing a traumatized fifteen-year-old girl who had been homeschooled and lived in her pajamas for the better part of the past decade.

My mother had let me grow up free yet sheltered. With her, I had never set foot in a classroom, never stayed in the same place for more than three months, and seldom played with kids my age. She'd taken me all around the world, and I'd learned everything school can't teach you: languages, culture, politics . . . My dad had been left to deal with everything else.

He did a fine job, considering that I made it through high school, stopped picking my nose in public around the age of twenty-two, and graduated from Columbia engineering with honors.

Anyway, what worried me the most at the moment was that my father knew about Dries. Back in the day, my mom had left out the fine print about her ex, but he had sort of guessed the guy was bad company. To the best of my knowledge, Dad hadn't made any attempt to reach me yet, but it was only a matter of hours before the hunt began—less, if luck screwed me. I got up from the bed with a sigh and did what I knew best: hover.

March's arm moved to catch me as I padded past him. "Come here."

He pulled me toward him. I relaxed in his hold and wrapped my arms around his neck, resting my cheek against his. I didn't mind the slight rasp of his five-o'clock shadow; it was an integral part of my little bubble of heaven, a warm, cozy place that smelled of soap, laundry, and mints.

I quickly scanned the pictures on the laptop's screen: mug shots of guys I'd never heard about, some satellite images of the wreckage. A tired smile stretched March's lips when I kissed the corner of his mouth. "Have you learned anything new?"

"Yes and no. Details about the crash . . . nothing conclusive. Bashir is off the grid, and the Saudis made it clear they don't want to see his name tied to the attack."

"Is that why the FBI is targeting Dries? Where is he anyway?"

He took my hand and pressed an absent kiss to the back of my knuckles. "No idea. Possibly still in Italy."

"Won't the Lions help him?"

"No. He wouldn't allow it. The brotherhood comes first: he'll let himself become a target if it means protecting the rest of the organization."

"You mean he'll take the fall for them?" I completed, an unpleasant weight in my stomach at the idea.

"Not exactly. I have no doubt that he'll indulge the authorities in a game of cat and mouse to shield the Lions . . . but I'm not sure that this"—he gestured at the screen—"is their work. The Lions are assassins, mercenaries. They cauterize strategic targets, destabilize local governments—"

"But they don't do mass murder."

"No, they are professionals fighting other professionals. I can't see them bombing a commercial flight, not even to eliminate a target."

I let go of him to lean against the desk. "They have bombed planes before though."

From the silence that followed, I gathered that March and I had been entertaining a similar train of thought. Who, in the CIA, could possibly be working so hard to convince the investigators that Dries was responsible for the attack on flight DL504?

Someone who had access to a considerable amount of data on him, of course.

Someone with a visceral, bone-deep hatred for the Lions.

Someone who believed Dries was responsible for shooting down a private jet full of Egyptian officials six years prior, and killing a CIA agent and his wife in the process.

I closed my eyes, fighting licks of pain beneath my temples. "Do you think he's behind this?"

There was neither anger nor smugness in March's voice as he answered, "I have no doubt he is."

THREE
THE BATCAVE

Have you ever tried Yaycupid? If you haven't, don't: that website is such a scam. They spam you with their e-mails and commercials about ordinary people finding love there, until you relent and give it a try. I'll tell you what Yaycupid did for me. Here are my stats:

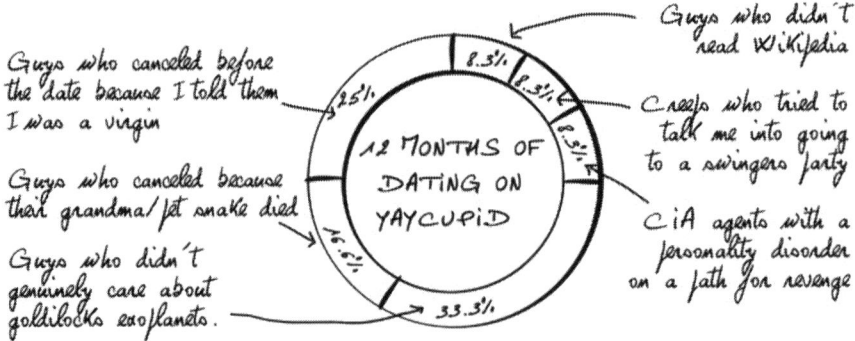

Look at that chart. Look at it well, because that's where Yaycupid got me!

The worst decision among the ones I listed above was a guy with a week's worth of stubble, the softest cinnamon eyes you've ever seen, and who, as it turned out, did *not* work in insurance. I guess every woman has her demons: Joy's was a clingy senior accountant better known under the code name clown dick; mine was a young CIA agent whose parents the Lions had murdered and who had manipulated me in a bid to get revenge on Dries.

Alexander Morgan: "Alex" during the two months I had dated him; "that nice boy from Washington," according to my father; and "Mr. Morgan" for March, who didn't like him much. Maybe because of all of the above. Or because the cinnamon eyes weren't so sweet once I tried to break up with him and the guy turned Mr. Hyde on me, complete with manhandling, psycho threats, and a side of bruises. In any case, Alex had made it clear that "we were only getting started" and that he'd eventually get to Dries one way or another.

Well, fate had just handed Agent Morgan the perfect astral configuration, and he had wasted no time putting it to good use.

March had left the room to go fix himself a second cup of tea. For the first time in three days, I found myself itching to contact Alex, to know whether he was behind Dries's outing and understand what was going on, even a little.

Of course, using my phone would be suicide, whereas a message in his Yaycupid account, sent via a proxy . . . I checked the bedroom's window and caught a flash of fiery gold. The sun was setting behind March, who stood on the patch of lawn surrounding his cubicle house, phone in hand. Probably Phyllis again. I already knew what he'd say if I came out to ask him whether it was a good idea to contact Alex. I gulped down my shame as I grabbed my laptop and opened it.

If this had been about hacking someone else's computer and posting naked pictures of them wearing both a Nazi armband *and* a One Direction cap, I'd have hidden my ass behind seven proxies. This was, however, about messaging Alex. I added an eighth one just for safety. It would be a long while before anyone managed to track my connection to Yaycupid as I gleefully bounced around random servers all around the world.

I was sort of pleased to see his account was still active, even if it meant he might prey on other unsuspecting girls. When it came to write the actual missive though, my fingers hovered over the keyboard in hesitation. Explicit accusations were out of the question, as was pleading Dries's case—not even Bob Loblaw could have taken that one. I went for something curt and easy to decipher but that couldn't be held against me, were I to end up in a pair of orange pj's.

 I've seen the news. Good job, I guess.

There. It'd trigger an instant notification in his e-mail account and right afterward, an alert on his phone—you simply don't escape Yaycupid. An entire minute passed, during which I rapped on the touchpad to refresh until I feared it'd break. Then, in my inbox, a tiny pink label lit up, announcing a new message. I held my breath as I clicked to open it.

 I was about to call you. How's the weather in Vienna?

Excellent, thank you. Especially since my proxy there appeared to be working just fine. Time to skip the pleasantries.

Nice media plan. Should I congratulate you? Or did someone else come up with this? Someone smarter?

His reply came almost instantly.

 Bangui? You move fast! I'm actually glad you wrote, need to tell you stg.

Something cold prickled down my spine. Needed to tell me what? I wasn't sure I wanted to bait him any longer to find out. While I debated with myself whether to log out, a third message appeared.

 Are you in Cape St Francis?

Panic sizzled through me as I rechecked the list of servers my connection had jumped through. Bratislava, Vienna, Ulan Bator, Bangui, Beijing, Lanzhou, Sucre . . . could he possibly know about the cubicle house? I typed my answer with trembling fingers.

 What do you want from me?

 Only to help you. Dries is going down, and I don't want you to be part of the purge.

Wait, wait, wait . . . what *purge*?

 What are you talking about?

His answer took a little longer this time. Was he trying to locate me? At last, a single line blinked on the screen.

 Island. Get away. Now.

Okay, things were getting way too creepy for the amateur spy I prided myself to have recently become. My hands jerked to close the browser and all connections.

The blood pounding in my ears covered the noise at first, but after a few seconds, it became clearer. The low thrum of a rotor in the distance. I looked through the window, where the dark shape of a helicopter seemed to undulate against the flaming sunset. Narrow, with straight lines and sharp angles. Goose bumps rose on my forearms as I mentally flipped through a zillion Wikipedia pages and B movies to stop on a specific entry: *Attack helicopter. Machine gun + rockets + antitank missiles = Large flying nope.* The stain against the horizon was getting larger, its buzz ominously louder, but I couldn't move a muscle. The vision felt so unreal that I couldn't believe it was really happening. I just stared in fascinated horror.

Until it occurred to me that March was no longer in the garden, at the same time that I heard his voice shout, "Island, under the bed!"

That's when the true rush of panic came, and my heartbeat picked up until it hurt. I rolled under the bed. There, cheek pressed to a floor where there wasn't a single dust bunny to be found, I had a good thirty seconds to go through the terrifying list of possibilities. Machine gun? A mattress wouldn't stop those. Missiles? Okay. I'd die a virgin and become a martyr for all nerds in the world. Then, something—someone?—crashed through the living room, and moments after, I felt the wooden floor shake under me.

It happened almost at the same time—me screaming as I fell down into March's arms, through a heavy hatch I had no idea was there and then . . . *whoosh*. A deafening, heart-stopping blast, carrying powerful flames I saw lick at the steel door right before March closed it behind us. Okay. Definitely some sort of missile, what with everything blowing up in the bedroom. My feet met the cold concrete of the basement floor as he helped me up. My back felt a little hot, but there was no roast-chicken smell, so I assumed I was good—well, medium rare at worst. My knees wouldn't stop shaking, and confused thoughts clanked around my skull like coins in a piggy bank as I held on to March's arm. That or my ears were still ringing from the explosion.

I had landed in the magic basement. Kind of the same as the magic suitcase that he always took with him for "work": a mystical place where he stored gardening tools and heavy artillery alike—yes, the pruners were for *gardening*. I refused to believe otherwise. I already knew there was a hatch leading to it under the rug in the living room, but I guess you can never be too cautious.

March smoothed hair away from my cheeks with his palms. His breath was a little short as it breezed over my face. "Biscuit. Are you all right?"

I looked down. My legs were still wobbling. "I don't know... Who are those guys?"

"Lions."

What? Was that the purge Alex had been threatening me with? "March, I need to tell you something!"

He squeezed my hands in his. "So do I, but it'll have to wait. We have less than a minute. All that matters is whether you're all right."

"Yes," I said reluctantly.

"Good." He turned to grab a brown fleece jacket hanging from a hook on the wall. When he dropped it on my shoulders, I gauged its unusual weight and stiff lining.

"You keep a bulletproof jacket for gardening?" I asked, zipping it up. I rolled the sleeves. Way too big.

"Interpersonal violence and gardening accidents rank among the leading causes of death in South Africa. Now, get in the truck."

I shook my head to dispel a vision of March getting shot while watering his plants of society garlic. The truck. Of course. A renewed surge of adrenaline steadied my legs. I stared at the long black Toyota pickup parked between a sleek motorbike and a lawnmower. Behind me, March had shrugged into his own impeccably cut bulletproof jacket, and he was already loading the back seat.

I figured whoever caught us would be sorry: freed from the many racks lining the basement walls and waltzing before my eyes were various types of rifles with their long suppressors, guns, more guns, and a fricking grenade launcher. Several tubes of mints joined this Prévert inventory, and my mouth fell open when I saw him lift a voluminous case into the cargo bed with a grunt. The Twitter bazooka. So, things were *that* bad. The magic suitcase itself landed last, next to a magazine of grenades.

March slammed the rear door shut and jumped behind the wheel; my knees jerked in response, and that was my cue to climb into the passenger seat. Above us, ominous creaking followed by loud crashing sounds suggested that nothing would be left of the little cubicle house at dawn. I fastened my seat belt with shaky hands, pondering whether there'd be anything left of *us* either.

"No, don't."

I stared at March with wide eyes as the engine started. For Mr. Clean to ask me to skip the seat belt was . . . unheard of.

He jerked his chin toward the cramped space under the dashboard. "Do you think you can fit under there?"

"Yeah." I slid down my seat and curled up in this improvised shelter. Outside, I caught the whirring sound of an electric garage door opening.

"Hold on; we're going out."

It was only when the truck's acceleration propelled me forward and I bumped my forehead against the seat that I caught on to the obvious. *Out?* Of the basement? There *was* a rollup door at the other end of the room, but I was pretty sure I hadn't seen any garage entrance near the house. So *how? Where?*

And yet we were already racing down a tunnel, and looking up through the window, I could glimpse fluorescent lights flashing by. After a minute or so, the ground under the pickup started to feel uneven. Darkness enveloped us, and I registered splashing noises, like the wheels were struggling through rocky ground and deep puddles. Then, I finally caught a glimpse of the cloudy night sky, and foamy waves crashed against the vehicle, sending a splatter of crystalline droplets on my window.

We were on the beach. Bits of our surfing session flashed in my mind, completing the puzzle. I had spotted a cave entrance, nested in the rocks. Upon my asking about it, March had made a passing comment that later he'd show me what was inside. I'd thought he meant more rocks and possibly some sort of hostile wildlife—never turn your back on a mantis shrimp, by the way. It was, however, becoming obvious that while he had kept his investment minimal when it came to his four-hundred-square-foot cubicle, March had otherwise built a goddamn Batcave underneath it.

The pickup took a series of sharp turns among the rocks, punctuated by my squeaks each time my head hit the underside of the dashboard and March's apologies. I held my breath until we were finally driving fast on a flat expanse of sand. I regretted my sigh of relief almost instantly though, because over the clatter of pebbles hitting the bumper, I could hear the terrifying thrum of the helicopter's rotor. Of course they could see us. The Bat Tunnel had earned us some temporary reprieve, but we were less than two hundred yards away from the remains of the house, and we made for a perfect target from above.

No need to tell March that: with the threatening droning above our heads growing ever louder and closer, the truck took another sharp turn and shook as we sped up through a tangle of coastal thicket. He was trying to get us back on the sinewy trail leading away from the beach and toward Saint Francis Bay. There was less than a mile to the road, but then what? Would they give up once we were driving among shops and villas? Doubtful, if the engine roar ahead of us was any indication. Another car? From my position, curled between the seat and the dashboard, I couldn't see anything.

"There's something on the trail! What's going on?" I shrieked.

Above the gearshift, March's hand froze, hovering like he was waiting for something. "It's nothing, biscuit. Stay down. It's going to be fine."

"You said we wouldn't lie to each other!"

A rictus tugged at the corner of his lips. "Modified Jeep, three passengers. Not from the neighborhood."

This last suspicion was confirmed when a first round of bullets crackled in the distance, simultaneously clanging against the magic pickup's sides. Those guys were trying to trap us in some sort of deadly sandwich.

"Island." My head jerked up. I didn't like March's expression; that seemed a lot like fear in his eyes. "I'm afraid those gentlemen above are getting ready to engage us."

Sweet Raptor Jesus. *"Any good news?"*

"One." His fingers closed around the gearshift with a white-knuckled grip. "I believe their rockets"—he brutally shifted down two gears and pulled the handbrake. Dirt screeched under the wheels as the pickup drifted to a brutal stop in the middle of the trail—"are unguided."

That's the exact moment I saw myself die. Because, staring up in panic at my window, I saw the helicopter right behind us. A flash of light illuminated the night: they'd fired a pair of rockets at us. I physically felt my heart stop, like it had turned to stone inside my rib cage and crushed everything in there. Yet the fireworks barreled past us, even as I could have sworn they'd grazed our roof. I guess it was only a side effect of the—literal—heat of the moment, since basic spatial geometry contradicts this version of events: according to my calculations, the rockets swooped a comfortable six feet above our heads.

On the other hand, I regret to say that they did more than just graze the evil Jeep. There was the blast of a huge explosion. I curled up and shielded my head as the shock wave shook the truck's solid frame and rippled through my body. When I felt the pickup steer away and resume its race down the trail, I summoned the courage to take a peek, only for March to shove my head down again at once. There wasn't much to see anyway—only the charred carcass of a vehicle engulfed in flames and a column of acrid black smoke rising in the air, permeating everything, even the inside of our own truck.

The trail was a small blessing: it zigzagged around rocks, rolled up and down between trees and bushes, making it difficult for the helicopter to accomplish much, save for following us. Still, the ever-present thrumming above us served as a reminder that it was only a matter of time before they got a firing window. That's where guided weapons would have made a difference, but fortunately, those guys had chosen the cheaper option, meaning they needed better terrain in order to lock down on us. They did make a couple of attempts with a machine gun—and I did come close to wetting myself—but the rounds missed us by several yards.

March drove us north, staying on the trail as long as possible. All too soon, however, a smooth surface under the pickup's wheels announced the start of a nightmare. Miles and miles of a straight road crossing through Saint Francis Bay on the east side. Nowhere to hide, and a potential collateral damage list that looked like Michael Bay's: slums, bungalows . . . Also, left-hand driving, but I don't think it was our most immediate issue here.

Those guys in the helicopter wasted no time. The machine gun crackled again behind us; March swerved right to avoid it, but we were now an easy target. I couldn't hold back a scream when a series of huge bumps appeared on the truck's roof, like we were being hammered by giant hailstones.

"Fifty BMG," March commented through gritted teeth.

Okay. Whatever that truck was made of had just stopped .50-caliber armor-piercing ammo. I was therefore driving in the closest thing to a tank I had ever seen. That was the good news. The bad news? Tears in the fabric lining the roof revealed some serious damage to the various layers of steel and composite material making up the armor.

"Can it take a second round?" I asked, contorting to peek up at my window, all the while staying hidden.

March's eyes darted to the mirror, and his reply came with a sharp exhale. "Barely. And certainly not a third."

Outside us, the thrumming suddenly changed, becoming more distant. March checked his side mirror and cursed under his breath before hitting the gas pedal hard. I had no idea what this could mean, until the noise returned, this time much louder and . . . ahead of us?

"Island, stay down!"

For the first time since the beginning of this hellish race, I registered undisguised fear in March's shout. Terror spilled through me in response, seeping into every pore of my body. My lungs struggled to pump air in rapid pants, tears of helplessness blurring my vision. The truck swerved left and right to avoid an enemy I couldn't see, to save us from a fate I couldn't even imagine. I gripped the passenger seat and dug my nails into the synthetic fabric, searching for something to anchor me.

I should have never done that. Because in a split second, I nearly lost my left hand. I knew the roof was no longer the problem. Just as I knew what the ear-splitting rattle above us meant. By the time my brain had formed the word *windshield* and I recoiled in horrified realization, diamonds were raining everywhere around me, and there was this loud buzzing sound in my ears, covering everything. All that was left of the seat I had been holding on to was an indiscernible mess of yellow foam and shredded black fabric.

Everything was happening too fast: my brain had slowed down and couldn't process it. *March.* For a second, I thought, *He's dead*, and something shattered inside me. But his hand closed around my shoulder and pulled me up, away from that slow-motion hell and back to reality. The first thing I saw clearly was the jagged hole in the windshield, where the bulletproof glass had been torn apart by the helicopter's powerful ammo. And the wheel. Empty.

"Island, the wheel! Take the wheel!"

March's roar achieved to clear my thoughts, and with it, chaos returned. The pickup was still driving fast in the middle of the road, facing that flying monster in the distance, which now hovered low enough to fire another round in what was left of our windshield. Gusts lashed at my face, covered the hum of the rotor, and March lay half sprawled between the seats, trying to grab something from the back.

On a normal day, I'd have commented that he had to be pretty desperate to allow me anywhere near the steering wheel, and that the seat adjustment was all wrong anyway. But, honestly, we were past that point. I went on autopilot, scrambling over his hip to take hold of the wheel and keep us from barreling off the road. I didn't even really think it'd save us; I just gripped the damn thing until my knuckles hurt and looked straight ahead, like a mosquito on a suicide mission against a halogen lamp.

Next to me, March raised something in the general direction of the helicopter. I thought a gun or a rifle wouldn't do much, until I saw the size of the barrel. Yes. Now was the perfect time to use the grenade launcher. Six detonations shook my frame in a matter of seconds. Most of them missed, because you're not supposed to shoot in a reclining position, at a moving target, in the dark, and through a broken windshield.

They retaliated with the machine gun almost instantly, and bullets clanked against the hood. One single grenade, however, hit the mark. It was all it took. A safety reminder for all criminals out there: under no circumstances should a live grenade make contact with the rotor mast of a helicopter. Not if you want it to keep spinning anyway. The explosion itself wasn't nearly as terrifying as that of the rockets, only a burst of light and some smoke. I should, however, have known better than to underestimate anything coming from March's magic basement. Ahead of us, the aircraft wobbled and started spinning down.

I pulled the handbrake with all I had. The tires screeched, and the pickup skidded to a stop as bits of the rotor flew in all directions, hitting the remnants of the windshield. I jerked back against March with a yelp when a burning metal fragment grazed my forearm. The blades bent, some snapped off, and one of them went flying toward us, scraping against the pickup's roof with a terrifying creak.

Now, there's this rule in movies that any flying object experiencing a crash must explode upon making contact with the ground. I threw myself over March between the seats and buried my face in his chest, bracing myself for the blast. It never came; the helicopter hit the asphalt with the deafening sound of smashed metal. I looked up to see the tail shattering all over the place before the battered cabin toppled over and finally came to a full stop. An odd peacefulness fell on the road, barely troubled by plaintive whirring sounds and clouds of steam hissing from torn wiring where the rotor had been.

So, no. It wasn't the crash that caused the explosion. Without a word, March carefully pushed me out of the way and stepped out of the truck. I extracted myself too and managed to stand on unsteady legs as he walked to the cargo bed and pulled out . . . the Twitter bazooka. Ukrainian technology, designed for the modern, connected man. An integrated app allowed the user to post a tweet that said "Boom" every time you fired it. I knew March had recently opened a

Twitter account on Phyllis's recommendation, but I gathered this had little to do with social networking. Watching him secure a long rocket in the tube and steady the beast on his shoulder with a deadly cold gaze, I knew, without a doubt, that this was payback for the little cubicle house.

A tiny part of me did yell that I should have stopped him, but I was riding a spectacular adrenaline low at the moment, and I don't think I could have moved even if I had truly meant to inquire about the status of the guys who had just tried to kill us with military-grade stuff. My jaw went slack at the same time that March pressed the trigger. And that is, indeed, how the helicopter blew up in a cloud of flames. We were standing far enough away, but I still felt the wave of hot air sweep over us. Burning fragments rained like shards of gold, some falling mere feet away from me. I watched the wreckage in a state of shock.

With the same apparent cool, March went to place the bazooka back in its case. He then produced a folded rag from a compartment in the cargo bed, which he used to wipe the case over and over for a good thirty seconds, until it sat oddly clean and shiny in a truck that was otherwise nearly totaled. I stepped closer and saw that his hands were shaking a little. When I touched his arm, the muscles bunched under my palm, and his fingers curled into fists. He turned to face me, and there it was, the mask I knew too well: icy gaze, courteous and empty smile, both letting nothing through.

In the distance, I could hear a siren. The helicopter had crashed less than a quarter mile away from a shantytown: we must have drawn some attention. March steered me toward the partly shredded passenger seat with a palm on the small of my back. "We have to leave. Are you all right?"

"Yeah, I guess. But you . . . Are you sure? Your hands—"

"Don't worry," March said as the engine coughed to a start. There was a little smoke coming from the hood; it didn't look like we'd make it far with the truck.

I wished he'd have dropped the act and let me in a little, but it'd take a while to make it past those walls—if I ever did, I realized, with a tinge of sadness. I fastened my seat belt and snuggled into his bulletproof fleece jacket. I had yet to tell him about my creepy little chat with Alex, and now that my mind was clearing up, I was beginning to see how badly I had messed up.

FOUR
VIVA POLO

That beautiful, annoying American girl had it all fucking wrong, and Dmitri would show her. He was Bratva. He didn't ask women out; he shoved them in his trunk.

—Abby Chuman, The Russian Mobster's Innocent Tourist

After March had texted Phyllis to let her know that, against all odds, she still had an employer, we drove east on a deserted country road, passing a few houses and larger properties I assumed were ranches.

A rising migraine throbbed under my forehead in response to the stress of the past hours. My body was exhausted and at the same time acutely aware of the slightest stimuli: the night breeze blowing through our now nonexistent windshield—March had done some cleaning up—or the faint tang of my own sweat. When he saw me massage my temples and forcefully dig my thumbs into my skull, he fished a pack of pain pills out of the glove box and popped one, which he handed me. I swallowed it dry, for lack of any water to help it go down.

His eyes darted over to me. "Will you be all right? Do we need to stop?"

"No, I'm okay . . . Don't worry about the car. I won't throw up."

"Island, I don't care about the car."

I slumped in my seat with a sigh. "You said the guys who attacked us were Lions. How did you know?" I sensed he was in no hurry to have this conversation. But we both needed it.

"Someone called me," he admitted.

I remembered seeing him on the phone in the garden moments before the house had blown up. "Phyllis?"

"No. Dries."

A bump on the road shook the pickup. The hood clanked loudly, as if to express a shock similar to mine. "He . . . Where is he?"

"Still in Venice. He called to warn me that there would be some cleaning up, and he requested my help."

"But who . . . Why would anyone want to clean *you* up? It's been more than a decade since you left the Lions, and they never went after you!"

"I'm not certain what's going on, but it would seem that the plane bombing put Dries in a precarious position, and the brotherhood made a decision to cut their losses."

The brotherhood? More like their commander, and the man my mother had tried to warn me against before her death—Dries's elder brother, *Anies*, aka the sketchy uncle. Inside me, confusion gave way to a rush of anger. "It still doesn't explain why *you* would pay for the attack."

March turned left onto a narrow trail. Trees and tall grass flashed by, briefly outlined by the headlights. "When a high-ranking Lion is cleaned out of the brotherhood, his closest disciples will often be cut as well. Anyone whose loyalty might be questioned. It's not just me. Dries has always entertained strong ties to his disciples. I can think of at least half a dozen men."

"This is insane! You dumped him, you sided against him, you

ruined his plans with the Cullinan, you destroyed his penthouse with a rocket, you killed all of his henchmen, you punched him in the face, you—"

He cleared his throat. "Yes, biscuit, I understand your point."

"How can they be dumb enough to think you'd still be loyal to Dries?" March went silent, and I felt my throat tighten at the implications. "Did you agree to help him?"

"No," he said, licking his lips, as if looking for his words. "But as much as I acknowledge our differences, I know what I owe him. Starting with your life, and mine, tonight."

I rubbed my forehead with the heel of my palm. "You agreed to help him."

"I did not. He simply gave me a contact. Someone who'll help us leave the country safely."

"Out of his good heart?"

"I didn't expect that from him, but I think he wants you safe."

I could believe that. While he didn't exactly qualify for a Father of the Year Award, I knew Dries secretly entertained regrets over my mother's death and all that could have been. It was in fact an odd, almost chilling hindsight that I could have been raised by him.

March, on the other hand, Dries regarded as some sort of lapdog he had trained. A dog he was proud of but still only a dog. And no matter how much he had accomplished on his own, March did feel the same, to some extent, as evidenced by his comment that he owed Dries somehow. So, if Dries was willing to help March out of the pool of crap he himself had dragged us into, it could only mean one thing: he wanted something from his favorite disciple.

"It's a trap." I sighed. "You know it's a trap."

"I don't. What I do know is that the Lions are playing at home, and they have much more reach here than they do anywhere else. If Dries can help me protect you, I don't care what it costs me."

That's when I felt really bad. No, that's actually when I felt like shit because there he was proclaiming that he'd protect me at any cost like some fairytale knight, and I still hadn't told him. Guilt filled me up, lapped at the back of my throat, making me nauseous.

I mentally went over the words again and again. My lips parted. "March . . ."

"Yes? By the way, we've arrived."

His announcement derailed the carefully crafted apology I'd been rehearsing. I checked the road ahead of us to see that we were driving toward a hangar. The doors were still open, illuminating a rusty façade on which a sign painted in bold black letters read Kromrivier Deluxe Garage. On each side of the doors, faded red and yellow logos encouraged customers to trust either Pegasus or Shell for their motor spirits. March parked his pickup in the courtyard. Before we'd even stepped out, a long whistle ricocheted in the quiet of the night, followed by an exaggerated groan. "Jesus *fokken* Christ, *bra*. What the *fok* is that?"

A lean form came out of the hangar, wiping his hands on baggy overalls. At first, all I could make out was a dark silhouette haloed by the warm glow coming from inside the hangar. As he staggered toward the truck, I made a note that the guy had a slight limp, but he sounded relatively young, no more than thirty.

March greeted the shadow with an apologetic shrug. "Good evening, Pieter. There was a slight incident."

"Man, when my pants fell off at Friendly, *that* was an incident. This . . ."

That Pieter person took a step closer, and the light revealed a youthful face, large round eyes, and equally large ears. A mop of curly black hair served to half conceal those cute satellite dishes. I decided I liked this guy, maybe because I too had once performed a literal walk of shame, pantsless, in the aisles of a French supermarket, thanks to March. Pieter scuttled around the truck, feeling the deep bullet impacts on the doors, and stood on tiptoe to take a better look at the roof.

He eventually stepped back and dragged his hand across his face. "*Fokken* shame."

"Shame," March agreed with a small nod.

"I told you. I told you this would happen!" Pieter squeaked.

My heart faltered. He knew? About the Lions and everything?

Turned out he didn't. Pieter's rationale was a simpler one. He kicked one of the front wheels, causing the hubcap to fall off with a clang. "Japanese car!"

"Well, those bullets were really big," I said, in defense of the magic pickup.

His face pinched. "That'd never happen with a Polo."

No, indeed, I thought. Because a Polo would have been blown to smithereens by the very first round of fire. I kept my snark to myself though; the sheer number of Polos I had seen since our arrival in South Africa suggested that, much like Peppermint Crisp, they were serious business around here.

Past the initial shock of discovering the state of March's truck, it seemed that a light bulb lit up under all that unruly hair. Pieter's eyebrows arched until deep creases appeared on his forehead. "Who's that?"

March cleared his throat. "Pieter, this is Island. Island, this is Pieter." He motioned to the mechanic. "Pieter took over his father's business and has done a remarkable job developing it." He paused, and I held my breath. "Island"—we both knew what particular word hung in the air. Would he say it? Or maybe it was too soon. Or . . . — "Island is my girlfriend. She's spending a few days with me here in Saint Francis."

Forget about those proverbial butterflies in one's stomach. The little assholes appeared to have migrated, and they were now fluttering everywhere in my body. Not only that, but I could tell my ears and cheeks were reddening out of control.

Pieter, on the other hand, seemed deflated by the news. "*Ag*, bummer. Always thought you'd stay single. No more *braai* nights?"

"I'm sure there'll be opportunities," March reassured him.

I looked back and forth between those two. So March did sometimes socialize like any other man his age. Knowing him, those barbecue nights with Pieter must have been pretty quiet—on his part, anyway. But they nonetheless qualified as bro dates. The notion brought me an odd sense of comfort on an otherwise disastrous day.

"So, came here to relax?" Pieter asked me, leading us inside the hangar, where an odd mix of decrepit furniture cohabited with brand-new equipment.

I grimaced. "Sort of."

He pointed to a blue stuffed chair facing what I assumed to be his desk. "Take a seat. And don't worry; I never ask."

So, Pieter did understand that clients—or friends, for that matter—weren't supposed to show up in the middle of the night driving a truck that was riddled with bullet holes. It wasn't clear how much he knew about March's former line of business, but that didn't appear to bother him. I plopped myself in the chair's well-worn cushions with a sigh, inhaling the delicious smell of gas permeating the garage. Meanwhile, Pieter and March had reached the other end of the hangar, where a few secondhand cars, Polos mostly, awaited a new owner.

Pieter reverently patted the side of a white one. "So here we have a Vivo GTI. Not even five hundred kilometers on the clock. Panoramic roof. Air conditioning. Front electric windows. Very nice." He opened the rear door and caressed the back seat covering suggestively. "*Lekker comfortabel.*"

March tipped his head toward a lone brown SUV. "I'll take this one. Phyllis will transfer you the money."

The corners of Pieter's lips fell. I shifted in my seat to take a better look at the logo on the large grille and had to clasp my hand over my mouth to stifle a snorting laugh. *Honda.*

"I'll do the papers," Pieter muttered. "But you'll be dead by morning!" he added, pointing an accusing finger at the vehicle.

Pieter lived behind the hangar, in a trailer he'd bought from one of his cousins who lived in Port Elizabeth. The guy worked at Ocean Basket and smoked too much dagga because his girlfriend had dumped him—it was a long story, but the point of it was that Pieter now possessed the trailer, and whenever he traveled to Port Elizabeth, the cousin would get him vouchers for free fried seafood.

Anyway, while its interior was a long shot from March's hygiene standards—which could explain why he spent less than five minutes inside to freshen up and change—the trailer was cool. It wasn't huge, and over time, the white walls had turned various shades of yellow, but there was a sink, a shower stall, and tepid water. Also, Pieter had this antibacterial shower gel that promised ten times more protection and "odor control" in stressful situations. I needed that.

I came out smelling of "sandalwood and masculine power," wearing a perfectly pressed white shirt March had retrieved for me from his magic suitcase, and felt overall very manly. Save for the yoga pants and red polka-dotted ballet flats, which might betray my gender to the most attentive observers. I trotted back to the hangar, where Pieter was busy filling out forms behind his desk.

Watching him print a small card and some kind of green diploma, both bearing the seal of the Republic of South Africa, I came to understand that what he had meant when saying "I'll do the papers" was "I'll forge the shit out of them." March was finished loading any intact weapons into the SUV's trunk and stood in the courtyard, drinking a coffee while his beer buddy now worked on affixing new plates on the vehicle. I joined him there, thinking of ways to free myself of the weight that had returned in my chest.

Upon seeing me, he quickly sipped the last drop of his coffee and threw the paper cup in a nearby trash can. "Do you feel better?"

"I guess. March, there's something I have to tell you."

His eyebrows drew together in a watchful expression, but he let me continue.

"Right before the helicopter, I was . . . I needed to know if Alex had anything to do with all this, Dries in the news, getting exposed like that." I took a gulp of air. "I knew it might not be such a great idea, so I set up all those proxies so he wouldn't be able to track me, and I used his Yaycupid address so the messages would be relayed by their servers. I'm sorry, I—"

"You contacted him." For an instant, his defenses crashed down, shock and hurt plain for me to see in his wide eyes.

"Yes."

"Behind my back."

He might as well have reached inside my rib cage and squeezed my heart directly with those three little words. There was no mistaking the anger hardening his voice as the cold mask fell back in place on his face. Trust in exchange for control: that was the name of the game, and it was difficult for March to envision a relationship any other way.

In truth, he himself wasn't above all reproach when it came to dissimulation, and deep down, he knew that he didn't need a subservient girlfriend who would turn him from a control freak into a complete tyrant. That was the theory. The reality was that I had broken his trust and, in doing so, reminded him that, indeed, he could not control me at all times. Add to that some degree of jealousy and territoriality because no guy ever wants to see the ex back in the picture, and there was an easy recipe for disaster.

I searched his gaze pleadingly. "I'm really sorry. I knew if I asked, you'd say no."

"And so you did it behind my back," he repeated, looking straight past me.

A tiny "Yes" whistled out of my throat.

He crossed his arms. "So was it worth it? Did you perhaps extort some sort of decisive intel from him?"

Choosing to ignore the undercurrent of irony, I answered in a steady voice. "He didn't say much. I think he was just playing with me."

A flicker of concern softened his eyes. "Playing with you?"

"I thought I was safe and he could see the proxies relaying my connection. But then he asked if I was in Cape Saint Francis, and he told me that there would be a purge and that I should get away." I shivered at the memory of that particular fear. Like standing right in front of the eye of Sauron.

"Go on," March said, glancing at me before focusing back on the trail in an elaborate display of indifference.

"That's when I saw the helicopter, and at first I thought . . . you know . . . it was like he could see me, and he knew what was going to happen." I wrapped my arms around myself. "But it doesn't make any sense, since you're telling me those guys were Lions. I think he tried to freak me out, and it worked, because he's good at it."

He still wasn't looking at me. There was a twitch in his jaw, as if his molars were grinding together. His eyes were set on the dark, flat line of the horizon where it met a bluish, starless sky. "They were coming from the east. Supposing they took off from a base in the Jeffreys Bay area, it would have taken them about twelve minutes to reach Saint Francis. Meaning they were on their way before you even messaged Mr. Morgan. That's a spectacularly lucky guess on his part."

I shook my head. "March, I honestly think he was trying to be creepy. I mean, he *could* have learned about your place somehow, and maybe he even suspected that the Lions would go after Dries's disciples, but he couldn't have known the exact time and location. It's not like they take their phone to warn the CIA of those things, right?" I reasoned.

"It depends."

My jaw went slack. "What is *that* supposed to mean?"

"Never mind. Mr. Morgan and his dubious sense of humor are the least of our problems right now."

I straightened up. "So you won't tell me anything?"

He looked at me at last—but only to flash me the cold-killer stare, complete with slanted eyes and all. "You're *not* off of the hook yet. If our circumstances were any different, I'd put you in the trunk."

"But you'll just be mad at me instead," I said softly.

"Not mad. *Disappointed*."

I flinched. Time to try the big sad eyes. I looked up at him and flashed him my wounded-kitten look. All fuzz and heartbreak. "Will it help if I put myself in the trunk?"

"No."

I followed him back to the hangar with a despondent sigh. When we entered Pieter's office, he appeared to be done and ready to hand the SUV's keys to their new owner. Before he could do so, a flashy green smartphone started rattling on his desk.

Pieter frowned at the caller ID but took the call nonetheless. "Thank you for calling Kromrivier Deluxe Garage. What's broken?"

He listened to the voice on the other end of the line and stared at me, his brow slowly rising until it became clear it would take off soon.

"Um, yeah . . . she"—*God*. That brow was reaching even higher. I didn't even think it was physiologically possible—"she's . . . here."

And he handed me the phone.

Oooh, the look March sent my way. The way his nostrils flared. One-way ticket to the trunk!

"I have no idea what this is about; March, I swear, this time I didn't do anything!"

Pieter's eyebrows landed back, but his eyes narrowed in suspicion. "You don't know any guy named *Colin*?"

FIVE
THE LEGEND

Never let him forget that there are literally billions of guys out there waiting for you, including your ex.
—Aurelia Nichols & Jillie Bean, 101 Tips to Lock Him Down

I knew a guy named Colin.

Colin Jeon. Twenty-seven. Teenage Mutant Ninja Turtles fan, genius hacker, slow runner, and who had therefore traded a 197-year prison sentence for lifelong slavery in the service of the US government. He and I had met during the Ruby case and teamed up to recover my boss's money. We had sort of hit it off, being both innocent nerds lost to a spiral of crime. I was well aware that, even restrained by the tight leash the NSA kept him on, Colin was capable of many wonderful and illegal things. I simply hadn't expected him to call Pieter's phone. To talk to me.

The youthful and frantic voice on the other end of the line was, indeed, unmistakable. "Are you okay? Like, not horribly maimed or anything like that?"

March took the phone from me before I could answer. "*How* did you get this number?"

Whatever Colin said, March didn't like it; he shut down the phone and removed the battery, handing them both back to Pieter. Less than five seconds after he had done so, a cheerful ringtone chimed from Pieter's computer. He jumped on the mouse to close the Skype window which had just popped up with a bubbly sound effect. He clicked over and over, to no avail. "*Fokken* witchcraft!" he hissed under his breath.

The accepted terminology was *backdoor* rather than witchcraft, because Pieter was probably of those unsuspecting souls who clicked on random ads when browsing PornHub, but the result was the same: the mouse no longer obeyed him, and the pointer moved of its own accord to launch a Skype call.

A familiar face appeared on-screen: a young Asian guy sitting behind a cluttered desk and wearing a pink Krang T-shirt. He brushed away a lock of jet-black hair curtaining his glasses. "Please listen to me. Sir, I swear I'm just trying to help! We shut down the feed; we're covering you!"

March's eyes turned to slits. "Who's *we*, Mr. Jeon?"

Colin gulped down in visible fear. "I didn't really get the details, but Hendry thinks you're going to kill his grandma if he sells you out. So we told Morgan we'd lost the signal. Because of a Vista upgrade. He actually bought it, but he sounded ready to kill someone."

I raised my palms in the air in a virtual effort to contain the flood of information pouring from that screen. Alex knew about the cleaning up, and he had watched us trying to escape? NSA bigwig Hendry was siding with March because of past threats against Hendry's grandma and her Chihuahua? The NSA used *Windows Vista* to run ECHELON? "Stop! Start again. Start with what you said about Alex," I said.

Colin gaped like a fish before he resumed speaking in a somewhat more composed voice. "So Morgan used his ID to request an emergency satellite tracking. I was there. I was with Hendry in his office, so we checked the coordinates before approving them, and then Hendry goes like, 'Fuck! It's the South African's house!'"

My legs still held me up, but I was reeling as if I'd been punched in the stomach. Pieter seemed completely lost but displayed a suitable amount of shock, while on his desk, March's hand curled into a fist. "Keep going."

"We watched, because we were wondering what the hell Morgan wanted with you. And after, I don't know, three minutes, we see a Tiger on-screen, and your house goes boom!" Colin concluded, with an eloquent gesture of his open arms.

"You said you shut down the satellite signal?" March asked, ice crackling in his voice.

"Right after you made them blow up their own Jeep. Morgan requested cross tracking and asked us to calculate all potential escape routes. Hendry said something smelled off, and he told me to stall. So I jammed the signal and bullshitted Morgan. And after he gave up, I tried to locate you and see if you were still alive." Colin paused, drew a deep breath, and when he spoke again, his voice held the reverence of a man beholding one of the rarest Crime Pokémons in the world. "I'm your biggest fan, sir; please don't shoot me with a bazooka."

"We'll see about that," March said coolly. Not that he meant it. I suspected he was in fact secretly flattered by Colin's awed terror and intended to cultivate his legend. Even now that he had retired from wet jobs to pursue a legitimate career as a "security consultant," March remained a mythical beast for those privy to the worst details of his résumé—kinda like Judge Doom but without the weird eyes and shitty toupee.

"So . . ." I ventured, before Colin had a chance to further digress and ask whether it was true that March had once put a Russian mobster's hand in a blender. "I guess you've seen the news too?"

He refocused instantly. "I know—that plane completely disintegrated! This is insane! Did you see the pics?"

"*I* have. And we will get to that part," March said. "But I'm more interested in what you can tell us about the prime suspect."

Colin fidgeted in his seat. "Sir, with all due respect . . . you know that man better than I do."

March's fingers drummed against Pieter's mouse pad. "Please spare me this, Mr. Jeon. Did Mr. Morgan leak the video?"

This time Colin's gaze set on me, nervous and sympathetic at once. "He got a green light. But I don't know about the satellite tracking. I think Morgan did that alone."

March crossed his arms. "I see . . . Mr. Jeon, you mentioned the pictures of the wreckage. I assumed you've accessed the early reports as well?"

"Yeah. Signs of a sudden decompression between twenty and twenty five thousand feet, fuselage integrity got badly compromised, and wham! Confetti everywhere," Colin said, counting each step on his fingers.

Behind us, Pieter went to fix himself a cup of coffee; we had lost him at the nerd rant. I shrugged. "Tell us something we don't already know."

A smug grin tugged at the corner of Colin's lips. "Did you notice anything about the wreckage pics?"

Above me, March sighed. "No. Did *you*?"

"There's nothing left of the roof. The largest fragment they found so far is half an inch long," Colin explained.

March raised an eyebrow. "Did you expect it to resist that kind of crash?"

"Actually yes," Colin said. "Let me show you something."

On the screen, a video popped up. March and I watched in mild confusion as a busty blonde proceeded to tell us about the miracle of Ceraglass®, a revolutionary transparent ceramic. Super light yet hard enough to resist depleted uranium ammo, with awesome bending strength and ultrasonic velocity, and a mind-blowing 98 percent transparency index—which the girl demonstrated by strutting naked behind a transparent wall—Ceraglass® was going to change our lives and step in everywhere glass and thermoplastic couldn't do the job. Also, Michael Cera had nothing to do with any of this: the guilty party was a company called Novensia, whose marketing department was apparently fearless.

Colin stopped the video with a self-satisfied nod.

I was starting to see his point. "That's what the roof was made of?"

"Yup."

I replayed the last frame of the commercial that showed a recap of the material's physical properties. "It's very resistant, and it bends easily enough, especially for a ceramic compound, so there should be significant pieces of the sky roof left in the wreckage. It's a little weird that it shattered that bad."

"Correct. And the rest of the wreckage doesn't look like the result of one single device exploding in the cabin either; it's like . . . like the whole thing disintegrated in a matter of seconds, from nose to tail."

"What is your own theory?" March inquired.

Colin rubbed his palms together nervously before he hunched to hammer at his keyboard. Another window appeared, this time with a 3D model of the AirBW 850. He slammed a key to rotate the camera angle, and several glowing tooltips popped up, connecting barely recognizable fragments to their theoretical location on the hull.

"I'm no flight engineer or anything, so take that with a grain of salt, but if I was a truther holding on to my tinfoil hat, I'd say that the so-called invulnerable sky roof was a shitty idea, and maybe it was faulty, brittle or something. It took a hit, came apart, and at three hundred and fifty miles per hour, that completely shredded the rest of the fuselage. If I'm right, then my bet is the Men in Black want me to look at the big bad terrorist, so I won't be looking at the worst industrial screw-up since radium face cream."

March crossed his arms, his mouth a thin line as he gazed at the screen. "The CIA doesn't work overtime to cover up industrial mishaps. If they suspected no foul play, they'd have let the press go after the manufacturer already. They wouldn't step in at all."

"What if they're just using the whole thing to take Dries down?" I ventured. "It could be more than just Alex's vendetta; maybe Dries did something that really pissed them off this time."

Colin's embarrassed shrug was self-explanatory: my genitor dragged the kind of unfortunate reputation that made it difficult for anyone to believe him innocent of anything.

After several seconds of silence, March's attention returned to Colin. "We won't hold you any longer, Mr. Jeon. Thank you for your assistance. Have an excellent evening."

Colin's mouth formed an O of surprise at this abrupt dismissal. The word *wait* was on the tip of my tongue, but before I could protest, March had shut down Pieter's computer.

I huffed. "That was *rough*."

"I was civil—"

"He tried to save our lives, and you tossed him like a Kleenex."

"I don't fully trust him," March countered.

"You don't fully trust *anyone*."

I wished he would have said I was the exception, but March looked past my shoulder and remained silent.

Now back with a mug of creamy coffee, Pieter stared at March, doubt and admiration written all over his face. "*Bra* . . . I always figured you did gas stations and grocery stores. But CIA and all that shit?"

I shook my head in compete disbelief. "You thought he robbed gas stations? With an armored pickup and a grenade launcher?"

He gave a half shrug. "Wel, dis Suid-Afrika." *Well, this is South Africa.*

We were all set. Pieter had given March a fierce bro hug, a thermos of coffee, and chocolate rusks for the road—although I entertained no hope whatsoever that I'd be granted permission to eat those in the car. My seat belt was properly fastened; March was behind the wheel, grinding a couple of mints between his molars. At last, the engine started.

Our destination? I had no idea, because I had been the recipient of a cold shoulder for the past hour. I craned my neck to sneak one last peek at the busted pickup truck behind us. "What will he do with your car?"

The cold shoulder demanded that he neither smiled nor looked at me and that I be left hanging for a minimum of forty seconds before any kind of vocal stimulus prompted an answer—if any. I knew from prior experience that March wasn't the type to explode with rage and simply be done. Equally certain was the fact that snark would get me nowhere as long as he was pissed. Which left me with a single option: as we progressed down the trail, I gazed at the gravel illuminated by the lights and waited.

"He'll take some parts and scrap the rest. I trust him to make it disappear," March eventually said, his voice cool and remote.

Forty-eight seconds. Still pissed. On my left, I caught rustling in the tall grass, and a dark shape galloped away, barely outlined by the lights. "What was that?"

Forty-two seconds and another mint later, he answered. "A bushbuck. They tend to be nocturnal."

His lips remained set in a hard line. An ache settled in my chest as I kept thinking about the pickup and, even more so, about the little cubicle house. Thank God Gerald had been moved to March's new place in New York and escaped being burned to a crisp. I didn't like that orange tree, its passive-aggressive game, always popping horribly disfigured oranges to bring March down. But I knew March liked Gerald more than he'd ever admit. Just as he liked his cubicle house and cared about its destruction underneath that layer of indifference.

It wasn't the first time that the notion nagged at me: guys like him had a completely different relationship to places and objects. They were trained to develop no attachment to those. Everything that makes our lives anchors us, whether we like it or not; it meant nothing to them, and if it did, they'd bury the feeling and move on.

"I'm really sorry about your house," I murmured.

Seconds stretched between us. Whether because he secretly reveled in punishing me like this—which I doubted—or because my words had hit too close to home, March remained obstinately silent.

I took a shaky breath. "If you want me to feel bad, it's working. I feel like shit. *Please* talk to me."

The SUV slowed down and came to a halt on the trail, in the middle of nowhere. He wouldn't look at me, but his features relaxed, the ice in his voice melting to let through genuine hurt. "I'm not angry that you contacted him. What I hate is that you felt you needed to hide from me."

His left hand dropped from the wheel to rest on his lap, and I covered it with mine. "Would you have agreed if I had asked you?"

He sighed. "No."

"Because of the risk?"

"Because it's him," he admitted.

I leaned on his shoulder. "You really have *nothing* to worry about."

His reply came with the brush of his lips in my hair. "Is that so?"

"He shaves his chest."

There was a beat of silence as March pondered this. "Is that . . . why you two didn't—"

My cheeks turned crimson. "Pleading the Fifth."

He started the engine. "I won't ask then. Although I did wonder—"

"March!"

I remembered Joy telling me once that it was one of the many facets of jealousy: the need to know everything about one's rival, no matter how creepy or intimate the details. March would have to live without that particular knowledge. I doubted I'd ever share how I had nearly slept with Alex, only to run away from his hotel room because *someone else* was on my mind.

As the road came into sight, I thought it safer to revert to a somewhat less controversial subject. "So, where are we going?

"Cape Town. Dries has a contact there who arranged a flight for us," he replied, pulling out his phone to sync it with the car stereo. "Now try to rest; we will be driving all night."

I shifted in my seat to watch March, my fears kept at bay by a warm cocoon I knew came from being at peace with him. When he pressed play, Conway Twitty's gravelly voice filled the car like a manly lullaby, singing to his girl that he'd love to lay her down.

SIX
THE MOTHER CITY

Preston tore away the greasy Whopper wrapper to reveal a small velvet box. "Yes, I only pretended to be a bum to see through you, Charity. And I have."—he went down on one knee—"So, Charity Angel, will you marry me?"

Alabama Skye, Her Billionaire Bum

During the months my mom and I spent in Pretoria, I saw very little of South Africa save for the quiet luxury of a rented villa in the secluded residential area of Waterkloof Heights.

    I remember long days spent in near silence, yawning in front of online courses and waiting for her to come home. Yet some details stand out, like colorful pebbles scattered in the sand. There was the laugh of our neighbor's kids as they came back from school and walked by our front yard. I was dying to go out and hobnob, but I wasn't allowed outside on my own, so I'd just eye them through the window like some creep. Even sharper was the memory of Dries's footsteps on the wooden floor, at a time when he was nothing but a shadow visiting my mother at night. And, always, the purple haze of the alleys of Jacaranda trees shrouding everything.

Discovering Saint Francis Bay had been my first inkling that there was so much more to this country than the vague patchwork I had in mind, made of crime statistics, Peppermint Crisp, and Johnny Clegg songs. This impression was confirmed by our eight-hour drive to Cape Town, chasing the sun as it rose over wild greenery and clusters of pink houses, on roads that stretched for miles and miles along an azure ocean.

And so, the Mother City, as they called it . . . Well, it was a shock, but not the kind of shock I'd been hoping for. I had been ready for a burst of light and colors, for palm trees and white sandy beaches overlooked by the massive silhouette of Table Mountain. I couldn't wait to see flashy colonial houses next to skyscrapers, to experience the spicy scent and dizzying hubbub of traditional markets . . .

Forget that.

The sun had just risen, and Table Mountain was little more than a bluish ghost in the distance as we drove along a highway in the airport area. A strong onshore wind swept over patches of dried grass and a few trees. The occasional green dustbin added a welcome touch of fantasy. After a mile or so, it became clear that the sparse houses scattered in the plain were getting more and more derelict as we progressed. March's fingers rapped on the wheel. "I'm sorry. Cape Town is a beautiful city, but this isn't the best neighborhood."

I gazed at a strip of houses that looked like they had been dropped there in an afterthought, their rusty tin roofs supported by cracked walls and wooden planks. "Where are we?"

"In the flats. This township is called KTC; it's part of Nyanga."

Nyanga. As a teen, I'd heard it mentioned a few times on television, spoken by our neighbors, always in hushed voices and with an appropriate amount of disdain. "A crying shame," they'd say of a township that held the dubious honor of being their country's murder capital. There, even more than anywhere else, unemployment, poverty, and violence prevailed, eating away at the community.

I gazed at the jagged ribbon of wooden shacks flying past us. I thought of Dries, back in Japan, six months prior, serving me a plate of caviar as he told me about March's father, a British immigrant who used to sell drugs in a similar hellhole in the flats. "Is it like that, Lavender Hill? When we were in Tokyo, Dries said . . ."

His eyes darted at me, losing sight of the road for a second. A rare occurrence for him, who made such a big deal out of road rules—well, most of the time anyway. "If you mean the township, yes. Lavender Hill is just as bad. But we lived south, in Marina da Gama."

My jaw went slack for a second. I honestly hadn't been expecting anything beyond a gentle dismissal. I pushed my luck. "So . . . it was better?"

"We had walls."

There was a lot packed in those three quietly uttered words.

"March, what were they like, your parents?" I asked tentatively.

His Adam's apple moved, but he remained silent. I thought maybe I shouldn't press the issue, that there were still so many layers to tear through. He let go of the gearshift and took my hand. His mouth worked in vain, as if words were on the tip of his tongue, but he couldn't assemble them into a coherent sentence. He shook his head in frustration. His fingers tightened around mine, his thumb stroking my palm over and over. "I'm sorry," he said.

I covered his hand with mine. "It's okay. When you told me about your Lion, and I asked about your name, I said you can tell me when you're ready. There's time . . . you just need to find where the tape starts."

He flashed me a curious look as he let go of my hand.

"You know, when there's too much data at once, and everything is linked and too complicated to sort out, sometimes the best way is to find the one thing that ties it all, and that's where you start. It gets easier after that," I explained with an encouraging smile.

He pursed his lips as if he were contemplating the notion.

I went on. "Like, for me, if I had to tell someone about my mother, about all I've discovered, I think I'd actually start with you. You're where my tape starts."

Surprise registered in his eyes, and I couldn't stop the blush I felt warming my cheeks. While I might be a step ahead of March when it came to opening to others, some confessions didn't come easily yet.

He nodded a few times, to himself it seemed. "I promise I'll try. Just give me a little time." At last, he smiled too. The hint of sadness, of caution that seldom left him, was still there, etched in his fine crow's-feet, but seeing the dimples appear on his cheeks, I felt lighter.

He pulled out at the next exit and took a few turns until we were on Klipfontein Road. The first quarter mile wasn't so bad, but soon we were driving in a bona fide shantytown—sorry, an "informal settlement." In the dark, those frail shacks on the outskirts of Saint Francis Bay had been easier to ignore. Or maybe I didn't really want to see, because it'd mean accepting a reality that people like me only glimpsed on TV. Twenty years after the end of the apartheid, there were still walls no amount of democracy could tear down. In those streets where trash piled up, where houses were little more than a patchwork of tin, wood, and cardboard, you could find all the colors of the rainbow nation, except one.

Music boomed somewhere to my right, barking echoed in the distance, and smoke rose from a repurposed red container, accompanied by the smell of fried food. Heads turned as the SUV drove past them; children stopped playing to stare. It wasn't that they'd never seen a car. What they probably didn't see that often was a couple of "whities getting lost" in this part of town, to quote a seemingly drunk guy who yelled at us when we drove past him.

I fidgeted in my seat, holding on to my seat belt.

March cast me a sideways look. "Don't worry. We're safe here. Safer than downtown."

As a general rule, I trusted him, but, really, there *was* reason to worry. A dozen guys covered with tattoos were now surrounding the car. Some lean, some beefy, most proudly displaying the saint trinity of any aspiring gangster: a soccer T-shirt, some amount of tasteful jewelry, and, of course, a "passion gap." Kind of like my gap tooth, except it was about pulling out your four top incisors to look dope, and that was too much dope, even for a rebel like me.

I shrank in my seat when a bony guy with one such gap wiggled his tongue at me through the window. I could guess what sort of message he meant to convey, but no thanks. A squeak escaped me when something slammed on the car's hood, and March pulled the brakes with a huff. Another soccer enthusiast, this one much fatter, was playing drums on our car's hood. He and his friends appeared inordinately pleased to see us.

Next to me, March shook his head and smacked his tongue in annoyance. He fitted his black gloves on before reaching under his seat . . . for an Uzi. I suppose our hosts didn't react immediately because the windows were a little tinted, so it must have been difficult to see clearly what was going on. I, on the other hand, stared at the long suppressor and elaborate optic mount and was close to hyperventilating. "March, I'm not sure . . ."

He shrugged one shoulder. "Don't worry; most of them are just kids."

Kids with guns, I mentally corrected, as one of them raised his red-and-white shirt to expose a toned midsection and the handle of the pistol he kept tucked in his jeans. March ignored him. He flipped on the laser aim of the gun resting on his lap and casually lowered his window. Those gangsters outside welcomed the first three inches down with victorious cheers; then March revealed the Uzi at the same time that a little red dot popped between the eyes of the guy closest to the window, a boy wearing a black Porsche cap.

"Good morning, gentlemen. How may I help you?" he asked in his smoothest, coldest voice. Solidified azote in a velvet glove.

In spite of my initial scruples, I had to admit that March's approach made sense. You should indeed always try to solve your problems in a courteous manner. A slew of profanities and the solemn promise to "kill us dead" reached my ears, but the boys all backed away from the car with slow, careful movements. Well, except Porsche boy. He remained where he was, bent in an uncomfortable position and facing the Uzi. He was sweating a lot.

"Uh," he said in an odd, high-pitched voice, "man . . . it's cool. You do your thing . . . and I do my thing . . . and I go."

March's head tilted. Oh my God. He was giving him the creepy poker smile. At that point, I felt bad for the kid, even if I now recognized that little prick as the one who had wiggled his tongue at me. "*Man?*" March repeated.

Surprising how fast the human brain works under stress. "*Sir!* I mean, can I go and do my thing . . . *sir?* Please?"

"Barely arrived in Cape Town, already sowing death and destruction in the flats!" a cheerful baritone suddenly called from behind Porsche boy.

March seemed to recognize its owner. He lowered the gun and handed it to me with a little wink. "Can I entrust this to you, biscuit?"

No, not really, but it would have to do. I took the Uzi, only to relax when I looked down and noticed the position of the tiny switch on its side. The safety was on. Still, I was the one with a gun now, so while Porsche boy slowly backed away from our car, I raised the weapon in warning and stuck out my tongue at him. Don't say it was petty: you don't understand the ruthless law of the townships like I do.

I looked over March's shoulder. A tall figure emerged from a wooden shack and strolled toward our car. A confident grin cracked through his ebony skin. With his tux and shiny brogues, he looked like he had accidentally been pasted in the decor. Oh, wait. His dress shirt was covered in blood, so it was okay: he had earned the right to "sow death in the flats."

The guy had a few years on March—early forties at least. Examining the razor-sharp lines of his buzz cut and his impeccable shave, I gathered they shared the same grooming habits. What I'm really trying to say is that I didn't need to see the scarification on his back—the way he carried himself, his predatory nonchalance, even that untied bow tie hanging from his neck, as if it was just another night of partying too hard: this guy had *Dries's disciple* written all over him.

March opened his door and took the Uzi from me to place it back under his seat. "It's all right; we can come out."

Still hesitant, I stepped out of the car, never losing sight of the young gangsters who now watched the scene from a safe distance.

The newcomer assessed me with an expression I couldn't quite decipher. Benevolent yet wolfish, if that makes any sense. "Pleasure to meet you. People call me Isiporho."

I shook the hand he was offering me. The grip squeezing my fingers spoke of contained strength. "It's a pleasure to meet you too, sir. I'm—"

"Little Island," he stated.

I startled. Not just because he already knew my name, but also since the only other person I had ever heard call me that was Dries. Isiporho then turned to March. "And this is a face I haven't seen in a very long time. I take it you had a rough night too, *broer*?"

"You could say that," March conceded.

I made a note that, again, like Dries's and March's, our host's South African accent had been largely tamed into something closer to an inconspicuous British accent. When he gestured for us to follow him, I hesitated. "Are we going to leave the car here?"

Yes, I was being guilty of social prejudice. But, *honestly* . . .

Isiporho's eyebrows shot up in mock incomprehension. "Well, yes. Why shouldn't we?"

All I could manage in response was an uncomfortable rictus. Best leave it at that, since March seemed okay with this plan. Our host, however, had something of a showman in him. He raised his arms, palms splayed flat like a preacher, and called to the scattered gangsters still glaring at us. In doing so, he revealed a double holster and two guns tucked to his sides. "Is anyone going to touch my brother's car?"

The men around us remained silent; the most impressionable ones shook their heads negatively. Isiporho flashed me a smug grin. "See? Safest neighborhood in Cape Town."

Right.

He led us to an isolated tin hut at the end of the road. Some cement bricks supported the structure, and it was a little sturdier than the cardboard sheds we had passed. March had done really well so far, ignoring the devastation around us and the junk littering the dusty ground, but when Isiporho opened the plywood door, I sensed him stiffen. I think it had to do with the notion of being trapped in a cramped space that might trigger every single one of his buttons and bring back memories that were best left buried.

I came in first to take a peek while he stood in the doorway. My chest tightened at the idea that someone lived in here every day, in that musty smell, with a floor made of cardboard and plastic sheets hastily taped over scraps of wallpaper. Seeing more plastic sheets covering everything in the main room, from the microwave to the old electricity meter, I came to understand that they were meant to contain the humidity that would seep into every corner when it rained.

March hadn't moved. He just stared, fists tightly clenched. I took his arm and squeezed it. "We have to go in."

"I know," he said tightly.

Isiporho gave us an odd look, which prompted March to finally move. Once he was in, his eyelids fluttered, like he was about to be sick, but he soldiered on, past the stained plastic bucket serving as a sink and through a pair of flowery curtains. I held his arm tighter. His hand found mine, squeezing it hard. It was all the support I could offer, but I was glad that he at least sought it.

The curtains shielded a camp bed on which a young man rested. His eyes were a striking green, but his face, which I gathered should have been a golden shade of brown, appeared a pasty gray under the ray of light filtering from a small window above him. Next to the bed, an old woman wordlessly tended to thick bandages around his right arm. Blood seeped through the white gauze in several different places, and he snarled, revealing clenched teeth. The old woman placed a hand on his forehead and mumbled a few words to calm him down. There was no apparent tenderness in the deep lines creasing her face, but from the way her fingers smoothed dark curls away from his face, I figured he was no stranger to her.

In that moment, I wondered if anything at all could scratch a dent in Isiporho's jovial mood. He was still smiling as he pointed to the guy on the bed. "As you can see, I had to improvise. That's our little cub, Dominik, here. Freshly carved by Dries and already retired. Dominik, say hello to our guests with your good hand."

Dominik was in no mood to say hi. Perhaps because his "brothers" had tried to clean him up mere hours ago. "*Fok jou, 'Porho,*" he croaked.

That earned him a reprimand and a little slap from the woman—on his good arm, indeed.

Isiporho shrugged. "I'd shoot him to teach him manners, but as you can see, it's already been done."

The old woman left Dominik's side, whispering a few words in Afrikaans that I couldn't understand, save for the word *drink*. She went to search a cupboard, from which she retrieved three glasses and a bottle of flashy green soda. Cream soda, in fact, according to the label. She wiped each glass with her sleeve before pouring soda in them. Isiporho accepted his drink. When it was March's turn, he seemed conflicted but took the glass with a gentle smile. "Dankie." *Thank you.*

I knew he wouldn't drink it. The old woman trotted back to Dominik's bed, chewing on another unintelligible sentence.

Isiporho toasted me with his glass and, in a conversational tone, asked March, "So, jy naai Dries se dogter?" *So, you fuck Dries's daughter?*

I choked on my soda, inhaling some and coughing it out forcefully, while behind us, Dominik let out a weak groan and hissed an insult between his teeth.

March took the hit without flinching. Technically, he didn't lie. He looked his "brother" straight in the eye and said, "No."

"*Fokken* liar!" Dominik spat, only to earn himself another slap from the woman I now strongly suspected to be his grandma.

Isiporho's shoulders shook with quiet laughter.

"In any case, I doubt Dries brought us here to discuss my personal life," March said, his tone suddenly a notch cooler.

I sipped my soda in silence, looking back and forth between those two. I didn't want to miss a single breath of what would follow. Isiporho glanced at March and tipped his head to the plywood door. "Buite?" *Outside?*

When I moved to follow them, they both turned with an air of surprise.

"What?" I asked.

"You can wait here with our little ray of sunshine, Dominik, if you want. There's plenty of Sparletta left," Isiporho said, pointing at the soda bottle.

I narrowed my eyes at him. "No, thanks. I want to hear what you have to say."

March's features softened; the corners of his lips lifted in an apologetic smile, and I knew what would come next.

I held out an accusing finger. "Stop. Stop this. You're about to biscuit me."

He raised his palms in a pacifying gesture. "No . . . I have"—he paused, considering his next words under Isiporho's incredulous gaze—"I have no secrets from you. You can follow us if you'd like."

I'm not fluent in hit man nonverbal communication, but I'm fairly certain that the way Isiporho's face pinched could be translated as *Dude, where have your balls gone?*

Regardless, he led us out and away from the house toward the wooden barrier enclosing the settlement, beyond which the highway stretched along the industrial area surrounding the airport.

"Malek, Beaunard, and Tjaard are dead," Isiporho announced, all traces of mirth gone from his voice—fellow Lions, no doubt. "But that old *chop* Dikkenek is fine. They don't know where he lives now, and since he's retired, I doubt he's their priority."

"Where is he?" March asked.

"In Venice. He's painting a house there. I didn't get all the details, but it made no sense. Sounds like the sort of thing he'd do."

"He's a weirdo?" I asked.

Isiporho shrugged. "No worse than March, I suppose."

"March isn't weird."

That prompted Isiporho to raise a dubious eyebrow at the interested party. "Dries showed me the website for that security business you set up in New York. Why the hell an ostrich?"

"It's an *emu*," March corrected with an aggravated sigh. "It's completely different. I encourage you to check Wikipedia."

Isiporho turned to me and raised his palms as if to say, *See?*

Well, that pic of an angry emu gracing the cover of March's

commercial brochure was indeed the subject of mild contention between him and Phyllis, because she had insisted they go for the emu when March's favorite animal was the ostrich, whose long lashes and tranquil gaze he believed reflected a deep, contemplative personality. I didn't dare contradict him, even though my own experience with ostriches at the Berlin Zoo had me convinced that they were in fact the skinheads of the animal kingdom: stupid, aggressive, and bald.

Anyway. We weren't here to discuss March's advertising strategy. "So that's where we're going, Venice? When do we leave the country?"

"Bi—" He held it back when I shot him a withering glare. "Island, all I want is for you to be safe."

One of Isiporho's large hands reached for my shoulder with the obvious intent to pat it. I dodged. It made him chuckle. "You'll be going with Dominik and me. I'll put you on a flight to New York. One stop in London and you're home."

I treated March to my best look of outrage. "Is that the plan? I wasn't aware we were parting ways."

When he answered, his gaze wouldn't quite meet mine. "I'm sorry. I can't take you with me. Phyllis will pick you up at Teterboro."

I looked down at the dust covering our shoes, incipient anger swelling in my chest, buzzing in my ears. "Isiporho?"

He flashed me a lopsided grin, waiting for the rest.

"March and I need to fight; can you give us a moment?"

Once he was a few yards away, waving March good luck with his back to us, I attacked. "What did you agree to do for Dries?"

He stiffened. "Island, I don't want you involved in his business."

"You said we had to be honest with each other. You bit my head off for contacting Alex . . . but it's always me who has to be an open book. You? You keep hiding stuff, and if I ask, you just clam up on me."

"I believe you're being very unfair, considering what I shared with you," he lashed back.

The briefest of flushes warmed my cheeks, but I knew he didn't mean *that*. It was true though: he had told me about the meaning of the scarification on his back and the code number the Lions had given him. And upon my asking, he'd revealed that the number my mother had tried to warn me about was in fact Anies's own code.

I drew a tired sigh. "I'm sorry . . . I just don't like it when you brush me off like that."

The tight line of his mouth softened. "I promise to be careful. But this is something I must do. The Lions won't leave Dries or any of his disciples in peace until either we're all dead, or Dries is able to clear his name."

"That's the deal? You help him find who framed him so you won't have to look over your shoulder for the rest of your life?"

"Hopefully."

"What if you fail? Or if it turns out that Dries is involved after all?" I knew he wouldn't answer that, so I moved closer and lowered my voice. "You'll have to make the good-bye kiss worth it, in case we never see each other again."

His lips quirked. "Not in public."

March might have cared; I didn't, especially after Isiporho had stated that he suspected the worst—or the best, depending. I rested my cheek against his chest and wrapped my arms around his waist. He still smelled a little of Pieter's manly soap, and through soft cotton I could feel the promised land: pecs and springy chest hair. I rubbed my cheek deliberately. A low sigh of appreciation rewarded my efforts.

Even so, March's walls were no easy siege. I let out a little huff of displeasure when his hands landed on my shoulders, maneuvering us apart. "Biscuit . . . not here."

I resisted. "Let's say you take care of keeping us alive, and I take care of the puzzle."

He cocked an eyebrow. "The puzzle?"

"It's not just about Dries. I want to know what really happened to that plane. Don't you?"

He schooled his features into a poker face, which I deemed a good sign because it meant he was trying to conceal genuine interest. "Where will you start?"

"With the data Colin sent you. Whoever outed Dries wants everyone's attention focused on him. Now, if you're certain he's not the one who did it, I'm thinking that maybe, in all that data, there's a trail of bread crumbs leading to someone else."

His lips pursed.

"Plus Phyllis and Colin will help us—"

"No."

"All right, Phyllis and Colin will help *me*."

"Island . . ."

I straightened to stand like a soldier awaiting orders. "I know the rules. When you say keep quiet, I keep quiet. When you say stay back, I stay back. When you tell me not to touch a weapon, I don't touch it."

March inhaled sharply.

As I had hoped, this particular comeback derailed his implacable logic, which dictated that he'd say no again, and, if meeting any further resistance, would shift to caveman mode. His jaw worked silently as he came to realize that those were the very rules he'd set during our first adventure in Paris. In his eyes, some measure of admiration warred with mild outrage—guess he didn't expect for me to steal his lines and turn them against him.

Eventually his forefinger landed on the tip of my nose, a last recourse he believed could keep me under control. "I see . . . I'm afraid, however, that you missed the memo."

I pushed the finger away and slanted my eyes at him.

"Additional rules: You will *not* leave the hotel room. You're not even allowed to go on the balcony."

"Objection—"

"And no room service."

I made a face. "Your program sounds a lot like a Norwegian prison."

My protest was met with the cocking of a haughty eyebrow. "Which means one of the lowest recidivism rates in the world. I'd say this is exactly what you need."

Dominik could walk but not without Isiporho's help. Not only had he been shot twice in the arm and shoulder, but one of his ankles had been sprained badly during his escape. The old woman patted his cheek and sealed a lunch box for his journey. By then, I'd learned that she was, indeed, his grandma—well, *Ouma*, really—and she was actually nice but didn't like to chat with strangers because she was missing most of her teeth.

Forced to hide his wounded comrade and himself somewhere he believed the Lions wouldn't look for them, Isiporho had quite simply brought Dominik back home. My best guess was that the "cub" therefore behaved like a douchenozzle because the move didn't sit well with him. Presumably for the same reasons March didn't want to tell me about his own family: they'd both signed a pact with the devil to escape a life wasted in the gutter, and neither wanted to be reminded of where they came from.

When March put a hand on my shoulder to signal that we were leaving, the old woman held me back and took my hands in hers. She squeezed them and mumbled a short tirade, which she concluded with a sharp look in March's direction.

He responded with an embarrassed smile. "Asseblief, moenie bekommerd wees nie, ek is nie so nie." *Please don't worry, I'm not like that.*

I smiled too and thanked her for her hospitality, because I had no idea what else to do.

"What did she say?" I asked March as we walked out.

Next to us, Isiporho snickered, and Dominik made every effort to avoid my gaze. March translated nonetheless. "She said that you shouldn't stay with me, that you think I'm nice now, but I'm nothing but a gangster and"—he cleared his throat—"when you become pregnant, I will leave you, and you won't have a nice home."

I blushed, cringed . . . and eventually chortled. "It's okay. I'll ask a PI to hunt you down for palimony. I know this agency in New York; I think the name's Struthio."

One mischievous dimple poked March's cheek as he said, "I'll keep it in mind."

On our way down the settlement's main alley, Isiporho kept staring back and forth between us with that deceptive grin of his. "The daughter and the *gunsteling dissipel*," he finally said. "Dries's ulcer must be torturing him."

Limping at Isiporho's side, his arm over his shoulder, Dominik shot a dirty look at March and muttered something along the lines of "*Fokken* disgrace." Since he looked still young, I wondered if he was going through some sort of fanboy phase when it came to Dries—you know what they say about new converts—or if he just took everything March did personally. At any rate, I was now privy to the fact that Dries suffered from a well-deserved stomach ulcer, and that it was common knowledge that March used to be his favorite. To be honest, I suspected he remained so, even after the events of Tokyo.

I asked March, "Is that why the Lions left you alone all this time, even though you were technically some sort of defector? Because you were the teacher's pet?"

"Possibly," he said.

"Too nosy for your own good," Isiporho tutted with a glance my way.

I ignored his taunting. "What about Anies? What did he think of that?"

Isiporho barked a laugh. March shot him a look of warning, one he gleefully ignored. "You mean after the brotherhood had lost half a dozen good men, and Dries shat all over the code and said 'Oh, he's my boy; let it go?'"

I cringed. "Yeah, after that, I guess."

A couple of mints made it from March's pocket to his mouth, only to be mercilessly crushed between his molars. Isiporho patted Dominik's back, his eyes never leaving us. "Let's just say that Dominik and I didn't get the helicopter. That's VIP treatment."

VIP, huh? I was starting to understand the roots of Dominik's discontent. March wasn't just your average defector. To the Lions, he not only embodied betrayal but also acted as a living testament of Dries's weakness. Dominik's idol was fallible, and every breath March took was a reminder of that. Anies, however, I had an inkling that *his* hand wouldn't waver.

"So Anies wants March's head to make some sort of point," I said somberly as we reached our SUV.

March's brow creased, but he didn't comment.

Isiporho sighed. "There's that . . . but, honestly, Dries's had it coming for a very long time."

"What's that supposed to mean?"

He shrugged. "Not your business. Not even mine, in fact."

A telling statement from a man who seemed to otherwise stick his nose everywhere. I rubbed my forehead, fighting off a faint headache and, all the while, sorting my thoughts. Did he mean that Anies had been planning to get rid of Dries for a while, and the plane bombing was a convenient opportunity to carry out that plan?

I was distracted by March's hand on the small of my back, steering me to the passenger door. He went to open the rear door so Isiporho could help Dominik inside. Once we were in the car, March behind the wheel and our companions of misfortune in the back seat, I fastened my seat belt and steeled my voice to play mini-me. "The car only starts when everyone has their seat belt on." My gaze fell on the stereo's screen. "And I hope you like Dolly Parton."

As I expected, a smile of approval lit up March's face, and I must confess, I felt a tinge of pride when I heard the twin clicks coming from the back seat.

From what I gathered, Dominik had "acquaintances" he could count on to provide discreet access to the tarmac. We met with a bunch of sketchy dudes in an abandoned warehouse that was part of the industrial area adjacent to the airport. The proffered deal was that they got to keep the SUV and all the weapons that weren't in the magic suitcase, except the Twitter bazooka, which Isiporho wanted for himself. March noted that the transaction was unsatisfying. He pulled out his phone, launched the calculator, and several minutes of tough negotiation ensued, which resulted in Isiporho agreeing to sign a lease on the Twitter bazooka with an upfront payment of 30,000 rand and the gangsters pledging to remit 37 percent net of tax on all profits coming from the sale of the car and weapons if such sale occurred within two weeks. If not, they'd have to pay March 30 percent of the goods' market value.

He warned the gangsters that he'd show up to collect if they failed to honor the preferential deal he was offering, and he gave them a glimpse of the suppressed gun under his jacket, which achieved to convince them that he was absolutely serious. In the end, two guys took off with the vehicle, after we received a loyalty card for crystal meth promising very attractive rewards for any purchase above fifty grams. The remaining thug, a teen wearing a flashy bandana printed with the American flag, guided us through the industrial area, where he met with a man whose turquoise jacket identified him as an airport employee.

A wad of cash changed hands.

After that, the newcomer took over. Through streets, parking lots, gates, and hangars, more handshakes were exchanged, along with a couple of bills every time, and soon we were standing on the tarmac of the cargo terminal. I prayed the few people in the distance wouldn't pay too much attention to Dominik's bandaged arm, Isiporho's bloody shirt, or even the large black case in which the Twitter bazooka rested. They didn't, and, his work done, our guide slipped away without a word.

Isiporho directed his gaze to a row of aging planes and winked at March. "Don't hold it against me; I was in a hurry."

He welcomed the comment with a good-natured smile. "I've flown in worse."

Agreed, anything would do as long as it got us away from the wrath of their brothers.

Isiporho walked to a blue plane next to which a pilot wearing a pair of sunglasses and crocodile boots awaited, a cigarette in hand. He threw it to the ground and mumbled a series of syllables punctuated by soft clicks of his tongue. Xhosa, presumably.

"Well"—Isiporho smiled—"that's our flight; we'd better hurry."

I shook his hand, but when I tried to offer the same to Dominik, he ignored it and locked eyes with March instead. Sweat beading on his brow, the "cub" swallowed and spoke in a low, threatening voice.

"I failed, and I can't serve him for now. So you go, and you *die* for him if you have to. You hear me? You pay your debt, and you die for him."

That was the kind of grasp Dries held on his disciples, I realized: complete trust and devotion, through good and bad, and to the bitter end. A marriage of sorts.

I stepped closer to Dominik and poked his chest. "Meanwhile, maybe you could do something about your grandma. She deserves better than KTC. Is that how Lions—"

"Island."

The latent warning in March's voice stopped me. Even after all this time, after all he had lost, they remained his brothers, right?

Dominik treated me to a level glare. "I respect your father, but you, you're no one to tell me what to do with her. You think I didn't give her money? She won't go. She's been stuck in there her whole life; she knows nothing else and . . ."—his voice faltered—"it fried her brain. What do you know about that? About being so poor for so long that even money makes no difference in the end?"

My cheeks flushed with guilt and some degree of shame as I saw myself through Dominik's eyes: a spoiled little girl prone to rash judgments. March's quiet gaze met mine. He didn't say anything, but I recognized the sorrow clouding the blue in his eyes. He didn't pity Dominik, but unlike me, *he* understood.

He tilted his head at Isiporho, who tried to ease the atmosphere with one of his infectious grins—sincere or not. "*Eish* . . . time to go. We don't want to miss our flight and neither do you."

March dipped his head. "Thank you, Isiporho. I wish you good luck."

He snapped his fingers. "Don't need any. I *am* luck."

March turned to leave. I stood in place. "Dominik, I'm sorry. I shouldn't have said that," I murmured.

He acknowledged my *mea culpa* with a quick duck of his head. I waved a stilted good-bye to him and Isiporho before I ran to catch up with March. What was it that March had said to Isiporho? "I've flown in worse"? Indeed. I knew that glass nose, with its characteristic lower deck. A synonym for extreme endurance, sketchy maintenance, shady cargo, and rare but grisly crashes: the glorious Ilyushin Il-76.

It was so weird to step into the hold; I'd never been in a plane like that, and I felt like Indiana Jones, even though all there was to explore were steel walls covered with worn tarpaulin. It wasn't full, but most of the shipment was constituted by pallets of cardboard boxes that didn't look very comfortable. I spotted one though whose load was secured by nets and looked somewhat softer. March watched with a tired smile as I poked and tested the supple plastic bags stacked under the net. I checked the labels to make sure I wouldn't be resting on stink bombs, whoopee cushions, or whatever.

It was nothing like that; but for the sake of full disclosure, if you live in London and purchased a crocheted springbok plushie imported from South Africa over the past eighteen months, know that my butt may have been near it. I climbed onto this improvised mattress and patted it for March to do the same. He seemed to hesitate.

I grinned at him. "Plush toys. It's pretty nice; you don't feel the nets so much. and"—I lowered my voice to a confidential whisper—"no one will ever know you did something wild!"

He gave in and, in a rare moment of pure playfulness, climbed on the pallet to lie by my side. He closed his eyes; I scooted closer to caress his cheek. His features relaxed as the hull started to vibrate. We were taking off.

I kissed his chin. "You need a shave, Mr. November, but I like you with those whiskers too."

March ran a hand across his face. "I'll pick the first option if you don't mind."

He stared at the ceiling for a while, before his gaze set on me. "Island."

"It's me."

His lips grazed my forehead. "I'm truly sorry . . . for all this."

"Don't be," I said, molding my body to his. "But when we find Dries, I say you hold him while I kick him."

A chuckle breezed atop my head. "With great pleasure."

SEVEN
STAATSSICHERHEIT

He would watch her closely . . . very closely.
—*Carla Danger, Secret Police: Forbidden Files*

We made a stop in Cameroon a little before sunset. It had been raining, and everything was gray: the wet tarmac of Nsimalen Airport, the sky, all shrouded in muggy, foggy weather. One of the pilots helped us out of the hold, and March guided me away from the plane and toward the jet terminal.

Once we were close enough for me to assess the aircraft that would take us the rest of the way to Venice, I addressed a silent prayer of thanks to both Raptor Jesus and Phyllis. This flight was her work, and it showed—because it was a Gulfstream, with one of those impossibly clean and comfy cabins. I inspected the cream leather seats with renewed energy before checking the contents of the minifridge.

Did I want a grenadine soda and a slice of banana bread? Absolutely.

March too seemed to appreciate this change of air. A long sigh of satisfaction escaped him as he flopped into a seat, watching me binge on banana bread with a moan of delight. He motioned to a black suitcase sitting in a corner of the cabin. "Phyllis took care of your luggage."

As soon I opened it, my knees grew weak. Oh God, yes. Yes to clean clothes and underwear—how the hell did she know I preferred hipsters? My eyes darted to March, who lounged in his seat, eyes half closed in a catlike expression, following my movements. I preferred not to imagine what conversation had taken place between him and his assistant. Would it qualify as yet another control issue if it turned out that he'd briefed Phyllis on what kind of panties I should wear? Definitively. But I would allow myself to be controlled until we landed in Venice. For the sake of clean undies.

There was a tiny shower stall in the lavatory, equipped with a shower head capable of spouting a dribble of lukewarm water. Pure bliss, in our circumstances. We waited until after takeoff to take turns showering and changing. An hour later, I wore a brand-new T-shirt and a pair of denim shorts; March had returned to his default wrinkle-free state, and the rebellious stubble of the past twenty-four hours had been cleanly shaved off his jaw.

Don't think for a second, however, that this abundance of comfort was enough to distract me from my goals. It had not escaped my notice that while Phyllis had done wonders to equip me, one item was conspicuously missing from my trousseau . . . I shot a sideways glance at the culprit, whose body appeared to have liquefied in a large seat.

If I wasn't allowed to have a phone, his would have to do.

"March?"

One of his eyes cracked open in lazy watchfulness. "Yes, biscuit?"

"Can I borrow your phone?"

What for? I could practically hear the question sizzling on the tip of his tongue, ready to spill from his lips, but he victoriously held it back. The tiny Stasi officer who lived in his ear and whispered bad relationship advice to him would probably recommend that he check the phone's logs right afterward anyway. I watched his inner struggle play out, the hesitation in his eyes as he unlocked the device and he handed it to me. "There you go."

I welcomed it with a little bow and a smile. A graceful blue-eyed ostrich stared at me disapprovingly on the phone's wallpaper while I sent a brief message to Joy and my dad to make sure they wouldn't worry. I was still in South Africa; everything was awesome except for the tragic news of the plane crash, *love you, Kthxbai*.

Joy had left work and was hurrying to the launch party of a painting exhibit in Tribeca with Vince-the-cutest-photographer-in-the-world. I had never really told her what the deal was with March's job, so all she knew about him was that he was an older guy with a dubious source of income, who had popped up in my life, handcuffed me in my bed, taken me to Paris, only to ruthlessly dump me . . . and pick me up again afterward. From her point of view, March thus belonged to the wide subspecies of sketchy and manipulative studs. She couldn't, in all conscience, recommend that I indulge in any sort of congress with him, but a stud was a stud, and a girl's gotta do what she gotta do. She sent me a link to a *Cosmo* article discussing the best positions for first-timers.

I stopped myself before I hit *Read More*—I *did* want specific drawn instructions on how to best achieve the "coital alignment technique", but not on March's phone. Besides, I noticed a series of new e-mails in my inbox: my dad had no articles to share with me, but rather repeated demands that I call him. To check on me, to know where I was, with whom? For how long? And, "Island, this is the second phone you've lost in six months!"

I considered his e-mails with a wince. Yeah, maybe that phone call could wait another half hour. I turned to March, who had been observing me with carefully feigned indifference. "Can you unlock those folders where you stored the data Colin sent you, please? I'd like to go through them."

My request was welcomed by the faintest twitch of his brow. "Do you need it urgently?"

I took a calming breath. I would not give up, and certainly not get angry, but I was going to win this. "No, nothing urgent. It can easily wait a few minutes if you have something else to do."

March straightened in his seat. "You seem exhausted; wouldn't you rather get some rest?"

"No, I'm good."

Facing unexpected resistance, he stood up and towered over me. "Can I offer you another drink?"

"I'm not thirsty. Can I see those files now?"

After thirty seconds of silence, he swiped a few times across the screen and handed me the phone with a sigh. "Island, this is external consulting. Nothing more."

I gave a firm nod. "Nothing more."

He settled in the seat across from mine and watched me go through the various documents Colin had sent him. Besides the early crash simulations, I found a copy of the passenger list and early reports from the National Transportation Safety Board. For almost two hours, I scrolled through the names, scoured the web for dozens of search engine results, feeling an odd sense of intrusion upon reading the place and date of birth, professional occupation, and personal ties of so many dead people. I was halfway through the list when I paused on a particular entry.

After Google confirmed my hunch was correct, I handed the phone back to March. "Do you believe in coincidences?"

He frowned at the screen. "Sabina Falchi, thirty-six, Italian. Her file is almost empty. Apparently she had a ticket but never boarded. Do you know her?"

"No," I said. "But it says she's a materials chemistry engineer. So I checked her résumé. Right after university, she spent four years doing R&D for a company called . . . Novensia."

"The manufacturer of the plane's roof? With the terrible commercial?"

"Yeah. Technically, they only provided that Ceraglass compound, and AirBW assembled the roof. They don't communicate much, but they're actually the second-largest industrial group in Italy. They specialize in construction materials, and they also branch in telecommunications and even dog food."

March's forefinger swiped down a couple of times as he skimmed through the search results. "Mr. Jeon did say he believed the roof could have been faulty."

I drew an excited breath. "I know. Of course, it could be a lot of other things, like another plane taking them out, and for the record I *refuse* to rule out an alien intervention. But honestly, if we take Dries's suitcase out of the equation . . . I think the first thing we need to know is why *she* didn't board."

As March's forefinger tapped the screen repeatedly, for the first time in twenty-four hours, the mints he always kept in his pocket in case of an emergency reappeared. He dropped a couple in his mouth and chewed them thoughtfully. "Sabina Falchi hasn't been seen since the plane took off; the Italian police are looking for her."

I leaned forward to check the data on his phone. "So they're tying her to the attack?"

"No. The file mentions an 'incident' shortly before boarding. No further details."

"Then we need to find her before they do."

"*We?*"

I got up from my seat to peck his cheek. "I mean you and Dries. I'll just be consulting around."

Outside the jet, the sun was setting. March watched me trot away with his phone to settle on a long couch at the other end of the cabin. He cocked an eyebrow in question.

I held up the phone with an apologetic grin. "I need it for a little longer. I gotta call my dad."

EIGHT
HER

Her voluptuous breasts rose with each feverish breath she took.
"What are you going to do to me?" she asked.
He eyed the mat at their feet. "How supple are you?"

Tawny Fawn, Bent Over by The Yoga Teacher

Twenty minutes had gone by already, and the Gulfstream now glided above a blanket of ink-black clouds. I sat very straight, holding March's phone at a safe distance from my ear while a storm of general displeasure and specific trap questions hailed upon me. I dodged and lied my tongue off, of course. My father and I did comment on the news of the plane crash with the appropriate amount of dispassionate concern, but Dries's name wasn't uttered a single time during our conversation. Yet I could feel his stifling presence enveloping each silence, each evasive reply, like a cloud of acrid smoke neither of us would acknowledge.

Inevitably, once my dad had ascertained that I was safe, and having exhausted our stock of mundane observations on terrorism and the state of the world these days, the topic shifted back to the most pressing issue: the no-doubt sordid intentions of the "shady forty-year-old dom" whose claws I had once again fallen prey to.

"Honey, listen to me—"

"Dad, please . . . I'm a little too old for you to screen my dates or anything."

"Island. I love you, honey, but do you honestly think I'm stupid?"

I was taken aback as much by the question itself as by the sudden gravity in his voice. "I . . . no. I'd never think that. Dad—"

"So you listen to me. I know you. If you could give me his name, you would. If you could tell me what he does for a living, or even where you met him, you would. Believe me, I know that tune already. If he was"—my throat knotted when I heard him take a gulp of air on the other end of the line—"if he was a good man, you wouldn't hide anything from me."

Touché. Business acumen wasn't his only gift—my father was much more insightful than I gave him credit for. But he was also wrong. "He *is* a good man, and I know you heard things through Joy. She was kidding; he's not, um . . . "—God. How do you tell your sixty-three-year-old dad that your boyfriend isn't actually into BDSM?—"He's not . . . kinky."

A heavy sigh rewarded my efforts before my father at last detonated. "Island, I wouldn't give a damn about that even if he was Dr. Frank N. Furter! You know what I'm talking about!"

The words had been shouted loud enough for March to hear them. He sent me a questioning look. I shook my head; involving him would only make the ordeal worse.

"No, I don't know, and I really wish you'd trust me," I hissed.

"Honey, it's not you, it's your choices I don't always trust."

His words slapped me in the face, the sting almost physical. "I understand," I managed. "I think we're done for now."

"Island—"

"Look, it's late. I'm going to bed soon. I'll call you tomorrow if I can . . . I love you."

I hung up before he could say more, guilt weighing heavy in my chest. The ostrich on March's wallpaper wouldn't stop giving that judgmental stare; I turned the screen off. I didn't notice he had moved until the sofa sank under his weight, and his arms wrapped around me from behind, pulling me in a comforting embrace. "I'm sorry it didn't go well."

I let out a shaky sigh. "It's not your fault. I just can't tell him. I can't tell anyone, so I try to dodge. I make up stuff . . . but there's no end to it, and now he says he doesn't trust my decisions."

March maneuvered us on the sofa until I found myself lying down, my head resting on his lap. One of his hands combed bangs away from my forehead. "Do you?"

I looked up at his heavy-lidded eyes, their blue depths clouded with doubt. "Do I what?"

"Do you trust your decision to follow me?"

"Haven't we been over that already?" I grimaced. "Please don't dump me for my own good again."

His mouth twitched. "I'd make sure to give you a parachute."

"See? That's why my dad thinks you're bad news," I said with a chuckle.

I regretted my words instantly when the smile left his face. "Island. He's right. If the hunt for Dries's disciples goes on, I won't be able to return to New York"—he paused and laced his fingers with mine—"at least, not officially."

"Mr. November and Struthio Security will have to vanish?"

"Yes."

I squeezed his hand. "We'll go into hiding then, with sunglasses and all." The beat of silence that followed was sadly eloquent. I trudged on. "I'll go with you. I mean, if you want me around." Relief welled in my chest when I felt him gather me closer in response. "I'll drive you crazy, but at least I'm more fun than Gerald," I said with a tentative smile.

"Biscuit, you have a family, friends . . . an entire life. And, after all, you barely know me."

March wasn't trying to convince me. He was trying to rationalize our situation so he'd find the strength to "parachute" me if need be—possibly literally so. Well, no. As far as girlfriends went, I intended to be the enduring type. Think of a strip of Velcro stuck to the back of an Angora sweater.

"It's sort of true," I admitted. "The other guys I dated, I'd know their birthday, where they went to school, this whole narrative about them, but in the end, I never really *knew* any of them. Not even Alex. You"—I raised a hand to caress his jaw—"you don't fit in any of the boxes people define themselves with, and it's true that I have no idea what to tell my father when he asks.

"But I know you always dress the same because it stresses you out to buy clothes of a different color. I know you like strawberries, and you make that little sound at the back of your throat in your sleep—I think you'll be a snorer when you get old. Also, I now know"—I stretched, intentionally giving him a peek at my navel—"that you *love it* when I do this."

March's hand moved to rest on the prize, his palm warm against the skin of my stomach. "And your point is?"

"All I'm saying is that, overall, I know you more intimately than anyone else I've ever known, except maybe Joy and my dad."

I wished he'd say something, because I'd basically admitted I'd follow him anywhere, and he was the most important thing in my life. March's fingertips stroked my belly absently, and I could see his Adam's apple working in his throat, but his lips remained sealed, and silence stretched between us. I waited, aware of the slightest shift in his posture, of my own heart beating in my ears.

"March twenty-sixth. That's when I was born."

I squirmed to a sitting position by his side. I just couldn't lay here like a log when he was crossing the Rubicon. No, wait, make that the freaking *Amazon*. "So that's why you chose that code name?"

Unexpected sadness suddenly weighed on his features, bringing the corners of his mouth down. I squeezed his hand in a silent plea to let me in.

"Dries used to say that it was like hiding in plain sight"—a derisive smile creased a dimple in his cheek—"because there was never any code name. It's the name my mother gave me. She liked it."

I had to take a deep breath, because otherwise, I knew I'd cry. I thought of that single letter, carved at the bottom of the lion scarification covering half of March's back. Forever engraved in his skin. H. The initial of his last name. All he should have kept from his past self after joining the brotherhood.

For a long time, I hadn't even been sure he had a real name. To me, he was March, but also Mr. April, July, May . . . and Mr. November. The man he had created for me, to be with me. A good citizen with a legit security business, an actual address. *"But I haven't found a good first name yet."* That's what he had said in Vaduz. I had told him to keep March. Just March. Because I liked it, unaware of what it meant to him. It was so much more than a code name. It was a part of himself he had clung to, obstinately. He was March H. Someone's son.

I curled against his chest, tucked my head under his chin. My hand never let go of his, afraid to break that precious connection, that single silvery thread. "What was she like?"

"A bit like you."

"Like me?"

He shook his head. "Messy. Candid. When I was still little, it was almost like growing up with a big sister. We'd stay home, play, and watch cartoons . . . She liked the dog musketeers."

"That old one where d'Artagnan looked like Snoopy? They aired it in South Africa too?"

A chuckle shook his frame. *"Brakanjan en die drie musketiers . . .* I wonder what Alexandre Dumas would have made of that."

"Your mom sounds like she was fun to be around."

He went quiet again for a while, searching his words. "She was . . . very young. The more I grew up, the more I realized she didn't. I think I was six or seven when I understood that she couldn't really take care of me. It had to be the other way around. She would"—March's tongue clicked in disapproval at his own memories—"she didn't pay attention to her money when we went to the grocery store.

She'd take things we couldn't afford and have to put them back on the shelves. And she couldn't take care of the house. Things would pile up. Empty boxes, clothes . . . trash. It drove my father mad when he was there."

A knot formed in my throat. "So you counted the money. And you cleaned."

He ducked his head with a sorrowful smile. "She called me her little lieutenant. Second in command, in charge of switching Chappies and Amarula for rice and cans in our cart and counting the change. I was also perhaps a little vainglorious about my ability to operate our old twin tub."

A seven-year-old child doing the laundry? I *was* admittedly messy and candid, but by March's account, his mother had been dependent. "But your father, didn't he—"

He cut me off, his tone suddenly frosty. "He wasn't home much. It was fine that way."

I probably should have left it at that, but upon finding out that March had grown up with his mother—as I had—I couldn't stop the next question forming on my lips. "How old were you when she died?"

I felt him stiffen. Around me his hold loosened, and I instantly knew I had stirred the wrong memory. "I was thirteen . . . but we can talk about it another day. Now you should try to get some sleep; we'll land in Venice at seven."

By the time he was finished speaking, he had risen from the couch to fetch a cover and a pillow for me from a cupboard.

I murmured, "I'm sorry. I didn't mean to hurt you."

He knelt by the couch. "You didn't, and I'm the one who should apologize. I shouldn't have been so crusty. As I remember telling you once, there's simply nothing glorious about my life. Just old stories not worth dwelling on."

I took the proffered gray fleece cover from his hands. I didn't want to insist—my foot was wedged far enough down my throat as it was—but how could he not see how wrong he was? Of course his past mattered to me. I didn't want any *glorious* tales, only to know him a little better, to understand him.

I wanted to be closer.

With a sigh, I squirmed forward to press my mouth to his. "I wish that couch was bigger."

This bold statement was rewarded by a quick swipe of his tongue at my upper lip. "Why, Miss Chaptal, how wanton of you."

That made my heart beat a little faster. "I didn't mean it like that. I mean, I know it's technically doable. But I think the couch would be an advanced level for me."

His lips quivered in that way they did when he was stifling a laugh. "Advanced level?"

I fought a blush. "Yeah, when we finally get to that, I prefer starting with the basic stuff . . . in a bed. One that won't explode. But I'm totally on board with experimenting later on, just not with weird upside-down positions. Because I get headaches when I try those during yoga . . ."

March wouldn't stop blinking, and it dawned on me that I was long past the point where I should have stopped talking. Completely.

His eyebrows pinched and jumped. "Biscuit . . . exactly what kind of yoga are we talking about?"

"*Normal* yoga! Sometimes we do inverted yoga positions. Like the plow"—I waved my hands, mimicking what I hoped were clear instructions—"with your legs behind your head."

His eyes remained slanted in suspicion.

"It's not sexual."

"I believe you."

I clasped a hand over my mouth, unable to suppress a nervous chortle. "*God* . . . all I was trying to say is that I wished we could both fit on the couch, because I really liked sleeping close to you, back at your house." I looked around the cabin, scanning the pairs of single opposite seats. "But I guess we'll have to wait until we're in Venice for that." *Damn.*

March's gaze followed mine, reaching a similar conclusion, I assumed. He drew the fleece cover to me as I let myself fall back down onto the couch. Once he'd flipped a switch above my head that dimmed the lights in the cabin, I struggled to keep my eyes open. The only thing keeping me awake was the delicious tickle of his mouth brushing my ear shell and his low purr. "Of course, you're aware that once we find a bed that doesn't explode, there won't be much sleeping?"

"I'll hold you to that," I whispered, while in the fog of my comatose brain, a little voice shouted at the top of her lungs: *You just wait, girl . . . He's gonna nail us like Jesus to the cross!*

NINE
A BATTLE OF WILLS

Make unforgettable memories together: a beach sunset, a fun boat trip . . . Create key-moments you can later use to remind him how important you are. **He didn't see Venice with Cherry; he saw it with YOU**.

—Aurelia Nichols & Jillie Bean, 101 Tips to Lock Him Down

The forty-five-minute ride to Venice in an overcrowded vaporetto was a long shot from the jet's luxury, but I've always loved water-buses. March . . . not so much. I guessed he had picked this particular mode of transportation because it was inconspicuous and made it difficult to track us. The boat, however, wasn't exactly in mint condition, and he stood stiff, surrounded by a subtle fragrance of gasoline, sun cream, and diaper. The latter could be attributed to a chubby tot lounging in his stroller, who engaged in a stare down with March.

That kid had no idea who he was dealing with—the fight lasted for a good minute, during which March fixed slanted, unblinking eyes on the enemy. The insolent little turd retaliated by ostensibly picking his nose and eating the fruits of his labor. March's nostrils flared. He stared harder, until the kid broke under the pressure—he looked away and started crying. I didn't miss the imperceptible curling of the victor's lips; I clasped my hand over my mouth to suppress a giggle.

Meanwhile, around us, the lagoon's backdrop had changed to a band of old brick-and-stone buildings, stretching along a blue-green sea. Towers and domes overlooked tiled roofs baked by the bright morning sun. Venice in a nutshell.

"I'm going on the deck to get a better look," I said.

March's lips pursed, and this time, it was *I* who could hear the cogs wheeling fast in his brain. Our agreement specified that I was forbidden to access balconies. But did a boat deck count as a balcony? And if it didn't and I went to the deck, what where the statistical chances that I might bend over the rail and fall into the water, only to be devoured by a giant Venetian clam shortly afterward?

At last, he gave a cautious nod. "We'll arrive in San Marco in ten minutes though. Be ready to disembark."

"Got it!"

I left him my suitcase and wasted no time squeezing among a group of retired French tourists to find a good observation spot. The vaporetto made a wide berth around a row of thick wooden poles emerging from the water to delimit a sand bank. Once again, I silently thanked Phyllis for a perfect shopping list. The red-and-white striped T-shirt and navy cigarette pants would allow me to blend smoothly with the locals. I leaned against the rail and closed my eyes. A pleasant morning breeze tickled the fuzz on my forearms. The squawks of seagulls ganging up on a trawler echoed in the distance. Nature in all its glory.

My head jerked at the sound of a police siren approaching. Around me, all eyes turned to a blue speedboat racing toward us, beacon light flashing madly. That's the problem with living a criminal's life: it makes you paranoid. After all, we had made it out of Marco Polo Airport with utterly fake passports without getting shot or anything. *No one cares about Mr. and Mrs. June*, I mentally droned. *No. One.*

"Island."

March's hand landed on my shoulder. He had seen the boat and came out to find me. It couldn't be good. I cast him a worried look, while around us, tourists were busy filming the police boat's arrival. It looped around the vaporetto to stop its course. Under our feet, the engine's vibrations died, and the boat slowly came to a halt, swayed by a lazy swell. My chest was starting to feel tight, but up until that point, I still wanted to believe that it had nothing to do with us.

The police boat maneuvered closer, but March wasn't looking at them; he was checking our surroundings. Another speedboat had stopped as well, some fifty yards away. White, no beacon lights on that one. I wondered if they meant to take pictures too—smartphones have ruined us.

I gritted my teeth when two police officers, a man and a woman, boarded the vaporetto and started searching the crowd, scrutinizing fidgety passengers. Through the speedboat's tinted windows, I could make out the shape of a third cop—the pilot, I gathered—waiting inside the cabin and observing his colleagues' progress. The woman noticed us, and under the long black bangs escaping from her cap, a flash of recognition sparkled in her eyes. The second cop muttered something into a walkie-talkie secured to the front of his navy uniform and made a swiping gesture with his arms for the other passengers to stand back. The woman's hand moved to the butt on the gun resting in her holster belt.

She gave us a nasty look. "Ci voglia seguire, per favore." *Please follow us.*

My instinct was to take a step back, but March offered the policewoman his most charming dimpled smile and moved forward. "Noi non opponiamo alcuna resistenza all'arresto."

He had a thick accent, but still, I had no idea he could speak Italian so well. Then again, when you kill people for a living, you best learn how to say "We are not resisting arrest," in case you need it someday. He motioned for me to follow him. "Come on, Island. Let's not make the lady wait."

Judging by her glare, she was supremely pissed by his calm attitude and the way he seemed to be addressing the crowd of passengers rather than her—a clear warning not to cause a scene with so many potential witnesses and side casualties. I complied, puffing my chest and holding my head up high to conceal my fear but also a good deal of humiliation. Like when you're the only one whose bag gets searched at the mall entrance, and everybody is looking at you as if you stole that cheese grater. At least the other passengers didn't dare take pics while the cops stood so close. I preferred not to imagine what would happen if my dad somehow stumbled on a pic of me getting arrested.

As soon as we stepped foot in the cockpit, the atmosphere cooled down noticeably. The pair, who had been guiding us out with a wary hand on their guns so far, drew them at once. I startled and raised my hands above my head. March didn't move. Not even when the boat started sailing away from the vaporetto, where dozens of people were still leaning on the rail, staring in disbelief.

The woman, who sounded like the boss, pointed at the bench seat and barked a single order. "Sedere!" *Sit!*

It was easy to obey: my knees more or less gave way under me, and I scooted to the right, as far away from her as I could. March remained still, the hint of a smile dancing on his lips. "Don't worry. They're not carabinieri."

Okay, now I was even more worried, especially since I noticed that the other white boat was following us, catching up fast.

Their fingers tightened around the triggers of the guns. The woman's tongue darted to swipe at her lips nervously. March went on, his expression turning feral. "If they were, we'd have seen reinforcements by now. And"—he tilted his head at the barrel of their guns—"I've never seen carabinieri equipped with anything else than a Beretta. A modified Smith & Wesson . . . it's so tacky. Very American. Let me guess: Foreign Operations?"

The man shot a glance at his partner, clearly expecting a scathing comeback.

She blew her dark bangs away from her eyes with an excited grin.

Her grip on the gun was so tight I could see each vein under her bronze skin. "Who knows? Now, take out your gun, with your *left* hand, and throw it overboard." Ten points for March. There was nothing Italian about that new accent. "And, please, *do* something stupid. I really want to be known as the woman who killed you."

March reached inside his favorite navy bulletproof jacket. "You will not."

When I glimpsed the grip in his gloved hand, I backed away as much as possible, readying myself for him to shoot them and, if they had the time to fire back, for them to shoot us. But March casually threw his gun into the lagoon. It was her cue; perhaps thinking he no longer posed an immediate threat, she lowered her own weapon to shoot him in the legs. A terrible idea, if you ask me.

In the instant that followed, March dashed to the left. Two bullets narrowly missed him and smashed into the cockpit floor, right before he grabbed the woman's now exposed wrist. I registered her scream over two other gunshots, but I didn't connect the dots until the guy who had been aiming at me staggered back, dark blood blooming around a wound right above his knee and seeping from a second wound on the hand that had been holding his gun seconds prior. He curled up on his side with a groan. I blinked rapidly, struggling to process what had just happened. The female agent seemed unconscious, and her wrist was broken—disarticulated, really. Her own gun now rested in March's right hand. Her colleague's bloodstained gun had landed close to me. I wasn't sure what I'd do with it, but I picked it up.

In the cabin, the pilot had turned around and pulled out a gun as well. I raised the semiautomatic reflexively. "You won't have time to shoot us both!" I yelled, praying he couldn't hear the tremor in my voice. No need for him to know that I'd never pull the trigger with March standing so close—bullets tended to bend at a ninety-degree angle when I was in charge.

March confirmed with a wry smile. "You heard my bodyguard."

The boat was still racing, bumping over waves. The pilot was breathing fast. His fist shook around the weapon's grip. Still aiming at him, March gave the slightest shrug of his shoulder, tipping his head to the water.

The guy grimaced, as if to say, *Dude, seriously?*

I made a show of adjusting my aim. So did March, black leather squeaking as his fingers tightened around the trigger. At that point, our adversary figured that some battles are better left unfought—he dropped his gun and came out, splaying his palms in a pacifying gesture . . . and jumped overboard.

Likely alerted by the gunshots, the white speedboat now raced fifty yards behind us, and I could make out several men kneeling on its deck. It was the moment their female colleague chose to come to her senses. Scrambling up with a gasp, she struggled to produce a combat knife from her jacket. She was fighting a losing battle with only her left hand, so March was a gentleman about the whole situation. When she threw herself at him, he had no choice but to head-butt her overboard too, but not before he growled, "My apologies."

I managed to wobble up and fought back a wave of nausea when I noticed that one of my palms was sticky from the blood of the guy still curled up in the cockpit and breathing hard. His erratic intakes of air and the beads of sweat on his temples were familiar; I understood his fear. But I knew something he didn't: March wouldn't kill a CIA agent. For years, he'd cultivated "cordial" ties with the agency by carrying out hits for them in exchange for an indulgent—if not blind—eye to the rest of his activities. They had even let him retire and set up Struthio Security on US soil. It was bad enough that the Lions wanted March dead; he wouldn't risk burning that bridge too.

"He's not going to kill you," I whispered.

The guy didn't reply; he just stared up at the gun still resting in my hand, his gaze empty, almost fascinated, as if he believed his fate was mine to decide.

March squeezed my shoulder with a fleeting look of guilt and gestured to the now empty piloting post inside the cabin. "Do you think you can?"

I hoped so. Apparently, we had this new rule that every time he needed both his hands for carnage, I'd be expected to copilot. Our options were limited anyway. We were headed straight and fast toward the Lido—way too fast—and the white boat was still in pursuit. I balled my fists, stepped into the cabin, and grabbed the wheel.

"Don't worry, I piloted a cruise liner in *Ship Simulator Extremes*!" I said, steering us away from the shore before we earned eternal damnation for crashing into the marble façade of Santa Maria Elisabetta Church.

March chose not to ask for details about my credentials, and I chose not to disclose that it was the *Titanic*, and that I had intentionally rammed it against the iceberg to perform a reconstitution. Over the droning of the engine, I heard a groan and some rustling in the cockpit. My eyes darted to the mirror. March stood on the deck. I glimpsed a flash of yellow and registered a splashing sound. The last guy had been granted the luxury of a lifejacket. March knelt over his magic suitcase to wipe his gloves with a wet towel and started rummaging in the compartments to assemble something. A sniper rifle.

The other speedboat was still gaining on us as we raced toward the entrance of the Grand Canal. Half of the buttons in front of me I didn't know how to use, but I had at least approximate control of the wheel and speed lever. March was now positioned at the rear of the boat, leaning on the bench to stabilize his rifle, and ready to shoot another bunch of fake Italians.

Our trip to Venice was starting well, if you're willing to overlook the fact that no version of *Ship Simulator* covered the topic of how to engage in a speedboat race on the Grand Canal. Forget about enjoying the surreal sight of renaissance buildings planted in water. Because of boats. Boats everywhere! Ochre, pink, red: a ribbon of colors flew past me as I swerved left and right, between water taxis and gondolas, barges and . . . a fricking *canoe*?

"Island!"

March's shout had me spinning the wheel just in time. As the boat veered left, there was a loud scratching sound, and I saw a ream fly past us from the corner of my eye. The sudden change of direction sent us bulleting straight toward a restaurant terrace, and I thought, *This is it. This is what they'll say in my eulogy—that I died boat crashing into a pizzeria.*

I didn't, but it was a close call; a vigorous swing of the wheel sent us sailing away from the panicked screams of people who had seen themselves die too, only eating calzones. Once we were back in the middle of the canal, I checked the mirror. The canoe guy was being pulled out of the water by a gondolier. He looked sort of okay, although I doubted he'd ever try paddling down the Grand Canal again.

Behind us, the white boat was equally hindered. A departing vaporetto forced them to make a loop in the middle of the canal, under the insults of several water taxis. March kept watching them through his riflescope, but apparently they weren't stupid enough to open fire while surrounded by tourists eating gelato.

"Are they after Dries?" I shouted from the cabin.

"An excellent question for Mr. Morgan—he looks very flustered!"

"*What?*"

It made sense. If Dries was still in Venice and the CIA was looking for him, then that's where Alex would go. But I wished March hadn't told me, because now I felt sick, and my hands were trembling as I pushed on the throttle lever. I didn't think it would get worse, until I caught a flash of blue beyond the massive white arches of the Rialto Bridge. Did we want to race past another police boat while ours was possibly stolen, and there was blood all over the cockpit inside which March sat holding a rifle? Maybe not.

I didn't have any plan; I steered all the way to the right and barreled into a narrow canal leading into the maze of old stones of the Castello district. The first gunshots crackling in the air reminded me that we were now away from prying eyes and that my ex-boyfriend was the clingy type. I buried my head in my shoulders and gripped the wheel harder. March replied with two consecutive shots. It was a dark epiphany to realize that I could tell when he was the one firing—not just because it sounded closer but because he seldom pressed the trigger twice unless he had to. An unpleasant pressure squeezed my lungs when I noticed in the mirror that the two men who had been visible on the deck of the white boat appeared to be gone. I hoped they were only wounded too . . . Could one of them be Alex?

"They're faster than us; we need to lose them."

I jumped out of my skin when March pulled me away from the controls. Desperately focused on not crashing into anything, I hadn't heard him retreat into the cabin.

I reluctantly let go of the wheel, and I crouched a little to shield myself. Mossy walls and dinghies flew past us. It was the sight of an eighteenth-century building that sparked a light in my memories. I had been there before, with my mother. It'd been more than a decade, but I couldn't forget that roman arch, flanked by a pair of unfortunately placed round windows. Just a little too high. The gondola ride had been a smoother and slower one, giving me ample time to stare and conclude that no one should ever build an entrance door that looked like the female reproductive system.

I grabbed March's forearm. "Take a left; take a left now! There's . . . a bridge, in that street!"

"Island—"

"*Now!*" I shouted.

To my amazement, he complied and swore under his breath right afterward. Too late to back out. I thought we'd make it through easily, but the pink bridge was even lower than in my memories. We bolted under the tiny arch. Something creaked and tore on the roof—the beacon light, judging by the blue shards of plastic raining into the cockpit. I was counting on the evil white boat to follow us, and boy, did it, in a terrible crash of plastic and metal. You see, the CIA was a generous mistress, one that provided bigger, faster, better crafts than those of the Venetian police. But mostly bigger.

March looked in the mirror at the pristine bow stuck under the bridge and the mess of floating parts surrounding it. Then his gaze fell on me. "The damage is superficial. And there's a larger canal running parallel to this one; it won't take them long to find us again."

My features pinched at the same time that his relaxed a little. "I am, however, impressed," he concluded with a wink.

I don't think March had ever played *Ship Simulator*, but in his hands, the wheel barely moved, guided by his palms. Our boat glided straight and fast down the ironically named Canale della Misericordia until we reached the north side of the lagoon. There he moored on a deserted wooden pier. Behind us, an alley the size of a needle's eye meandered back into the paved streets of the Cannaregio. We were already running away when I looked over my shoulder at the police boat secured to a red-and-white striped post. "Your suitcase, you forgot it in the cockpit!"

He hadn't. In guise of answer, he squeezed my hand harder, pulling me toward him. A couple of pigeons took off ahead of us. I was distracted by the soft flapping of their wings, the flash of iridescent gray, almost black against the glare of the sun. Behind us, something blew up on the pier. I held my breath when the booming shock wave reached us. People were yelling. They sounded fine, but there was an undercurrent of stupor to their voices, like they couldn't believe it. *I could*, because I had gotten used to the fact that things often exploded around March.

I kept looking back at the cloud of black smoke rising above the tiled roofs. March dragged me so I wouldn't stop running. "I'm sorry for that. I prefer not to leave anything behind."

Understandable, I thought, my breath short from the effort to keep up with him—Damn you, tall people! In the middle of it all, I made a mental note that my own suitcase had lasted all of twelve hours . . .

I had no idea where he was taking me. We turned left and right, our shoes clattering on the pavement as we raced past cracked walls and colorful shutters. I wondered if March knew—sensed—something: he'd sometimes pause briefly, hesitate between two streets, and always pick the darkest, less touristy one. We ran and ran, until flowers and light burst into view. Water trickled from a stone fountain in front of a small renaissance church. We'd reached a rather large place, and this time there would be nowhere to hide.

March stopped dead in his tracks. His eyes scanned the buildings, the tourists chatting in front of a gift shop. It always made me feel half blind when he did that, because there were so many things he saw that I would never have noticed. Like the guy in a worn leather jacket sitting with his back to us under an umbrella at the table of a trattoria.

I should have recognized him though. He turned to greet us. A warm, peaceful smile cracked under a week's worth of dark stubble, and he had the softest cinnamon eyes.

Alex's eyes.

TEN
DEAD BALL

Christie caressed the soft swell of her belly with a despondent sigh. It had only taken one night of devastating passion for Xander to score both in her heart and in her uterus.

Becky David, Under Penalty of Love

March's eyes darted up to one of the windows above the trattoria. The shutters were slightly ajar, and he didn't seem to like it much. Meanwhile, Alex crossed the place like any other tourist, his hands in his pockets, and that boyish je ne sais quoi on his features, which seldom left him. I glanced down. His pants were still damp, the only sign that he had just narrowly avoided dying at the age of twenty-eight, smashed like a pumpkin against a Venetian bridge.

He looked me straight in the eyes, and his lips curved down in the semblance of a compassionate frown. "Baby, are you okay?"

Before I could snap back something I'd regret, he turned his attention to March. "Quite a run you gave us, Mr. November. But working with you, I learned you're not so good when you get drawn out of the shadows." He gazed at the place around us. "I've got a team in place, and you left me half of the other one. I wouldn't do anything rash if I were you." He narrowed his eyes at me, just for a second, and there it was, the other Alex, the one I'd come to know on the side of a mountain road in Switzerland. "She's slow. You're dragging her, and you know it. Even if you could escape, I'd just make sure she gets shot and never walks again."

He winked at me then, and two scenes flashed in my mind: March, severing the spine of a guy named Rislow, in part to settle an old score but mostly as punishment for having tried to dismember me on an operation table. And later, Dries threatening to do the same to me to reassert who was the boss in his evil lair. It was apparently one of the Lions' favorite punishments, called a *forty-five*, and consisted of cutting between the fourth and fifth vertebrae, so the recipient could still breathe on his own but was left a quadriplegic. I wondered if Alex was aware he used the same kind of threat as the man he had sworn to kill.

March took a step back to stand behind me, shielding my spine with his own. I clenched my fists. Anything, *anything* but this. He returned Alex's tranquil smile, as if they were just a couple of old friends about to meet for drinks. "Forgive me, I'm a little confused. I must say I'd been hoping for a romantic escapade in Venice, rather than, well"—he smacked his tongue—"enlighten me, Mr. Morgan. What is it that you have in mind?"

"Listen to me, asshole. You wounded five agents, nearly killed one. Whatever deal you had with the agency is off. Now you're just another name on the long list of people I'm free to wipe out any way I want."

"Yet I'm still standing," March noted.

"I want Dries, and you're going to help me find him."

"I'm afraid there isn't much I can do."

The soft cinnamon gaze turned stone cold. "You're gonna help me, because I'm your only chance to ever return to that shitty Good Samaritan life you tried to make for yourself. Give me what I want, I clean up your file"—Alex snapped his fingers—"just like that. Think about it. You can go back to your little business, chase cheating husbands and lost cats"—he flashed me his most convincing good-guy smile—"and fuck my spoils after dinner."

I took a sharp breath. "Alex."

"Yes, baby?"

Don't. Call. Me. Baby.

"I hope Poppy never finds out what kind of turd you are."

The nice smile distorted into a snarl. Alex didn't like it when people brought up his dear little sister, who lived the carefree life of a sixteen-year-old in Washington's suburbs, unaware that her brother traveled around the world killing people in the name of the greater good. Or just to satisfy a hunger I had yet to fully comprehend.

He shrugged. "She won't. But you will if I don't find Dries. You're his accomplices. Him"—Alex jerked his chin at March—"he'll escape, or get himself killed. But *you* . . . you'll get life without parole in maximum security, so the good people get to see some justice."

Neither March nor I reacted to these new threats. Whether intentionally or not, Alex had provided us with a considerable piece of intel. He *knew* Dries had contacted March. Otherwise he wouldn't have been so sure March and I were part of some evil terrorist plot. Which brought me back to the same question I'd been asking myself back in Cape Saint Francis: *How?* March had sort of hinted at the possibility that Lions occasionally make their plans known to the CIA. Or was it the opposite? But Alex made no secret of his beef with their (now former) vice commander, and he had burned Dries, badly. So why would the Lions want anything to do with him?

"Island, baby?"

I glared at Alex and took a cautious step back. He turned his head to a lone figure standing at the other end of the place in front of the church's marble stairs. "Can I ask you to follow Agent Stiles without making a scene? Mr. November and I need to finish this conversation alone."

I glanced over his shoulder. I recognized the loose-fitting suit concealing a brawny build, the blond buzz cut, and that perpetual air of innocence, even as he tried to look stern. A fleeting sense of relief eased the tension in my limbs. We were being marked by a bunch of invisible shooters waiting for Alex to give his go, and he wanted to use me against March to force him to talk. But in this dark hour, I had a Facebook friend.

Special Agent Joshua Stiles, forty years old, ten of which spent in the shadow of assholes like Alex at the CIA's Directorate of Foreign Operations. Enjoyed *Dukes of Hazzard* reruns, pizza rolls, and . . . cats. He and I had met in New York during the investigation of the Ruby case. We'd barely spent fifteen minutes alone together in Bellevue hospital's garage, while Alex and March were busy having yet another pissing contest over me. Short as our encounter might have been, it was bromance at first sight: Here was a man who wondered whether Guantanamo provided smaller orange pj's for short people like me, and spent a considerable amount of time posting cat pics on Facebook during work hours.

He had sent me a friend invite, with the promise of the hottest videos I'd ever see online, and that's how everything had begun. Our forbidden passion had been consummated during my trip from Vaduz to Cape Saint Francis, when I started liking said videos one after another in the plane. I didn't know how to tell March about Stiles and his secret hobby without it sounding weird, or even dangerous, so I had kept this new relationship a secret.

I waved timidly at him. He didn't wave back. Heartbreak and betrayal? So soon?

"Island . . ." Alex's warning held the amusement of an adult scolding a child, but I could see no trace of humor in his eyes.

I moved away from March slowly, searching his face for any sign that he had a plan. He merely nodded once and watched me leave. Halfway across the place, I stopped.

Certain moments in life call for an organ solo. Such as the horrifying second of doubt you experience right before ripping out the band of wax you just placed on your armpit. Or when you're being hunted in the streets of Venice by your creepy ex-boyfriend, and, in front of you, the heavy wooden doors of a church open to reveal a funeral procession. As if to remind you that yes, you are indeed *that* screwed.

A whiff of incense reached my nostrils at the same time that Stiles turned to check the newcomers. The procession was pretty standard, as far as burial ceremonies go: A dozen people of all ages and sizes dressed in black, a couple of old women sobbing. Four men carried a black coffin. I noticed that they were all wearing homemade yellow armbands bearing the emblem of the local soccer club, the Venezia F.C. In the same spirit, the spray of white and purple chrysanthemums sitting on top of the coffin had been arranged to form a shape reminiscent of a soccer ball.

A dedicated fan had left this world.

We all watched, for a moment suspended in time, as they walked down the smooth marble steps and crossed the place in quiet solemnity.

Until something shook, rolled, and clanked inside the coffin.

The men dropped it in panic. Under their black lace veils, the old ladies squeaked. March and Alex drew their weapons at once. Red dots appeared on the walls and started a hesitant waltz between the coffin, the mourners, my chest, March's head, and even Alex's, because I guess even the black ops have their twits. Combined horror and bewilderment took over me when the black lacquered wood emitted the faintest squeak.

I'm a woman of science, and up to a point, a rational person. But I also watched *The Sixth Sense* in the dark as a kid, and since then, I never really stopped worrying that the dead might actually be creeping all around us. So, when I saw the top of the coffin shake, the smoke seep out—*straight from hell*—I'd tell you that my blood chilled, but that's not even close. Every square inch of my skin prickled in horror. My jaw started quivering, and I just couldn't stop the chatter of my teeth.

A broken cry made it past the lump in my throat. "March. *March!*"

From where he stood, maybe he could already see the soccer zombie. I'm not sure. He yelled for me to stay down, but his voice was covered by a loud bang. The coffin burst open in an eruption of white, icy smoke. An actual soccer ball went flying in the air, along with the top of the casket, and I caught a flash of red spinning toward the sky. I heard Alex bark some kind of order; I didn't wait to find out what it was. The gas surrounding us was stinging my eyes, burning my lungs, and I could no longer see March. I ran blindly toward the church, to seek refuge and get a better view of the place.

Once at the steps, a hand clasped around my wrist and hauled me all the way behind one of the doors, to safety. Stiles. I glanced up at him, and he responded with a quick nod of reassurance. I squeezed his arm; I hadn't lost my new Facebook friend after all. Absolute chaos ensued. People fled the place with panicked shrieks, gunshots echoed through the mist that was now enveloping March and Alex. Bright-red dots danced madly, seeking a proper target. Several shots were fired into the coffin, causing a limp, pasty-white arm to jerk up and dangle out of the wooden box.

Once the white cloud had dissipated, I realized that this apocalypse had been provoked by an extinguisher, which had exploded inside the unfortunate soccer fan's coffin. Whether this tasteless prank had anything to do with us, I had no idea, but it'd changed the game. Alex now stood in the middle of the place with several guys holding assault rifles or guns. He did glance at the church's doors, but he had more pressing concerns: March was nowhere to be seen. He wasn't far though—as the men looked around, swiping the area with their laser pointers, one of them collapsed without warning, hit in the knee.

The group scattered behind the fountain and the tables of the trattoria. Shielded behind a corner of the building, Alex was beyond himself with rage. His voice boomed in Stiles's earpiece so loud I could hear it. "Fucking *find* him!"

I gripped Stiles's arm harder. "I swear we had nothing to do with what happened to that plane! Alex, he's—"

"I can't let you go," he said, his southern drawl enveloping each word. He shook his head, conflict obvious in his pale blue eyes. "But I'll do what I can to make sure they treat you well."

Two other gunshots tore the silence, taking out one of the guys positioned around the fountain. He fell to the ground, hit in the leg and arm. Then, nothing, just the howl of a police siren in the distance. The block was enclosed by canals. They'd be here soon. Stiles and I stood still, entirely focused on the remaining agents spreading around the place to either find March or escape.

Did you know that eardrum degeneration starts in your twenties and will first affect high frequencies and progress throughout adulthood until you lose your ability to hear low frequencies as well toward the age of sixty? What I'm getting at is that me being fifteen years younger than Stiles is probably why I registered the soft clatter of soles on the marble before he did. I spun around. In the shadows of the deserted transept, a man stood, wearing a three-piece suit and shiny brogues. But mostly carrying a gun. Stiles turned too, a second too late. I saw the glint of metal and the outline of a suppressor.

"Stiles! Watch out!"

He was much heavier than me, so I rammed into him with all my strength. He lost his balance, staggered back and caught himself on a prayer kneeler. The round of bullets missed him by a hair, smashing into the marble with a crackling sound. Stiles struggled back to his feet to aim at the ghost. He fired once; at the same time, our attacker breezed past me to finish him. A powerful kick sent the gun flying from Stiles's hand; it bounced on the floor and landed spinning a few feet away. He managed to get up on his knees, only to be kicked again, this time in the chest. When he hit the floor, he was breathing heavily and seemed disoriented.

I wouldn't have thought I had it in me to do something like that—spurred by pure adrenaline, I latched on to the shadow with a battle cry, grabbing the back of his jacket to stop him any way I could. The distraction sort of worked, but it also backfired fast. I barely had the time to inhale a familiar scent of wood and spice before the man contorted to brush me away as if I were nothing but lint. I landed on my ass with a yelp. I looked up in terror at the face that was now outlined by the light coming from the doors. Through shimmering dust, I saw a short, graying beard and hazel eyes that could have been mine . . . only a little more golden.

Dries?

I scrambled up and kicked him in the shin so hard I hurt my toes. "Don't you *dare* kill Stiles!"

ELEVEN
THE LADY-KILLER

"Yes, Paola, I'll break society's rules for another taste of you! Call me your stepfather if you want, but it won't stop me from loving you!"
La Passione Dei Cuori, *episode 827*

"He's down. Not worth killing."

Dries and I had been reunited for less than thirty seconds, and yet, watching him sneer at Stiles's fruitless attempt to get on his feet, I was already mentally starting a dick-move counter. Shitting all over a persistent adversary who also happened to be a really sweet guy: +1.

Outside the church, more gunshots echoed. Alex's little chess game with March wasn't over. I pointed to the fountain, next to which one of Alex's men held his thigh with a grimace of pain. "March is still out there!"

Dries shrugged and adjusted a golden cufflink, half concealed by a gray sleeve. "I gave him an extinguisher and a soccer ball; he'll be fine. He'll keep that little piece of shit busy for us."

"But . . ." Did he mean Alex? Did Dries know he was the one behind this manhunt?

Before I could ask, he was already pulling me away toward a small door behind the altar. "Little Island, I'd love to sit down for a chat, but I'm afraid we have to take our leave."

He was right. Outside, the sound of boots smacking the pavement was getting closer. Alex had sent someone to check on me and Stiles. I ran behind him as he led us out of the church, across a bridge, and into an exiguous alley whose decrepit walls I doubted ever saw any sunlight.

"Where are we going?"

He slowed down to hustle me into a covered walkway made of stone arches running along a shallow canal. "I never answer that kind of question."

"But, March! How will he find us?"

"I'll leave him some bread crumbs. He deserves a little whipping; it'll do him good."

"Seriously? He came all the way here to help your sorry ass!"

Dries snorted. "And he brought you with him."

"Because I asked him to—"

A loud splash and the screams of a group of tourists interrupted our dispute. A chubby teen had fallen into the water, shoved out of the way by three men running toward us. One of them, wearing a black hoodie and conspicuous sunglasses, pulled out a gun. On TV, they always make it look easy to shoot people while running, but it's actually tricky. I'm sure that guy was well trained, but all he accomplished was scaring the crap out of me and making me run even faster when bullets shattered windows and stone carvings behind us.

We were almost at a bridge linking two islets, where tourists gathered, attracted by the windows of a supermarket. The gunshots scattered them like pigeons, leaving free range to our pursuers. This time Dries turned back. He didn't entertain the same kind of qualms March had about shooting CIA agents. He raised his gun, pulled the trigger, and the man closest to us, hoodie-glasses, fell like a rag doll, hit between the eyes. Our pursuers dealt swift retribution: limestone fragments exploded all around us as we crossed the bridge. Something brushed my hip, leaving a burning sensation in its wake. My heart faltered. I'd been shot. No. Almost. In any case, I could still move. A little blood seeped through my T-shirt, but I was even more scared to look than to stop running.

We'd reached the other side, but I could see no escape route, save for a large street with nowhere to hide.

"We're going down!"

What? Dries pulled me to him, wrapped his arm around my waist . . . and threw us over the bridge. I expected water; I met the hard pavement of a short pier and his chest, which cushioned my fall to some extent. Above us, one of the two men yelled to his colleague to follow us down there. I staggered up, and finally saw what Dries had seen. On one of the buildings, a door opening to the canal had been left ajar. We barreled inside and climbed up a series of musty stairs leading to the roof.

The footsteps smacking the wood weren't far behind us. Dries shot the lock of an iron door and dragged me across the roof under a rickety pergola. When I figured out where this was headed, my legs froze. "No, I'm not . . . I can't!"

"Island, I don't have time for this," he growled.

I stared at the ledge on the adjacent building, a good twenty feet above the ground. It was easily accessible—just one big step—but that building could be what, five hundred years old? The stones could have become a pile of giant wafers by now! I wasn't given a choice. Dries gripped my arm hard enough to leave a bruise and yanked me toward the empty space between the two buildings. I wobbled forward with a gasp, and all that was left to do was take the jump or fall. It must have been no more than three feet, but it felt like a hundred. I looked down and caught a glimpse of the street below: the sight of a green trash can knotted my insides like a Brazilian bracelet.

"Almost there," he said in what I understood to be his best attempt at a reassuring tone, but it still came out a little gruff.

I pressed my body against the sun-warmed wall, unable to look elsewhere, and especially not at the ten-inch-wide ledge on which I now stood. My hand found Dries's, and my fingers dug into his palm as we took the few steps needed to reach the nearest open window. He helped me over the railing of a wrought iron balcony and, like a pair of nosy cats looking to their next misdeed, we slipped into an empty kitchen. Dries immediately closed the window behind us and drew its lace curtain. Through the gauzy fabric, we watched as, on the opposite roof, two figures burst through the door we'd left open, searching for any sign of our presence. One of them pressed a finger to his ear, perhaps receiving new orders. We moved away from the window. I followed Dries, shivers coursing through me as I tiptoed—well, broke, really—into a stranger's home.

It was an old Venetian apartment, one of those places where time stands still. The green mosaic tiling on the floor and faded yellow of the furniture suggested that the clock had stopped ticking sometime during the midsixties. Half covered by the loud hum of a rusty fridge, the sound of a television echoed through the walls. Dries brought a finger to his lips and pointed to the kitchen door leading to a long corridor. There, countless paintings and photos served to conceal faded, flowery wallpaper. As we treaded on the parqueted floor with excruciating care, it struck me that even at his age, Dries retained the same sort of inexplicable feline grace I had witnessed in March. He must have weighed twice as much as I did, yet he moved like a shadow. My chest tightened unpleasantly at the thought of all the people he must have killed, sneaking up on them in the same fashion.

The background noise of hurried Italian speech mingled with the dramatic sigh of violins was getting louder. A soap opera was airing, and a good one, I reckoned. Dries held his hand midair to stop me. A pair of French doors opened to a living room. I could make out kitschy furniture covered with lace doilies and a burgundy couch. Dries's finger curled around the gun's trigger. For the first time, I noticed the inscription engraved in the long black barrel. I wouldn't allow this. We would *not* shoot an elderly person with a Desert Eagle. I placed my hand on his, shaking my head with an imploring look.

Under his silvery beard, the corner of his mouth twitched. He took a deliberate step forward; I dove to stop him, and we found ourselves standing in an awkward position in front of the French doors, no longer hidden.

The couch was in fact empty, and someone in there was even quieter than a Lion. An old lady wearing a mauve robe over a long nightshirt stood in the middle of the living room, staring back at us. Now, if I had seen a guy like Dries pop in my hallway, holding a big semiautomatic and wearing a three-piece suit, my first thought would have been *Mafioso* and the second one *Oh my God. Call the police!* That woman? She didn't seem to mind, and I was willing to bet that my heart was beating faster than hers at the moment.

She kind of ignored me, looking Dries up and down instead. He straightened and dusted his jacket as if this were an ordinary encounter. "*Scusami*," he whispered in a husky, almost seductive tone, bringing his forefinger to his lips like he had done to silence me.

My jaw hit the floor when she responded with the hint of a shy smile. Was this all it took, even in such a situation? An old-school playboy vibe, an admittedly good suit, and shazam? What kind of mojo was that?

I'd have asked for some details, but the shrill buzz of her doorbell killed the moment. Dries's eyes narrowed. He waved with his gun for our sort-of-hostage to go answer. As she did so, we retreated to the farthest corner of her living room and hid behind a mahogany hutch. By the time her fingers touched the lock, the buzzing had been replaced by impatient knocking. I was still waiting for her to freak out, but I guess I was the only chicken—well, chick—in this apartment. She opened the door and greeted her visitor with a tone of regal superiority, regardless of the fact that she couldn't have been more than five feet tall. A man spoke in broken Italian with a thick English accent. My pulse revved. They weren't stupid after all—they'd figured that the fastest way to escape the roof of the adjacent building was to jump onto the ledge of this one.

Dries's finger curled around the trigger. I listened, petrified, as the old woman lied with surprising ease, claiming that she had no idea what Alex's goon was talking about and even going so far as to berate him for his lack of manners. A slew of angry accusations rolled off of her tongue, while in the living room, playboy Massimo had just revealed to innocent nurse Paola that Giorgio, her three-year-old little brother, was in fact his own son! He had donated to a sperm bank, and Paola's evil mother had plotted to be inseminated with his swimmers in a bid to force Massimo to love her and raise the child with her. But now Paola too was pregnant with Massimo's child, and with these shocking revelations, she found herself expecting her own stepsister!

In the hallway, a shrill yell informed us that shit had gotten real. "Sciò! Vai via di qua!" *Shoo! Get out of here!*

The man did make a feeble attempt to question the old lady further, but before he was able to put together a comprehensible sentence, the door slammed in his face strong enough to make the walls tremble.

We left our hiding spot as she marched back into her living room and readjusted her robe. She planted herself in front of Dries, sizing him up again. Waiting for something. He flashed her a smile that I regret to say could only be described as carnal, revealing the same gap tooth I had inherited from him. He then bowed with flourish. The killing move was administered under the form of a long, mildly upsetting baise-mains, complete with some mandatory eye contact at the end. I couldn't help but wonder how many women had fallen for his shtick since my mother.

The lady eventually snatched her hand back, but the flush in her cheeks didn't lie: Dries had scored. Hard. She trotted back to her couch and patted the cushions with an inviting smile. I briefly feared this situation would degenerate into something I did not want to witness, but that wasn't the point—we just needed to make sure those guys looking for us would be gone before we could sneak out of her apartment. Also, I think she really wanted to watch the remaining five minutes of her episode of *La Passione dei Cuori* with Dries. I was *so* torrenting this series as soon as I got home.

"We need to find March!" I repeated for approximately the tenth time as we made our way through the crowd on the Rialto Bridge. Drowning in a sea of backpacks, I could barely discern the white limestone arches sandwiching each side of the oldest bridge crossing the Grand Canal. Not that there would have been much to see—the whole place was just an endless stream of shops selling plastic gondolas and glittery carnival masks.

Dries snorted, looking almost offended by my insistence. "I sent him a rendezvous point; what more do you want me to do?"

"Check if he's fricking *alive*!"

"I'd forgotten you were so difficult. Just like your mother."

I bit back an insult. "Oh, I'm sorry; you don't care about March? Then why don't you tell me what was in that case you gave to Bashir instead?"

Surprise flashed across his face, but he quickly regained his composure. "What would you do with that information?"

How could he not see? I massaged my forehead forcefully, fighting the waves of pain crashing in my skull after our wild chase. "Nothing. I'll do nothing, Dries . . . It just . . . It *matters* to me if you killed six hundred innocent people."

"I didn't. The case contained a pair of plastinated testicles, since it *matters* to you."

My arms dropped at my sides. "Plast . . . what the hell?"

He made an evasive gesture with his hand. "Some cultures attach more importance than others to the purity of a daughter." He gave me a pointed look. "I was personally solicited to help rectify a situation."

Rectify . . . March sometimes used that same word. Like when he'd admitted to having once shot someone in the knees with expanding bullets in his wild days. I wanted to believe that the guy had it coming because he was a gangster, but sometimes I feared I was living a lie. Would it similarly comfort me to know whether Dries's victim was still alive? What if he was dead? Was it a case of avenging rape, or had Dries crushed a pure love like Sanchez cutting out the heart of his girlfriend's lover before her very eyes in *License to Kill?*—he was really one of the worst James Bond villains. Jerk totally deserved to die in the end.

I worded my next question carefully. "Would you say that, within your moral frame of reference, this guy deserved to be . . . uh . . . to have that done to him? Because he had committed some sort of crime?"

"Irrelevant. Plastination is, however, a fascinating process."

"Come on! I'm trying to find you excuses, and you're just being an asshole!"

"Careful, little Island." We both knew the threat was—almost—empty; he pulled out a tiny black smartphone and shot me a condescending glare. "There. March is on his way. Happy now?"

"Is he okay?"

Dries removed a toddler out of his way, casually lifting her by the handle of her Mickey Mouse backpack, under the parents' horrified stares. "I certainly hope not. That idiot let Morgan escape. He'd better show up with a missing leg for it."

Morgan? So, Dries already knew that the leak had come from Alex. What else exactly did he know?

He took us through a maze of backstreets, zigzagging away from the Rialto and into San Polo. A long-suffering sigh reached my ears. "What did I hire him for?"

"You didn't hire March. You whined for help because you're burnt like toast," I muttered.

"As you would be, were it not for my generous intervention."

I nearly choked with indignation. "Because it was entirely your fault in the first place!"

He paused midstep, a dangerous gleam in his golden eyes. "It was. However, imagine my surprise when I told March that a cleaning team was on its way to his house, and he informed me that you were in said house." I opened my mouth to protest. He cut me off. "I remember stating you didn't have my blessing."

"I'm sorry, but it doesn't work like that. What I do, and who I do it with, is none of your business, Dries."

His chest heaved as if he was going to lose his temper, but whatever rage had been boiling in there he kept in check behind a mask of disdain. "Betrayed by my own blood. *Twice.* Now, hush and walk. We will have this conversation again, young lady."

TWELVE
THE GOLDEN MOUNTAIN

In her palm, the meatballs felt hot, moist and heavy.
—*Terry Robs*, The Italian Chef's Secret Sauce

The pizza boxes and soda bottles overflowing from the trash cans made for a decent sundial: I'd say we reached the quiet neighborhood of Campo San Tomà around lunchtime. We slipped into a passageway so narrow Dries and I could barely walk side by side. He stopped in front of a tall door recessed in an arch that was supported by two sculpted columns. The building was in poor condition, as evidenced by the bricks showing under what had once been a layer of plaster and red paint. The intricate Moorish designs and latticed windows suggested a fifteenth-or sixteenth-century house, the sort of gift Venice bestowed upon those brave enough to get lost in its streets until nightfall.

I wondered if he owned the place, since he made it past a rather complicated door code. Ahead of us, a corridor led to a wrought iron gate barring access to a private Eden: a small patch of garden where thick foliage surrounded cascading glycine and fragrant rosebushes. I couldn't wait to take a better look, but the gate refused to budge when Dries turned the knob. He slammed his thumb on a plastic intercom on the wall. "Dikkenek, maak oop die hek." *Dikkenek, open the gate.*

Dikkenek? Wasn't that the name Isiporho had mentioned in Cape Town? Another Lion then. The lock clicked, triggering loud barking and the heavy patter of claws, first on the floor above us and then in the garden's gravel. I jumped back, and Dries closed the gate just in time, before a hurricane of brownish hair and flappy jowls rammed against it. Through the rusty-iron bars, a fat bulldog snarled at us. Dries rang the intercom again with an irritated sigh. "En neem beheer van jou hond." *And control your dog.*

A gravelly male voiced thundered from somewhere inside the house. "Andrea, zwijg! Kom hier terug!" *Andrea, be quiet! Come back here!*

With a final reluctant yelp, the dog retreated, and this time legitimate footsteps crushed the gravel. Before us stood some sort of . . . old Viking. Think Jeffrey Lebowski—The Dude—but with bright-yellow paint stains all over his T-shirt and cargo shorts and even some clinging to his mess of shoulder-length blond hair. I paid little attention to his right hand until he pulled the gate open. Alerted by an unexpected whirring sound, I looked down. The sleek carbon fiber reached all the way up his arm and under the sleeve of his T-shirt. I made a note that the metallic joints had amazing coordination: his elbow and fingers moved smoothly as he showed us in.

I tried to avert my eyes, but he noticed I'd been staring. "Feast your eyes; I don't mind. You can call me Jan, by the way." His accent was different than Dries's, a little softer maybe. In any case, save for the beer belly, this guy looked strong enough to open a thousand pickle jars.

"You look worse and worse every time I see you, *broer*," Dries said with a smirk.

Nice greeting, especially to a guy who was obviously going through the trouble of hiding us.

"And you've come a long way down, Vice Commander," our host shot back. The curl of his lips under that yellowish beard belied the harsh statement.

Once in the garden, I basked in the scent of flowers and crushed leaves hanging in the air. Andrea now lay sprawled in a bed of violets, watching us through heavy-lidded eyes. *God,* that dog was a zeppelin.

"So is it *Dikkenek* or Jan?" I asked the guy as he opened a worm-eaten wooden door leading inside the house.

That made him laugh, but I received no further clarification.

"He was from Brussels, and he always had a big mouth," Dries commented with a shrug, as if it explained everything.

It sort of did. Past tense: Jan's career was over, likely because he was missing his right arm. Different accent: The guy was from Belgium, where *Dikkenek* was not-so-nice slang to designate a boastful, big-mouthed type of individual.

Andrea's frenzied bark broke through our chitchat. The front door had been opened; someone else was inviting themselves into Jan's little paradise. I ran toward the gate, with the dog springing after me—his owner grabbed him by the collar with a powerful left hand, otherwise this story might have ended then and there. I jumped into March's arms when he walked in. "Are you okay?"

"Yes." His hand brushed down my side, where a bullet had grazed me and left a smarting sensation and a little dried blood on the torn cotton. "We need to take care of this."

I looked up to see that he had earned a gash of his own, under his ear, and much closer to his carotid than I was comfortable with. "I'm fine; what happened to you?"

"Mr. Morgan was very insistent I should spend the rest of the afternoon with him."

"The little shit's father taught him well." Dries stood with his arms crossed, dark amusement in his eyes.

I balled my fists, willing myself not to react. Alex's father? How well had Dries known him before his death?

Against me, March stiffened. He planted his gaze in his mentor's. "Speaking of that . . . we need to talk."

Before Dries had a chance to say a word, Jan waved his prosthetic arm to the open door revealing the half-painted walls of his living room. "Band-Aids and pasta first?"

If it had been up to me, I'd have followed March to a room upstairs to help him take care of his neck—and provided all manner of physical comfort in the process. *Hélas!* Dries stated that he didn't want the two of us alone together, and I guess it would have been awkward anyway for us to disappear into a bedroom, even just to kiss. Because, you know, not in public. Even behind locked doors.

So, after having disinfected my own scrape and put a Band-Aid on it, I found myself helping Jan cook pasta in a kitchen that was okay by my standards and a lot less so by March's. I sliced an onion on the stone counter while he opened a box of spaghetti with the consummate skill of a man who lived alone. At Jan's feet, Andrea didn't miss a detail of the preparation, his tongue dangling and salivating in a disgusting manner when Jan grabbed a large box of meatballs from his freezer. For having a "big mouth," the man was oddly quiet though.

"It's a beautiful house," I said, hoping to strike up conversation while he put the meatballs in the microwave, inside which enough food splatters remained to make a second meal.

"Bought it for my wife. She grew up in the area, and she wanted to renovate it." He glanced at the half-painted yellow walls of the living area behind us. "Now I'm doing it with Andrea, but I'm not sure about the colors . . . and he doesn't even see them."

I scanned the haphazard paint strokes and brand-new red tiling around us in the kitchen. "Did your wife leave?"

"She died last year. Cancer."

My hands let go of the knife. *Good job, Island!* "I'm really sorry."

"Yeah . . . she was a fine woman. Damn shame."

Remembering March's conversation with Pieter, back in Cape

Saint Francis, I submitted to the custom Jan had no doubt adopted during his years in South Africa and confirmed his statement with a little nod. "Shame."

He resumed watching the bubbling water. I hesitated to tell him that it wouldn't boil if he kept looking at it—a well-known, albeit inexplicable, scientific phenomenon. Considering my previous misstep, however, I decided to tread on safer ground. I pointed at the line of golden trophies on top of a cupboard. "Wow, you won the . . . um . . . *Montagna d'Oro* cup? Several times?"

"Not me, Andrea."

I turned to the culprit, sprawled on his side and watching my every move as I started stirring the tomato sauce. "Wow . . . like some kind of"—I cringed, noticing that drool had started to pool on the terracotta tiles under Andrea's glistening chin—"*pageant?*"

Jan gave me a look mirroring that of his dog. "It's fried polenta. A fried-polenta eating contest."

"For dogs?"

"Yup. They hold it in Ca' Savio every summer. They set up a tent on the beach; people come to watch."

"No way!"

At last, he threw the spaghetti in the boiling water with a prideful grin. This baby here"—he pointed his finger at Andrea—"can eat six pounds of polenta in four minutes and twenty seconds. We smashed that Great Dane last year!"

"Sweet Jesus! Does he throw it up afterward?"

"Sometimes."

"You know, maybe it's bad for him."

On Jan's forehead, the lines deepened. "You're judging."

"Absolutely not. But he's already really fat—"

"We tried the local pet fit club; it wasn't his thing."

Arms akimbo, I forced an air of severity on my face. "I don't see any pet food—you're only feeding him leftovers, right?"

Jan took a wary step back. "It depends. He doesn't like—"

"Will you need any help, Island?"

I whirled around. How long had March been standing there? And, more importantly, how the hell had he managed to clean up so fast? Even the fresh bloodstains on his collar had disappeared, a slight dampness the only indication that a miracle had taken place. My man was a wizard.

"No, we're almost done. Can you just bring these outside?" I said, handing him four plates to be set on the table standing in the garden.

He took them, his gaze traveling between Andrea and Jan. "Weight Watchers, perhaps?"

It was like a weird family lunch, where half of the guests wore holsters, one kept feeding pasta to his dog as if we wouldn't notice, and March and I stole glances at each other every time Dries looked down at his plate. Cutlery clinked softly; the Parmesan mill traveled across the table. No one dared to say a word until the patriarch of this clichéd play poured himself a second glass of priceless red Quintarelli to go with his frozen meatballs.

"I'm going to have to supervise your dating. I have a few names in mind, nice boys," Dries said, almost absently.

The shot was, however, precisely calculated. Across the table, Jan cast me a look of sorrow.

March paused halfway in the process of dividing a meatball in four perfect quarter spheres. "I don't remember that we came here for that."

Dries's eyes sent daggers my way. "And, yet, poor choices were made that brought us together here and now. Were you happy to see Mr. Morgan again, by the way?"

I welcomed the blow with gritted teeth. Point made. He'd somehow learned of my involvement with Alex and expected me to go through each Station of the Cross to beg for forgiveness. I wouldn't. "Stop this. Alex is trying to destroy you because you killed his parents. Don't make this about me." On my plate, the tomato sauce now looked mildly disgusting. "I was just a means to an end."

Across the table, Dries leaned back in his chair. "Always so blunt. If you insist, let's get it out of the way. Yes, I got rid of Morgan Senior.

Yes, there were unexpected side casualties. We all live with our ghosts, and we don't let them get in the way of the job—that's how it works."

Our "ghosts", huh? Like my mom. Just a ghost that got in the way of the job. I dropped my fork onto my plate. I would have preferred some sob story about a botched job, sprinkled with a few regretful sighs, rather than this cynical detachment.

I rapped my fingers on the table. "Good for you. I mean, if you're cool about it. I guess it's easier for Alex to hate you that way."

March covered my hand with his to stop the rapping. "Why did you kill him?" he asked Dries.

"He'd served his purpose, and I didn't trust him much." I noticed Jan's imperceptible nod of approval as Dries concluded with an exasperated sigh. "Are we going to go over every single frumentarius I ever erased, or can we move on?"

I looked up from my plate. *Frumentarius?*

March's reaction was different than mine. Not curiosity, but rather pure shock as his eyes fluttered wide open, and the muscles in his jaw contracted. "I'm sorry, come again?"

THIRTEEN
THE GRAIN COLLECTORS

Neither his pungent garlic breath, nor the thick layer of fat protecting his middle from sword cuts could stop her: She wanted this powerful warrior passionately.

Hope Knight, The Gladiator's Sheath

"The father was a frumentarius. I thought you'd have figured it out by now," Dries said to March, helping himself to a couple more meatballs.

I had no idea what he meant by that, but March seemed to be reeling, an infrequent occurrence for him . . . except around Dries. "Is Mr. Morgan aware of this?"

A barking laugh burst from Dries's chest. "I hope so. If I recall well, his boss didn't exactly try to stop us, back then. Erwin was done with him too. Gladly threw him to the Lions, in fact."

March shot up from his chair, nearly toppling the table over. My heart jostled. All color had drained from his face, and his features seemed paralyzed, as if he were struggling to curb the kind of rage no one wants to be on the receiving end of.

Here we go. Erwin. Again.

Alex's boss. I preferred to call him "the Caterpillar," because the guy enjoyed cigarillos, and he was a pretentious asswipe who deserved to get knocked off of his mushroom—said mushroom being a shadow subdivision of the CIA's Directorate of Foreign Operations, for which March had carried out some nasty wet jobs in his former life. Erwin and March shared a long and grisly history together, punctuated by minor incidents such as Erwin pushing one of his agents into March's bed, only to later send her to her death during a mission in Ivory Coast. Nothing huge. It wasn't like March had dragged around some serious emotional trauma for years after Charlotte's horrendous death.

Why was I not surprised to learn that a manipulative asshole like the Caterpillar had hired and groomed a young Alex after he had engineered his father's death? Did Alex know any of this?

Next to me, March spoke to Dries without even looking at him, each word enunciated slowly, dangerously, balanced on the edge of a razor blade. "A word with you."

I sprang up too, only to be stopped by his palm on my shoulder, gentle but inflexible. "Island. No."

He and Dries left the table and disappeared into Jan's house. In his own chair, our host appeared curious but otherwise unaffected. I wondered how much he had seen in his life, how many secrets he had kept to become so jaded. I took a calming breath and sat back. "What's a frumentarius? What did Dries do this time?"

Jan's shoulders heaved in a lazy shrug. "Nothing he hasn't done before."

Shouts in Afrikaans suddenly burst from the house. My head jerked up to a window on the second floor. Behind the reflection of the afternoon clouds in the glass, March's silhouette paced in a room, tearing Dries's head off about something. I could only grasp a few intelligible bits of his booming voice. "Is hy? . . . Het Anies . . . ?" *Is he? . . . Did Anies . . . ?*

"Jan, *what* are they talking about?"

His features pinched. He looked left and right, stroking his bushy beard. "The Frumentarii . . . you could call them spies. I say they're just assholes who're not brave or skilled enough to join the brotherhood."

I moved my chair to his, my voice down to a whisper. "Spies for the Lions?"

He lowered his voice. "Actually it means *grain collector*. In the old times, they were legionnaires spying for the Roman Emperor . . . and for us. There's no grain left to collect, and the empire is long gone." He winked. "But we're still here, and there are other empires to spy on. They don't get carved. Most of them work for other chicken coops. They're our foxes."

Good thing I was sitting. Because as it turned out, Alex's dad had been a double agent feeding intel to the Lions. I remembered March's words at Pieter's garage, when I'd asked if Lions ever took their phones to let the CIA know of their plans: *It depends.*

Alex had known that the Lions were coming to blow up March's house . . . did I even want to go there? Not really, but my neurons were already busy laying the first brick of the scenario: Alex pretending to be cool with his father's death, becoming a frumentarius and some kind of triple spy, all to frame Dries and watch him get destroyed by his own brotherhood. But wouldn't the Lions have seen him coming a mile away, waving a sign that said *disgruntled orphan*? Plus, in this scenario, Alex couldn't ignore that Erwin was at least in part responsible for his parents' deaths.

"Enlighten me. What's in the deal for those guys?" I asked Jan.

"Often money. Sometimes they have a lot to lose if they don't play along; some want to join the brotherhood."

"Can they?"

"Rarely. And never on Dries's watch."

I glanced up at the now silent window. "He doesn't like them, right?"

"Once burned . . ."

In the house, two pairs of feet thumped down the old wooden stairs before I had a chance to ask who had "burned" Dries. I immediately dragged my chair back to its initial place while Jan leaned back with an air of innocence that didn't really suit the lines of experience on his tanned face.

Dries strolled to the table, self-assured and impenetrable, back to his default mode. March returned to his seat. Next to me, I could feel the tension still thrumming through him, flowing to me. I caressed his forearm in a bid to ease it a little. His skin was warmer than usual, like he had a fever, and the muscles twitched under my palm. He let out a long exhale, relaxing under my touch. It brought me a sense of relief that I was able to accomplish that. Against his own not-in-public rule, and possibly to stick it to Dries, March bent to nuzzle my hair and press a kiss to my temple.

It worked. I couldn't stop the lovestruck smile I felt tug at my lips, and Dries looked ready to shoot us both. He clapped his hands, calling the end of the break he had been the cause of, and gulped down the rest of his wine. "Let's get down to business. We have someone to find."

One of March's eyebrows arced in doubt. "I don't think Bashir planned the bombing. He's gone into hiding too, and his future looks quite compromised at the moment."

Dries waved his hand dismissively. "I'll take care of him later. First, I want that girl, the one who didn't board and Interpol is looking for."

My eyebrows jumped. "Sabina Falchi? The engineer? How do you know about her?"

"Don't insult me," he said with a haughty look that was in fact directed at March.

"So you know she used to work for Novensia?"

"Who manufactured the glass roof? Yes. Have you seen their commercial?"

March cleared his throat. "We have."

Dries's mouth pursed in appreciation. "What a fine piece of advertising . . ."

So, that made at least one mystery solved: Who was the target demographic for an ad that relied on a naked blonde to sell polycrystalline transparent ceramics? Heterosexual men in their fifties.

Dries clasped his hands. "Let me show you something, rookies."

That was Jan's cue to rise from his chair. He went to fetch a laptop in his living room, which he set on the table, next to the meatballs. A sleek, sexy silvery little thing—I'd have to ask him where he'd bought it. He pressed a key to launch a video. We all moved closer to watch as, on-screen, travelers hurried across a long hall encased between a glass wall overlooking the tarmac and a row of duty-free shops. A red crosshair appeared on a lone figure sitting next to the windows.

"How did you get your hands on the airport's surveillance footage?" I asked Dries.

A lazy smirk revealed what could have just as well been a fang. "Morgan isn't the only one with a taste for cinematography." He paused the footage. "That's her. It's 9:41; she's sitting in the boarding area. At that point, she looks perfectly fine."

Indeed, on the grainy surveillance tape, Sabina Falchi could be seen reading a magazine as she waited to board the flight.

"And here's a guest I want to know more about," he explained as the tape resumed playing.

On the screen, a second crosshair blinked, this time to single out a lean, hooded figure. A man, most likely, wearing a pair of jeans and sneakers. He went to sit right next to Falchi, his back to the camera. At first, she didn't seem to care, but he spoke to her. I watched in perplexity as she let go of her magazine and jumped back in apparent surprise, before her hands flew to her mouth, like she recognized him. She considered him hesitantly, scooted closer, and it seemed they started chatting.

Around them, passengers were lining up in front of the Delta Air Lines desk, and boarding started while their conversation went on. March fast-forwarded through their exchange, until 9:58.

"She's trying to leave," he said as Falchi got up, only to be stopped by the hooded figure.

He was gripping her shoulders, not very tight, more like he was imploring her not to go. She tried to free herself; he blocked her. The friendly reunion was taking an unpleasant turn. Near them, the passengers were finished boarding, and a ground attendant spoke into a microphone, presumably calling any remaining passengers. Falchi and the man both turned to the desk. But she didn't move. She looked back and forth between her mysterious visitor and the ground attendant, in some kind of daze. The man insisted, wouldn't let go of her hand, and she allowed the flight attendant to leave, without signaling herself.

It was 10:12, and Sabina Falchi had missed her flight.

She seemed to get agitated, then angry even, as if she'd just realized that guy had made her do something stupid. She yelled at him, but he just stood there and, after a minute or so, left. He entered the men's room and never came out. *Dammit* . . . the footage ended there, and we had no clear shot of his face.

"So you think she knew what would happen?" I asked. "He warned her?"

"I don't know. She doesn't seem to panic; she's not trying to alert anyone," Dries noted, stroking his chin. "But he popped up from nowhere and made sure she didn't board. I want to hear more about our mystery man."

March frowned at the paused footage. "Where do we start?"

"Anyone want to finish those?"

We all turned our heads to stare at Jan, holding the meatball pot. A deep silence fell on the table. He eventually threw the leftovers to Andrea, who raced with surprising agility to eat them in the grass.

Ignoring both the chewing sounds behind him and my question, Dries got up and motioned for Jan to follow him as he strode toward the house. A few hushed words were exchanged in Afrikaans, and when he came out, he was wearing his suit jacket.

March cast him a questioning look, and I jumped to my feet to protest. "Where are you going?"

Dries just waved at me without turning back as the gate creaked open. "I won't be long. Why don't you go help Dikkenek with the dishes?"

A hot wave of patriarchal douchebaggery hit me and made my

blood boil; I ran after him, only to be outsped by March, to whom Jan threw his own jacket. I lunged to catch him and demand an explanation, but he slammed the gate closed behind him. "I'm sorry, biscuit," March called before disappearing in the street. "I'll be right back."

By the time I made it past the gate too, and tumbled in the street, they had vanished around a corner. I balled my fists and yelled, mostly to the attention of the neighborhood, "Well, screw you too!"

FOURTEEN
L'AUTRE

"Cherchez la femme !"
Alexandre Dumas, *Les Mohicans de Paris*

I paced in the garden, glancing at the gate every five seconds or so. Jan and Andrea lounged together in the grass under a pearly sky. Curls of pungent smoke swirled around them: he was drawing on . . . not a cigarette.

"Where did you say they were going?" I asked for the second time.

"Near Santa Lucia Station. They have a guy to see. Jukebox. Guy came here from Bulgaria, has ears and eyes everywhere in Venice. It shouldn't be more than an hour; don't get all worked up." He patted the ground with his free hand, causing Andrea to startle with a grunt. I took the invitation and sat next to him, at a safe distance from the dog.

He pulled the joint away from his lips and held it up, looking up at me with one eyebrow raised in question.

I shook my head. "No, thank you. I don't want to get stoned. And March would bite my head off anyway. Drugs are marginally worse than murder in his book."

He guffawed in a cloud of smoke. "Always been like that, broom up his ass and all."

"I kinda thought all Lions shared that trait until I met you," I countered.

"No, it's professionalism. It's not the same. We're professionals, and we do the job. March, he's a pro, but he's also completely *gek*," he said, spinning his forefinger against his temple.

"He's not like that. He's just a little different. But so is everyone else, in some way."

He stubbed his joint in the fresh grass and stared at it pensively. "Ah, young love. You know this is driving your pa crazy, right?"

"You mean Dries?"

"Got another one?"

"Yeah, actually."

He coughed a laugh. "Complicated family."

It was. While Dries wasn't exactly my "dad," the more I discovered about him, the more I thought of him as a second father in a weird, instinctive way. Even worse, I was tempted to trust him, when every rational fiber of my being told me I shouldn't.

Jan looked up at me. "When Dries showed up and told me what was going on, honestly, I thought, *He just called March so he can kill him faster.* He's still raw about that diamond thing too. What a mess . . ."

I shrugged. "I'm not sorry for him. Dries made it clear I don't have his consent. But I made it clear I don't need it."

The corners of his lips tugged down in disapproval, which made me wonder if every man possessed a secret dad mode, regardless of whether he had kids or not. "Well, I'd say he's right. But I remember the time when *he* was the one losing his mind over a girl, and anyone who had anything to say about it, they could go fuck themselves—but only if they ran fast enough for him not to kill them first."

My heart skipped a beat. Did he mean my mom? Back in Tokyo, Dries had claimed without flinching to have never loved her. Yet he had later admitted that he wished she would have told him about me, given him the choice to stay in the picture or not. Until now, I had always thought of their relationship as a destructive and one-sided passion, a fifteen-year-long storm that eventually led my mother to her death, because she couldn't resist Dries's pull or think straight around him. It was an odd epiphany to figure out that I now stood in the exact same place. I trusted March. Needed him, even when we fought. Would *I* ever be able to leave him if I had to?

"Come here; I'll show you something."

Jan had gotten to his feet. He dusted blades of grass from his shorts and bent down to pat Andrea on the back. When I didn't get on my feet and looked at him in question instead, he flashed me a conspiratorial smile and jerked his head toward the second floor's window. "Come, get up. Wouldn't want to get caught by Dries showing you."

I scrambled to my feet. He led me up a flight of creaky stairs and to a dark hallway. Here too, there was a lot of work, but the original hexadecimal tiling and some of the paneling had been preserved. I caressed the smooth wood carvings, amazed at the idea that centuries ago, corseted ladies had walked on that same floor.

We passed two closed doors. The third one looked like a library turned storage room. Bookshelves lined the bare stone walls, and approximately a million plastic boxes were stacked on top of each other, containing magazines, linens, dishes . . . A mattress and a sleeping bag lay in a corner of the room, next to a threadbare dog bed.

Jan rummaged through a specific box. After some struggling with a handful of postcards that kept slipping from his carbon fiber hand, he retrieved a large leather album. "I'm not really supposed to have this. He doesn't like that kind of trace."

We sat together on the mattress, and when he opened the album and started flipping through the yellowish pages, I held my breath. He had kept pictures. And not just that: there were also newspaper cuttings, most of them announcing either the murder or "accidental" death of various officials. Like a seventeen-year-old Justin Bieber fan, over the years Jan had put together an album of his favorite kills and many travels.

He skimmed past entire sections, and I tried to ignore some of the worst pictures, like the one where he could be seen posing next to a dead crocodile still holding a dismembered leg in its mouth, or that polaroid selfie with a black guy I was pretty sure was Idi Amin Dada. He eventually paused to point at a specific page. *1988, Monte Carlo.*

My pulse picked up as I scanned the page. A cut from *The Monaco Times* recounted the gruesome execution of a Colombian drug lord and his entire escort in a suite at the Hôtel Métropole. Next to the article, Jan had pasted a single Polaroid, taken on a road overlooking a turquoise sea. My fingertips instinctively moved to caress the plastic film protecting the picture.

My mother must have been twenty-two. She looked so young . . . I couldn't remember ever having seen any pics of her before my birth. The oversized top and wild red curls held by combs on the sides were indeed typical of the era. She was leaning next to an equally young Dries against the hood of a black BMW, caught off guard by whoever had taken the pic, it seemed. Her smile was gentle, part amusement and part exasperation. Clad in a pair of jeans and T-shirt that were a far call from the perfectly cut three-piece suits I knew, Dries was scowling at the camera. A third figure stood away from the car with his arms crossed. The short brown hair and thick eyebrows were familiar. Kind of aristocratic but with something unpleasant in his sharp features: perhaps the cheekbones, too high, or the nose, a bit too long. Someone who looked a lot like Dries but wasn't Dries.

He wasn't looking at the camera. His eyes were set on my mother.

My forefinger lingered on his gray dress shirt. "Is that Anies?"

Jan gave a noncommittal grunt.

"What's he like?"

He rubbed his thumb against his lips. "I don't really know. He was already our boss back then, so I never talked that much with him. Anies, he was the quiet type. Most of the time you couldn't tell what he was thinking."

I thought of my mother's last letter, of the way she had tried to warn me against I2000009, Anies's code number. "And my mother? Did she know him well?"

He suppressed a smile. "It was complicated."

"Define *complicated*."

He mumbled in his beard. "Broers delen alles." *Brothers share everything.*

I considered asking him to repeat that. I didn't understand Flemish that well; I could have misinterpreted his words. It had to be that. Because I didn't want to consider the possibility that Anies . . . No. It was bad enough that my biological father was Dries—no need to envision a worse scenario. My fingers drummed on the album's page. "You're wrong; my mom didn't like Anies. She didn't . . ." I hesitated. Could I tell him this? He seemed to know a lot about the three of them already anyway. "I think she was afraid of him."

"I know," he said quietly.

Our eyes met. I tried to decipher the conflict lurking in those washed-out blue irises. After several seconds, he finally spoke. "I said brothers share everything . . . I didn't say Dries wanted to share."

Oh. I looked down at the picture again, at Anies's dark gaze focused on my mother and at Dries's left hand resting possessively on the small of her back. "So it was a problem between them, Dries's relationship with my mom?"

He scratched his beard. "Not so much when she was alive. Like I told you, Anies wasn't the kind to say anything. But honestly, another man guesses those things. I remember times when you could have cut the tension between the two of them with a knife."

"And after she was killed?" I prodded.

"It changed everything. Dries was mad, because of the frumentarii. After that, he and Anies both rose in the ranks, and they took over the brotherhood together, but it was the one thing they could never agree on."

"What do the frumentarii have to do with this?"

Jan's eyes darted toward the door as if he was worried Dries and March would show up any moment. "The 'tarii, they've always been

Anies's playthings. He used them for everything, recruited dozens, then hundreds. Dries didn't like it, because he thought we shouldn't trust them. The day your mother died, your father didn't even know his sniper was one of them: Anies had assigned that guy to his team without telling him."

My stomach heaved. The man who had shot my mother wasn't a Lion, as I had first been led to believe, but a spy working for Anies. Dries hadn't lied when telling me in Tokyo that the sniper had disobeyed his orders.

Was it Anies's orders he had followed instead? Because even after all this time, Anies still resented my mother for choosing Dries over him? I found it hard to believe that the commander of the Lions would have wasted any amount of time and resources over a petty grief. Frumentarii could, after all, be double agents: that guy could have been working for anyone who held a grudge against my mother.

Taking in my distress, Jan went on in a lower voice. "There was nothing left to do, since Dries had already killed the guy, but after that, he made a point to *always* get rid of his 'tarii as soon as he was done with them, even if it pissed Anies off."

I chewed on one of my nails as I took in this new information. Whether Anies was responsible or not for my mother's assassination, one thing was sure: Dries had retaliated the only way he could, by making all frumentarii pay for the crime of a single one. And among those unfortunate men had been Alex's father. Yet another life wasted in a vicious circle. Once again, it struck me that Dries and Alex had, in fact, a lot in common.

I gazed at the picture again, trying to remember every detail. I wanted to keep it, but it was Jan's, and with his wife gone, all he had left were Andrea and his albums. I hadn't realized my hand still hovered above the plastic film. I snatched it back.

When he saw that, he removed the photograph from his album and placed it on my lap. "Keep it. I have better ones anyway."

"Are you sure?"

"Yeah. I have pics of your dad bathing an armadillo."

My eyes went wide. "Seriously? But . . . *how? Why?*"

He let out a heavy sigh, as if recounting some grisly tale of war. "Bolino the armadillo . . . It's a long story. He stole it from a circus when he met your mother. Gave it to a zoo afterward. They don't make good pets, and that one was a complete asshole. Antisocial or something like that."

Wait . . . Hadn't Dries said something about it, back in Tokyo? About how he could never kill an armadillo? I blinked stupidly, picturing a younger Dries chasing an antisocial armadillo rolling away in a tight ball, and I wondered what sort of role my mother could have possibly played in this. "I'm sorry, but, again. *Why?*"

A grin pierced through Jan's golden beard. "Well . . ."

Outside, a light rain had started to fall, rustling through the leaves, pattering against the windows. He paused. Andrea's sudden bark alerted us to March and Dries's return before the gate even had a chance to creak.

FIFTEEN
GTA

He laid her carefully on a bed of kale and daikon radish, and there, under the hot summer rain, he planted his secret seed in her.
—Calypso Cooter, Enslaved by The Billionaire Microgreens Farmer

"But why is he so sure that woman is suspicious?" I asked March, after he had given us a brief account of his and Dries's meeting at Santa Lucia Station with the snitch named Jukebox: His mom had a cousin who knew a guy who worked at the reception of a seedy hotel located in the industrial area of Mestre, Venice's continental half. He had welcomed a woman in her midthirties two days ago. She had the same long black hair as Sabina Falchi, didn't carry any suitcase, looked completely haggard, and had remained locked inside her room since.

"The receptionist was worried because in the past forty-eight hours . . . she hasn't received any clients."

Dries nodded. "Confirmed by the owner of the sex shop next door."

I cringed. "It's that kind of hotel?"

"Primarily," March admitted. "They've joined online booking websites to diversify their clientele, but with little result so far."

Wow. That Jukebox guy really knew *everything*. Jan seemed unimpressed though. He shrugged. "Did Jukkie get you your stuff?"

"Yes," March said. "He does offer very competitive prices. Speaking of which"—he fished for a black phone from his pocket and handed it to me—"you might need it."

My heart swelled. A fake iPhone running on Android! I hugged him in front of a mildly disgusted Dries. "Thank you!"

"Island."

I paused in my examination of this marvel of Chinese technology.

March seemed conflicted, his eyebrows drawn in a halfhearted scowl. "I trust you," he eventually said.

"I understand."

There was no need for more. Jan and Dries didn't get it, of course, and they stared at our exchange as if he'd just asked for my hand in marriage: amusement on my left and barely contained irritation to my right.

Now that I potentially had access to my mailbox and Candy Crush account again, there was one last practicality nagging at me. "Jan, your guy . . . aren't you worried that he's going to sell his intel to other people?"

He looked almost offended. "He doesn't talk to the cops."

"And to, um, *noncops*?" I insisted.

Jan's eyes narrowed. "You're judging again."

"He calls himself Jukebox."

March exchanged a look with Dries. "It's a possibility. But if that guest is Falchi, it's worth a try."

"So when do we leave?" I asked.

I expected I'd have to fight to come with them, but there was no patronizing retort nor any attempt to outmacho me this time. "Now," Dries replied. "We've already imposed for too long."

More like: *I don't want to stay in the same place for too long*, but it made sense anyway. I felt my back pocket to make sure Jan's Polaroid was safely tucked in there, slipped the phone in my front pocket, and I was good to go. Because I was learning to live with nothing but my life and my dreams!

Dries exchanged a bro hug with Jan. March bade him a polite good-bye, all the while trying to escape Andrea, who wanted to lick his hand—he made it clear that it would *not* happen. When it was my turn, I wasn't sure what to say, because I owed this near-stranger so much, and yet I didn't even know his last name, or if we'd ever see each other again. I gave him an awkward bro hug too, which he returned loosely, as if he feared he'd break me to pieces.

I took one last look at the garden under the rain and smiled at him. "Jan. Are you on Facebook?"

After a short and thankfully safe walk through the backstreets of Santa Croce, we reached Piazzale Roma, a large square serving to park the countless cars and buses that were banned in the historical center. A few concrete buildings announced the return to the twenty-first century and the last stop before leaving the lagoon. Whether he could be trusted or not, Jukebox had delivered so far—true to his word, he had arranged for one of his uncle's friends to wait for us with a black Audi. Our new vehicle came complete with free German road maps, Fruitella candy in the glove compartment—or the cubbyhole, as Dries said when he took one—brand-new plates, and even a booster seat! *Ready to be wrecked*, I thought with a touch of fatalism. Before he took the wheel, March gave back the booster seat with a passing comment that the car was "perhaps a little too fresh." I shushed my conscience, because it was this or walking all the way to Mestre.

By the time we reached the Ponte della Libertà, a long bridge linking Venice to the continent, the windshield wipers battled against a downpour. The horizon had been swallowed by dark clouds, leaving nothing but grayish paint daubs that were supposed to be cruise ships.

In the passenger seat, Dries had intended to light up a cigarillo and chill, but March gave him the pigeon eye, the one where he peers at people sideways like they just committed a mortal sin: intense, judgmental, inescapable. So Dries closed his silvery cigarette case and focused on harassing me instead. "Do you ever stop playing with your phone? If you don't stop, I'm throwing you out of this car."

"Empty threats," I quipped from the back seat, without raising my eyes from the screen.

"What are you doing anyway?"

"I was liking that Roomba cat video a friend posted on Facebook."

"Roomba what?"

"Look." I gave him the phone. "He has several cats, and also a Roomba. So he films them riding the Roomba."

Dries watched the orange tabby amble around Stiles's living room, sitting regally on the little vacuum-cleaning robot. In the background, he could be heard taking pics and encouraging Ron—that was the cat's name. "Yes! Give me that look! Blue steel!"

"Why in the world is that animal wearing a frog hat?" Dries asked, pausing the video.

"Because it's funnier this way."

He handed me back my phone with an air of consternation. As he did so, I noticed a new notification under the video: *DKK & Andrea likes this*. I squirmed in the back seat, performing a little victory dance.

"Dries," March said, turning right past a gas station and a few residence buildings.

We were almost there, driving on an avenue no doubt lined with trees to conceal the many plants and tagged warehouses surrounding us. To our right stood the sex shop Dries had mentioned earlier, a sad, neutral showcase promising personal booths—thank God!—but none of the moist heat of *Enslaved by the Billionaire Microgreens Farmer*.

The hotel stood a little farther down the road. It was one of those austere three-story cubes from the sixties, made even gloomier by the pouring weather. An empty bar occupied the first floor, its windows covered with flashy ads for the latest scratch games.

One thing didn't belong in this decor though: a red Alfa Romeo roadster. Not much to do with the dad cars and light trucks lining the parking lot.

"Someone won the lottery." Dries chuckled, but he didn't look particularly happy.

"Island, I'd prefer you stay in the car," March said.

Dries turned in his seat to scrutinize me. "Can she be the driver?"

"No."

I resented March's answer. I wasn't that bad with a wheel!

"Then she's coming with us," Dries decided, to March's apparent irritation.

In the lobby, the yellow-painted walls and airport seats offered little for potential tourists to dream of. A few posters of Venice had been hung on the wall, but otherwise the place looked like a DMV office, down to the gray linoleum my hair was dripping onto. March and Dries walked to the desk, where a single employee snoozed behind an artificial orchid.

The receptionist, a young guy with prematurely thinning hair he combed forward like Donald Trump, never got up from his office chair, choosing instead to wheel himself to the other end of the desk. "Buona sera, signora e signori. Per un'ora o per la notte?" *Good afternoon, lady and gentlemen. For an hour or for the night?*

I fought an eye roll. He wasn't even trying.

March leaned on the counter with his most charming smile. I'd have run if I were that guy. He showed him a picture of Sabina Falchi on his phone. "Numero di stanza?" *Room number?*

The receptionist gave him shifty eyes and answered in English, with a thick accent, "I don't know if she's in her room, sir."

March's smile was softer than ever as he opened his jacket, just a fraction, to let him see the gun inside. "Please, can I have her room number?"

Behind him, Dries crossed his arms and watched, manifestly pleased by this turn of events.

The young man staggered back and rummaged through a set of drawers behind the desk. He retrieved a key to room number 205, which he gave to March. "No trouble in the hotel?" he asked, his voice a barely audible squeak.

March wouldn't lie, so he remained silent, while Dries strolled toward a narrow staircase leading to the first floor. "Never any trouble," he said, almost to himself.

I was ready to follow, but March's eyes darted to the plastic seats against the wall. He fished in his pocket for the car keys. "We'll be back shortly; can you wait for us, please?" I was about to protest when he lowered his voice and dropped the keys in my hand. "If anything happens, don't wait for us. *Leave.*"

How I wanted to go up there and question our mysterious witness while smoking a pipe. But he had a point: if a questionable surprise awaited them, I wouldn't help much in a gunfight. I went to sit with a dejected sigh.

That Italian Donald Trump made a quick phone call, and once he was done, he wouldn't stop looking at me, as if my face could tell him what March and Dries were doing up there. He wasn't the only one interested: some grandpa who wore a leather jacket and too much cologne strolled past me with a girl about my age clinging to his arm. Her dress should have been short enough to warrant his undivided attention, but he leered at me anyway and stopped to whisper something in the receptionist's ear.

The young guy shook his head. Unconvinced, the grandpa sent another scorching look my way and, to my and the receptionist's horror, made a come-hither gesture. The move angered his escort, who expressed strong disapproval, emphasized with a firm statement that she was not interested in any form of *bunga bunga.*

I shrank in my seat. I wasn't interested in a mini-orgy either, but that creepy old fart was already walking toward me, unfettered by the receptionist's weak protests. The girl warned she'd leave without him, which would make me the only target left. I got up from my seat warily, and I glanced at the outline of the black Audi on the parking lot, blurred by the raindrops pit-patting against the lobby's windows. Waiting in the car didn't sound like such a bad idea after all.

When the old guy was close enough for me to count the leather fringes dangling from the sleeves of his jacket, I shook my head vigorously and hurried past his slew of amused protests. The moment

I stepped outside, something red flashed in my field of vision. The red Alfa was leaving. I wiped the raindrops clinging to my eyelashes and checked the driver through the windshield, almost mechanically. Woman, pretty. Black hair.

Like . . . Sabina Falchi?

I caught sight of Donaldo Trumpo through the window. Our eyes met. His face fell like melted mozzarella, and it was all the confirmation I needed. Forgetting about the hours, days, weeks of purgatory potentially awaiting me for breaking March's rules again, I raced to the Audi and jumped in the driver's seat. A flicker of guilt, and no doubt puppy love, had me put my seat belt on . . . before I started in third gear.

I bulleted out of the parking lot, scraping a couple of bumpers in the process. Hand on the brake, I spun the wheel like Bo Duke in his General Lee to take a turn on the road we had arrived on. Once I was more or less in the lines, driving fast through the industrial area, a red smudge appeared in the distance. I followed the Alfa as it took a left on a road lined with stacks of containers, the wipers flapping back and forth madly to fight that never-ending rain. A flash of lightning tearing ashen clouds warned me that the weather wouldn't get any better soon. We were leaving Mestre, and that's when she noticed me, presumably because I kept swerving and passing cars to catch up to her.

Surf formed under the Alfa's tires as it sped up. I imitated her, choosing to ignore the three-digit number on my speed counter. In the same instant, the Chinese iPhone vibrated in my pants pocket. Picking up at 110 kph would certainly be against road rules, but March was probably mad, worried sick, and I needed to tell him I was tailing Sabina Falchi. My left hand never leaving the wheel, I pulled the phone out of my pocket, dropped it in the cup holder, and quickly tapped twice to both accept the call and activate the speakerphone.

I shouldn't have done that.

March's roar exploded through the speaker. "Island!"

I gripped the wheel with a grimace. "I'm so, so sorry, but I can't talk right now, I'm right behind her. The Alfa Romeo, it was hers! I think the receptionist warned her you were coming."

I could practically hear his teeth grinding together as he digested the news. "Where are you?"

"Um . . . I think I'm on Via dell'Elettronica, in the industrial area."

Dries's voice took over. "I *will* strangle you for this, but for now, check under the seat—he always keeps a spare gun there. And get me that woman."

"Don't listen to him! Keep following her at a distance and for the love of God, *wait* for us!" March insisted.

"Yeah, I'll do that. I'm not shooting anyone."

"And don't hang up. I want you to tell me exactly where you're going."

I picked up background noise—the revving of an engine: they were driving too. Someone would be pissed when searching the parking lot for their car. Shaking the thought away, I focused on Sabina Falchi's car ahead of me. The road was getting smaller; we were out of the industrial area, racing fast along a river. I glanced at the GPS and yelled in the speaker.

"We're on via Moranzani. She's headed to the seafront. I think we got her; she's minutes away from a dead end!"

March's voice answered me, now back to a cooler, professional tone. "Good. Don't try anything; just park sideways to block her exit if you can."

I squinted at the road ahead, which had turned into a grayish mist by the heavy rain. It split into two smaller alleys. One led straight to the sea and was the dead end I could see on the GPS's screen. The other . . . didn't really exist. It was just a path winding through a grove, which had been barred by a row of garbage bins belonging to a nearby camping. There was therefore no valid reason to take it, and, Jesus . . . was she seriously going to?

The contents of a green bin went flying my way as the Alfa Romeo rammed into it and forced its way onto the trail beyond. Soda cans clanked against the windshield; through the speaker, March asked what was going on, and Dries whether I was dead yet. I ignored them and crushed the gas pedal, not even caring that a close brush with a glass bin had probably ruined the Audi's right door.

"I'm still after her!" I gasped when the car started to shake on a gravelly path, and the sea came into view. "She went off the road!"

"And *you*?" March asked, nearly shouting that last word.

"Oh, I followed her. But it's okay!" It wasn't, I realized, as both our cars burst out of the grove and onto a walkway stretching along the raging sea. Now was the time to pull on the brake hard or end up in the lagoon with Sabina Falchi. I didn't think she'd be the first to give up, but she did. The Alfa drifted to a stop sideways and hit the iron railing lining the walkway.

I could see her through the window, trapped, blinking at me madly through the droplets snaking down her car's windows. Black tresses fell on her shoulders, curtaining part of her face. One of her hands still gripped the wheel, and she too held her phone in the other. Sensing victory at hand's reach, I stopped the Audi inches away from her car and blindly searched for the gun Dries had mentioned. I felt the cool metal of a barrel. Once I had a firm grip on the semiautomatic, my first impulse was to jump out and proceed to a citizen's arrest—regardless of the fact that the safety was still on.

I'm glad I didn't do that. Because I had been so busy mentally rehearsing a badass line, I didn't see the gray SUV coming from my right until it was too late, and I could do nothing but watch in slow motion as it crashed into the Audi's passenger side.

The next couple of seconds were the very definition of a moment suspended in time. A bad moment, where my heart stopped, and everything felt slow and unreal. The airbags bursting all around me muted the moan of metal being crushed and glass shattering. Pain erupted like fireworks in my chest and limbs as my body slammed against the door. Around me, the seafront became a blur as the Audi went spinning out of the way. It veered as if it'd topple over. I braced myself. Nothing came, and the car eventually stopped moving.

I wasn't dead—yet not quite back in this world. I coughed out the talc swirling in the air as the airbags slowly deflated. My phone had been sent flying under the dashboard. I had this odd thought that it might be broken, like it mattered. It still worked though. I registered March's voice calling my name through the speaker, shouting that he was almost there.

Through the cracks in the window, blurry shapes moved and came into focus. Having shoved the Audi out of the way, the SUV was now positioned parallel to Falchi's Alpha. A couple of men in suits helped her out of the car. Taking her? My right hand jolted. I was thinking of March's gun, but my body seemed to be having some trouble connecting intent with movement; I slumped in my seat and tried to record everything, anything.

I felt strangely calm, dazed and bruised in the carcass of that stolen car, surrounded by the storm and the silence. Outside, Sabina Falchi looked shaken. She wasn't fighting these guys though. More like holding on to one of them as he helped her inside the SUV. She cried out. A sound so earnest and desperate that it broke through my stupor. "Lucca! Dov'è Lucca?" *Lucca! Where is Lucca?*

Right then, I had the intuition, the certainty even, that she wasn't being kidnapped. She was being rescued. The operation, however, was cut short by the sound of tires screeching. A single gunshot echoed through the rain, taking out one of the men before he had time to climb in the vehicle.

I lolled my head to the left and pushed the now flappy airbag hanging from the ceiling and covering my window. A tiny blue Italian car—the kind the French would commonly refer to as a "yogurt tub"—had burst from the grove and sped toward the gray SUV, its toylike wheels barely touching the ground. The passenger door was open, and March's upper body was visible, half outside the car, gun in one hand, while he held on to the roof with the other.

I croaked his name and made a feeble attempt to unclasp my seat belt. To my right, the SUV backed up and took off, way too fast for the brave little yogurt tub to stand a chance. The tiny car skidded to a halt a few yards away, and March ran to free me from the Audi's wreckage.

His face was pale, his jaw clenched tight as he undid my seat belt. I held out my arms to reach out to him, but he stopped me, his hands gentle but his tone brusque. "Don't try to move."

I let him examine me, searching for whiplash or fractures, checking my pupils for signs of a concussion. In his, all I could read was distress. It hit me then. March and I had gone back to that same place, together, ten years ago, on a crowded Tokyo avenue. Me, trapped in the wreckage of my mother's car, next to her lifeless body, watching the hood catch fire, unable to move or even scream. And him, for the first time, getting me out of that car, gathering me in his arms. It was the day both our lives had changed, spun in new directions.

March drew an unsteady breath.

"I'm sorry," I murmured. "I didn't want—"

He averted his eyes. "You're all right; it's all that matters for now."

"But they got away—"

"We can deal with that later," he snapped, even as he carefully lifted me from the driver's seat.

March wanted to carry me, but I tried to stand: I needed to feel the ground under my feet. I leaned on him and took a few cautious steps on grass made squishy by the rain. Dries had gotten out of the yogurt tub as well and joined us, looking majorly pissed. Leaving him to support me instead, March went to circle Falchi's red Alfa Romeo.

Dries watched him open the rear door with a scowl. "May I suggest we leave?"

"Give me a second. I think our new friends forgot something in their haste," March said, reaching to retrieve a gray tote bag.

A warm weight settled on my shoulders. Dries had removed his jacket and was busy adjusting it on me.

I managed out a small "Thank you" while March searched the bag and retrieved a black laptop. With a bullet hole. The three of us stared at the bag, where a similar hole had pierced the leather, then at the Alfa Romeo's door. One of March's bullets had missed the SUV but made it through Falchi's car like a knife in butter.

Dries patted my shoulder with a grunt. "See, that's his kick: he's always liked testing my patience."

SIXTEEN
RELATIONSHIPS 101

Don't argue with her feelings and opinions. Take time out and discuss things later when there is less emotional charge. Practice the Love Letter technique as described in chapter 11.

–John Gray, Men Are from Mars, Women Are from Venus: A Practical Guide for Improving Communication and Getting What You Want in Your Relationships.

Crime pays. A lot, considering that Dries's plan B was a yacht. His yacht, to be precise. Slower, but makes it easier to cross borders. I had seen very little of it so far, save for the cabin I was resting in: all sleek wooden panels and art deco lamps. We were sailing away from Italy in a continuous hum. I sat up on the bed and gazed at the evening sky outside the bay window, the moon's silvery reflection shimmering on the waves.

After leaving Venice for good, we'd driven a few miles south in the stolen yogurt tub to a port where the ship and its small crew awaited. A doctor had briefly come on board to check on me, a man, I think, but he might just as well have been a unicorn: with a raging migraine kneading my brain, I floated through the exam. I wanted nothing but to rest, primarily to avoid the anxious and angry blue gaze watching the doctor's every move. March had since left, but I knew I'd have to face him sooner or later. A storm was coming in the wake of my stunt with the car, and so, I courageously pretended to be too tired to talk.

I drew a long sigh, studying the black terry robe one of the crewmen had brought for me, with a little lion head embroidered on the pocket. It was so tacky; Dries's conquests must love it. I got out of bed and walked to the bedroom's door, intent on exploring the yacht. The doorknob wouldn't move.

Aw, come on...

I let myself fall forward, my forehead hitting the smooth mahogany. "March. Let me out."

On the other side of the cabin's door, I caught Dries's hushed voice. "How long are you going to keep her in there? I need her to look at the laptop."

"She won't," March snapped.

I banged my fists on the door. "I can hear you! I know you're there! I said: *Let. Me. Out!*"

"Can't you at least sedate her?" Dries groaned.

"No. She will calm down."

That seemed to amuse Dries—as his footsteps echoed away from the bedroom's door, he called out to March, his voice filled with a joy only known to vindicated parents. "To your newly single life then."

There was no visible clock around, so I'm not sure how long I yelled while March waited behind that door for me to cool down. Maybe half an hour. I eventually ran out of fuel, and when he deemed I'd been silent long enough, the doorknob clicked. I stepped back. He entered the room in a whiff of fresh laundry and mints, wearing what can best be described as Simon Cowell's "It's no" face.

I watched him from the corner of my eye, still seething. "So that's how things are gonna be between us? I wait around for you, and if I'm not compliant enough, you just lock me up?"

"If that's what it takes to keep you safe, yes," he said, no emotion filtering through his voice.

"And if I don't want that?"

He drew a slow breath, his eyes never leaving mine. He wouldn't say it. I knew that the answer to my question was something along the lines of "my way or no way," and for the first time since we'd met, I truly got scared of my feelings for March. Scared that he'd never compromise and that I could never find the strength to walk out. Scared we would end up hurting each other like Dries and my mother.

Better put that to the test now. "I'm going to look for Dries," I announced, taking a step toward the door. "I want to see Falchi's laptop."

As I padded my way around him, March caught my waist, his hand gentle, but unyielding. "Island, we need to talk about this."

I fought his grip to no avail. "If you're going to lock me up again, I don't think there's anything to talk about."

March didn't let go. "We had an agreement."

"Which I tried to respect, but I didn't have a choice—"

"You did. You could have called me," he retorted, his voice deepening with suppressed anger.

"She was already getting away. I couldn't just stand there and watch!"

Around my waist the grip loosened, and March plunged his gaze into mine. His irises seemed darker than usual, around pupils now widening as if their depths meant to swallow me whole. One of his hands let go of me to retrieve something from his wallet. "I found this in your pocket," he said, handing me Jan's Polaroid.

I took it, gulping past the laces I could feel tightening around my windpipe. "Jan gave it to me. It's just a souvenir."

Surely he'd say something, accuse me of playing detective around the kind of suspect who'd better be left alone, threaten to sentence me to a week in the trunk. He didn't. In a breath, his head dipped, and he kissed me. Although I could taste the familiar sweetness of way too many mints on his tongue, it was different from usual. I liked March's kisses because he took his time: as his ex told me once, he wasn't the volcano type, which suited me just fine. But this... I was having a hard time keeping up with the onslaught as he cradled the back of my head. His chest was heaving, and there was something akin to desperation in the way his lips tugged at mine, as if I might dissolve any second and he meant to capture a little part of me for himself.

He finally ended it when I gasped for air, his palms lingering on my cheeks, stroking them. "How do we make this work?"

"I don't know," I admitted. "I know you want me to stay away, but I can't, because all of this... Alex, Dries, Anies... it's personal to me."

March's anger abated in a long, tired sigh. I startled when his fingers caressed my collarbones before they glided down and parted the terry robe. The belt slipped undone without much resistance. I shivered, finding myself in foreign territory, where being naked was no longer new, but at the same time nothing casual yet: ours was a Map of Tendre where much remained to be explored. I held my breath when his hand reached inside the garment. His fingertips grazed the fresh bruises on my side, the Band-Aid concealing the spot where a bullet had grazed me during our chase in Venice.

His free hand cupped my jaw. "*This* is personal to *me*."

I wrapped my arms around his torso and held him tight. "I'm so sorry... I know you want me to have a normal life. But I can't. I lost my job because of Ruby, and now I think the thug life is calling me."

On March's lips, a sad smile returned. He pressed a kiss to my cheek. "I know. I've been thinking about how to handle... things between us." He let go of me to search his pocket and produced a folded piece of paper. "I need you to hear this."

I blinked as he proceeded to read the paper out loud, his tone flat and a little hurried.

"Dear Island, I am angry that you keep taking risks without telling me. I am disappointed that you didn't trust me enough to tell me about your discussion with Mr. Morgan, or the picture Jan gave you." He cleared his throat. "I'm extremely worried for your safety. You are more vulnerable than you realize, and I regret that you won't be reasonable and let me protect you. I want to pursue this relationship nonetheless, but I don't want to have to tie you up in order to keep you safe."

He folded back the note and gazed at me, half anxious for my response and, might as well say it, looking immensely pleased with his intervention.

I had no idea what to say. My eyes were as wide as saucers, and my brain was working fast to sort out the facts. Deep within, there was a part of March that would forever remain overcontrolling and more than a little macho. But, contrary to my fears, he was actually working on himself: he'd just inflicted the five-point "love letter" technique on me, something I gathered he'd found in *Men Are from Mars, Women Are from Venus: A Practical Guide for Improving Communication and Getting What You Want in Your Relationships*. Impressive.

He deserved an A for effort and honesty, I decided. Not only this, but he was right about one thing—whether I wanted to or not, I did interfere with his work. While I had no intention to stop doing so, we needed to find a safe way to collaborate, or else we'd both die stupidly someday.

"I understand," I said at last. "I want to make this work too. I *need* answers, and I can't always stay on the side and watch, but I get that sometimes you need me out of the way. I can hear that, and I don't want to endanger you. Thank you for being so honest and for all the great communication."

He reached for the paper again. "I wrote one regarding the state of your apartment too."

I placed my hand on his wrist. "It's okay . . . I think I can imagine what's in it. Maybe you can read it to me later?"

His lips pursed. After a moment of hesitation, he put it back in his pocket. "Certainly."

"So, what now?"

"Falchi's laptop was considerably damaged. Dries wants you to take a look at it, see if there's anything recoverable."

My body quivered with anticipation. "I can do that!"

A genuine smile pinched his dimples. "Excellent. We're making good progress."

Whether he meant in our investigation, or in our attempts to communicate as different species, I didn't know.

Dear Island,

I am frustrated with the state of your apartment. You and Joy need to fold your clean laundry, pick up after yourselves, and also clean your bathroom and kitchen more regularly. The candy wrappers scattered on the counter are especially unacceptable considering that you have a trash can under the sink. Some of the food in your fridge is expired. Please don't eat the turkey + swiss.

I am sad that you keep refusing my help in improving your living standards, and that you threatened to change your locks.

I do not want you to die of food poisoning or share your premises with an army of dust mites.

I regret that I'm forced to have Maid Magic intervene without your consent.

I forgive you for your poor housekeeping skills, I appreciate that you are now rinsing your dishes and placing them in the dishwasher. Most of the time.

Affectionately,

M.

SEVENTEEN
THE CANNOLI

Ô temps ! suspends ton vol, et vous, heures propices !
Suspendez votre cours :
Laissez-nous savourer les rapides délices.
Des plus beaux de nos jours !

—Alphonse de Lamartine, *Le Lac*

Damn. It is nice to have your own yacht, I thought, padding across the aft deck to find Dries and March waiting for me on a long semicircular couch. The evening air was warm and the motor's sound surprisingly low, considering how fast we were sailing and the massive trail of foam we left in our wake. Ceiling spots bathed the sitting area in a soft golden light: Dries would have made a great cruise operator.

Well, except for the crew. I wasn't entirely comfortable yet with the four men in black polos roaming silently through the ship and watching our every move. One of them had given me my clothes back though, freshly stitched and laundered after my recent adventures. It was nice of him, but I didn't know what to think of his yakuza sleeve tattoos, or the gun tucked in his back. At any rate, everyone seemed okay with it, so I decided not to bring it up.

"There she is. I have work for you," Dries announced, gesturing for me to join them.

He had changed into a blue shirt and a pair of khakis, and it felt odd to realize that I was seeing him out of a three-piece suit for the very first time—well, if you except Jan's Polaroid. He patted the space between him and March; I settled there, feigning to ignore that a light meal had been served on the coffee table—the cannoli were chanting my name. Next to Dries's razor-thin laptop sat the blue one March had inadvertently shot.

"Can you do something about it?" Dries asked.

"Maybe. Let me check it," I said, rubbing my palms together in anticipation.

Once I'd dragged the KO'd laptop to me across the table, I examined it carefully. "You're lucky," I said. "The bullet missed the lithium battery; otherwise the whole thing would have gone up in flames. I think the hard drive might be okay. Do you have a toolbox? Also I need this." I extended a greedy hand toward Dries's nice little laptop.

He gave me a suspicious look but nonetheless gestured to one of the crew members, who returned with a fully equipped toolbox less than a minute later. At last, in this life filled with violence, heartbreak, dark secrets, and sexual frustration . . . some pleasure.

I lined up several screwdrivers of various sizes and four Nutella-filled cannoli in front of me and got to work. March and Dries watched me disassemble Falchi's computer with undisguised interest. Once I had freed the hard drive, I was pleased to see that my diagnostic had been accurate—it looked more or less intact. Now all that was left to do was test it. I moved to grab Dries's laptop, but it wouldn't budge. Because his hand was on it.

"I need it to plug Falchi's drive."

"You're not allowed to disassemble it."

I feigned outrage. "Of course I won't. I just need to open it a little."

His fingers flattened on the lid. I let go with a sigh . . . and pulled again fast, as soon as his grip decreased, holding the loot against my chest. In his eyes, the golden glint turned dangerous. Good thing I was his daughter, and I could get away with it. Also, if he tried anything, I'd just let March handle him.

After half a dozen cannoli, the partial dismemberment of Dries's laptop, and some careful fiddling with the hard drive because it wasn't spinning as it ought to, we found ourselves looking at 97.1 percent recoverable data, scattered in hundreds of folders.

I pointed at the screen while Dries considered the screws coming from his laptop with no small amount of annoyance. "There's a little work to go through all this, but hopefully we can find some interesting stuff."

The news seemed to satisfy him. He stuffed his face with two cannoli in a row under March's disapproving eyes. Looked like we had more in common than a gap tooth and too many moles. A sweet tooth as well.

When I didn't move immediately, he stopped chewing on the pastry. "What are you waiting for? Now get to work, and tell me what's on that disk. I gave your mother ten million dollars so you'd go to college. I want some return on that investment."

I'd have eaten my fourth cannoli, but it slipped from my hands.

Ten million dollars. Roughly half of everything my mother had left me—43.86 percent, taking into account the current exchange rate, if we were going to be picky. Sitting cross-legged on the tangle of black sheets on my bed, I was trying to concentrate on the thousands of files in Sabina Falchi's laptop, but Dries's words wouldn't stop bouncing around my skull. Had my mother asked for this? Or was it something he had decided himself, because he knew he'd never be there for me?

For the first time since we had met in Tokyo, I felt an inexplicable guilt. I had never thought of Dries; I didn't even know he existed, and once I did, I rapidly came to the conclusion that he was an arrogant asswipe and a menace to society. But *he* had thought of me, and the idea filled me with a sense of regret, like sand slipping from my fingers that I could never catch again.

Would Dries have made a good father? March was trying to change for me, to leave his past as a hit man behind and become a good citizen. Was it something Dries would have ever been capable of, for my mother and me? She'd said in her good-bye letter that she didn't believe so, that he'd never choose us over his brothers. It seemed Dries wanted to believe the same, but I had this intuition, like a painful weight in my chest, that both of them had been terribly wrong, that maybe, if they'd talked to each other . . .

It was all in the past though. I already had a father—whom I would need to call again eventually. Dries and I could never recover the memories that weren't, but I could at least try to clear his name. Well, of the plane bombing anyway.

I stirred with a yawn and locked my eyes on the screen of the laptop. There were years of research on that drive, but the only files Falchi had flushed were an archive containing ten-year-old e-mails and PDF scans. She'd apparently spent the first weeks of 2005 helping another intern with his thesis paper on titanium-based glass, and after that, it was mostly mundane communications with her boss or someone from HR.

Until May. I went through a particular series of e-mails; she'd been getting closer to a guy named . . . *Lucca* Gerone. Their exchanges often contained scientific discussions, but he was clearly interested in more. He'd been the one sending the scans in the archive. I opened the first one and blinked. Over a page where he had initially printed complex chemical model equations, Gerone had drawn Sabina. The portrait was a little manga-ish and overall pretty bad; I found it incredibly sweet.

I went through more scans of the same type, containing either doodles or chemistry jokes, until I reached a large drawing, covering a double page. For the first time, Gerone had drawn himself holding

Sabina, ascending in a rocket toward a flying potato. No wait. The moon. A title had been hastily added with an orange highlighter: *Another Practical Use for DPC: Taking You to the Moon and Back*. My gaze lingered on the text I could make out under the drawing.

Nanocrystals explosion.

My pulse increased steadily as I zoomed on the paragraph. Dynamic Prismatic Crystals... kinematic analysis... ultrasound-induced structural stress... molecular single crystals mimicking mechanical processes at macroscopic levels... When exposed to ultrasound waves within the aforementioned range... fragments travel up to 10^5–10^9 their own length... High risk of instability.

Now, that was a good start—or a terrible one, whichever you prefer. A recipe involving yttrium, aluminum, and neodymium—those crystals had been one of Gerone's research projects at Novensia. According to Gerone's notes, the resulting nanopowder would enhance Ceraglass's optical properties and shock resistance, effectively creating "a new generation of highly resistant light-transmitting material."

I browsed through the remaining scans feverishly. Failed attempts to stabilize the formula, more jokes about the danger of possible practical use. One folder contained a video shot inside a test chamber. A couple minutes long, it was a practical demonstration of the chain reaction Gerone's notes hypothesized: microscopic crystalline structures vibrated and popped apart one after another under the effect of the chosen ultrasound wavelength. The whole thing might have looked underwhelming—anodyne, even—to the untrained eye, but a brief scale calculation told me all I needed to know about what kind of energy would be released and what sort of damage might occur if playing the same game with several tons of those.

Yet Gerone hadn't seemed too worried about what might happen if his crystals ever landed in the wrong hands... or the hundred-foot-long sky roof of a jumbo jet.

A soft knock at the cabin's door startled me.

"Biscuit? Can I come in?"

"Sure, you need to see this!"

March entered the bedroom like a ghost, careful to close the door behind him without so much as a whisper. He walked to my nightstand and placed a bottle of water there. "For the night," he said.

He had noticed. This man had officially become my boyfriend less than five days ago, but he had already figured out that I woke up at night to drink water and would wander to the nearest tap if no bottle was available. I took a reverent sip, my eyes never leaving him as he sat next to me on the bed.

"You said I needed to see something?"

"I think I found what Dries was looking for. Well, no, it's not what he was looking for, but check this . . ."

For the second time, I went through Falchi and Gerone's tender exchanges and showed March the files: the fun doodles of the beginning, which progressively became more, his declaration of love, drawn on a printed version of his research paper about the ultrasound-sensitive crystals, and the experiment footage.

I paused on a particular file containing various sinusoidal graphs and comments. "You see those lines? They describe the minimum frequency and amplitude you need to expose the crystals to, in order for them to explode—243 kilohertz, it's in the lower spectrum and way beyond the human-hearing range. You need special equipment to generate that."

March nodded, his perplexity artfully concealed by a frown of concentration.

"You believe that's what happened to the plane? The sky roof material reacted to some kind of . . . high frequency signal, and it triggered an explosion?"

"It's possible. That kind of frequency is short range, and according to Gerone's data, it triggers a chain reaction in the crystals. Supposing someone built a transducer that's powerful enough to emit the signal and placed it less than ten feet away from the sky roof, concealed as a laptop for example . . . I think it would work. And it could make it past security: no liquid or explosives involved."

"What about Gerone himself? Did you find anything else about him in Falchi's files?"

"Nope. I looked him up online, but I found almost nothing. It's like he lived in a cave after Novensia: no address, no résumé, no search engine results, no social media . . . zilch."

"I see. I'll send your report to Phyllis; she'll research his whereabouts."

"Okay. You know, the more I think about it, the more I'm convinced that this has nothing to do with a terrorist attack at all. Maybe something happened to Gerone while he worked at Novensia, and Sabina Falchi knows about it." In my mind, the airport footage replayed. Sabina Falchi's surprise, their long exchange, then her sudden distrust when he'd tried to hold her back. "And if our hooded guy is Lucca Gerone, that'd explain why he saved Falchi: he knew the roof's material was contaminated with his crystals, so he stepped in."

March stroked my arm pensively. "That would also imply he knew what would happen. Perhaps Pio Maraì will be able to tell us more about him."

"Maraì . . . Novensia's CEO? Do you think he knows what's going on?"

"I'm tempted to believe so. Phyllis and I did some research of our own: he left Rome in a hurry shortly after the crash."

"Seriously?"

He winked at me. "But no mortal can escape the claws of the fearsome Phyllis. Novensia operates a secluded research center on the island of Vis in Croatia. Maraì sometimes retreats there to conduct operations. His private jet landed in Zagreb thirty hours ago. He probably fled to escape an upcoming crisis."

Impressive. I had no idea if I should be glad or horrified that for the past six years Phyllis had put those skills to the service of helping March screen his "clients." I looked through the window. It was past 1:00 a.m., and we were sailing south fast. "That's where we're headed?"

"Yes."

I closed the laptop and let myself fall flat on the mattress. "Okay, I think the last drop of my energy just left me. Heard it run off down the hallway."

He bent down to brush his lips to mine. "Good night then. Sleep tight. It's been a long day."

"A bold understatement, Mr. November." I tugged at his hand. "Will you stay?"

His arm extended over me to turn off a lamp on the wall next to the headboard. "Perhaps until you fall asleep?"

"You need to relax too . . ."

I could tell he was tempted: his shoulders were slouching already. I wrapped myself around him, hoping to crumble his last defenses. March let his body fall onto the mattress, taking me with him. His lips found mine in the dark; his palms cupped my cheeks, so warm, even as he said, "I should let you rest."

No. Not when I could taste coffee and sugar on his tongue. Not when he had sworn to me he would take me with the strength of a thousand suns as soon as we found a bed for that. Yeah, I'm quoting from memory. Maybe he didn't say it exactly like that. Regardless, there was no longer any hesitation in March's gestures as he lifted my T-shirt, mindful to kiss and nuzzle each square inch of skin he uncovered. In between delicious shivers, I returned the favor the best I could, working the buttons of his shirt with shaky hands.

At some point, an unidentified elbow—okay, mine—nearly kicked the laptop to the floor. This required an awkward pause in order to move it to safety on the coffee table, along with our respective clothes, which had somehow been properly folded in the meantime. Don't ask. It's like when I saw that both his gun and a couple of condoms had materialized on the nightstand: there are levels of organizational skills modern science can't explain. I felt March's body stretch atop mine, our underwear the last obstacle in the way of savage, breathless LEGOing. In a bed that was unlikely to explode. Also, this time we had protection. And still, my neurons kept flipping through the list of terrifying scenarios that might somehow prevent successful intercourse.

Tsunami? None recorded in the area recently, as far as I knew.

Meteorite? Odds were 1 in 700,000 in a lifetime. Low—but very real.

Random bum attack? Improbable. But we had a gun anyway.

Phone call? Oh no. Please, *no*.

Or maybe it just wouldn't work. Or it would hurt too much . . .

I closed my eyes and tried to clear my mind, inhaling March's clean, soapy scent. I thought of the way they say it in French: la première fois. *the first time.*

"Are you all right?"

March's strained whisper snapped me out of my linguistic considerations. I had spaced out, and he needed me to tell him if it was okay to keep going. His hands stroked my sides gently, tickling me a little. Was it the same for him, was he . . .

"Are you nervous too?" I asked in a voice so small that I barely recognized it as mine.

There was a hoarse chuckle in the darkness before he buried his face in my neck. "Yes. You have no idea."

"Why?"

"Because it's been a little while for me. And you'll only have one first time." He pressed a kiss to the corner of my mouth. "I almost wish I was strong enough to wait a little more."

"I'm not sure I want to stay a virgin forever," I mumbled.

"You won't."

Indeed. As if to give some literal weight to this statement, March molded his body into mine. And I felt everything. Hot skin, the muscles coiling underneath in anticipation. The mystery bits too, and the caress of that soft, sexy, manly chest hair against my skin—divine fleece! Rug of Eros! I'd have to tell him someday. But not tonight, because I wasn't sure how he would react to that strange fetish of mine.

I opened my eyes wide and tried to memorize every detail, the way the moonlight coming from the window chiseled his features, his eyes boring into mine, and the soft smile I knew was for me only. I touched my lips to his and pushed him back, just a little. Enough for me to wiggle to a half-sitting position. He watched, still as a lion about to pounce, as I removed my bra and tossed it across the room.

If it ever registered in March's brain that the move constituted a blatant act of littering, he chose to overlook it. Because breasts. Fun size ones, to quote him, but the magic works with those too. He was back atop me in a heartbeat, and I welcomed his onslaught with a giggle ... then incoherent whimpers. I remember the exact moment, by the way. My fingers were digging into his scalp, urging his mouth on, when a sudden rush of air cooled our skin. The cabin's door slammed open so hard I heard the wood crack, and the lights came on. Lightning fast, March let go of me to reach to the nightstand. Less than a second later, I lay on the bed, stunned, while he stood in his boxer briefs, gun in hand.

In the doorway, Dries looked livid. Possibly because my bra had landed at his feet and his ex-favorite disciple was aiming at him. Flushing a nice shade of Tabasco red, I rolled swiftly to wrap myself in the comforter like a libidinous burrito.

Dries's gaze swiped from the flimsy piece of white cotton on the floor to my face sticking out from the covers before settling on March. One of his eyelids twitched, but he schooled his features into a derisive sneer. "And now, on top of that, you're going to shoot me, *Judas?*"

March lowered the gun with a sigh. "Can I ask you to please *knock?*"

The culprit brushed off imaginary lint from his shirt. Ice crackled on the walls as his voice filled the cabin. "I believe your own room is at the other end of the hallway," he told March. "As for you, young lady, weren't you supposed to be working on my disk?"

Seriously? Did I say something earlier about a sense of guilt, regret, or whatever over my relationship with Dries? Please give me a moment to go fetch a giant eraser and a jug of White-Out. I mean, watching him stand there, playing the part of the outraged father, when, honestly, he was just smug about successfully cockblocking March. I popped a hand out from the comforter to point at the laptop sitting on the coffee table. "All my notes are in a folder on the desktop, along with the files we found. I'll be more than happy to debrief you, but can you just *go away*? This is a little awkward."

A sardonic smile twisted his lips. "Now, is it?"

I saw March's fists clench at his sides, but he held his anger at bay, unfurling his fingers in a slow exhale. "Dries, I'm willing to take responsibility and discuss the matter with you but not here and not like this."

How chivalrous, and a lot more diplomacy than Dries deserved. I squirmed to a sitting position and held my head high, mustering as much dignity as I could, given the circumstances. "It's okay, March. He knows that we're adults, and we don't owe him any kind of justification." I slanted my eyes at Daddy Capulet. "Get out, *now*. And wait for me on the deck. You and I need to talk."

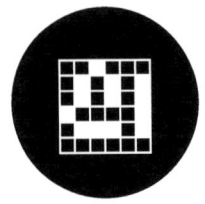

EIGHTEEN
THE MOUNTAIN DEW

"Aye, lassie! Let me tickle yer innards!"
—Diane MacRoth, *Kilted Need*

After I had given March a hundred of kisses to make up for what I feared might become the worst case of blue balls ever recorded in medical history, I trotted to the upper deck. As agreed, Dries was there, leaning on the bow railing, gazing down at the dark waves. I approached him slowly and rested my back against the railing, arms crossed.

Until I met Dries, I always thought I had inherited my ability to settle in angry and uncomfortable silence from my dad, who'd be in the Guinness World Records if they had a category for that. But I was now considering the possibility that genetics were involved: Dries was a passive-aggressive black belt, masterfully building a stifling, nerve-racking atmosphere, rhythmed by his occasional intakes of air and the swells crashing against the hull.

He won. I spoke because it was either that or trying to push him over the railing. "Look, this needs to stop—you, treating me like I'm sixteen, and the way you barged in back there, it was unacceptable. And also completely creepy. Whatever your problem is, let's talk it through. Like adults."

It took him a good minute to answer. When he did, his voice held an unfamiliar edge: not just cold anger, or even exasperation, but perhaps an itsy tiny bit of hurt. "I dragged that little punk out of the dumpster he lived in. I trained him. I gave him everything. For Christ's sake, I bought him his first crosswords! Me. Not his junkie mother! Not that good-for-nothing father who loaded her with speedballs until they picked up her body from the bathroom floor. Does he think he takes after him? I don't think so." He paused and pointed an accusing finger at me, although I suspected it was March he was seeing. "*I* made him. I made that boy, and all the reward I got was that he took off, cost me two billion dollars, and hooked up with my daughter."

A painful weight set in my chest as I tried to connect what Dries had just said with March's words back in the plane. *She couldn't really take care of me . . . he wasn't home much. It was fine that way.* March, king of understatements. Who loved his mother so much he wouldn't taint her memory with the truth, who wouldn't even mention his father, probably because he couldn't forgive him.

Because someone had replaced him anyway.

It was the word *boy*, the way Dries said it. To the best of my knowledge, I was his only child. His years forming March might be the closest thing he had ever experienced to a father-and-son dynamic. March too had found in his mentor what his biological father had been unable to embody: a role model, someone to believe in his potential and tear him out of his chrysalis. Maybe the reason Dries made such a huge deal of our relationship was that, consciously or not, he regarded it as incestuous.

Still, lots of shortcuts and self-victimization there. I turned around to rest my elbows on the railing as well. "I already told you it doesn't work like that... Just because you think March owes you doesn't mean you get to choose who he sees. And it's the same for me—I liked him before I even knew you existed."

"He can sleep with you over my dead body."

I fought the urge to roll my eyes. "You do realize you sound like some crazy bigot who hunts down his daughter's suitors with a shotgun, right?"

"Isn't it what Simon does?"

Simon? As in *Simon Halder?* "Hold on, you know my dad?"

He shrugged. "Shared a drink with him once."

"Seriously? Where did you—"

"In London. It was a few years after your birth. I was curious to meet him. I joined him at the Kensington's bar, I believe."

I was trying to picture them sitting together at a table. Night and day, the hyper-anxious banker and the glacial hit man. "How did it go?"

"Well enough. I asked for some financial advice. He seemed to know what he was doing. A very cautious, analytical mind, I remember." A curve that wasn't quite a smile appeared on Dries's lips as he went through his memories. "Toward the end, I told him he was raising my daughter. And I told him what I did for a living."

Cold spilled in my stomach. I'd always wondered how much my dad knew. *That* much. No wonder where all that helicopter parenting came from.

"He said he wasn't afraid of me," Dries went on with a snort. "He was lying. His hands were shaking."

"Glad to hear you had fun," I said cuttingly.

"I didn't. He told me he pitied me." He paused, staring down at the glitter of the moon on ink-black waters. "I thought of following him back to his hotel and slicing his throat."

Blood rushed to my head; I grabbed his arm. "Don't talk about him like that!"

Dries looked at me then. The same way he had in Tokyo—like his walls were down and those expressionless eyes, that emptiness, they were his true self, and all he'd ever have to give. My chest hurt, as if my heart were physically breaking.

"But I didn't kill him," he finally said.

My mother had been in my place. She had seen the emptiness too, dug until she hit that same icy kernel, and she thought he couldn't let her in, could never change. I understood now how powerless she must have felt. I didn't want to talk anymore—I didn't feel strong enough for that at the moment. Dries watched me back away with hesitant steps, until he seemed to make up his mind and moved to stop me.

His hand hovered over my shoulder without touching it, as if he feared I'd leave for good if he did. At first I just looked at his neck, the silvery stubble and the wrinkles there. The tiny flat moles, just like mine. I forced myself to meet his eyes. In the dark, they no longer seemed so golden, just a sad hazel.

"Why didn't you kill him, if it was so easy?" I asked.

"Because you needed a father."

I breathed fast to stop the prickling in my nose. I wouldn't let him make me cry again. "Then why the fuck didn't you do the job?"

"Léa went off the grid without even telling me she was pregnant. I took it as a clear message that my presence was not needed, or wanted, for that matter."

It sounded like another of the shortcuts he liked so much, a convenient blanket thrown over God knew how much rage and how many tears. The tension in his voice, the way his hand lingered on my forearm though, those were real.

"Maybe she wanted you to find her," I said softly.

I practically heard iron gates slam shut as he moved away. "I did, and I got her killed. Any other insights to share for tonight?"

Jan's voice echoed in my ears as he recounted the circumstances of my mother's death, the trail of bodies Dries had left behind him after that, to make sure that no frumentarius would ever have a chance to betray him again. Was there any going back from that?

I blinked back those goddamn tears and steadied my voice. "You're making everybody pay. Alex's father, all the other frumentarii, me . . . Did Anies pay too?"

A smirk tugged at his lips; he shook his head. "Dikkenek . . . always there to help. Always talking too much."

"This has nothing to do with him. I'm asking *you*—"

"About things that are none of your business!" His sudden bark startled me. Regaining his composure, Dries let out a weary sigh and averted his eyes. "Now go back to your room and"—he waved a hand to the stairway leading back inside the yacht—"not with him. You can do better, little Island; trust an old Lion on that."

I could have dealt him the finishing blow by observing that he was the one who had brought March and me together in the first place. I chose not to. I was shaken; he looked bitter and tired. Maybe it was best we both get some sleep.

"I'm sorry to hear you say that," I simply said, before turning away.

When I looked back through the bay window, I saw him standing alone on the deck. He ran a hand across his face. Dries still wasn't very good at the whole parenting thing.

There was no trace of March in my cabin, so I crept down the hallway to his, avoiding the suspicious look Dries's men shot my way when I walked past them. I turned the doorknob with excruciating care, even if I knew he wouldn't sleep through someone intruding in his nest anyway.

He was still awake, resting in his bed with a tablet in his hands. With a smile, he set it on his lap and tapped the mattress to invite me under the covers. It would have been rude to decline; within seconds, I was pantsless, sucked in by the warmth of his body and, well, the comforter.

March draped an arm around my shoulder and pulled me close. Our animalistic urges temporarily curbed by Dries's intervention, I reveled in the growing sense of intimacy between us, a pull that was physical yet not necessarily sexual. As his palm skimmed up and down my arm, I kissed his shoulder and stroked the outer ridge of his lion scarification, the rough tissue catching my fingertips.

"How did it go?" he inquired. "I assumed you'd scream if you needed help."

"It was okay . . . We talked a little. I think he wants to be able to play the dad card when it suits him, to stick his nose into my business. By the way, he said you can sleep with me over his dead body."

A heavy sigh fanned against my cheek. "Then let us live on borrowed time."

"Exactly." I eyed the tablet still lying on his stomach. "Were you working?"

"Well, I reread your report about Lucca Gerone. I assume Dries will do the same once he's done—"

"Sulking."

March shook his head. "Something to that effect. In any case, I'd be lying if I said I was working when you came in."

I watched in curiosity as he unlocked the tablet's screen, and a crossword grid appeared. Sitting up, I scanned the jumble of words with no small amount of admiration. He'd beaten some pretty tough definitions. Some of those I could have found out, but others I had never heard of. "Levantine coffee cup": a *zarf*? That sounded like *Star Trek* stuff. "Tuberous crop": *Excalibur* . . . Sweet Jesus!

The grid was almost complete, save for a few squares awaiting the last missing word. I gathered that's what he had been torturing himself with before my return. I raised the tablet to get a better look at the definitions.

"Try *monadic*."

March's fingers hovered above the screen. "Are you sure?"

"Pertaining to a programmable semicolon, in seven letters. Trust me, it's *monadic*. It's functional programming stuff."

He filled each square diligently. Once he was done, the grid flashed twice, and applause boomed from the tablet's speaker, prompting a self-satisfied smile on his lips. A pop-up with a timer announced that March had conquered the crossword app's ultimate monthly puzzle in record time. As a result, he'd won a twelve-pack of diet Mountain Dew and a branded green-sequin cap. I watched him close the pop-up without claiming his prize.

"You don't want the cap?"

His lips pursing in the slightest hint of regret, he considered the finished grid. "It's the first time I ever won, but it wouldn't be fair. You helped me."

I was tempted to argue that we should share the prize then, but with a steady tap on the screen, he opened the app's menu and deleted the grid. I checked the high scores; somewhere in Oklahoma, Grmaof4_39 had just beaten the puzzle too. A gold star appeared next to her name.

"She's getting the Mountain Dew," I noted.

"I know." March placed the tablet back on his nightstand before he gathered me in his arms. "But I already have everything I need."

His unexpected candor took me aback. My mouth worked in vain. All I could feel building was a premature declaration of total love, something so intense I feared it couldn't be contained in my body and might ooze out in some horrific way. I think I eventually said something lame like "me too," and I just held on to him, caressed the bristles on his nape, kissed the fuzz I loved so much on his ear.

After March had turned off the lights, it took me a little while to fall asleep. I kept thinking of Dries and my mother. I listened to his steady breathing, felt the weight of his arm on my hip, and I told myself I never wanted to make the same mistakes they had.

NINETEEN
THE RITUAL

He threw her on the bed roughly and tore off his embroidered vest. His eyes were dark and smoldering with molten desire. "Darling, I'm going to teach you how to play the Alphorn," he said hoarsely.

Kendra Sparkle, Surrendering to The Swiss Cowboy

When people conjure up visions of heavenly European sceneries, of old stones, verdant maquis and turquoise waters, they'll usually think of the Mediterranean Sea: the French Riviera or the Italian coasts, that kind of thing. You seldom—if ever—hear them bring up the Adriatic. Too bad, because Vis, a ten-mile-long jewel stretching off the Croatian coast, possessed all the wild charm and idle insouciance of Saint Tropez's backcountry and none of its insufferable jet-set drama-llama shit.

Dries's yacht was anchored south of the island, at a safe distance from the coast. On the deck, I watched the sun rise over a handful of tiled roofs scattered along pine trees and sandy beaches. Perched atop a cove enclosed by tall rocks, a complex and uneven geometric structure reflected the golden light on its glass exterior. Novensia's research facility shimmered like a giant crystal; the irony wasn't lost on me. I munched on a brioche roll, observing the occasional speedboats gliding through the natural stone arch guarding the cove.

Meanwhile, Dries was basically planning Pio Maraì's kidnapping.

"The entire area is privatized. They control the creek, and access to the north trail is restricted. The security perimeter is three hundred meters," he explained to March, zooming on a satellite map on his laptop's screen. "You have a series of underwater caves connecting to the creek's lagoon. The DPV will take you there easily."

I wanted to ask what he called a DPV, but first, I preferred to hear the rest of what sounded like a plan to kill March under the guise of finding Pio Maraì.

Dries swiped to display pictures of a crescent-shaped beach stretching at the foot of a cliff. "Once you've reached the creek, as long as they don't detect you, the rest is child's play: just a little climbing," he concluded as a sinuous green line appeared on-screen, tracing the optimal path up a hundred feet of steep rock and all the way to the glass façade of Novensia's building.

"But how does he get inside and find Maraì? And aren't you going with him?" I asked.

"I'm not going because it is my understanding that someone needs to stay with you," Dries replied, sending a sharp glance in March's direction. "And for hell's sake, if he can't break through a window and find an unarmed clown in a science lab, *what* do you see in him?"

Neither of us took the risk to comment on this. Dries was evidently still sore about the prior evening's incident, even after three cream-filled cornetti and a pint of cappuccino.

"March, are you sure about this?"

His arms crossed, he gazed at the maps and calculations on-screen. "It's feasible but admittedly a little daring." *It's complete bullshit, and I don't want to have to do this.* "But Island is right: the facility is about four thousand square meters on ten stories. I'll need a way to locate Maraì precisely." *Why don't you ask me to kidnap the entire Duggar family instead?*

"Actually, he doesn't know us. Why don't we just go there and say we believe his company has something to do with the crash and see how it goes from there? If he kicks us out, then you can always go scuba diving and climb up a cliff to break into his building and kill everyone," I suggested.

March looked at me curiously at first, but after a few seconds, he seemed sold on the idea.

Dries got up from the couch and towered above me as if I were some bug he was about to squish. "Young lady, that's not how we do things in this family."

I held my head up high and sustained his icy glare. "Then maybe *we* should do things differently, because *our* plan sucks and might get March killed."

The briefest flutter of his eyelids the only sign that he was in fact upset, Dries ignored me to speak to March instead. "I see your earlier point more clearly now; let's lock her up."

I retreated behind March, just in case.

"I believe," he said cautiously, shielding me from paternal wrath, "that we have enough cards in our sleeve to approach Maraì."

"What do you do with the welcome committee?" Dries asked, tilting his head to the laptop's screen, where a zoomed picture revealed armed guards.

"I'll go alone, and if discussion isn't possible after all, they will be *my* problem."

Dries frowned. "No. If you manage to meet Maraì, I want to be there."

"Me too."

Two pairs of eyes rolled at the same time to stare down at me. I still wasn't welcome in the little killer club. Oh well, worth a try.

March confirmed the sentence. "I'd prefer you wait for us here, Island."

Remembering my earlier pledge to let him keep me safe, I bit back my frustration. As I considered asking him to wear a wire for my benefit, a black-clad figure emerged from the stairs leading to the aft deck: Moritz, Dries's cook and overall handyman.

I'd run into him a couple of times on the ship. He'd smiled at me, and we'd even exchanged a few words: a considerable improvement from the silent treatment I got from the yakuza guy or the pilot and engineer. He was about my age and originally from Bern; I found him oddly lean for someone who baked so many pastries. Speaking of which, he was bringing another tray of Nutella-filled cornetti—Dries was in excellent shape, but I was starting to fear that Moritz meant in fact to fatten him for some dark Helvetic ritual.

I smiled when I saw the Nutella. Moritz smiled too, just a little too sweetly—maybe I was scheduled to be part of the ritual sacrifice too.

March didn't smile. At all. He considered the newcomer warily and wrapped an arm around my shoulders. "Perhaps you'll be safer with us after all."

And so, the wheel of destiny spun, because even in the heart of the most civilized gentleman sleeps a red-ass baboon.

TWENTY
THE EMPEROR'S WIFE

Ramirez squeezed one of Rica's luscious and perfect breasts with a salacious smile. "At long last, Rica, you are mine!"
She looked away and wiped a tear from her beautiful eyes. "No, Ramirez. I am only your prisoner."
—Kerry-Lee Storm, The Cost of Rica III: Shackles of Lust

Forty minutes after our family had made the decision to not only renounce violence but also support women in the workforce, Dries's yacht was anchored ashore from the seaside village of Marinje Zemlje. We rented an old white Mercedes from a local garage whose owner didn't seem to care much for a valid proof of ID. Soon we were driving up a trail among fragrant pine trees and cypresses, surrounded by a bunch of cicadas shaking their asses—sorry, their *timbals*—like there would be no tomorrow. We passed a few houses and vineyards, until a tall barbed wire fence barred the trail.

Maraì had chosen to isolate his facility completely: beyond the fence, the only land access to the glass building was a footpath zigzagging through dense maquis shrubbery. A steel gate guarded the entrance to the compound. There was no visible intercom, but less than a minute after we'd stopped the car, a pair of bodyguards clad in dark-gray fatigues appeared on the other side of the gate.

I had a moment of mild embarrassment when I realized that I was the only one not wearing sunglasses here, so these guys would immediately know I wasn't the real deal. From the back seat, I glanced at March's aviators and made a mental note to find myself a pair of those. Dries and I watched him step out of the car and stroll to the gate. Once there, he produced a printed version of one of Falchi's scans from his jacket that he slipped through the steel bars. "Good morning, gentlemen. Can I ask you to give this to Mr. Maraì and tell him we would like a word with him about Sabina Falchi?"

Hard to tell what could be going on behind the guards' own sunglasses. They took the paper and disappeared down the footpath without a word. March returned to the car and leaned against it, waiting. It took almost ten minutes before they returned, this time with a couple of friends, who weren't even trying to conceal their holsters and the guns inside.

Dries lowered his sunglasses and winked at me in the mirror. "Shall we?"

Too late to chicken out. I didn't want to wait alone in the car in the middle of nowhere anyway. I followed him out of the car, puffing my chest to inspire some measure of respect from our hosts. We earned a body search before being allowed past the gate. I worried that March's and Dries's best friends would be a problem, but the guards just took those and placed them in barcoded Ziploc bags, and that was it. As if it were a common occurrence for Maraì's visitors to conceal carry. What kind of world do we live in?

Once they had—hastily—ascertained that we posed no further threat, we were guided down the tortuous path leading to Novensia's research facility, sandwiched between the two pairs of bodyguards.

When the cove came into view, I forgot about the purpose of our visit for a moment. From above, the place was even more beautiful, its water among the purest I'd ever seen. On the creamy sand, turquoise green bled on azure blue like watercolor.

Up close, the building wasn't so much an architectural marvel as an aesthetic one. The design of the massive crystal-like structure was more complex than I'd previously thought: each irregular pentagon-shaped face was made of smaller triangular facets forming recursive pentagrams. Geometry and engineering in the service of witchcraft. Very reassuring.

Esoteric considerations aside, the facility seemed more or less deserted as we entered. A few papers still lay forgotten on the reception desk. Through glass partitions, an empty open space and several meeting rooms were visible. There'd been people working here until very recently, but now it was just us and the bodyguards leading the way.

At the other end of the lobby, doors slid open, whose outline I'd barely noticed in the smooth brushed-steel wall. The guards gestured for us to stop there. March assessed with a wary gaze the second group of four men approaching us. I clenched my fists. It looked a lot like we were being surrounded. Behind the newcomers, a silhouette moved, held back by a fifth guard, it seemed.

March and I watched in mild shock as Sabina Falchi came forward. The men stepped aside with a scowl, apparently hesitant to touch her. Dries crossed his arms, gauging her with a feral twist of his lips. Now wearing an elegant tapered teal dress, high-heeled sandals, and a ton of conditioner on the black tresses framing a flashy diamond necklace, Sabina looked nothing like the woman who had been rescued less than eighteen hours ago . . . possibly by the same guys. She was deadly pale though, and no amount of makeup could conceal the dark circles under her eyes.

I took a cautious step forward, only to be stopped by March's hand on my shoulder. "What are you doing here?" I asked. "Do you know what really happened to that plane?"

The car chase was probably still fresh in her mind: her face pinched into a grimace of fear as her gaze met mine. She reined in the emotion in a long exhale and stared at Dries with an intensity I couldn't decipher. Obviously she recognized him.

He tilted his head and answered her scrutiny in a velvety voice. "Lady Luck herself. Are you as happy to meet me as I am to meet you, Sabina?"

I can safely say that the last answer any of us expected was that soft, breathless "Yes."

March and I exchanged looks as one of the guards split from the group and crossed the lobby to call an elevator. Whatever game she and "Lucca" were playing, and whether Pio Maraì had anything to do with it . . . we would know soon.

"We must go upstairs now," Falchi announced, each syllable rolling with a soft Italian accent.

Dries shook his head with the faintest curl of his lips. "Oh Sabina . . . did you arrange a party for us? You shouldn't have." He beckoned March and me with his hand, as if he were onstage performing some kind of twisted play. "Come on, you two, let us not make the empress wait."

Something flickered in her gaze when he said this, a spark of surprise, admiration even.

As the guards crammed with us in the elevator, March's hand sneaked around my waist. I closed my eyes briefly, grateful for that tiny, invisible bond between us, even when my nose was ten inches away from the barrel of a rifle.

"I didn't picture you as a man with an interest in history," Sabina told Dries, once the steel doors slid closed.

His golden eyes softened—whether there was any sincerity to it, I couldn't tell. "Well, I like a woman of character, and Emperor Hadrian's wife didn't lack any."

Her chest rose with a sharp intake of air. "It was also the name of Nero's second wife."

It was the way she said this, like a warning: licks of cold fear prickled down my spine as the doors opened to a vast penthouse overlooking the creek. We crossed a living room that could just as well have been a museum: minimalistic, impersonal, the pure-white lines and touches of wood only here to showcase the antique sculptures and paintings on the walls. Sabina whirled around and stared at Dries again for a moment, an unspoken plea in her eyes, as if he held some answer neither March nor I did. She then seemed to make up her mind and walked across the room to a spiral staircase leading to the tenth and last floor. "This way."

We followed her up the stairs. When we reached the top, March's hand brushed my arm in silent reassurance. I thought of Moritz. I almost wished he hadn't decided to feed me Nutella cornetti and hit on me right under his nose.

The tenth and last floor must have been where Maraì lived. From the kitchen to the couch and bookshelves, the atmosphere was different in this room, made warmer by a little mess and colorful cushions. In a corner of the room, a stereo was playing. I recognized Mozart's Requiem, or more precisely, the soft, ghostly choirs of the Agnus Dei. Okay . . . let it be a coincidence.

In front of us, a bay window opened to a terrace that almost looked like it was floating on the horizon's line. There, two men facing away from us appeared to be enjoying the warm morning breeze. My pulse picked up. Next to a brown-haired man lounging in a deck chair, a hooded figure sat crouched.

A soprano's crystalline voice was begging God to welcome us in his light, and Sabina had lost a good deal of her countenance. Her fists were balled in an effort not to shake. Tears were welling in her eyes, which she struggled to hold back. "Lucca. Loro sono qui," she managed out. *Lucca. They're here.*

The hooded guy got up on his feet. He was lean, graceful; his navy hoodie and gray jeans could have been those of a student. He turned to face us, and all of a sudden, I found myself tumbling down the uncanny valley. Looking back at us were empty eyes, human features lacking any asperity, any life. The blissful and impenetrable smile of a Japanese Noh mask.

TWENTY-ONE
JUS IN BELLO

Lamb of God, who takes away the sins of the world, grant them everlasting rest.

–Wolfgang Amadeus Mozart, Requiem

The Noh mask fascinated me, with its pale oval and the slanted eyes. The mouth was small, feminine, revealing a row of square teeth. I couldn't tear my gaze from that eerie smile, and it took me several seconds to figure that the guy in a suit resting on the deck chair was probably Pio Maraì, and that he wasn't going to move because he was dead. I stepped back instinctively, meeting the comforting planes of March's chest. His hand moved to rest on my shoulder.

The hooded man moved too, and my stomach twisted because I thought he meant to reach for me, grab me. It was in fact Sabina he pulled to him and gathered in his arms. He held her tenderly, like a lover would have, stroked her face and the wavy ribbons of black hair. It looked like he meant to kiss her but couldn't, so he touched his cold lips to hers and spoke, in a voice that was just as inhuman as this parody of affection.

"Io non voglio che tu sia triste." *I don't want you to be sad.*

The unexpected metallic, robotic accents turned my bones to brittle ice. It was a machine speaking. The intonation sounded surprisingly natural though: just as soft as his fingers caressing her glittery necklace. She sniffed quietly in response. This woman wasn't sad. She was legitimately terrified. It was becoming obvious that over the past eighteen hours, Sabina Falchi had come to understand she had made a terrible mistake in resting her fate in the hands of whoever Lucca truly was. Which, by the way, begged to question our own immediate future.

He must be used to people being weirded out. He let go of Sabina to study us through the tiny holes in his metal mask. I couldn't see his eyes, and that made him even scarier. "I'm sorry; this part is always a little awkward." He touched the side of his mask. "It reads neuroelectrical signals from my brain and muscle activity on the upper half of my face, and it crosses the data to restitute natural speech. I'm very proud of it. Although, I must warn you that my words aren't always exactly the ones I mean, and I apologize for any misunderstanding as a result."

So whatever the mask concealed was bad enough that he could no longer speak. Jesus, this was wrong. I just couldn't reconcile this computerized voice with the rest his body . . . The skin, the veins on his delicate hands, the hair on his knuckles—those were flesh and blood; they belonged to a human being. More specifically, a psychopathic asshole.

"Who are you?" March asked, his own astonishment enveloping each word.

"No one of importance." The Noh guy tilted his head, and I knew that behind the black slits, his gaze was traveling between me and Dries. "You do look like each other. She's your daughter, am I right?"

He knew? *How?*

Dries's fists clenched in response, but his expression remained one of self-assurance. "Answer the question. Who am I talking to? Or perhaps should I say, *what*?"

"You are being hurtful." There was an odd accent of sincerity in the synthetic harmonics. "I don't like you."

"I don't like you either," Dries went on. "And what I like even less is waking up to my own face on TV. I'm afraid you have a lot of explaining to do."

The Noh mask's shoulders shook in silent laughter. "You are like Pio. An old, desperate man who can't see he has served his purpose and needs to go."

Upon hearing this, Sabina sniffed quietly, and her mouth twisted to reveal gritted teeth.

The Noh mask placed a not-so-comforting hand on the small of her back, and his synthetic voice went on, the slanted eyes set on Dries. "You need to go. Everyone needs you to go. That's why you're here. So I can solve this problem."

I saw Dries's lips part to say something, but I spoke before I could stop myself, spurred by an equal amount of fear and anger. "You're Lucca Gerone, right? I read about your research for Novensia, the crystals. Is that what happened? Did you use some kind of ultrasound frequency against the plane?"

Sabina cast a desperate look my way. All the confirmation I needed. I jerked my chin at her. "But then you realized she would be on the flight, so you went to the airport, and you saved her life." I pointed to the lifeless body slowly cooking under the sun with a trembling finger. "No such pity for Pio Maraì though." Behind me, I sensed March shift. Could he tell I was trying to play for time? I raised my voice. "*Why*? What happened to you, Lucca?"

The Noh mask let go of Sabina, but he barely acknowledged me, speaking to March instead. "I like her better than her father. You have nothing to worry about; she will be spared. You have to leave us too, but I want you to know no one will hurt her even after you are gone."

My heart rammed against my rib cage. Somehow Gerone's promise scared me more than any death threat would have. Because of the finality of his words as he voiced his intent to kill March. Void of anger. Matter-of-fact. Why would he spare me anyway? I had nothing to do with whatever insane scheme he was trying to pull. Did he even know March to address that promise to him specifically?

"How generous of you," March replied, a cold smile stirring his lips.

As he said this, his posture straightened imperceptibly. The black leather of his gloves fitted around his knuckles with a faint squeak. Something moved at the edge of my vision—the guards who had led us to the penthouse had positioned themselves in the living room and on each side of the window. I could see their assault rifles reflected in the glass balcony. Dries sent me a sharp look, and I noticed Sabina was inching away from Gerone and toward him. I couldn't blame her. I had been through enough over the past six months to know that sometimes immediate emergency dictates you pick the fire over the frying pan.

Inside the penthouse, the Requiem was still playing. An unpleasant pressure squeezed my lungs when the eighth and final movement started. "Cum Sanctis tuis in aeternum" *With your Saints, in eternity* . . . how about *no?*

Gerone extended his hands in my and Sabina's direction. "Ladies? I believe it's time for us to go."

I stood frozen in place, looking up at March helplessly, while Sabina shook her head and staggered backward until she stood at Dries's side. Some of the guards reached for their guns. She begged Gerone through choked sobs. "Lucca . . . lasciami andare. Non mi uccidere! Per favore!" *Lucca . . . let me go. Don't kill me! Please!*

My first instinct was that she was wrong, that, twisted as he may be, he loved her enough to have rescued her, so he wouldn't. But he stiffened, as if he were surprised with her refusal to join him, and reached in his pocket, palming something there. That's when she panicked. Her hands flew to the intricate diamond necklace around her neck, trembling, clutching and unclutching, yet never making contact with the jewelry. Her sobbing had become hysterical. "No, no! Non farlo . . . Lucca, per favore!" *No, no! Don't do it . . . Lucca, please!*

My gaze was locked on her fingers, the shimmering stones they wouldn't dare to touch. Bits of Gerone's research flashed in my mind. *When exposed to ultrasound waves . . . High risk of instability.*

Crystals explosion.

Oooh. Shit. Ultron dabbled in jewelry too.

Gerone's hand remained in his pocket as he faced Sabina. "You're making a scene. Your mascara is running. Come, please," the synthetic voice ordered.

All guards stared at Sabina through their badass sunglasses, waiting for an order from Gerone. Dries winked at her. She was panting now, her stomach undulating under the tight material of her dress, beads of sweat rolling between her breasts.

I didn't think Gerone would do it. Even knowing he'd likely killed six hundred people without a trace of remorse, my brain refused to compute that one human being could blow up another's head like that. I barely saw Dries move. Sabina shrieked in horror even as he tore the river of crystals from her neck and hurled it to the ground. I'm not sure the necklace even touched it, the deflagration happened too fast. *Holy shit, he did it. He seriously tried to . . .* March shoved me to the ground and shielded us with his bulletproof jacket from the storm of white-hot crystals hailing our way. I hissed when I felt some hit my legs, the burn seeping through the fabric of my pants.

By the time my vision cleared, several of Gerone's men were already taking him to safety back inside the penthouse. Flattened to the ground under Dries, Sabina emitted a series of panicked hiccups, a sure sign that she wasn't dead yet. In the two seconds it took for the remaining guards standing on the terrace to recover and set their sights on killing us, March grabbed the barrel of the rifle closest to him and spun it around, shooting its unfortunate owner in the face.

At that point, I think they got really angry with us. Bullets started flying in all directions, smashing into the teak floorboards, shattering the glass balcony, transpiercing the deck chair where Pio Maraì still rested. Dries rolled toward the deck chair. I thought he meant to shield himself, but he toppled it over with a kick. I heard Sabina yelp when the corpse fell heavily, landing inches from her. The chair went flying across the terrace and hit a guard square in the face. My breakfast threatened to geyser back up when he collapsed in a splatter of blood and—*God*—a few teeth. Dries picked up the man's gun, and that was terrible news for his two remaining colleagues, who fell dead shortly afterward.

Someone grabbed my legs, and I almost kicked back, only to realize that March was dragging me back inside the penthouse and into the space between the kitchen counter and island. On the terrace, Sabina made an attempt to get on her feet, but Dries knocked her out unceremoniously with an encouragement to "be a good girl, and wait here." She dropped unconscious near Maraï's waxy body. For those of you reading this and wondering where the gentlemen have gone, that's where—beating up women in Croatia.

March knelt by me and squeezed my hand. "Others are coming up. Stay here, and *please* don't do anything. Wait, and stay hidden until I come back for you."

"What if they come for me?" I asked between two panicked breaths.

I shouldn't have. He didn't need to think of that. His brow quivered, as if his brain were trying to work through an equation that wouldn't compute.

The answer came from above, tossed in my lap by Dries. "Then you have my permission to use this. Last resort."

I took what looked every bit like be a pair of aluminum USB keys. "What's that?"

"Concentrated C-4. Press both sides simultaneously to arm them. You have five seconds after that. Daddy loves science too."

C-4? As in, *Boom*? Was there a manual for this? I didn't want to make anyone explode! *Sweet Raptor Jesus*, what was it that March and I had discussed on the boat, about me being safe and staying clear of the thug life?

March seemed conflicted about Dries's "last resort" plan. He pressed a quick kiss to my temple. "Don't touch it. Trust me, when the way is clear, I'll come back for you."

My fingers closed around the strangely heavy metal dominoes as he and Dries hurried toward the staircase. New gunshots crackled in the air, which made me curl into a tight ball. The noises progressively grew fainter until I was alone in the penthouse, a few feet away from several dead bodies and a passed-out Sabina, who wasn't giving any sign of coming to her senses.

Above the counter, a brass clock on the wall ticked off the seconds steadily. Gerone must have fled the building by now. I couldn't hear any noise coming from the floors below. Something flared at the edge of my vision. I glanced outside to see the noon sun hitting the building's façade, turning each glass panel into a gleaming-white jewel. On the terrace floor, hundreds of crystal fragments coming from Sabina's necklace still lay scattered, some turned brownish by the heat of the explosion. That's when I started to envision the possibility that I was in fact trapped on the top floor of one massive pile of Novensia glass. I preferred not to explore the ramifications of that particular scenario.

A minute passed, which is in fact a very long time when your heart is beating so fast it hurts. At last, footsteps slammed onto the steps of the staircase. My initial reaction was one of relief, and I slumped against the cool brushed steel of Pio Maraï's dishwasher . . . Except there had to be more than two pairs of feet, some sounding particularly heavy, and that no one was calling me "biscuit" or telling me that it was all right, and I could come out now.

What I heard was a deep voice muttering orders in a thick Eastern European accent. Boots clattered on the parqueted floor. It was as if my windpipe and lungs were being crushed, and I couldn't breathe, suffocated by a paralyzing fear. On my left, the bay window reflected a dark shape creeping toward the kitchen counter, half crouched, holding a gun.

He mustn't come near me, I thought. If he moved any closer, I'd be within shooting range, and I was toast. I clenched my fist around Dries's pocket C-4 bombs. *Last. Resort.* I told myself I could earn a little time, find something to make them back off until March and Dries returned.

Yeah, I know a jar of olives isn't exactly military-grade stuff, but it was the only decent weapon sitting on the shelves of the island. I grabbed it and threw it over the counter, in the general direction of the living area. The jar crashed to the floor in a din of broken glass. A round of fire in the island welcomed my initiative. Bullets banged against the steel, hard enough to make the structure shake, but, thankfully, none made it through. The guy moving toward me stepped back. In the window, I saw him make little hand gestures to whoever had opened fire.

I'd earned a ten-second reprieve, but now they knew I had no gun. I was desperately trying to think over the pounding in my ears, and I couldn't bring myself to do it. I threw a couple of caviar tins because I thought it'd earn me five more seconds, and maybe March would show up and save me. There was another round of fire, caviar in my hair, and March wasn't there.

The footsteps came closer, and my hands were shaking so hard I could barely find the strength to press each side of the metallic rectangle like Dries had told me to. I repeated in my head, like a mantra, that once I let go of the buttons I could feel clicking under my thumb and forefinger, I'd have five seconds left until . . . Before I knew it, I'd tossed the pocket C-4 over the counter. I had a terrifying vision that the device would somehow remain stuck to my hand and blow my entire arm off. It didn't. I registered a faint clatter as it landed on the floor.

Boots thumped around the living room before it was all swallowed by a loud explosion, much worse than the necklace's. I felt the shock wave travel through my body, all the way to the tips of my toes. Shards of wood and burning plush flew above my head and landed on the counter. I clamped my hand over my mouth and nose to stifle my own cry of surprise.

Then I heard it. An agonizing howl coming from the other end of the living room. "Oh God! Oh *God*, I'm hit! Man down! Man down! It's . . . it's everywhere! There's blood everywhere on me!"

"Shut up, Karl!" hissed the big voice I'd heard before. The boss, surely.

"I can feel myself going. There's a light, I—"

"Someone make him shut the fuck up!" A third voice growled, echoing his comrade's callous order.

My breath coming in gasps, I thought of that poor guy, agonizing just a few feet away. I had done that. Admittedly to defend myself, but without thinking of the consequences. I was responsible. Was my soul as dark as Dries's after all? Like it was genetics? I pressed a palm on my chest to calm my racing heart and, in as loud and steady a voice as I could muster, called out to him. "Sir, are you mortally wounded?"

I didn't miss the sharp clicks of guns being reloaded and armed as I spoke, but Karl ignored his teammates to answer me.

"I don't know." He moaned. He had a slight accent I couldn't place, and his voice sounded a little less urgent than it had moments before, but he was clearly in horrifying pain. "I-I have a bulletproof vest"—I distinctly heard someone behind him whisper, "Let me shoot that cocksucker," but he kept talking—"there's blood on my leg . . . It's . . . aaaahhh . . . I think it's the femoral artery. God, I'm gonna lose my leg, I can't feel it anymore!"

Panic throbbed in my forehead: I had to do something, quick. A roll of paper towels had landed next to my feet when everything had blown up. I grabbed it and threw it over the island, like I had the C-4. A new round of bullets clanked into the wall of steel shielding me. I covered my ears until there was only silence again.

"Thank you!"

I let out a breath of relief as Karl confirmed the safe delivery of the paper towels.

"It's probably too late for me already, but it's a very good brand. Very absorbent!"

This product review spurred another aggravated roar. "Seriously? Will you fucking *shut up*? We're in the middle of somethi—"

It's sad because those were that guy's last words, and he wasted them insulting Karl, when he could have been paying attention to his surroundings. He'd have noticed that March and Dries were done with his colleagues and were back to finish the job.

Or maybe it would have made no difference, given how fast the bodies hit the ground after each shot. One gave a low moan, followed by a gurgle, before collapsing less than two feet away from my hiding spot. I screwed my eyes shut to block the sight of his blood spilling from his neck on the blond floorboards. I suddenly thought of Karl: a burst of renewed adrenaline gave me enough courage to crawl out and toward Dries's shoes as he moved to finish a guy wearing a balaclava and holding a roll of paper towels to his chest.

I scrambled to my feet just as March came behind me to help me up. "Don't shoot him!"

Dries's finger paused on the trigger, and he cocked an eyebrow at me.

I joined my hands in prayer. "Please! He's badly wounded!"

He stepped over Karl with an air of disgust. "He's perfectly fine, and he'd better get up if he wants to live." Done with his diagnostic, Dries ran to the terrace to haul a barely conscious Sabina to her feet. She was limp in his arms and struggled to even stand up. Frustrated, he pressed his thumb against her carotid to knock her out again, before he hauled her over his shoulder like a bag of potatoes.

"March," he said, an undercurrent of warning in his voice.

March took my hand in response and dragged me fast across the living room and after Dries.

I turned to look at Karl, who had gotten up, and was following us, paper towels still in hand. "You said your femoral artery had been torn," I said accusingly, while we barreled across the ninth floor among dead bodies and damaged furniture.

"*Must* have been," Karl whined. "It sure felt like it!"

In front of me, I heard Dries mutter, "That boy's just a *poes*."

It started when we reached the elevator. Not a noise at first, just a strange pressure in my ears and my chest. Then, as the doors slid closed, the glass walls outside started to make these low crackling sounds. March, Dries, and I looked at each other. All around us, the vibrations intensified. Understanding dawned on us. March's hand squeezed mine urgently.

Trapped on the top floor of one massive pile of Novensia glass . . .

He was about to press on the first-floor button, but Karl lunged to punch sublevel five instead. Before I could stop him, March grabbed him by the collar and slammed him against the elevator's wall, while around us the building structure seemed to be shaking more and more, and I was getting frankly nauseous.

"It's the caves!" Karl yelled. "It's safer down there!"

March released him. It was too late to back out anyway. We had just glided past the ground floor. Through the holes of his balaclava, Karl's eyes were wide with panic. That didn't look like the face of a man with an evil plan B. To be honest, I wasn't entirely sure he was smart enough for that.

The elevator doors opened to some sort of dark basement. I glimpsed fluorescent lamps and some numbers painted on the walls. The next thing I knew was pain. Above us, a detonation shook the ceiling and the elevator, so loud, so violent that it felt like my very bones were shattering inside me. My ears were ringing, buzzing; I couldn't hear anything. I ran because everyone else was running, and March wouldn't let go of my hand, but in truth, I had no idea how my legs were even moving. Plaster and gravel fell on our heads, and I kept running, down a corridor, toward a glimmering blue light. I saw turquoise spots dancing in my vision, outlining March's back as he pulled me with all his strength.

Then the solid ground was no more, and we plunged into dark, cold water. Fully clothed, my body felt heavy, like the black depths were calling me, and I'd never breathe again. Bubbles swirled around me, and the turquoise light was getting brighter. I thought I saw a veil, something white and beautiful wrapping around March and me as he held me tight against him and swam us up to the surface.

The paper towel roll. That shit was everywhere. Emerging from my daze, I removed a towel clinging to my forehead and spat salty water. The sun was blinding me, my eardrums still hurt, but we were alive; March's drenched cheek against mine told me that much. We were floating right outside the entrance of a cave leading to the facility's private cove. Above us, the building was a blazing steel skeleton, shedding burning debris down the cliff and onto the beach's pristine sand. A few feet away, Karl was fighting his way out of a wet paper roll but was otherwise fine.

"It's over; it's going to be all right," March said with a gasp of effort, keeping me afloat until I remembered how to move my legs.

I looked around frantically. "Dries! Where is he?"

March looked back to the cove. "He split from us in the cave."

The roar of a motorboat had me pedaling in the water toward the source of the noise. I drank a mouthful when a white shape bulleted through the natural stone arch giving access to the cove, splashing us like only a nefarious asshat would have.

Wide eyed, I watched the boat race west and leave us behind. I recognized that patch of green: Sabina's dress. "He's not seriously leaving us here and taking off with her?"

March swam closer to me. "He wants to be alone with her."

Deep inside, I knew why. But wanting to believe otherwise, I forced a smile onto my lips. "She won't sleep with him after he knocked her out like that."

March gazed in the direction where the speedboat had disappeared, anger knotting his brow. "I don't think that's why he took her."

I kept quiet as we swam back to the beach. I couldn't find any way to sugarcoat the fact that Dries simply didn't want us around while he . . . *questioned* Sabina Falchi. Sweet Jesus, I hoped he'd limit his efforts to scaring the ever-loving crap out of her like I knew he could.

By the time we got out of the water, police sirens echoed from above our heads. I looked at the top of the cliff. They'd likely come by the road, alerted by the explosion. We'd have to find another way out, which is where Karl came into play. Now a full-time member of our team and not at all a shady character wearing a balaclava and following us around with a wet roll of paper towels, he led us to another boat, moored to a wooden pier in the creek. He didn't have the keys but instead hotwired the ignition with the ease of a true professional. Or, at the very least, a professional more used to petty crime than paramilitary action.

Minutes later, March stood behind the wheel, and I sat curled up next to Karl on the boat's back seat as we glided away from Vis on a smooth sea. Karl twisted around to get one last look at the blackened skeleton of Novensia's building, shrouded in a dark smoke cloud that swelled toward the sky.

"Whoa." He let out a low whistle. "They weren't lying when they said the rehearsal would be something crazy."

March's hands dropped from the wheel. In the blink of an eye, Karl was up on his feet and struggling against a powerful headlock. Mr. November was past any sort of courtesy, and his growl boded nothing good. "What did you say? What rehearsal?"

Nearly as freaked out as Karl by March's sudden outburst, I snuck around them to keep a hand on the wheel, my eyes jerking back and forth between the strip of land stretching along the horizon and Karl's interrogation.

Through the holes in his black hood, his eyes became big green marbles. "It's just something I heard from the others—"

"What else did you hear?" March asked, tightening his grip around the poor guy's windpipe.

"Nothing, I just—"

"Stop it, please!" I yelled over the engine sound. "Let's find somewhere safe, and then we can chat!"

March let go of him with a huff. "You're right. Let's get out of here first."

The moment he was free, Karl collapsed in the back seat, gasping for air in exaggerated gulps. He sounded suddenly very young and very lost as he cradled his head in his hands and moaned. "I can't believe they told me to join because Croatia was nice at this time of the year."

TWENTY-TWO
THE INVITATION

The kind, considerate, and presentable son-in-law your parents love will <u>invariably</u> turn out to be a lying, cheating sack of shit. So, take the time to gauge their reactions. They hate him? Good. He's a keeper.

—Aurelia Nichols & Jillie Bean, 101 Tips to Lock Him Down

March said that it wasn't really stealing because we'd drop that black Golf in front of a police station once we were done with it. Also, he'd make sure to return it with a full tank and after a ride through a carwash. Emergency borrowing, that's what he called it.

Palm trees flashed past us, and Croatian pop poured from the speakers, filling the car with its mandatory accordion chorus. March's eyes were on the road and the few tourists on the sidewalk, his mouth a stern line as he drove us through the streets of Split, a large coastal city two hours away from Vis. There we'd—hopefully—be able to find a safe place, acquire some "equipment," and work on finding Dries and Gerone. In the mirror, a brown-haired guy with a patchy crew cut stared at us. He couldn't have been more than twenty, and his air of innocence seemed completely at odds with his now-dry fatigues. Karl had removed his balaclava, but he still held on to his paper towels.

I turned in my seat to look at him. "So who hired you, the guy with the Japanese mask, Lucca Gerone?"

"Not him directly, but yes. I applied on Yaythug. They have a Swedish version now, very nice."

So, dude was from Sweden. Where citizens enjoyed such a degree of freedom and Nordic efficiency that you could apparently apply online to work for supervillains. "Um, *Yaythug*, is it like—"

Karl nodded. "Well, it's not just for dating; they do classifieds and job offers too. It's on the darknet, but I don't think it's run by the same guys who made Yaycupid."

"It isn't," March commented soberly.

It puzzled me that someone like Karl could have spiraled into a criminal career. I examined his nose, as I often did when assessing reprobates. I found it a little big, but from an evolutionary point of view, if nasal cartilage had been a determining factor in making someone a gangster, someone like, say, Pablo Escobar would have carried his around in a wheelbarrow. So it wasn't that.

March's voice cut through my musings, intentionally cold. "You said what happened at Novensia was a rehearsal. What does it mean?"

Karl looked down, studying his combat boots. "I don't know the details; I just heard . . . things."

"Like what?" I prodded, more gently.

"That the Whisperer wanted to test the cannon on something big, like Novensia."

The cannon? March and I exchanged tense looks. It wasn't impossible—sound cannons existed, which operated on a similar principle: exposure of a target to a specific frequency capable of causing physical discomfort or even material damage. But something like what had happened back at Novensia? That was another level.

"When you say the Whisperer, are we still talking about Lucca Gerone?"

"That's what he calls himself: the Crystal Whisperer. I think it's because he likes to blow up glass. He's some sort of scientist. Very rich too. I've never worked for someone so rich, you know?"

So there was a tacky code name to go with that Noh mask. Hopefully we'd live long enough to get to the bottom of this. "Karl, what's that cannon you're talking about, and what's after the rehearsal?"

He shook his head sadly. "I don't know."

As we reached the historical center, the ruins of Diocletian's Palace came into view. It was an odd sight, all those colorful houses and restaurants leaning on thousand-year-old stones and pillars. Split's center had literally been built inside and around what had once been a Roman emperor's three-hundred-thousand-square-foot retirement crib. Goes to remind you that a couple thousand years from now, somebody will be running a fast-food joint inside one of Bill Gates's twenty-four bathrooms.

March's fingers rapped on the wheel in frustration. "What about Maraì and Sabina Falchi?"

Lines of concentration formed on Karl's brow. "The Whisperer knew him. And Maraì knew it would end like that. When we took over, well"—Karl scratched his nose on his forearm—"there was nothing to take over; everyone was gone already. He was alone."

"Did Maraì say anything?"

"He cried. He said things in Italian. I didn't understand. But he yelled stuff at the Whisperer's girlfriend, Sabina. That's when she got afraid, and I think she didn't want to be with him anymore, but he said, 'No way.' Well, it was in Italian, so maybe he didn't say it like that."

Considering Sabina's state of panic when we had found her, and Gerone's attempt at killing her, Karl's version of events confirmed our findings so far: Lucca Gerone, aka the Crystal Whisperer, enjoyed using an unidentified technology of his making to blow up anything made of Novensia's "revolutionary" Ceraglass. Sabina knew why, and she wasn't so smitten with him once she found out what her savior was up to. But Dries had taken off with her, so there went our key witness. As for Maraï's role . . .

In the mirror, I studied the dispirited features of our second-most-important witness . . . who didn't understand a word of Italian. I sighed. "Please try to remember. Did anything stand out?"

Karl released a deep breath, like he was trying to contact spirits. "Not really. You know, most of the time, I just took care of the boxes."

March's eyebrows jerked. "What boxes?"

"Back in Dubrovnik, they made us fill a plane with boxes that we were sending to France. So I took care of that. I was in charge of the tape."

Maybe Gerone was just moving into a new place, but I doubted he'd have needed to recruit men on Yaythug for that. "Do you remember where exactly they were sending those boxes?"

"The street, no. Too complicated. French stuff." His face pinched in intense concentration. "But I know that the town's name sounded like Range Rover . . ."

Uncharacteristically, March twisted his neck to look at Karl, road rules be damned. "Rangiroa?"

"Yes, yes! Rangiroa in France!"

I shook my head. "That sounds Tahitian; is it—"

"Yes," March confirmed. "It's an atoll in the Tuamotus."

So, French Polynesia, a mere ten thousand miles away from Paris. What the hell was Gerone planning there?

As if to answer that question, one of March's hands left the wheel so he could properly drag it across his face. My initial thought was that he was running on empty, having slept too little and run too much since our escape from South Africa. But there was something else. His cheeks were pale, his features taut. It was possibly the first I'd ever seen him . . . freak out.

"This is going to be a problem," he murmured.

"What do you mean?"

In the mirror, Karl too followed our exchange, his mouth slightly parted in anticipation.

"The Poseidon Dome. Have you ever heard about it? It's"—March fished for his phone in his pocket, unlocked it, and handed it to me—"you can look it up."

I felt the blood drain from my cheeks, and without looking, I knew I was making a face similar to March's. "You mean the glass dome, the resort? I heard about it"—I launched the search, and on the screen appeared a series of vacation pics in a tropical heaven—"I knew it was in Polynesia, but . . ." *Oh my God.* He was right, the Poseidon Dome *was* in Rangiroa, well, not exactly: according to their website, the resort stood on a *motu one*—a tiny patch of emerged sand—150 miles northeast of the atoll, in the northern Tuamotu Islands, indeed. Rangiroa was probably the closest place Gerone could get his "boxes" delivered without arousing too much suspicion.

I opened another pic. Framed by two palm trees standing on a pristine beach, a massive bubble seemed to emerge from a turquoise sea on the horizon. My eyes skimmed through a page advertising delights of "a week in a partially underwater luxury resort protected by a two-hundred-yard-wide transparent dome." *Sweet Jesus.* "Please don't tell me Novensia had *any* part in this."

March took the phone back from my hands and did the unthinkable: he texted while driving. "Phyllis will help us answer that."

I turned to Karl, whose mouth had yet to close. "Do you know anything about this? Are you sure there's nothing else you can tell us?"

When he shook his head slowly, I insisted, my voice becoming urgent. "Karl, this is really important. You know what Gerone did before Novensia, right?"

His gaze instantly dropped to his boots. "I'm not sure."

"I'll tell you then. He—"

"I know, okay? I heard the others talk about it." His tone had suddenly become cutting, and the green eyes that wouldn't meet mine seemed even more like a teenager's now.

"There were a lot of people on that plane. Children, babies, even!"

"But that's not what *I* do! I just . . . don't go putting it all on *me*—"

"Quiet, please."

March's command effectively shut Karl up. I registered the low buzz coming from inside his jacket while he parked by a tiny square on the port.

"Good afternoon, Phyllis," March greeted, before turning the speaker on. "You couldn't have called at a better time. We're going to need some assistance."

"And that's my middle name. Regarding the dome, I'm waiting for confirmation. But the project involved several European companies, so yes, I'm afraid we're gonna see Novensia's name come up. By the way, Scar is still with you?"

I cringed at this new nickname for Dries. Seemed like Phyllis had a variety of expletives ready for her "favorite bedside rug."

"No, which is my other concern," March admitted.

Karl chimed in. "But I'm here."

"Who's that?" Phyllis asked.

"Me. My name is Karl. I'm being held hostage. It's a pleasure to speak to you."

I think Karl would have said more, but in the mirror, March stabbed him with the cold-killer look, and he shrank in the back seat in response.

Phyllis's voice held a note of uncertainty as she asked, "Should I worry about that?"

"No," March replied.

"All right, then back to business. There was actually a reason for my call, besides the dome. I think you made quite an impression in Venice. I just received an invitation for you."

I scooted closer to the phone. "From Dries? Where is he?"

"No. From Director Erwin."

Reading March's and my facial expressions, Karl feigned shock and genuine interest, while *we* picked our jaws from the Golf's floor mats.

March cleared his throat. "That's . . . unexpected. I don't suppose he was willing to provide any kind of details?"

"Time and coordinates, nothing more. I think the message here is basically, 'Take it or leave it,'" Phyllis replied, distrust obvious in her tone.

March's gaze fell on me. "I see. Send those to me, please."

"Done. What else do you need? I can book something at the Atrium and have a suitcase delivered there. Fresh car too?"

"Yes, thank you."

After he had hung up, March leaned back in the driver's seat and stared at the fat palm trees lined in front of the car, the white bench where an old lady sat, searching her colorful bag for a city map. He remained silent.

I touched his forearm. "Can we talk?" My eyes darted to Karl, watching our every move in the mirror. "Outside?"

March nodded. Without so much as a glance for our "hostage," he opened his door and told the boy, "Wait for us in the car, please. If you try anything, I'm afraid I'll have to kill you."

To be honest, the threat was unnecessary, but Karl's head bobbed up and down in agreement anyway.

Once we were outside, I sat on the Golf's hood, reveling in the late-afternoon breeze that carried the scent of the sea, laced with that of fried food. A small blessing after the day we'd had so far. "Are you going?" I asked.

March's eyebrows drew in a pleading expression. "Island, I can't take you with me."

"I thought you'd say that," I said quietly. "But Erwin is going to want me too. I bet he thinks he can use me to bait Dries."

"The idea crossed my mind as well," March agreed.

"What if you go and there's no deal? What do I do if they arrest you?"

A tired smile etched a dimple in his cheek. "I won't be arrested."

No, I thought, *you'll be killed.* "I don't think you should go," I eventually said. "I think we should follow Karl's lead and go directly to Rangiroa. We might even find Dries there too, if Sabina Falchi talked to him."

March stepped forward. Not too close. Because not in goddamn public. "Island, if I keep running"—he drew a heavy sigh—"if we can't strike a deal, you'll lose everything too; your life, your friends, your family . . . You'll be a fugitive."

"I'll go with you. I already told you I will. I don't trust that old fart Erwin. Please . . ."

I saw the moment I had lost that battle before he even spoke. It was the way his spine straightened, the clenching of his right fist. A decision had been made, and any further arguing would be in vain. "I'm going to take you and that bumbling idiot to a hotel downtown. You will wait for me there. If anything happens, Phyllis will arrange for you to be extracted out of the country. If I come to a satisfying deal with Mr. Erwin, I'll come back for you."

I pursed my lips tight and acquiesced. I didn't trust myself to speak with the mix of fear and disappointment welling in my chest.

March's hand reached for my waist in a bid to pull me to him.

I avoided his gaze and squirmed away. "What about Karl? Do we let him go?"

He looked back at the Golf's windshield, through which the interested party watched our exchange with wide, attentive eyes. "No. He's our only witness. We might still need him."

. . . *To bargain with Erwin*, I mentally completed.

TWENTY-THREE
THE BAIT

Carly was mortified. The mysterious Sugar Daddy she had surrendered to was in fact her boss! Hot and powerful billionaire Redmond Velvet!

—Lena Raven, A Mouthful of Red Velvet

"Have a pleasant stay Mr. August. Would you like me to call someone to carry your luggage?"

"No, I'll be all right, thank you."

Next to a giant vase of flowers, Karl and I stood stiff as March finished check-in. With a congenial smile, he took the metal case that had been waiting for him at the reception desk of the Atrium, a nondescript business hotel a mile away from the crowded seafront. Phyllis worked fast. And, indeed, it was preferable that no overzealous groom was called to handle a suitcase that was undoubtedly full of guns and ammo. Our disheveled little group treaded across a sleek, soulless lobby. The whole thing almost reminded me of an actual office building, made of white walls and black glass panels encasing each area, complete with the mandatory wooden inserts to create some illusion of warmth.

An elevator took us all the way to the top floor, where March led us inside a suite so impersonal it looked like an IKEA display. Studying the many shades of gray of the carpet and bed linen, the black-and-white pictures on—you guessed it—gray walls, I wondered whether someone had forbidden the designer to use any color. Oh well, the bed wouldn't be any less comfy.

By then, I thought our relations with Karl had warmed to the point of being courteous—if not cordial. Wrong. The moment the doors had closed behind us, March laid the new mystery case on the bed, unlocked it with a six-digit code . . . and took out a pair of hinged handcuffs.

Karl cowered. "I wasn't actually planning to escape."

March's gaze flitted to me before it settled on our guest, unforgiving. "You tried to kill her less than six hours ago." He tipped his head to the bathroom door. "Please follow me."

His head hanging low, Karl complied, and March secured the handcuffs to a towel radiator next to the sink. Karl let himself slide down the black-tiled wall with a despondent sigh and gave me a beaten-puppy look.

I responded with an uneasy smile. "Sorry about that. Maybe I can get you something from the minibar?"

"Yes, thank you. A soda. Like, a Fanta, if there's any."

March's head jerked up, scandal written all over his face. I decided to ignore the unspoken message. *Yes*, I was aware that any snack eaten from the minibar would be billed to us. Yes, I knew that it would be cheaper to drink liquid gold than to grab a can from there. And it was Karl, and we didn't want to spend money on him or hand-feed him. Because we didn't like Karl. When I left the bathroom to start a quest for orange-flavored soda anyway, March followed me and closed the door behind us, leaving our prisoner to his own—limited—devices.

"Island, that can wait," March said as I knelt in front of the minibar. He walked to the bed where his suitcase still rested, and patted the comforter, inviting me to sit by his side. "I'll leave in thirty minutes. I need to give you something before I go."

I joined him, and my eyes widened in curiosity as he unlocked the new magic suitcase. He opened it, revealing a collection of many horrible and interesting things, all perfectly organized. One side was lighter than the other and appeared to be reserved for personal items, such as passports, a medical kit, and a change of impossibly wrinkle-free clothes. The other side, that one was the real deal. Four guns rested on the top layer, encased in black Styrofoam compartments, along with various accessories. Some I recognized, like suppressors or magazines; others I had never seen before—a flashlight, maybe?

March freed a semiautomatic that seemed a bit smaller than its siblings and held it in front of me. "This is a compact CZ 75. Czech. Excellent quality and very accurate aim." Thumbing a button on the side of the grip, he dropped the magazine. "You have fourteen rounds and one in the chamber."

I looked back and forth between him and the pistol in confusion. "Take it."

Before I could object, the CZ rested in my hands. His own hands cradled mine to help me rack the slide. "Now, the hammer is cocked, and if the gun was loaded, you could fire it. This, here, is the safety." There was a black switch on the side that he flipped down, revealing a red dot painted on the black steel. "If you can see the dot, it means the safety is off."

I pulled the trigger, experiencing a strange chill when it offered no resistance.

March guided my hands as together we loaded the magazine and repeated the same routine. Rack. Hammer. Switch up. "Now it's loaded, cocked, and locked. You can flip the safety anytime and fire."

As soon as he had said this, I laid the gun on the bed, safely away from my hands. He searched the magic suitcase's compartments and retrieved a black cylinder, almost as long as the CZ itself. "The suppressor will reduce the recoil. It might be best for you."

His mouth twisted as he screwed it to the barrel. Maybe he remembered the way the aforementioned recoil had sent me flying to the ground when trying to handle an assault rifle for the first time in my life in Paris. I hoped that the guy I had shot in the legs in that strip club was getting better, by the way.

I poked the silencer gingerly. "Why are you doing this?"

"It's yours. I don't want you to use it unless it's absolutely necessary. But I trust you with it." His brow quivered. Not quite a pleading expression, but he wasn't the type to get on his knees, after all. "If I can't come back for you, you'll have to leave. Promise you won't try anything . . . crazy."

Promise me you won't try to find me. Promise me you'll just run without looking back. I couldn't. I didn't even want to consider that outcome. I took the CZ. It felt heavy in my hand. Placing it on my lap, I drew March closer to kiss his cheek. "Don't go. You know Alex will be there."

He nuzzled my hair. "Officially, I am to meet outside the city with local agents acting on behalf of Erwin. Nothing else transpired."

"He'll be there. He wouldn't miss the opportunity."

"Island. Trust me."

I looked up at his eyes, startled by the sudden burst of confidence in his voice. There was a hard glint in his irises, but they also seemed brighter, as if some of the exhaustion of the past few days had lifted, revealing a new determination.

"I still have a few cards up my sleeves. Erwin knows it, and Mr. Morgan isn't all-powerful as he likes to believe."

"What kind of cards?"

He gave a faint shrug. "I know a lot of things. I too could take an interest in journalism if I felt like it."

Blackmail, huh? "But you'd rather not, right?"

"Pour vivre heureux, vivons cachés," he concluded with a wink and the most delicious accent. *To live happy, live hidden.* Old French adage, probably something he'd learned from Kalahari, his—nice—ex, who was married to a former French spy and ran a beauty salon chain in Paris. A chain March possessed stakes in. I couldn't stop a grin from tugging at my cheeks. There it was, the little spark of weird that made him so damn special. The reason I loved him.

The fleeting joy turned to an ache in my chest. I threw my arms around his torso and hugged him tight. I wanted to memorize the heat of his body, even the tang of sweat and smoke that clung to his clothes after our encounter with Lucca Gerone. "You need to change. Gotta look your best for that party."

He squeezed me in return before letting go to rise from the bed. "Indeed."

"Oh and, March."

"Yes, biscuit?"

"Let's just untie Karl. I honestly don't think he'll go after me at this point." I rolled my eyes. "And you're gonna need that bathroom. Do you really want to share it with him?"

"Mr. March, he's your boyfriend, right?"

I paused in the obsessive pacing that had no doubt started to leave marks on the carpet by now. The afternoon was reaching its end, and March had been gone for a little over thirty minutes now. Sitting in a black leather sofa, Karl hadn't taken his eyes from me since March's departure, his staring punctuated by slow sips from a fifteen-dollar Fanta bottle. The handcuffs were still on, March's only concession being that our prisoner was no longer chained to the towel radiator. Because sometimes, when you had a bad day, you just want to be alone in the bathroom, rather than with a stranger sitting at your feet and commenting on the softness of the hotel's towels while you shave.

Yeah, that's how Karl got himself kicked out of there.

"Yes," I admitted. "We're together." I crossed the living room to sit next to him. "My turn: how old are you?"

"Nineteen."

That made me smile. "I was pretty sure you were younger than me."

He shrugged. "Probably not that much."

"I'll be twenty-six in September."

Karl looked up from the half-empty Fanta to gauge me with incredulous eyes. I knew that stare all too well. It was the same one I'd received a couple of years ago upon showing up at a Thai restaurant to meet a guy who told me he was 100 percent sure I couldn't be legal, but he'd come anyway because it was "a total turn-on." An expeditious date ensued: We didn't have much to say to each other. Especially after I pulled out my ID.

Karl's eyes narrowed. "You know, it's cool; I understand if you want to be with an older guy." He looked around the suite. "And he's rich."

"Karl, I really am twenty-five, and March is *not* my sugar daddy!" And if he was, what a terrible investment he'd made so far . . .

He took a sip of Fanta. "I totally understand."

He didn't.

I leaned back into the couch's soft leather and let myself sink in the cushions. "How did a guy like you ever end up being a criminal?"

"My stepfather says we're victims of social determinism."

"What does he do for a living?"

"He deals cars."

In spite of my parents' teachings about observing the world with an open mind, I raised a suspicious eyebrow.

"Other people's cars," Karl clarified. "But it's not violent. They just take the cars when people aren't looking, and they resell them afterward. Their insurance covers that."

Sure. That made it okay. I shook my head with a sigh. "So your stepdad is the one who taught you how to hotwire like that? March didn't say anything, but I think he was impressed by your technique."

A cocky grin rewarded my compliment that sparked life in his green eyes. Oh, once he grew out of that lanky, clumsy body, girls would like him . . . a lot. "Yes, he says that I'm crazy, but I have magic hands."

"You're not crazy. I think you're the good kind of weird—"

The phone's ring made me jump out of my skin. Karl dropped his Fanta on the carpet at the same time that I leaped from the couch and flew into the bedroom to grab the receiver sitting on a nightstand.

On the other end of the line, a heavily accented female voice greeted me. "Mrs. August?"

"Yes, yes, it's me."

"Mr. August on the line for you."

I had to take several breaths to calm the drumming in my chest. "Yes, please, put him on!"

"Of course."

There was a clicking sound, then a few bips. Then I heard people mumbling to each other in Croatian because, I surmised, something had gone wrong with the transfer. More bipping. *Dammit* . . .

"Biscuit, I'm on my way. I'll be here in ten minutes."

Upon hearing March, a zillion tiny knots instantly loosened in my body. *Thank you, Raptor Jesus.*

"How did it go?"

There was some continuous background noise—he must be in a car. In his voice too, relief filtered, equal to mine. "Surprisingly well, considering. I'm coming back as fast as possible. Wait for me and don't move. There've been recent developments."

"What do you mean?"

A cheery Southern drawl burst from the speaker. "It's gonna be okay; we got you back on the right side of the law!"

Stiles? He was there too? This time I couldn't contain the joy bubbling inside me, like a backlash to the past hours' stress. "Okay, I'm waiting, and you'll tell me everything," I said excitedly.

"I'm coming for you." With this, March hung up.

I stood in front of the nightstand for a few seconds, dazed, my heart still pumping fast.

Behind me, Karl balanced his torso forward to rise from the couch with cuffed hands and trotted to the bedroom. "Is it good news?"

"Yeah, I think we're gonna be okay."

The wait seemed endless. I cleaned Karl's Fanta from the carpet to pass time and because I knew March wouldn't like the stain. Five minutes after that phone call, I felt like I'd been mopping soda with toilet paper for a thousand years—which sounds like a mythological punishment from a perversely creative deity. Until at last there was some rapping at the suite's doors. I felt each knock from the top of my head to the tip of my toes. Karl and I looked at each other and waited.

A muffled male voice called, "Room service."

Panic sizzled down my spine when I didn't recognize March's voice. My first instinct was to take the gun, which still rested on the bed. Contrary to popular belief, I felt even more scared once I held it firmly in my hands. It felt heavy. Cold. I flipped the safety off with my thumb. *Loaded. Cocked. Unlocked.*

I swallowed hard and steadied my voice. "We didn't order anything."

Outside, I registered a heavy sigh. "Jesus . . . baby, I was joking; it's me."

Alex.

Karl's brow jerked up, his round eyes wordlessly questioning me. *Dammit!* Of all the people Erwin could have sent to get to me faster than March . . . That old turd sandwich had to have done it on purpose. Just to mess with us a tiny bit more. I took hesitant steps toward the set of double doors and extended shaky fingers to the handle.

The doors came unlocked with a single click. A whiff of the good-guy cologne I knew all too well reached me before I even saw him. Brown leather jacket, worn jeans, white shirt. I didn't look up at his face. I didn't want to.

Alex took a step back. He'd seen the CZ in my hand. "Whoa, easy." He sighed. "You're becoming too rough even for me."

I kept my eyes trained on his chest. There were four other men behind him. Jackets, jeans, one in cargo pants. Other agents wearing the same kind of worn, unremarkable clothes. Guys you might pass in the street without ever suspecting they were CIA. "Why isn't March with you? I know he has a new deal with Erwin, so don't even try—"

"Cool your jets. I'm only here because I have orders to pick you up. Erwin's business is his own, and believe me, I'm done with it."

I summoned the strength to meet his gaze. There was no anger to be found in the soft cinnamon eyes, just some mild exasperation. I knew better than to trust that candid façade though. I moved back.

He rubbed the bridge of his nose tiredly. "Island, I deliver you, and I'm done. I don't care what happens next . . . who strikes deals with who."

Through the pounding in my temples, the insidious pain rising in my skull, I tried to keep cool. "Okay. March said he'll be here in a few minutes. Let's wait for him and go."

"Acceptable."

I nodded, my lips pressed tight.

"Baby?"

Don't call me baby. Don't. I bit back the words and just said, "What?"

He smiled. "Can you drop the gun?"

Around the CZ's grip, my palm was sweaty. I could. I didn't really want to though. Then again, shooting Alex on the spot might significantly undermine March's effort to haul us back on the US government's good side. I retreated inside the suite and slowly lowered it. That was all the good will I felt capable of at the moment.

Next to me, Karl still hadn't said a word. No unfiltered input on the situation, no request to drink another Fanta before the CIA picked him up. He was staring. Just staring. I followed the direction of his gaze to one of the men accompanying Alex. Big guy, taller than him. No more than forty, with a shaved, balding head. Never seen him. Karl's brow quivered. He wouldn't look away.

The guy noticed him, focusing hard gray eyes on him.

They recognized each other.

Whoever that guy was, Karl had seen him before . . . while working for the Crystal Whisperer? He darted fearful eyes at me, as if I were supposed to know what was going on. I didn't. A rush of terror electrified my limbs, and my fingers tightened around the CZ's grip. Did *Alex* know?

Oh, yes, he did.

His eyes briefly fluttered closed, and he shook his head. "Why can it *never* be easy?"

I'm not sure the question was addressed to me, or anyone else in particular. My legs were paralyzed as I went through our options and tried to assess how much longer it would take March and Stiles to get here. Alex's arm moved. Too fast.

I saw the gun in his hand. Four detonations exploded in my ears. I raised my own arm as a reflex, but my fingers remained paralyzed while Karl flew backward and crashed loudly onto the glass coffee table. The second after, Karl lay still on a bed of glass shards, blood pooling on the carpet around him. I pulled the trigger blindly. One of the men cried out and staggered back, and his colleagues drew out their own weapons. Like the crack of a whip, a surge of raw, overwhelming fear set my legs in motion. I spun on my heels and clambered toward the bathroom door. I knew I was trapped; I just thought of hiding, of putting at least a door lock between me and them.

I barely made it past Karl's lifeless body before I was hauled backward. Someone wrenched the gun from my hand and pulled my hair hard, hands clasped around my legs, my arms. I let out a series of shrill screams, summoned every ounce of strength I possessed, desperate to slip away from them.

Alex roared. "Fuck, give her something!"

A sharp pain cracked in my shoulder, like a powerful sting. I howled louder, harder, until my throat hurt, as if it could delay the inevitable numbness spreading through me. At some point I thought I'd rolled away. No. Someone else had done that, flipped me on my back. I saw Alex's face, blurry. I tried to claw at it as he picked me up. *Bait for Dries. You're bait for Dries*, a little voice repeated in my head.

Until it went quiet.

TWENTY-FOUR
THE LITTLE PRINCESS

"Sometimes I do pretend I am a princess. I pretend I am a princess, so that I can try and behave like one."
—Frances Hodgson Burnett, *A Little Princess*

Whatever they had injected me with didn't last very long. By the time they dragged me to a car in a backstreet, my mind was clear enough for me to register that I had been handcuffed, blindfolded, and that I was in as deep a shit as could be. The memory of Karl's lifeless body sent a renewed surge of distress in my brain, and my lungs were struggling for oxygen as the vehicle's tires screeched on the asphalt.

I had no sense of time or direction. Alex remained silent throughout the ride, but I knew he was here, no doubt in the driver's seat—I recognized the constant accelerations and rough turns that characterized his driving, until it all came to a stop. I was taken out of the car with surprising care, compared to the violence with which they'd taken me from the hotel room. Alex's scent no longer lingered; he was gone. For now.

Someone undid my blindfold with rough gestures, pulling at my hair in the process. At first, everything was just blurry sequins glittering all around me. Faces came into focus. I shook my head and stared blearily at the two armed men flanking me, then at our surroundings. My best guess was that the end of the world had occurred at some point during my kidnapping, and I'd awakened aboard mankind's last hope for survival: a massive flying saucer.

Okay, maybe the ship was going nowhere because it was in fact an abandoned building planted in the middle of a forest. We stood on the ruins of a patio atop the saucer's first floor. In the center of what I surmised to have once been a garden, pines and cypresses soared toward the sky, completely out of control. Above us, hundreds of identical square windows—most of them broken—lined a circular platform supported by concrete pillars.

Sandwiched between the bald guy Karl had recognized and a second, younger man, I was led inside the building, through a lobby that looked like a war zone, and up a long incurved ramp leading to the second level I had seen from outside. We made our way through a decrepit hallway circling around the saucer. Doors lined the opposite wall, some opening to what must have been bedrooms. Empty bed frames and broken chairs still rested on the dusty floor, as if their owners had fled and might someday return to this rotting dream.

I didn't really mind the atmosphere itself, and I'd have found the paint peeling off from the walls oddly romantic hadn't it been for my dire circumstances. This would certainly fit March's personal definition of hell, though. Wherever he was, now would have been be a good time to barge in and shoot everyone except me.

I held my breath as one of the doors creaked open. So, Alex hadn't been far after all. His brown curls were damp with perspiration. He raked a hand in his hair, combing it back. When he walked up to me, I inched away from the reek of sweat overpowering soapy cologne. His hand reached out for me, clasped around the nape of my neck. I jerked back to no avail as he brought my face closer and pressed his lips to mine.

I had suffered through some not-so-great kisses during my early dating experiments, but they were nothing compared to this. Whatever I had felt when Alex used to kiss me, what little chemistry had ever bound us . . . it was gone, and when his tongue forced its way inside my mouth, slithered against mine, nausea swelled at the back of my throat. I tried to break the kiss and bit his tongue, hard enough to taste the metallic tang of blood. He drew back, and I saw his arm rise. I braced myself, but his hand stopped in midair. He lowered it with a deep breath. In his eyes, the anger had evaporated already; they were as soft as ever.

"For old times' sake," he said.

I clenched my jaw tight, since all I could feel building in my mouth were insults, and I knew I had to keep my cool. I had to get through to him somehow. "What is this about?"

He cupped my jaw and ran his thumb across my lips. "You don't get it, do you?"

I shook his grip off, held on to my rage to help me focus and keep the fear at bay. "Enlighten me then. Does Erwin know about this? Or is it some shitty stunt to bait Dries so you can kill him yourself?"

Alex indulged in a chortle. "Erwin can go fuck himself. He's days away from retirement. And Dries . . . he didn't die today. Fine, he'll die tomorrow. He's done; he just doesn't realize it yet."

Gerone's words came back to me. Hadn't he said the same? He'd called Dries an old man who couldn't see he had served his purpose. He'd said Dries had to go . . . and Alex seemed to already know that Dries had narrowly escaped death earlier today.

What did I have to lose at that point? I decided to tip my hand and see how Alex would react. I took a circular look around the room, at him and his men. "You're all Frumentarii." I jerked my chin at Alex. "You, you're walking in your father's footsteps. He was a frumentarius too, and Dries murdered him and your mother. And now that Anies wants to take Dries down, you're all too happy to help, aren't you?" I went on, fixated on the slow expansion of Alex's pupils as he listened to me. "Gerone is part of the plan too. Dries took the heat for the plane bombing and kept everyone busy while Gerone got ready for his pièce de résistance in Rangiroa. And now Anies no longer needs Dries, and he's becoming too much trouble anyway. So he wants him dead."

I held my breath, praying that Alex would let something slip, help me fill the largest blank in this picture: how the hell did Lion king Anies and faceless mad scientist Lucca Gerone connect, and why would the Lions try to blow up the Poseidon Dome?

Alex mimicked some lazy clapping. "Bravo. See? You get it like a big girl."

No, dammit. I did *not* get it, and that was the problem!

"So what am I in all this?" I asked again. "Bait?"

He gave a weary shrug. "I didn't lie to you, you know. I'm just here to pick you up and deliver you. Honestly, you're lucking out. When this is over, Dries and March are gonna end up in a dozen bags"—he rolled his eyes—"but God forbid anyone touches the little princess."

I let that sink in. Deeply. Gerone too had promised March I'd be safe, and back in Cape Saint Francis, Alex had warned me to get away from the house. He'd requested satellite tracking on us. I was starting to understand that even then, he had been working on recovering me alive and unharmed for Anies . . . because brothers shared everything?

I held out my handcuffed wrists to Alex. "Take these off."

He smirked. "I think we'll leave them on, if that's okay with you."

"Take them off. Or I'll have to tell Anies I wasn't exactly treated like a princess." I studied Alex's reactions to each word, the way his lips thinned. "I'll have to bring up those *impulses* you seem to have trouble reining in."

A muscle twitched in his jaw. Behind him, the bald guy Karl had recognized crossed his arms. From the looks of it, I'd just hit the bull's-eye, and we were about to know exactly how much my dear uncle valued his little princess.

A whole lot.

I tried to control my surprise and feign cool detachment as Alex fished a key from his back pocket and freed my wrists from the steel cuffs. I wouldn't be going anywhere though: around me, baldie and his two colleagues moved closer, like the bars of a cage.

Alex considered me thoughtfully. "I always knew you couldn't be that innocent. No one ever is."

"Not even Poppy?" I shot back, wanting to hurt him, to wrestle his true self out. "What's gonna happen to her if you switch sides? Surely you can't imagine Erwin is that dumb—"

"Island, you mind your business, and I'll mind mine."

It was as if his face had suddenly turned into a mask of wax. No life in his gaze, just a blank expression. Threatening in a way no snarl could have been. I had a feeling that my status as Anies's very special snowflake wouldn't weigh much in the precarious balance of Alex's mind if I kept taking jabs at his sister. I decided to leave that rock alone, be it only to live through dawn.

"So what now?" I inquired, keeping my tone casual.

"We wait. Our little party back there attracted more attention than I'm comfortable with, so we'll have to lay low until my colleagues pick us up." He walked to a broken window and leaned by its dilapidated frame. Outside, a gust of wind whispered through the pine trees, making the heavy branches shiver. "Do you know what this place is?"

"No."

"The town is called Krvavica—pardon my French—and this is an abandoned children's hospital. Spooky shit." When I remained silent, he prodded on with a humorless smile. "Are you afraid of ghosts?"

I stood taller, straighter. "No. Are you afraid you're gonna end up like your father, Alex?"

He stared at me, unblinking, leaving me a spectator to whatever sick internal dialogue was playing behind those soft brown eyes. After a while, he ran a hand across his face, his fingers lingering to scratch the stubble on his chin, as I knew he did when something wouldn't compute. He walked up to me, too close, verging on invasive. Just the way he liked it. I staggered back, my battered ballet flats crushing leaves and paint chips.

Alex cracked his neck with a tired groan. "Oh, baby . . . you think you're getting off easy, huh?"

Not really, no.

"Then let me tell you this: I know him. He won't touch that little doll face, but"—he lowered his voice, his words a secret between us—"he's gonna . . . *Fuck. You. Up.*"

For some reason, *Boxing Helena* came to mind. I let the chills racking through my body run their course, focusing my efforts on standing still, straight. I didn't want him to see that, right now, I felt like a six-year-old huddled under her covers in a dark bedroom, staring wide-eyed at the closet door behind which all the other kids claim a monster lives. Chances were Alex could smell that particular fear though, and either the Lions or the CIA must have taught him that building anticipation is 50 percent of the pleasure.

Behind me, I registered movement. Baldie had pulled out his phone and nodded to Alex, who flashed me an adolescent grin. "We're moving."

One of the men went to open the room's door, and I was escorted out, Baldie and Alex leading the procession.

With the multitude of identical doors and windows, our walk down the darkened circular hallway felt like being thrown inside a spinning zoetrope, so much so that I was becoming dizzy—but it could have been the aftereffect of the drug they had injected me with earlier. Once outside, a light breeze caressed my face, which turned the sweat drops dampening my temples to ice. Half concealed by a bed of fragrant humus, a concrete path led away from the saucer and into the woods. In the distance, something roared and breathed. The ocean. The sound was getting clearer; we must be no more than a few hundred yards from the shore.

Treading deeper in a labyrinth of oddly angled trunks and gnarled branches, I thought of March and Stiles probably looking for me anywhere but here. I shivered. Beyond the woods, lurking in the dark, an ogre awaited. And he'd sent a boat—between two pine trees, a strip of sand appeared, fifty yards down a gentle slope. Dark shapes moved in the distance around what could be a Zodiac. Ashore, a single yacht awaited, all lights off, its bow a razor-thin black blade against the horizon: something designed for a fast break.

I squinted my eyes at the slope to my left. The trees and shrubs formed a mesh so thick in places that the beach was no longer visible. We would reach it soon though. There, in plain sight, there'd be no hope left for escape.

Do you remember Arnold Schwarzenegger in *Predator*? Covered in mud, crawling in the woods, setting up traps and singlehandedly offing a beefy alien with dreadlocks and a bad braces job? Yeah, I'm not like that. I'm not sure I would have found the strength to make a run for it, had it not been for the sudden beam of blinding white light falling from the sky and swiping through the trees ahead of us.

Because I had precisely been contemplating pulling a Schwarzie on Alex and his men, the first words that flashed in my brain were: *alien abduction*. The distant droning of a rotor, however, suggested a helicopter instead.

Alex grabbed my arm, and he looked up. "Shit, we got company. Hurry up."

I had no idea what was going on; I didn't even care if the chopper was here for me or if the Croatian police were just totally hardcore about people hiking outside designated trails. I wrenched my arm from Alex's grip with a scream and, without thinking, leaped down the slope in the dark. It was a hard landing, to say the least. Pain tore through my left wrist, shooting up all the way to my shoulder as I rolled down a bed of dirt, pine needles, and, unfortunately, rocks. A long-dead trunk stopped my fall at the same time that gunshots cracked above my head.

I caught Alex's furious hiss. "Hold your fire! I need her alive."

I curled into a fetal position behind the thick trunk, nursing the throbbing pain in my wrist. I prayed it wasn't broken, but I could barely close my fingers, making me fear that some bits weren't where they should have been. Thank God I couldn't see how bad it looked in the dark. That helped me keep it together. At the top of the slope, heavy footsteps crushed twigs as Alex and at least one other guy attempted to skid down in the direction I'd thrown myself.

I heard his voice call to a third man. "Get down here with me. And *no one* shoots. If she needs to be neutralized, I'll do it myself."

"Okay," a gruff voice answered.

It was that moment the helicopter chose to return with a vengeance, thrumming closer and closer. When the beam reappeared less than twenty yards away from me, I saw Alex, briefly bathed in white light, gun in hand, before he disappeared, swallowed back by the night. I breathed through my nose and desperately tried to think. Progressing any lower down the hill would not only deprive me of the relative protection offered by the dead trunk but would also get me closer to the beach and the Zodiac waiting for my sorry ass there. And—*God*—the pain in my forearm was relentless, hot, *raw*.

I sniffed back tears and rolled to my side, careful not let my injured wrist hit anything else. Maybe the trunk was large enough for me to slip inside and hide in there. Alex and his men needed to escape the helicopter's insistent search too. Their boat was waiting, and the clock ticked against them. Maybe if I could just scrape enough time . . .

"Baby, we don't have all night. Don't make me shoot you in the knee. That shit hurts."

Alex's voice petrified me. He was closer than I'd thought. I could pick up his soapy cologne over the mingled scents of earth and pine. Above us, the helicopter's persistent noise felt like a drumroll in my skull. I flattened my body to the ground, deadly still. I didn't dare release a single breath. One set of footsteps seemed to move away from the trunk, but another remained, its movements now almost imperceptible save for faint creaking sounds.

"Island. Get out!"

I saw Alex's legs, less than ten feet away, recognized his rugged boots. The gun's barrel glinted in the obscurity. I willed myself smaller, flatter, merged with the dirt and leaves. Invisible.

Beyond Alex and the tormented shapes of the trees, something flashed twice. A signal, coming from the beach.

A voice bellowed. "Morgan, we need to move!"

Alex swore under his breath. "Go ahead. I'll join you in a minute!" To himself, or perhaps to me, he growled. "Shit . . . you're here. I know you're in here."

When new gunshots echoed from the direction of the saucer, I figured Alex's men had just decided to ditch his orders and try to randomly shoot me. Bullets crashed into a tree right over me. Wood splinters landed in my hair, on my face. I bit the inside of my cheek not to scream and tasted blood. Tires screeched at the foot of the building, and the gunshots were getting closer. Alex took cover behind a tree and fired a series of shots. By then I was shaking so badly I thought that alone would give my hiding spot away.

That's when Raptor Jesus came down from the sky in his white toga. Except it was rather the helicopter's beam . . . But one thing is certain: Agent Alexander I-refuse-to-give-up Morgan retreated. With a final expletive, I saw his boots run past me and skid down the rest of the slope, toward the beach. I didn't try to move to see whether he was gone; I just stayed there, shielded behind my trunk, one with the earth, listening to new footsteps coming toward me. I didn't even want to know, especially when the razor-thin red rays of laser pointers started to appear all around me. I feared my earlier guess regarding the strict enforcement of hiking policies in Croatia was correct, to the point that it involved enrolling help from special ops to take down the offenders . . .

The footsteps stopped, and I thought I heard a whisper, something unintelligible. The flurry of red dots whirled my way, clustering on the trunk and the trees surrounding it. Every single muscle in my body froze.

A terrifying bark reached me. "Get out, with your hands in the air!"

American accent. Erwin's men? For real this time? In any case, I couldn't comply. My legs were shaking so badly I'd need both my hands to haul myself up, and that just wasn't happening, not with the pain still pulsing through my wrist in tune with my heartbeat.

"I can't get up." The words were a barely audible whistle. I gulped down and gave it another try. "I can't . . . I can't get up."

"Island!"

March's shout pierced through my daze. I rolled onto my back, keeping my wrist tucked against me. For the first time since nightfall, I noticed the stars, like millions of diamonds in the clear indigo sky. Combat boots trampled the bed of pebbles and pine needles I rested on, and soon, a group of men hovered above me, looking like big insects with their black gear and round infrared goggles. I didn't care; I could hear March wrestling his way to me past a guy telling him to stay back. I registered Stiles's voice too, asking one of the soldiers if I was wounded.

At last, March knelt by me. "You're going to be all right. I promise—"

"I know," I said, my voice oddly calm, even to my own ears. "But Anies is going to be pissed."

TWENTY-FIVE
BONE-DEEP

**Long has paled that sunny sky:
Echoes fade and memories die.
Autumn frosts have slain July.**

–Lewis Caroll, Alice's Adventures in Wonderland

No one would tell me anything at first, but I gathered that Alex's defection and Gerone's plans to blow up the Poseidon Dome had set the CIA's wheels in full motion: the unmarked ambulance I had been carried into was part of an entire convoy headed south for Dubrovnik—the closest airport.

And so, around 9:00 p.m., I lay in the back, on a fairly comfortable stretcher, while a quiet Croatian female doctor finished placing a purple sleeve around the fresh cast encasing my left hand and forearm. Clean Colles' fracture, she'd said, showing me the broken radius in my wrist on the screen of a portable X-ray. That thing was no bigger than a two-inch-thick iPad, and I decided I needed one. For science.

Sitting by my side, March watched her every move like a hawk, his eyes occasionally narrowing whenever a particular step made me flinch. It was only after the doctor allowed me to rest my forearm on my chest and she started disposing of the remaining strips of damp cast tape in a plastic bag that he seemed to relax. He drew a deep breath and briefly closed his eyes.

I reached for his hand with my good arm, linking his fingers with mine. "Are you okay?"

The quirk of his lips was anything but happy. "I should be the one asking you that."

Of course I wasn't okay. Not by a long shot. And I don't mean the wrist; that was almost a detail. "Karl had family; he mentioned his stepfather." I blinked back the tears I could feel building in my eyes. "I don't know his name. I just know he steals cars."

"In Stockholm," March confirmed. "Mr. Stiles's colleagues were able to identify him. I'm so sorry, biscuit. His body will be brought back to his mother."

I sniffed. "Will they tell her?"

"I believe the Säpo will leave out some details," March replied, evidently on the same wavelength.

"He was only nineteen."

"I know." His eyes grew unfocused, the silence between us thick with regrets. "I made a mistake. I shouldn't have handcuffed him."

"It wouldn't have made any difference. It went very fast; Alex didn't leave him a single chance."

Upon hearing Alex's name, March darted a look to the doctor. Her face shielded by a curtain of brown curls, she had been busy filling some sort of report on a laptop, perhaps overzealously so, in an obvious effort to give us as a little privacy in the cramped space. Noticing March's gaze, she pointed at the lampposts flashing by through the rear windows, and said, "It's okay, we're almost there. I'll go."

Indeed, moments after she'd spoken, the van came to a stop. I craned my neck to look outside. All I could make out was a nondescript parking lot.

The van's doors opened, and Stiles's grinning face appeared. "Final stop, Dubrovnik Airport."

I managed a stiff smile. "I desperately need a shower. Do you think I can take one, like in the business lounge, maybe?"

Before he could answer, the doctor squeezed past his solid frame to step outside the van, mumbling a final warning for me not to forget to protect my cast from water. Stiles watched his colleagues escort her toward a strange burrito-shaped terminal and returned his attention to me. "Actually, I think you'll like the shower in the plane even better."

Next to me, March went rigid. "I don't think Island will be flying with us."

Now why wouldn't I?

Stiles scratched the blond bristles on his skull. "Ah, yeah, about that . . . I think you should discuss it with him. He wants to see you."

"The Caterpillar?"

March and Stiles gave me odd looks.

"I mean, Erwin. He came all the way to Croatia?"

Stiles confirmed. "Yup. Normally he doesn't do fieldwork, but when he got the news about Morgan, he was a little upset."

As March helped me out of the van, I pondered the Caterpillar's sudden appearance. On March's wrist, the black dial of his watch indicated 9:55. Meaning it had been less than five hours since Alex had barged into our suite at the Atrium to take me. So either the US Army had dropped the Caterpillar's sexagenarian ass into an F-35 and flown him to Croatia faster than the speed of sound, or he had gotten there the old-fashioned way, and that meant an eight-hour flight from the East Coast—at the very least. In other words, that old scumbag had known something was off before we'd even set foot on Novensia's compound.

There were half a dozen other vehicles on the tarmac, and only one plane, an unmarked 787 Dreamliner, if my memory and my endless lurking on Wikipedia served me well. Oh, government . . . why can't you ever enjoy the small things in life instead of the big ones?

Standing near one of the black SUVs was a dark-skinned figure whose classy trench coat looked familiar: the ever-stoic Agent Murrell. I knew almost nothing of him, save that he was part of Alex's division and, from what I gathered, above Stiles in their internal hierarchy—that or he just liked bossing people around, and Stiles was too nice to make a fuss about it. He was the silent type, and I couldn't say he and I had hit it off when working on the Ruby case, but at the time, Murrell had struck me as a decent, reliable guy who did what he had to.

March greeted him with a slight tip of his head, which he returned. When we both walked up to the car though, Murrell's right hand jerked. "I'm sorry, Mr. November; for now, it's only Miss Chaptal."

"Our agreement specified otherwise," March retorted icily.

I laid a soothing hand on his arm. "It's okay. I'm not going anywhere."

He appraised me with anxious eyes, his gaze lingering on my cast, which I kept folded against my chest—I had this irrational fear that if I let it hang at my side, the bones wouldn't stick back together because of gravity or something. Medical hazards be damned, I forced myself to unfold my arm and held up the cast with a grin. "Don't worry—if he messes with me, I can whack him on the head."

March nodded with a tentative smile of his own. "I'll wait here."

Murrell opened the rear door for me. Immediately, the familiar whiff of sweet tobacco smoke hit me, different from the faint scent of cigarettes that always clung to Murrell's trench coat. My heart raced a little as he helped me climb in, carefully supporting my arm. The door slammed behind me, and I was sinking in a soft leather seat, alone with the Caterpillar—or Director Erwin, if you prefer.

The cigarillo was balanced between his index and middle finger. His suit was the same silvery gray as his hair. Nothing filtered through the deep creases around his mouth, the many lines canvassing his face. Seeing him again, I was once again struck by how much Alex's boss reminded me of Dries, as if some men were just destined for that life, and it was only a matter of choosing your side. I mean, even the cigarillo, right? Cigars for drug lords and Hannibal Smith, cigarillos for villains who fancied themselves too classy for the blood splattering on their suits.

His lips parted, filling the car with the gravel of a voice made hoarse by way, way too much smoking. "How have you been, Miss Chaptal? Enjoying yourself in Croatia?"

I had no choice but to inhale the curl of pungent smoke stretching between us. I looked down at the purple cast around my forearm. "Not really."

"Ah well . . . Ours is an unpredictable business."

"I'm not in the business."

He coughed a chuckle. "I'm afraid that's my call."

No, it wasn't. But I wasn't here to discuss that. I looked him straight in the eyes and, for the first time since we'd met, noticed they were a shade of brown so dark they almost seemed black. "So you knew about Alex?"

"Of course. The brotherhood approached him shortly after he had joined our ranks. Mr. Morgan was very enthusiastic about following in his father's footsteps, for reasons I used to think were obvious."

"He's good at making people trust him. I bet you were looking for weaknesses to exploit, and he showed you exactly what you wanted. Alex, he's like a mirror. You never see *him*; you see what he knows you need to see reflected back at you."

A humorless smile pulled at the corners of his lips. "Spoken like a true connoisseur."

I shrugged the compliment off. "So you planted him as a frumentarius. Or rather, he planted himself among you."

"I take risky bets. Most of the time I win, and our country wins with me."

"Except when you lose. When did you figure he had turned on you? I know it was before he kidnapped me."

He sighed a cloud of smoke. "When did you become so straightforward? Has the company of Mr. November hardened you so?"

"I won't talk to you if you keep me in the dark."

"I'll indulge you then. I was . . . intrigued by his handling of your father's case. He spared no efforts to hunt down Mr. Kovius—that, I expected—and he was onto Mr. November the minute his house was targeted, but when Sabina Falchi's name came up, it took him eight hours to even start looking for her, and by then, I was informed that her trail was cold. He's not that sloppy; we both know that, right?"

I pursed my lips in guise of an agreement. "But you didn't know there was a personal beef between Anies and Dries. Otherwise you might have seen it coming."

"So you too believe that his elusive brother threw Mr. Kovius under the proverbial bus? May I ask what the 'beef' was about?"

In my back pocket, I could still feel Jan's Polaroid. "Irreconcilable differences."

"Very helpful." Leather squeaked as Erwin leaned back in the seat and crossed his legs. "In any case, I knew there was a degree of rivalry between the brothers, but I underestimated it. As I underestimated Kovius Senior's influence on Mr. Morgan. Which brings us to our current agenda: what do you suggest we do now?"

"I don't know. You're the secret spy; you figure it out. I'm almost certain we'll find Gerone in Rangiroa, but I honestly have no idea what his connection to the Lions is, or why he wants to blow up that dome . . . I mean, other than because he has some serious issues."

The cigarillo hanging from his lips, the Caterpillar studied me for several seconds, concealed behind a smoke screen I was starting to think of as a metaphor for his very self. "Miss Chaptal, how many languages do you speak?"

I gave him a wary side-eye. "Um, apart from English and French, not that many . . . I have a decent grasp of Japanese and Italian. The other languages, it's more basic knowledge and intuition, enough to figure out what's going on around me, like"—I counted off on my fingers—"German, Russian, Afrikaans and Dutch, Spanish, Korean . . . I learned a little bit of Chinese too, when I was twelve."

"Do you speak Croatian?"

"No. I only recognize some words because of the Slavic and Latin roots. Like I said, intuition and etymology help."

Through the smoke, he bobbed his head slowly. I waited for him to clarify his intent.

"Miss Chaptal, what can you tell me about my watch?"

This time I nearly eye-rolled. What next? Would he pop out a Ouija board? I lowered my gaze to the brown leather band holding a rectangular dial peeking from under his shirt cuff. No need to see the brand; the shape spoke for itself. "It's a Jaeger-Lecoultre Reverso," I said. "It's a Swiss brand, and it's called a Reverso because you can slide the dial in its case and flip it around." I mimicked the gesture with my good hand. "That way the glass is facing your wrist, and it's protected from shocks. They invented it for British polo players in the thirties, because they'd break their watches during the games."

He crossed his arms and remained silent.

"I'm sorry, sir; where are you going with this?"

At last he stubbed the cigarillo in a door ashtray I was willing to bet had been installed just for him. "Don't expect to get paid if I don't see results. Don't expect to get rescued if you get caught. And don't *ever* expect to escape me, Miss Chaptal. Mr. Morgan is about to learn that the hard way."

A chill crept up my spine. "Are you forcing me to work for you again? I don't think that March—"

"I own him. And now, I own you too." His tone had noticeably cooled down. I shrank in my seat as he went on. "Welcome to our little family. As you can understand, we don't hand out written contracts."

I stared down at the cast on my lap. The meds the doctor had given me were wearing off. Slowly the pain was coming back, swelling, pulsing under my skin. "March is going to kill you for this."

The Caterpillar let out a dry laugh. "When he's fifty, and I'm a bag of bones in a wheelchair, that's when he'll come for me. Until then, I suggest we focus on the task at hand."

"I see. I have one last question."

A sigh of impatience fanned my way that carried terrible smoker's breath. "All inquiries can be addressed to either Murrell or Stiles."

"No. I want to know what will happen to Alex's sister now. Will Poppy be safe?"

His eyebrows jerked. "*Poppy?*"

"Yes, his sister. She's sixteen."

On his lap, his fingers clenched. Weird that, of all things, bringing up Alex's sister would make him nervous. "Miss Chaptal, when was the last time you spoke to . . . Poppy?"

"Actually, I've never . . . Back when Alex and I were together, he'd sometimes call her or text her, but, you know . . . he never let me get that close. Looking back on it, I don't think he ever intended to introduce us," I concluded, feeling suddenly a little queasy at the memory of the months Alex had spent manipulating me.

"I see." The Caterpillar gazed through his window at his agents hurrying around the plane outside, loading suitcases, making phone calls. "I doubt you'll ever meet her, indeed. Not in this life anyway."

I had a bad feeling about this. "Sir—"

"Her mother wanted to show her the pyramids. Something anyone should see at least once in their lifetime, right?"

For a second, the car and Erwin ceased to exist. I was free-falling, and my internal organs were knotting from the sudden vertigo. "She was in the plane?" I croaked out.

He dragged his gaze back to me and nodded once.

Dries's words came back to me. *We all live with our ghosts.* Poppy was one of them. A sixteen-year-old girl her parents had probably wanted to impress by taking her on a private jet to see the pyramids. And Alex . . . he carried her with him. He lied about her to keep her alive. It worked. If not in the flesh, Poppy had lived in my mind for months. He had shown me pictures of her, and a bubbly, snarky teen with a mop of brown curls had taken form in my mind. She was an integral part of the madness he'd spiraled into. My forehead throbbed with a pain that rivaled the one now blazing in my forearm.

And I was going to be sick.

When I lunged at the door handle, it resisted at first, but the Caterpillar flicked his wrist and the driver opened the door. I tumbled out, bumping into Murrell and March. He tried to catch me in his arms, but I pushed him away and staggered back. My stomach heaved, once, twice. I bent forward, braced my right hand on my knee, and curled my left arm against my breasts. Within seconds, I was done emptying the meager contents of my stomach onto the tarmac.

Once I was done coughing and drooling bitter vomit on the asphalt, I felt March's arms come around me, helping me up, bringing a tissue to my mouth. Part of me was aware of what it must cost him to get anywhere near that kind of filth. That mundane thought was the last straw. The tears came, hot, unrelenting. Because I felt so dirty and powerless—over Karl, Alex, Poppy, my mother . . . all the lives that were lost, broken, and that I could never fix. March anchored me, squeezed me tight as I heard myself bawl, "I'm sorry . . . I need a shower. I just want a shower!"

TWENTY-SIX
THE OSMETERIUM

He had her in his claws, and no matter how hard she fought her instincts, Lexie could no longer deny the raging chemistry between her and Bobby.

–Lane Tempest, Kiss of The Lobster Shifter

The shower helped. Stiles had given me a plastic bag to wrap my cast into, and after a good twenty minutes spent emptying minibottle after minibottle of shower gel, shampoo, conditioner, body lotion, hand cream, foot cream . . . I felt focused enough to come to the conclusion that the Caterpillar was robbing the taxpayers blind.

Because dude, dat 787!

With its ceiling shower system, golden taps, and the buttload of miniature shit lined on elegant ebony shelves, the bathroom I stood in represented only a fraction of the madness that was this plane. I had seen the Caterpillar in a Cadillac limo back in New York, and that alone had gotten me suspicious of the way that old fart handled government money. But we were dealing with a fricking airliner here, complete with two sleeping cabins and a conference room. And don't get me started on the walnut burl inserts and gilded stuff everywhere, around the windows, in the armrests—which were all fitted with black suede, by the way!

In the cabin adjacent to the bathroom, several bags and boxes sat on the bed: Stiles had raided the airport's sole duty-free shop while I scrubbed myself. Something else had been laid next to the pillow—by March, I was almost certain of it. Next to my precious polaroid lay the compact CZ 75 Alex's men had wrenched from my hand in the hotel room, its black steel glaring against the snowy-white linen. I stared at the gun for a while before I resolved to tuck it, along with the Polaroid, inside a little green shoulder bag Stiles had found for me. Someone needed to give that man a medal.

I damn near moaned at the feeling of clean underwear and silently thanked him for the ample cream tunic I could easily slip into, even with my cast. A pair of navy leggings completed the ensemble. I used a wet wipe to clean my ballet flats, and I felt *pea-chy*. No, on the verge of physical and mental exhaustion actually. Also those noises coming from my stomach didn't sound right. Low growls and ritual chanting too, I was pretty sure of it. A gate to hell would open in there real soon if I didn't eat something.

I came out of the cabin with the firm intent to find a fridge in the plane while around me everyone took a seat. The Caterpillar's agents were finished loading their stuff, and it appeared we'd be taking off in a few minutes. March was nowhere to be found, but before tumbling into the shower stall earlier, I'd heard him mutter that he wanted a "word" with the Caterpillar, so I figured they'd isolated themselves either in the second cabin or in the conference room. I feared there'd be in fact several words, like *no, unacceptable, the terms of our agreement*, and also *no*.

Rather than a fridge, I found a fully equipped kitchen at the other end of the sitting area. There too someone had raised trembling fists to the sky and yelled, "More walnut burl, more gold!" Noticing Stiles approaching behind me, I poked gingerly at the windows of a small . . . lobster tank. "Don't you think that this a little too much for governmental equipment?"

He had the good grace to cringe when a brownish crustacean waved at him through the glass. "I know, but changing everything would cost too much at this point."

"Well, maybe you guys shouldn't have bought it in the first place," I said tartly.

"It was actually a gift."

"Really?"

"Yes, from a Russian businessman."

I seized a fat chocolate muffin and gobbled it in three bites with a sigh of delight. I wiped the crumbs from my cheek. "So he gave you his plane, just like that?"

"Well, we inherited it, really."

"He's dead?"

Stiles shrugged. "They haven't found the body yet, but don't worry about that."

I looked over his shoulder. March and the Caterpillar had reappeared, both looking tight as violin strings. It was the first time I saw the guy standing on his legs, and he was shorter than I'd imagined, no more than 5´8˝. He went to sit in an isolated area where smoked-glass panels surrounding a large seat offered some degree of privacy. Nearby, a blond flight attendant was searching a cupboard for a bottle of cognac and went to serve him a glass.

"Stiles!" I hissed. "He's drinking before we've even taken off. Also, I think he stole this plane!"

He looked more than a little embarrassed as March joined us. "Well, he really liked it, and trust me, no one is going to come forward to claim it back."

"That's . . . hardcore."

I took a fearful peek at the man who'd proclaimed himself my new employer. After he'd downed his cognac and put his seat in sleep mode, the Caterpillar appeared dead to the world. Stiles went to sit across from Murrell, who had something to show him on a tablet, and at last, I was able to sink into a seat facing March's.

"How did it go?" I asked, while he helped me buckle my belt.

"You don't have to worry. I will find a way out of this. Until then, I don't want you anywhere near that dome."

"It's okay. I don't think I'll be much use to him anyway. Once he figures how bad I am at the spy stuff, he's gonna pay me to quit."

"There won't be any of that!" March snapped. "You have no idea what he's capable of asking—"

"I know."

He went silent, and his gaze drifted to the Caterpillar's agents, checking whether they might be listening to us.

"I haven't forgotten the story Kalahari told me in Paris," I said.

We wouldn't have that particular conversation here, surrounded by CIA agents, and less than twenty feet away from Erwin, but March knew exactly what I meant. Charlotte Covington was a ghost from March's past, who had visited me six months ago and never really left since. I think Kalahari told me about her so I'd know March was capable of loving just like anyone else, so I'd understand where he came from.

In a quiet bedroom in Paris, I had listened as she told me how the Caterpillar had sent Charlotte to March's bed, how he'd fallen in love for the first time in his life, despite knowing she was a spy. He'd told her, laid his heart at her feet . . . and she'd dumped him—along with her mission—because she couldn't deal with that level of complication.

It should have ended there, as nothing more than a painful lesson and a love forgotten, drowned in a whisky bottle. But a few months later, Charlotte was sent on a risky job in Ivory Coast, in the middle of a civil war. She was captured, along with several of her colleagues. As per rule number two—Don't expect to get rescued if you get caught—the Caterpillar issued a burn notice. I feel bad even using that term, since Charlotte ended up being tortured and burned alive before March could rescue her. By the time he found her, it was too late. There was nothing left to do, and he made the decision to end her suffering. That single shot and the memory of Charlotte's disfigured body haunted his nights for years afterward . . .

Back to the two of us, sitting in that ridiculously kitsch plane with the lobsters watching us. The vibrations of takeoff filled the cabin, and I let them wash over me, lost in March's eyes. There were so many things passing between us in that moment, words we couldn't say.

Once the 787 was gliding high above the clouds, March leaned forward, and with great care, caressed the fingers of my left hand that were peeking out from the cast. Only I could hear his softly whispered words and the determination in his voice. "It won't end like that. I'll do anything . . . I won't let it end like that."

I knew he meant it, and I was all too aware that "anything" meant a lot of people would die if it was the price to protect me. Yet, not for the first time since I'd met March, I wondered if I'd end up like Charlotte, like my mom: someone else's ghost. My throat tight, all I could say was, "It's okay. I know we'll figure this out."

"Sorry to interrupt."

March let go of my hand, and we both looked up at Stiles, who gestured to the conference room occupying the center of the plane. There, Murrell and another agent fumbled with the remote to a large mounted screen, reinforcing my deeply ingrained belief that there is no such thing as videoconference equipment that "works," only tears, self-loathing, and faulty HDMI cables.

"We got a meeting"—Stiles checked his watch—"in five. But we can get some sleep after that."

TWENTY-SEVEN
THE WHITLOW

She could run, she could hide, but it would be no use. He was a patient wolf; eventually, he would grab that pussy.

—Raquelle Montana, The Cat Breeder's Dark Obsession

True to my prediction, March and I had the time to eat two chicken sandwiches each and an entire bag of beet chips before Murrell was finished wrestling the wiring into submission. Thirty minutes later, the four of us were sitting around a long glass table. Water bottles had been placed in front of each seat, as well as complimentary notepads bearing the CIA's logo. They had given us pens too. I was so keeping those.

"Isn't Erwin going to join us?" March inquired.

Murrell shook his head. "He doesn't like meetings. I'll report to him later." With this, he grabbed the remote and pressed a button.

Around us, the glass panels isolating the conference room instantly turned a milky white to give us privacy.

I couldn't resist the urge to get up from my seat and go poke one with my good hand. "You guys have electrochromic glass here? This is so cool."

"I know, right?" A young male voice laughed.

I spun around to find that the large screen mounted on a wall at the end of the room had been turned on. His desk was still a complete mess on which sat a half-assembled server; today was, uncharacteristically, a red He-Man T-shirt day, and Colin looked fine overall.

He gauged us with round eyes from behind black-rimmed glasses. "Are you guys okay? I heard that there's been some action."

Some, indeed . . . I gave a sheepish shrug. "Yeah, sort of. We're good. Well, alive, anyway."

"Cool. And no news from Morgan, right?"

Murrell pursed his lips. "His file has been locked following the incident in Kv-Kravat . . . vica. We won't be discussing his case for now."

Colin gave an uneasy nod and directed his gaze to March and me. "So we did some research on Lucca Gerone based on what you gave us."

"What happened to him after Novensia?" March asked.

"Nothing that left any public trace, but you already know that. No known issue during his postdoc there, nothing from HR. But in December 2005, he got admitted into intensive care at the American Hospital in Rome. His file says 'lab accident.'"

I cringed. "Like?"

"There's nothing about the circumstances, but it says he had a severe facial trauma, third-degree burns on his arms and thorax. They also mention skin grafts and maxillofacial surgery."

"Something blew up in his face," Stiles concluded.

Colin tilted his head. "Like his own crystals, maybe . . ."

Some rustling followed by a muted grinding sound caught my attention: March had pulled his precious tube of mints. "Mr. Jeon, apart from the facial trauma, what else can you tell us?"

"Well, he's dead."

My eyebrows sprang up. "I'm sorry, what?"

"Yeah. He went into cardiac arrest during his surgery. They signed everything. I even got an autopsy report in Italian. How cool is that?"

I deflated in my chair. "And that's it? Just a cool autopsy report?"

A grin split Colin's face. "Of course not. I just wanted to amp up the tension. Remember how I said it was a lab accident? That also means a work accident. And guess what?"

I thought none of us would bother with offering any kind of astounded repartee to urge Colin on, but Stiles indulged him with a wink. "Tell us, please?"

"He settled out of court," Colin said with a dramatic swipe of his arm. "Four weeks after his death, a Panamanian foundation named Salieri Fondazione signed a confidential agreement with Novensia for almost a hundred million euros. His only living relative was his mom, and the agreement basically stated that neither she nor anyone else could sue over the incident. The thing is, Salieri Fondazione was three days old at the time, and if you dig hard enough . . ."

A humorless smile creased one of March's dimples. "Gerone was the sole beneficiary?"

"Almost. Him and his mom. But she died a year later. The foundation is still listed as being active though, and by the way, Novensia patented the Ceraglass three months after Gerone's 'death,'" Colin finished, with air quotes and a grimace of disgust.

Murrell opened a small laptop. "Can you send me all that? Who organized the settlement, by the way?"

"Studio Legale Aureli-Cesari. I guess that doesn't ring any bells?"

"None."

"And if I tell you that Antonio Aureli was, until very recently, Pio Maraì's personal lawyer?"

March's knuckles rapped against the shiny wood. "He was disfigured, left for dead, and Maraì paid him, so he'd disappear for good."

"That's what it sounds like. That way no one would ever know that Ceraglass presented a risk. Novensia made some serious money with it . . . Maybe the settlement wasn't good enough, and Gerone couldn't forgive them," Colin said with a shrug.

I noticed that Murrell was going through a series of files on his laptop. "The Poseidon Dome is the largest use ever made of Novensia's Ceraglass: twelve hundred tons for the dome alone and another three hundred tons all over the resort, in windows, balconies . . ." he muttered. "Let's say Gerone hated Maraì, and he wanted to destroy him completely. It'd make sense for him to want to take down that kind of symbol. But that doesn't tell us what the Lions get from that."

"Indeed," March concurred, his gaze unfocused.

I massaged my temples, sorting out my ideas. "Actually . . . I don't want to extrapolate too much from what Ale—Agent Morgan told me, but I got the feeling that to the Lions, the plane and Novensia were just massive decoys. We were all looking at Dries while Gerone tested his technology, and so he had free range to take his revenge on Maraì and Novensia. That worked for Anies because he wanted to kill everything about Dries, him, his reputation. And the plane crash did just that. The entire planet saw his face linked to the attack, like he was Bin Laden or something: there's no going back from that. We all know"—I looked around the table—"that even if we catch Gerone, you guys won't make the truth public. It'd be too messy."

Stiles and Colin carefully avoided my eyes, while Murrell cleared his throat.

I turned to March. "So that was step one. I think step two is about power. Anies wanted Dries out of the way to take control. Back in Tokyo, Dries said something to you about how the Lions could become more, train millions of men, grandiose stuff like that. On the roof, you remember, right?"

For some reason, March looked uncomfortable. Pissed even. "Yes, I remember."

"Well, maybe that's what Anies wants too, and there's something about the Poseidon Dome that's important for him, in that grand scheme. The Lions wanted the Cullinan because it was worth two billion dollars, and it'd pay for their dream—maybe that's a question of money. Maybe taking down the dome would profit them somehow."

Stiles chimed in. "We found no ties between the Poseidon's owners and the Lions, but it could be something less evident." He looked at March. "There're at least three thousand people in there, and the only access is by air or by sea. Do you think they could go for a good old-fashioned hostage taking?"

March still seemed distracted, like he barely saw Stiles sitting right next to him. "That would be new for them."

"All right," Murrell said. "Colin, you keep running everything we know against our databases; see if anything comes up."

"Got it. But so far we've been combing through the list of every guest, member of the personnel, accredited contractors . . . we got nothing. Most of them have a clean record, and those who don't, they just have no link to Gerone or the Lions." He skimmed through the data on a screen to his right. "Famous French chef who used to beat his wife, a few tax evaders, and . . . oh—"

Stiles frowned. "*Oh* what?"

"Anyone looking for a German pedophile?"

Murrell rubbed his eyes tiredly. "No, we got enough on our plate; thank you."

March too ran a hand across his face. He wouldn't show it, but I feared he too was completely exhausted. "I contacted a friend before we left. He might be able to help."

Interesting . . . "Who?"

"Ilan."

Murrell's brow creased in apparent worry.

"He's cool," I reassured him. "He's this super dangerous guy who used to work for the French secret service, but now he's like Stiles, a fairy godmother, but for criminals." I left out the part about him being the husband of March's ex: they didn't need to know that.

Stiles side-eyed me. "A fairy . . . godmother?"

"I mean it in the best way possible."

The Caterpillar had locked himself inside one of the cabins to get some sleep. March eventually did the same. I kissed him good night but didn't join him. In part because I felt it would have been awkward to follow him in there with the Caterpillar's agents watching us over their snack trays but also because I wanted to let him get the rest he desperately needed.

For my part, I just couldn't close my eyes. So much had happened over the past few days, and it was like my brain was running on overdrive, refusing to shut down even for a minute. So I stayed in the conference room to browse the Internet and read articles and technical data on the Poseidon Dome, until Stiles joined in for a little movie session.

"See this one," he said, launching a video of a fat Maine coon sprawling itself directly in front of a white Roomba so that the side brush would scratch his belly. "See how he angles his body, and the Roomba keeps spinning. It's a symbiotic relationship."

"You're making me want one."

He drew out a world-weary sigh. "It's a huge responsibility. Don't take it lightly."

And who could know better than the man who secretly ran YouTube's most-watched Roomba cats channel? Like I said earlier, I didn't know how to explain to March the bond Stiles and I shared. It had nothing to do with sexual or romantic love: Stiles was as deep in the friend zone as one could get, and he was perfectly content with that. Back in New York, Murrell had called him my soul mate, and while I disagreed because I wanted to believe that March held the position, there was a bit of truth in that. Stiles and I shared the same sort of ardent dedication to the things most people don't care about.

Like dressing up his four cats and filming them interacting with his Roomba.

As the video ended, another started automatically. My mouth fell open. Someone out there was seriously raising the bar. Stiles, for his part, appeared unimpressed. He watched, with a contemptuous sneer, the Roomba cat ambling around a kitchen, dressed as a shark, while a bulldog dressed as a duck sat in a corner, next to an actual duck. The duck kept waddling, quacking, until at the end of the video, the owner dressed it with the shark costume and placed it on the Roomba in its turn. I couldn't look away, mesmerized.

"Show off," Stiles said with a little snort.

"New to the business? I've never seen her channel before."

And yet, OregonGirl80 already boasted a staggering six hundred thousand views for this video alone.

"Yeah." He glowered at the screen. "Ain't gonna be around for long."

Ouch. Stiles was getting all emotional about the meteoric rise of shark cat. That girl didn't know it yet, but she was in for a bad time.

His soft Southern drawl enveloping each word, Stiles explained to me that beyond buying the costumes and filming, he dedicated a fair amount of his free time to eliminating competition—something made easier by his particular reach and abilities. Don't worry—he never killed anyone . . . where Roomba cats were concerned. Just some subtle tipping of the universal balance, now and then, when a particular YouTube account started to accumulate more views than it should have. Like that ninth grader from Washington, who had to shut down hers after someone mailed her parents a report card suggesting her grades were slipping because she spent too much time on the Internet, or even the dental assistant from Maryland and her five Siamese cats—aka "the Chocolate Point Crew." Her rise to the top was thwarted when it was discovered that she helped her boyfriend grow pot in their basement—they never found out who had tipped the police.

"What are you gonna do?" I murmured, after he was done revealing the ugliest secrets of his hobby.

He scooted closer. A conspiratorial whisper tickled my ear. "She filed a false 1099."

"Island, what are you doing?"

Oh shit. I jerked away from Stiles, my cheeks reddening with irrational guilt. Another video of Roomba duck wearing a pink thong was playing in the background.

March's brow furrowed in suspicion. "We'll be landing in Los Angeles in a few minutes. I believe we must return to our seats."

I got up on my feet, and he offered me his arm with a wary look in Stiles's general direction. For now, his inner caveman was in charge, and he wanted me away from the Roomba cats.

The break on the LAX tarmac felt like the calm before the storm. It was 3:00 a.m. The tar still glistened black from a recent downpour. Workers hurried around the Caterpillar's stolen 787, their fluorescent vests flashing in the night. Conspicuously followed by three agents, March and I strolled around the plane, stretching our legs, breathing the humid air and a touch of kerosene fumes. At last, I could feel my body giving up. Even with the constant ache in my left arm that the painkillers wouldn't dim, I knew I'd fall like a log the moment we returned to the plane.

"I could let you go." March's hand squeezed mine as I gazed sleepily at the gracious arches of the Theme Building glowing blue in the distance. "I could take care of Erwin's men, and it's a short run to the nearest terminal."

I snuggled closer to him. "And they'd catch me before I could make it out of the airport. I have a gun and no passport." Dangling at my side, the little green shoulder bag suddenly felt much heavier.

"Island, we didn't have many options in Croatia, but this is US soil. We could alert your father. Erwin doesn't want any more publicity for now—"

"If Dries is there, I *need* to see him."

"Because of the picture?"

"Among other things, yes. I talked to Jan while you were at Santa Lucia Station. He kind of implied that Dries and Anies had fought over my mother, and I'm thinking that maybe it has something to do with all this, the way Anies is trying to destroy him like that."

March stroked my cheek. "I don't know . . . but I doubt you'll see him. And it's better this way. I don't want you anywhere near Morgan or Gerone."

I forced a grin on my face. "I'm armed and dangerous."

"That you are." March's mouth twitched involuntarily despite his somber mood. "Would you like to hear what Erwin told me about you?"

"I suppose."

"He called you an agent of chaos. 'Worse than a whitlow,' to be precise."

It felt good to laugh; I let each burst shake my frame in earnest. "I hope you defended me."

"I did. I said"—he threaded his fingers in my hair, a wistful expression softening his features—"that you don't see the world the way we do, and that, mistaken as you may sometimes be, I try to follow you . . . because I think you set me on the right path."

I hugged him tight, unable to control the quivers in my body, the glow I could feel inside me. "Did you really say that?"

"Yes. Now he believes I'm clinically insane."

Shaking with renewed laughter, I held on to him, rubbed my cheek against his chest the way he liked. And I didn't give a damn if the Caterpillar's agents saw me.

"March," I murmured. "There's something else I need to ask you."

"What is it, biscuit?"

"You seemed weird, back in the meeting room, when I brought up what Dries told you in Tokyo. You were thinking about something. What was it?"

His hand rubbed my back. "Nothing. I suppose I'm just a little tired; don't worry about it."

It was the second time it happened, and now I recognized the feeling, that pressure in my chest, like my rib cage was suddenly a size too small for my heart.

The feeling you get when someone you love lies to you.

TWENTY-EIGHT
DECLARATION OF WAR

On the battleground of passion, his mind and his breeches warred relentlessly.

—Jade Mulhouse, *Raked by the Duke*

This could be a tale about me and my chalk-white skin catching fire the second I stepped out of the plane and running around Rangiroa Airport like a human torch. But Stiles had remembered to take sunscreen, so I survived that too. We landed around 11:00 a.m., and as soon as we were standing on the tarmac, I was swallowed by wind and light. Everything was so incredibly blue, the sky, the turquoise sea beyond. My tunic was flapping in a strong breeze, and I couldn't stop staring up at the clouds stretching above us.

Once I did look down, I realized that there was a welcome committee: several Jeeps and a sedan waited at the other end of the tarmac. I overheard someone saying that the Caterpillar had requested reinforcements from the Honolulu station, in case things went really bad. I wondered what they'd do though, if the Crystal Whisperer managed to blow up the dome. An army wouldn't suffice.

A bit farther, a different sort of company awaited us: a couple of armored station wagons that screamed French secret service. The Caterpillar walked to them with an escort. Indeed, armed men came out, along with older guys wearing linen suits—no doubt local caterpillars. A heated negotiation began, which I gathered went along the lines of "This is our country, and we're totally in control of the situation." "Fuck you, cheese-eaters, this is our investigation, and mine is bigger." "*Non*, mine." "Someone find us a ruler, terrorism can wait!"

Stiles scratched his head. "It might take a while . . ."

"Then perhaps we should leave these gentlemen to their administrative concerns," March said, observing the palavers disdainfully. "Besides"—he squinted his eyes in the direction of the airport's low building and its traditional tiled roof. There, a tall guy in a yellow Polynesian shirt and cargo pants stood, his arms akimbo—"I believe my friend is here."

I think he said something else to Stiles, but I was already running to greet Ilan, so I didn't listen. When the two of them followed me, one of the Caterpillar's agents yelled that we couldn't do that. That's all he did though, because he didn't have the balls to stand up to March, now that most of his pals guarded the Caterpillar and were busy stare-fighting with the French.

Unlike mine, Ilan's leathery olive skin didn't fear the tropical sun. He greeted me with a wide grin piercing through his silvery stubble. "Alors, on continue de foutre le bordel partout où on va ?" *So, still wreaking havoc wherever you go?*

"Ouais, ça va . . ." *Yeah, kinda . . .*

He frowned down at the purple cast around my wrist. "C'est pas beau ça . . . c'est récent?" *That doesn't look good . . . happened recently?*

"*Je t'expliquerai. Mais le résumé c'est: évite la drague sur le net.*" I'll tell you later. Long story short: stay clear of online dating.

Ilan nodded in puzzlement and raised an eyebrow at March, whose jaw clenched in response. It didn't make me happy or anything, but I was almost certain that if March caught Alex, the first damage he'd inflict would be a clean fracture of the left wrist.

I decided to change the subject. "Kalahari va bien?" *How's Kalahari?*

"Pretty good," he went on in English once March and Stiles had joined us. "She has some news for you two; she'll call you when you're done destroying the country."

"Hopefully we won't have to," March said with a weary sigh. "Thank you for responding so quickly."

Ilan towered over his old rival—just because he could—with a benevolent smile. "Don't mention it. Besides, I know half of the guys baring their teeth to Erwin back there." He rubbed his hands. "Couldn't pass on that kind of thrill. Who's the guest, by the way?" he asked, noticing Stiles behind March.

The interested party stepped forward and extended a hand that Ilan proceeded to crush in his big paw. "Special Agent Joshua Stiles, Directorate of Foreign Operations."

"Ilan."

"Yes, I heard about you." Stiles quickly retrieved his hand and shook it discreetly after the introductions were done.

"So you're with them?" Ilan asked, jerking his chin at the Caterpillar's agents waiting near the plane.

Stiles turned around to confirm, and his eyebrows shot up. "They" had finally noticed that we were leaving without them and were running toward us, guns in hand, while the Caterpillar watched the scene from behind his sunglasses.

"And here I was wondering when we'd start to run." Ilan laughed.

"Is it ready?" March asked, his gaze cutting to a big silvery helicopter.

Ilan gave a firm nod. "My guy is waiting for you."

March glanced at Stiles's colleagues, now less than a hundred yards away, and adjusted one of his cuffs. "All right." He planted his gaze in Ilan's. "Je te confie ce que j'ai de plus précieux." *I'm entrusting to you the most precious thing I have.*

When Ilan winked at him like it was a done deal or something, I took a gulp of air and my mouth opened, ready to protest and share my outrage. No sound ever came out, because March's hand went around my waist and his lips crashed on mine—in public! The kiss was brief but laden with a familiar urgency, the same as when he'd kissed me on Dries's yacht.

"Trust me," he whispered.

No. Watching him climb into the helicopter without looking back, my legs shaky, my heart all over the place, I didn't trust him. I hated him a little, in fact, for shunning me again. Especially when I feared he was hiding something big from me. I wasn't exactly superspy material, and that damn cast didn't help my street cred, but I wished he'd have at least told me what was on his mind before running away.

I jumped a little when Ilan's hand landed on my shoulder. "Let's move."

Stiles watched the chopper rise above us with a deafening noise, visibly confused. "I wasn't supposed to let him out of my sight."

"Where are you taking me?" I asked Ilan.

"To a nice hotel on an islet across the atoll. It's called Le Sauvage. No phone, no Internet, need a boat to get there: you won't get any safer than that."

More like a fricking cage . . . "Was that March's idea?"

Ilan gave a noncommittal shrug.

Of course. I had to think fast, because once Ilan got me locked up on that island, there would be no way out until March returned. If he ever did. The very idea that he might die hunting Gerone and Alex made my skin prickle with horror. My right hand went to rest on the heavy little green bag hanging from my shoulder as I mentally leafed through the possible scenarios.

"Okay, but I need to use a computer first. Obviously, I can't do that once we're at Le Sauvage." I turned to Stiles. "Do you think you could help me with that?"

"Sure."

Ilan considered us warily.

I joined my hands in a pleading gesture. "It won't take long."

He relented with a sigh. "All right."

Stiles led us to a white Jeep around which several of his colleagues still waited. He retrieved a bag sitting on the back seat and took out a laptop that he opened and unlocked. "Here."

When he, Ilan, and the guys behind them all stared at me expectantly, I retreated inside the Jeep. "I have to call my dad. Does everyone *have* to listen?" I asked, before slamming the rear door shut. I saw Ilan's arm move toward the handle, but Stiles appeared to reason with him, presumably arguing that a lady sometimes needed her privacy.

Being around March, I'd caught on to a few things, like what protocol and software he used to make video calls to Phyllis. What caller ID he entered. What PIN code he used to secure the line. I was disappointed to discover that the CIA's laptops weren't the crazy secure stuff I'd expected to battle with. Within minutes, I'd overridden the admin rights and installed the extensions I needed to make that call. It was early morning in New York, but I figured Phyllis would be up and ready to rock when March needed her the most.

I was right. At the second ring, her tired face appeared on-screen, a tangled heap of flaming-red curls cascading down her shoulders. "Hey! How's the wrist?"

"Good enough, I guess. The painkillers make it bearable."

Her head bobbed up and down, her expression turning serious. "Good, good . . . You gave my boss a cold sweat."

"I'm sorry. I know it's been a pretty rough week for everyone so far."

She shrugged. "That's the business. Sometimes you can't tell when the lemons will stop raining."

"Hopefully soon."

A clear laugh burst from the speakers. "What can I do to help you?"

"I have a question, and I need you to tell me the truth, even if March ordered you not to."

The mirth died in her eyes. "It depends . . ."

"No more lies," I said, a little more harshly than I intended to.

She gave a silent nod.

"March knows what's going on, right? He knows why Gerone is

targeting the dome."

"What makes you think that?"

"He's been weird, shifty. He knows. I can tell he knows," I insisted.

On-screen, Phyllis buried her face in her hands. "He's gonna kill me for this. Or he's gonna cut my bonus. More likely." She composed herself with a sigh. "He's been to Rangiroa before. Once."

"For a job?"

"No. It was a few years after he started working for the Board. They were very satisfied with him, and he was invited to the dome . . . to be introduced."

"You mean, to the Queen? That's when he met her for the first time?"

"Yes."

"But . . . do you think there's a link to all this?"

Her eyes narrowed. "Now you know how March met the Queen. Do you know how *I* met him?"

"He didn't give me the details, but I know he met you in Macau, that you were working in a casino there."

"Yes. A casino that belongs to the Board, the Goldmine. Code name HKS4MS17, which stands for HongKong Sector 4, Macau Subdivision 17. I was their accountant."

I filed every word, working the Rubik's Cube in my head as she spoke.

"And because I know their business inside out, as does March, I can tell you that if someone managed to pull apart the web of shell companies and foundations that own shares in the Poseidon, they'd eventually find a single entity named FPS3TS1."

I ventured a guess. "French Polynesia Sector 3, and—"

"Tuamotu Subdivision 1," Phyllis completed.

"The Poseidon Dome belongs to the Board. They gather there," I chewed out each word slowly, digesting the news.

"It's a multipurpose investment: good for money laundering, profitable on its own, and it's both remote and crowded. Hundreds of people come and go all day long, dozens of boats and helicopters. Who's going to notice a few businessmen gathering for a seminar?"

"Do you think that's what's going on? That the Board is calling a meeting, and Gerone is gonna to try to blow them up?"

"I have no way to be sure, but that's what it smells like."

I clenched my right hand into a fist to stop its shaking. Anies wasn't just getting rid of Dries; this was his big night. That insane turd was going to war. The Lions were done serving the Board, and the Board was likely done with them as well, after the way they had tried to keep the Ghost Cullinan for themselves. So Anies was going to try to destroy them and clear the path. And March stood in the middle of this mess, trying to warn the Board before it was too late, because even if his days as a hit man were behind him, he remained loyal to the Queen. As for Dries . . . did he know about this? Where the hell was that guy when you needed him, dammit?

"If March lets the Board know, they'll evacuate, right? And it's over?"

On the screen, Phyllis's pale-gray eyes avoided mine.

I smacked my forehead. "God . . . they'll pretend everything is cool to bait Gerone and try to shove his mask up his ass, right?" *And if the showdown goes wrong, three thousand people will pay the ultimate price*, I mentally completed.

Phyllis leaned back in her chair, arms crossed. "I can't imagine the Queen running away from that sicko. That's not the way she deals with threats, and she can't afford to show any weakness. Plenty of guys willing to take her place if she misses a step."

"Phyllis, I need to get to the dome. I can't just stay here and wait."

"There's nothing you could do, and March'd kill me if I sent you there and something happened to you. He seriously would," Phyllis retorted, a sudden gravity in her eyes.

I didn't believe March could ever hurt her, not even if I died, but I gathered Phyllis lived in a world where even undying loyalty never got in the way of some measure of caution. Begging her wouldn't work.

"I've seen Alex's men. I could recognize them."

She shook her head. "Island, I like you, but right now, whoever takes you to that dome lands on March's personal hit list."

"I understand." Yes, I did . . . and I knew exactly whose name I was going to put on that list. "I have to go. Thank you. Thank you for telling me the truth."

"Island, wait."

She combed back a red lock behind her ear with nervous fingers. "Don't do anything stupid. He's not"—her voice quavered—"he's not as strong as you think. He needs you. Alive."

"As I need him."

TWENTY-NINE
DA BOSS

He was done taking orders from the bigwigs in DC. He'd go alone and nuke Colombia if he had to in order to find her. His mission order was love.

—*Tiffanee Thunder*, Delta Heat#2: Bogota Fever

Ilan was steaming mad. I didn't dare meet his eyes as on the tarmac the Caterpillar's men surrounded us. Meanwhile, that flaming douchesac smiled at me, the usual cigarillo glued between his lips.

"And here I was afraid you'd bail on us, Miss Chaptal."

I sustained his mocking gaze with a blank expression. "We're a *family*; we help each other out. I can identify the men who tried to kidnap me, and I can also help you find Gerone's sound cannon. I wouldn't want to sit by and watch."

From the corner of my eye, I saw Ilan's fists clench.

The Caterpillar smirked and blew a spinning smoke ring in my face—his favorite trick. "Very well. Agent Stiles will take you to the Poseidon Dome along with Delta A1."

I looked past him at the few men standing several yards behind him near a second Jeep. They reminded me of the guys who had shown up with Alex in Croatia, all wearing unremarkable civilian clothes: jeans, Dockers . . . and even an actual Taco Bell T-shirt. On a two-hundred-pound beefcake who had probably never set foot there. I bit my tongue and wrestled the urge to ask if they were Delta Force for real, whether they'd heard of the Delta Heat series, and if any of them had ever led a secret operation in the Colombian jungle to save the woman he loved.

"I'll be going with her," Ilan stated.

I shook my head. "No, you don't have to take that risk."

"Then you should have thought about that before you made your decision," he snapped. "I took responsibility. I'm coming."

The Caterpillar was bored with us already. He sized up Ilan with a disdainful eye. "Suit yourself. But consider yourself on your own, and if your presence hinders my men in any way, they have my permission to dispose of you, Mr. Menahem."

It was the first time I'd heard Ilan's last name, and it served as a reminder that the Caterpillar was anything but a fool. Could he possibly know about the dome too? I knew from past experience that the CIA did not face the Board frontally but rather embraced a comfortable status quo where they tolerated most of its shady activities in exchange for self-regulation efforts and even a little collaboration now and then.

Behind me, Stiles clasped his hands, as if to disperse the explosive mix of contempt and anger hanging in the air between his boss and Ilan. "We're ready to move."

He turned his head toward the end of the airstrip, where a blue civilian Chinook was landing with a loud hum. I tugged at Ilan's flashy shirt with my right hand. "Let's go."

On our way to the helicopter, I mumbled. "I'm sorry. I just couldn't stay back."

I felt a big arm sneak around my shoulder, and a note of humor was back in his gravelly voice as he replied in French, "Franchement, tu serais ma nana, j't'assommerais et on en parlerait plus. Mais c'est pas moi qui décide pour toi, et le nouveau féminisme, j'y comprends rien." *Frankly, if you were my woman, I'd just knock you out, and that'd be the end of it. But I don't call the shots for you, and I have no idea how feminism works these days.*

"Toi et March, vous êtes bien pareil," I yelled cheerfully over the droning of the blades as we approached the Chinook. *You and March really are the same.*

He helped me inside with the hint of a prideful smile, and I watched the sunburned tarmac shrink away as we took off and headed for the ocean. It was my first helicopter ride, and even with a headset that kept slipping because the headband was too loose, it was damn cool. The colors appeared even brighter from above, the palm trees and pristine sand banks merging in a thousand shades of tourmaline, only to be abruptly swallowed by deep blue waters. Once again though, I did feel a little singled out, because while I tried to get used to these new flying sensations and the powerful vibrations of the rotor, everyone had pulled out sunglasses. I was starting to wonder if there was some kind of peer-pressure phenomenon going on regarding those in the espionage and crime sectors at large.

It took less than an hour for the dome's outline to appear in the horizon. We were flying over an increasing number of yachts and cruise ships, all ferrying lucky vacationers to this modern Elysium. Blood chilled in my veins when I realized the implications of that particular point.

"Ilan, please tell me they're not taking new guests . . ."

"They are. Apparently the Poseidon will keep operating normally until further notice. The owners and the DGSI don't want to start a panic. To be honest, they don't really believe the Americans' story about that masked guy." His gaze cut to Stiles. "They think one of your agents went rogue, and you're only trying to come up with something to cover your mess."

Stiles's face fell. "Really? It's . . . uh . . . outlandish."

Ilan appraised him with piercing green eyes but didn't press the issue.

As we approached, the details of the massive lenslike structure emerging from the water became clearer. I pointed at a series of incurved triangular blades overlapping to form a crown at the base of the dome. "It's the top of the iris. It's part of the elevating system."

Stiles squinted at the resort beneath us. "What is it for?"

"I read articles about it; it's amazing," I yelled into my microphone. "The whole resort is built on giant hydraulic jacks and can be partially immersed. When they do that, the triangles rotate over each other, like an iris, to form a steel belt that seals all accesses on the first level, like windows, terraces, doors, that kind of stuff. All the sundecks around the dome are retractable—how cool is that?"

Stiles scooted closer to me to look through the window. "But if the dome explodes, the iris won't resist, right?"

I gazed at the gracious curves sadly. "Even if it does, it would become completely useless."

The Chinook circled around the dome slowly until it landed on a floating helipad connected to the building by a ramp. Three larger docks served cruise ships and yachts.

After Ilan helped me out of the aircraft, I looked up at the sheer mass of concrete, steel, and glass engulfing my field of vision. So close to the Poseidon Dome, I felt like an ant. Through the windows, I could glimpse the paradise brochures and websites promised: several stories of shops, hotels, swimming pools, palm trees everywhere. This "resort" was really a huge mall built in the middle of the ocean. Like Phyllis had said, profitable, indeed. I personally preferred Rangiroa's deserted beaches, and some real sand between my toes.

Ilan led us to a white spaceship-like hall where visitors were being "welcomed"—as in searched and requested to provide a credit card imprint. Our little group, however, was escorted by security through a side door.

Once inside, we were swallowed by a wave of humid heat, artificial perfume, and tropical ambient music. Half of the people around us wore bathing suits, and cocktail trays swung past us, carried by nimble waiters. This was clearly the mall area I'd seen from outside: scattered on circular platforms whose balustrades overflowed with plants and flowers, the shops were installed inside fake tiki huts, complete with palm trees. A tangle of escalators and the massive spiral of a staircase linked the stories together.

At the confines of this consumerist heaven, screams and splashing sounds announced the dome's water park. Dodging a tray of mojitos, I looked up at the giant kakemono hanging from a balcony. Under the hourglass figure of a woman dressed in a black glittery gown, a bold title announced a representation of Mozart's Magic Flute in the dome's concert hall.

Ilan placed a hand on my shoulder. "Yeah, I meant to tell you about it. March mentioned your guy was a homicidal maniac who liked Mozart."

"Yes."

A smirk revealed Ilan's incisors. "And if I told you that tonight they're planning to submerge the dome fully during the show?"

"That sounds like a proper finale for the Crystal Whisperer," I said, unable to look away from the poster.

Stiles patted my shoulder, "Don't worry; we have a second team ready in case we need reinforcements." He checked his phone with a frown. "The French are sending a . . . joint but separate task force."

"They're just gonna compete with you guys for who gets Gerone first, right?"

He winced. "Yeah."

As he said this, the Taco Bell task force that may or may not have been composed of actual Delta Force dudes split from us to spread throughout the resort and start the hunt. After they were gone, Ilan took us away from the tourist crowd, into a quieter area where tall windows opened to a terrace overlooking the Pacific. A few people lounged on deck chairs, but there was definitely more fresh air and privacy. I liked that.

We all sat around at a table under a beach umbrella. Once he'd settled in his chair, Ilan pinned me in place with a hard stare. "So why are we here?"

Stiles too was looking at me with guileless, expectant blue eyes. I fidgeted in my seat. Nice soft cushion by the way. "I wanted to help you guys find Gerone, like I said."

Ilan's brow lowered, and his gaze turned dark, drilling holes in my head. "Santa knows when you're lying."

Santa was very perceptive, but admitting the truth in front of Stiles was out of the question. What if the CIA didn't know about the dome being the Board's property? The Board might later investigate the leak and come to the conclusion that either March or Phyllis was responsible for spilling the beans. What would happen to them then?

I was noticing the ache in my arm again, and the more I tried to think, the more it hurt. I gave up. "I can't tell you anything." I breathed through my nose. "I'm sorry. I can't."

Ilan attempted to glower me into submission, while, unexpectedly, Stiles's gaze softened.

"It's okay," he said. "We knew before Mr. November's assistant told you. Well, I mean, not everyone. But Erwin and I knew. And a third agent, from another directorate too, I think."

A sudden cold sweat made the light cotton tunic cling to my back. "Um—"

Stiles went on, with a sheepish smile. "It was my car and my laptop, you know. I keep an eye on them."

Ilan's gaze flittered between us, waiting for the rest. Stiles dealt the finishing blow while I disintegrated on my chair. "The whole resort belongs to the Board. Once in a while, the Queen and the Towers gather here, to review sectoral performances, mostly." When he saw us both blinking back at him, he added. "Tower is a code name for some sort of super sector manager. There's about twenty of them—we don't know them all."

Ilan leaned back in his chair and let out a low whistle. "So that Crystal Whisperer guy is"—he cleared his throat, like something was stuck in there that wouldn't go down—"he's singlehandedly taking on the entire Board?"

"Well, more like his employer is," Stiles corrected with a shrug. He paused to look up at the trail left by a little Cessna circling the dome. "Your uncle is a very ambitious man."

After he placed his hands on his lap as if to signal he was through blowing our minds for now, I sat there, stupidly, staring down at my cast and wondering if Alex and Murrell had ever realized that neither of them was Stiles's boss.

It was the other way around.

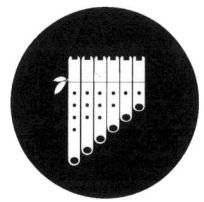

THIRTY
THE MAGIC FLUTES

Her sensual and perfect mouth played his big instrument, his voluptuous growls the soundtrack to their effervescing passion.

—Tory Fierce, Chamber Music

"So what do we do now?" I asked.

Still sitting on the terrace, Ilan and I gauged Stiles with uncertainty. He hadn't physically changed over the past five minutes. The blond buzz cut was still the same, and his worn gray suit retained the same unfortunate cut, just a little too big. But it was kind of like when the Canadian devil appears in *South Park*: You know he's not so bad, and he won't do that much damage, mostly flying around farting fire. Still, he's a devil nonetheless.

Stiles had pulled out his phone and finished typing something. "I updated Mr. November on our current situation." A few seconds passed, and he looked down at an incoming message. His eyebrows jumped. "He says he's going to kill me, and that sublevel four is well guarded, but there's no sign of the guests yet. They are expected to arrive tonight."

"Sublevel four, what's that?"

"It's a level that's closed to the public, located at the base of the resort, underwater."

"Is that where they meet?" Ilan asked.

"Yes," Stiles said, before he looked down at his phone. "Mr. November will join us in front of the flutes in fifteen minutes."

I tried to look at the screen, in vain. "The flutes?"

Ilan tipped his chin toward the mall. "I think he means those guys doing a show inside."

Trusting Ilan's eagle eye, Stiles and I got up to follow him back inside the resort. We strode past luxury stores and expensive restaurants toward the central area of the mall. The Poseidon, fortunately, wasn't full. Listening to the tourists chat, I gathered that July would be the height of the season—by then, people would be bumping elbows in the pools and restaurants. Next to me, Stiles was busy scanning the crowd—literally so, I realized, when he angled his sunglasses on the bridge of his nose, and his forefinger tickled the left branch repeatedly, as if scrolling through something.

"Oh my God, can you see them naked?" I whispered in horrified awe.

"No, just their rap sheets," Ilan commented with a smirk. "Nice toy, by the way."

Stiles acknowledged the compliment with a duck of his head. "Thank you."

Looking back and forth between them, I was practically drooling. "Can I . . ."

"Have fun," he said, taking off the glasses and handing them to me.

They weren't significantly thicker than a regular pair of Ray-Bans, but they did feel heavier in my hand, made of metal rather than plastic. I put them on, and my mouth formed an admiring O. Augmented reality at its best! Relying, I figured, on the NSA's considerable databases, Stiles's glasses performed multiple real-time face recognition scans and returned any relevant intel to the wearer. Such as the fact that the fat guy currently offering a chocolate cone to an unsuspecting little girl was Colin's German pedophile!

"Stiles!" I tugged at his sleeve. "It's him!"

Ilan's hand moved to his back and the gun no doubt concealed under his shirt. Stiles stopped in his tracks and looked around. "Who?"

"The pedophile! The one with the ice-cream cone, between the palm trees!"

He swiftly took the glasses back from my nose to check for himself. The corners of his lips tugged down. "You two wait here."

It wasn't part of his mission, but Stiles did great. He just casually walked past the guy, and all of a sudden, *bam*! He grabbed the chocolate cone and squished it on his face. Temporarily blinded, the German staggered back toward a wooden bench. Stiles kneed him in the balls, sending him falling onto his ass, before a swift karate chop rendered him unconscious. The whole thing didn't even take ten seconds, and the German was left sprawled on the bench, looking like a shit-faced unicorn. After he was done rescuing the little girl, Stiles smiled to her, but she ran away, crying to her parents, because kids are just ungrateful little toads really.

We resumed our quest, walking through a seemingly endless maze of tiki huts selling golf clubs or Roberto Cavalli dresses, until we reached our goal. The water wall that stood at the center of the mall's first floor had been turned into a spectacular background for a Magic Flute–themed mall show, clearly aimed toward a young audience. Cartoonish characters inspired by the opera sang and danced on the small stage, while parents forced their kids to applaud like puppets.

The problem with mall shows is they're often the product of a short chain of command, where bad decisions are made under pressure and without any rational counterpoint. Regardless of whether the underlying artistic concept makes sense, the organizers are given little time and budget to see the show through, and no one cares. Until it's too late, and a couple of dudes prance around dressed up as giant soprano flutes and... blow each other's beaks to the sound of an actual flutist playing in the background. I'm sure they didn't mean it like that, but a few parents glared at the stage and left with their children. Someone would certainly get fired over this.

Anyway, the flutes didn't matter as much as who I saw walking on the opposite platform, invisible to all in his "I love Polynesia" T-shirt, even to the magic glasses, who ought to have known better.

I gripped Stiles's forearm, my breath suddenly short. "On the other side of the bridge, walking toward the escalator, gray T-shirt, shaven skull."

"Who is he?"

"He was with Alex. He's the guy Karl recognized." I gulped, fighting a wave of nausea at the memory of Karl's lifeless body on that bedroom's floor back in Croatia.

Stiles turned to Ilan. "Okay. You stay here with her and wait for Mr. November. I'm gonna follow him."

"Are you sure?"

There was nothing tender in his baby-blue eyes as he said, "Yes."

Ilan held me back, and Stiles vanished before I had a chance to protest. With nothing else to do until March came for us, we waited and watched the ballet of unsuspecting tourists coming and going in this trap of steel and glass. Seldom had I felt so powerless, knowing that the worst might happen, but there was nothing I could do for now. Yelling for everyone to evacuate would at best cause a panic and at worst get us arrested by security—who, by the way, had been called on the giant flutes by an angry mom. The twerking had been the last straw, and the audience was now convinced that there was some sort of double entendre to their performance, which did not serve the cause of opera in any way.

Ilan had seen the ruckus too. He ran a hand across the stubble on his chin with a sigh of consternation. "N'importe quoi, putain . . ."

Fucking nonsense . . .

March wasn't there yet, and the flutes were fighting back, with claims that art knew no limits, except those of right-wing censors and, might as well say it, Nazis. Nothing suggested that those security guys were SS, but they certainly weren't joking: A brawny Polynesian headbutted one of the flutes, prompting the other one to denounce a case of police brutality. The second security guard said they weren't cops anyway, and Tasered him under the discreet applause of the most conservative onlookers.

Someone brushed past me. I ignored them, my eyes glued to the pair of guards handcuffing the protesting flutes to take them away.

"Good riddance. I would have shot them," a deep voice remarked.

I jumped out of my skin at the same time that Ilan spun on his heels. There was the answer to my earlier question: *Where* was Dries? Standing before us, watching misunderstood artists getting beat up.

Ilan's hand hovered near his back, but he looked mostly nonplussed rather than about to shoot the newcomer. As for me, I was just angry. There he was, looking just fine and smug in his cream linen suit, hiding behind a pair of goddamn sunglasses. How nice to know he'd found the time to tan a bit while I broke my wrist in the woods!

"What the hell? Couldn't you let us know . . ." I was trying to keep my voice low, but a young couple stared at us suspiciously.

Dries casually raised my cast to examine it. "Vis?" He asked.

"No, it was after that. But wait . . ."

Ilan's hand rested on the gun at his back, and he looked ready to pounce. "I don't care who you are. You step back. Now."

It would have taken a lot more to impress Dries. He cocked a condescending eyebrow at Ilan. "You may not care, but you know exactly who I am. Don't worry; I left my black helmet and light saber at home today."

I smacked his arm with my good hand. "Very funny. How long have you known Alex was a frumentarius?"

"I was on the fence in Venice."

In other words, basically from the start. I searched his gaze. "Erwin told me about his sister . . . He said she was in the plane. She was only sixteen. Did you know?"

His arm sneaked around my waist. "How about we go somewhere a little more private to chat?"

I slipped away. "Did you *know*?"

Something flickered in his eyes, perhaps the closest thing to regret he'd ever allow himself to feel. "I told you before, little Island. I live with my ghosts. All of them."

I looked away. "How do you sleep at night?"

"Sweetie, I don't have time for this; follow me—"

"No, March is going to look for us."

Dries huffed. "Now don't worry about that. Look—there he is."

I whirled around to see a familiar silhouette in a navy blue jacket and jeans striding toward us. I have to give credit where it's due: Nothing filtered on March's face. His features were a perfect blank mask as he stopped in front of us. Impressive, when I could tell he was in fact utterly, epically, a century-in-the-trunk mad.

THIRTY-ONE
THE PLAN

Rhäpihst had ruled over the Secret Vampire Billionaires Brotherhood for over a thousand years. Now the council wanted him dead, but he wouldn't go down without a fight. He would become the garlic to their bread, the silver spoon in their mouth!

—*Forest Belle*, Secret Vampire Billionaires Brotherhood #1 - Sucked

Even king of brazen assholes Dries sensed the danger. A smirk still hung on his lips as March approached us, but his shoulders rolled back and his spine straightened. He was getting ready to dodge a potential punch.

It was Ilan who stepped forward though, his expression somber and apologetic. "Stiles ditched us after he spotted one of Morgan's men in the mall. He went after him. He's gone silent since, and"—his gaze cut to me, filling with guilt—"I am responsible for this."

March barely acknowledged him, his gaze settling on me instead. Arctic cold. "No, Ilan, you are not."

He moved close enough for me to smell the mints, feel the anger roaring inside him. "I had a discussion with Phyllis regarding your . . . initiative. She no longer works for me, and I'm getting you out of here immediately. You'll wait for me at Le Sauvage as you should have, and when I return, we'll talk."

He scared me, and I hated that. I didn't want to feel like that around him. I needed our bond, the one that always made me safe, warm . . . and that was nowhere to be found. Inside me, too, resentment surged, swelled into rage. It felt like I was punching a mile-thick, sky-high concrete wall with my bare hands, banging, banging desperately, so much that my fists were getting bloody . . . yet I could never break through. We still couldn't understand each other. My right hand moved before I knew it, to push him back.

My palm met the very wall I'd been picturing—it was actually me who staggered back, while March's own body remained rooted in place. I stared down at the marble floor and the tips of his shoes, spit shined. "You lied to me. Again. I came here for you because I was scared to lose you. And"—my voice broke—"I can't believe you fired Phyllis."

I registered his hand moving, reaching for me. I recoiled.

"Don't touch me. I won't go back to Rangiroa. I'm going to stay here and help you lure Alex and Gerone out. And when it's over"—I pictured myself standing at the top of a building, overwhelmed by that mysterious urge to jump. *L'Appel du vide*, as the French call it. I swallowed the lump in my throat—"when it's over, I don't know if we'll talk. Maybe . . . it might be best we just go our separate ways."

March's hand dropped at his side. I still couldn't meet his eyes as he simply said, "Very well."

Not a word was uttered while Dries led our little group away from the mall and toward the entrance of the resort's palace. In the lobby, an interior designer had been let loose and covered the place with tropical plants and flowers, to the point where I could hardly see the walls underneath. March kept his distance; even in the elevator, he leaned against the wall opposite, as far as possible from me. I felt a little nauseous, physically ill at the realization that I'd gone too far and said words I wasn't certain I meant . . .

Numbers flashed one after another on a screen in the wall. I felt a weight on my left shoulder. Ilan's hand squeezed it, a tentative smile stirring his whiskers. March didn't react, apparently now reduced to a wax statue. Dries watched us drift apart with impenetrable golden eyes, until the elevator stopped on the fifth floor, and he gestured for us to step out.

I found my voice again as he swiped a card to unlock the floor's only door. "Sabina, she's with you?"

He smirked. "Yes. We've been chatting a lot. I believe she's warming up to me."

We followed him inside a lavish suite with a view of the ocean. A bucket of champagne still rested on the carpet. The king-size bed was undone, embroidered covers strewn in complete disarray. Ilan and I exchanged looks. The fragrance of a vase of orchids standing on the coffee table covered a different scent, a faint, musky note I now recognized, although my own experience in this department was meager at best. A blush crept to my cheeks.

I side-eyed Dries as he crossed the room to casually open the doors to what seemed to be the bathroom, judging by the white tile I could glimpse.

Splashing sounds and a yelp reached us.

Dries grinned like a schoolboy. "Get dressed, sweetheart. We have company."

"I don't even wanna know." I murmured.

"Neither do I." March's voice cracked like a whip. He sent Dries a chilling glare. "Was she able to tell you anything?"

"She led me here. She believes Gerone will strike during the opera tonight. That repugnant clown intends to be part of the show." He rolled his eyes to the ceiling. "God, I hate his kind. Why does everyone need to be so showy these days? What happened to solving your problems with a bullet between the eyes?"

"Is that how you'd have wanted Anies to deal with you?" I lashed out.

"Yes, in fact," he shot back, without missing a beat.

"You know why he sent Gerone here, right?"

The wry smile that was his self-defense mechanism was instantly in place. Of course he knew. With the Lions, Dries had started serving the Board long before March had. Surely he too had one day been "introduced" to the Queen and those Towers people who managed her empire.

Dries's gaze drifted away from me to the windows, losing itself in the blue immensity surrounding the dome. "I've sometimes heard idiots say that Anies took over because he was the firstborn, and that being the younger one, my legitimate place was second to him." A dry laugh burst from him. "As if the brotherhood ever cared for primogeniture ... This isn't the British crown. He just had what it took. I didn't. I wouldn't have been capable to pull the trigger on him. And"—he shook his head—"I never, *ever* thought of taking down the *fucking dome*."

"You're not a good man, but you're better than him."

We all turned to look where that soft voice and its Italian accent had come from. Sabina stood in the bathroom's doorway, regal, wrapped in an oversized white terry robe I suspected to be Dries's. Her long black tresses had been chopped and the remaining bob dyed a caramel blond. Even so, she was beautiful, on top of holding a PhD in chemistry. I hoped Dries at least understood how lucky he was that this woman clearly picked her dates wrong.

He crossed the room and pulled Sabina to him. "I appreciate the thought, but stay out of my business," he drawled, his lips inches from hers.

Before she could react, he silenced her with a scorching kiss, complete with a halfhearted struggle and a little moaning on her side. Dries let her go with a slap to her butt that made me cringe and wish some things could be unseen. Meanwhile, March and Ilan had the presence of mind to avert their eyes from this regrettable display of

Cold War–era machismo.

Coming to her senses, Sabina pushed him away with a huff. "I *am* your business."

"True," I chimed in. "You're going to need her tonight."

Dries flashed me a disdainful look. "Am I?"

"Well, you want to find Gerone and Alex, right?" I shrugged. "Stop looking. You have her; you have me. The three of us are like giant bait: just let the birds come to you."

He crossed his arms. "Are you suggesting we go see a bit of opera tonight?"

"Pretty much. Once Gerone figures Sabina is here, and she hooked up with you, there's gonna be a whole lot of crazy under that mask." I saw her flinch, and I did feel bad for stating things so crudely, but I went on anyway. "You? Alex will"—my voice faltered when I thought of Poppy. Of what Dries had done—"Alex won't miss an opportunity to kill you. As for me, well, you'll be pleased to learn that Anies holds me in such high regard that he sent his minions to kidnap me in Croatia because he wanted me safely out of the way while he killed you and March. I'm sure he'll be delighted to learn I'm inside the dome he's planning to blow up," I concluded.

Next to me, Ilan moved to plop himself into a chair with a puzzled grimace, while March crossed the room and towered over me with a cool glare. "Brilliant idea. I was thinking we could lower you into the middle of the opera hall in a harness, and perhaps wait for Anies's men to come up and catch you. Do you believe we should wound you first? How about a little blood to attract them faster?"

I held his gaze and squared my shoulders. "Actually, that's exactly what I had in mind. Do you think you can get us a well-exposed booth, somewhere everyone can see us?"

March's chest heaved, and I sensed I was seconds away from being flung over his shoulder caveman-style. Dries too picked up on the imminent burst; he stepped between us and placed a hand on my shoulder. "What if Anies decides he can live without you and gives his go to Gerone to blow up the dome?"

For once it was my turn to smirk like a James Bond villain. "Oh, the Crystal Whisperer isn't going to sink this dome. We are."

THIRTY-TWO
THE ELEVATOR

"I thought like, you can't, like, get pregnant if you do it in an elevator. Because it's made of metal."
—*Broke Teen Moms*, Reality Broadcasting Channel, 17 Sept. 2013.

I had been, of course, expecting to produce some effect on my audience with that dramatic statement, but the results were far beyond my expectations. Sabina's jaw went slack, Ilan's eyebrows hit his hairline, and even March's poker face fell, despite years of practice. Dries rubbed his hands gleefully. "I like that. You're going to tell me more about it, but first, I need to show you something." He winked at Sabina. "Darling, show them the drawings you did for me."

Sabina walked to the bed, and from the drawer of one of the nightstands, she retrieved a pen and a notepad bearing the logo of the Poseidon. "Come here, please," she said, padding to a couch and a pair of armchairs disposed around a coffee table at the other end of the room. Dries and I joined her on the couch, while Ilan and March claimed each armchair.

One of Dries's hands moved to rest on the nape of Sabina's neck, tangling in her hair. I would have been hard pressed to tell whether the gesture was a tender or menacing one, and perhaps that was his true skill with women . . .

She leaned into his touch nonetheless before she started flipping through a series of doodles. She paused at a particular one and placed the notepad on the table for all of us to see. Albeit represented with questionable skill, the dome was recognizable. At its extremity, a stage had been drawn crudely and on it stickmen wearing dresses. Like her old flame, Sabina liked to express herself with a pen. "The concert hall is here, close to the dome's transparent walls so that they serve as background for the stage. When the dome is immersed"—she pointed to snakes, or rather waves, she had sketched all around the structure—"it will be like a huge fishbowl, and the top of the bubble will still peek out from the water.

"Now, I saw something on Lucca's computer, the night after he . . . took me." I could tell she had been about to say "saved," and she seemed upset, but she composed herself and continued. "It was like an LRAD, and I think that's what he placed somewhere in the opera hall." On the stage she doodled something that was more reminiscent of a large frying pan than an actual Long Range Acoustic Device, which she hastily colored in black. She then added red lines coming from the pan, to figure ultrasound waves hitting the Ceraglass bubble. "It's probably very powerful, but even so, at this frequency, it needs to be close to the glass, a few meters at most."

I leaned over the sketch. "So that sound cannon would need to be either onstage or in the wings."

Sabina nodded. "That's what I think. At this distance, if the weapon is powerful enough, it will take less than a minute for the chain reaction to start, and when it does"—she proceeded to add a waterfall coming from a hole in the dome, right above the scene, and tiny stickmen drowning in the water. Sweet Jesus, that was dark—"once the dome has been breached and the superstructure is weakened, the weight of the water does the rest, and it destroys everything."

March studied the schema with slanted eyes. "What's the actual size of this thing?"

"Fifty to sixty inches wide," Dries said.

March frowned. "And why in the concert hall and not anywhere else? Did Gerone say anything about that?"

"Not really," Sabina said. "But before he killed him, Lucca told Pio that when he destroyed the Poseidon, it would be poetic, special. When I saw the opera, I knew that's where he would want to do it. I also think that in the concert hall, the cannon would be closer to one side of the dome." She pointed at the extremity of the dome that was supposed to act as an aquarium-like background for the stage. "That wall won't resist long."

Meaning that the stage and audience would get instantly crushed by several thousand tons of water moments before the dome collapsed on itself and turned the Board's supersecret sublevel four to a concrete-and-steel pancake.

Having listened to the whole thing with a stony face, Ilan asked Dries, "Did you search the concert hall already?"

"Yes," Dries confirmed. "I did a little reconnaissance last night, but I found nothing like what Sabina described. The Queen's security is fairly tight, rooms are searched regularly, and there are quite a few hidden scanners throughout the resort. If Gerone managed to get that cannon inside the dome, I'm thinking he disassembled it and hid the parts somewhere else, ready to be moved at the last minute."

I sprang to life. "That's why I told you we should sink the resort ourselves."

Again, my evil plan garnered me the attention of every pair of eyes in the room, including March's, for once. "I was thinking that if we want to derail Gerone's plans, we need to pull the rug under his feet. Dries, do you have a laptop in here?"

"Of course."

Dries rose from the couch to search a stack of metallic cases. I caught glimpses of enough weapons to start a war, but I chose not to comment—No wonder he worried about hidden scanners. He came back with a small black laptop that I greedily took from his hands as soon as he'd logged into his account.

"Check this." I opened one of the many articles and videos I'd binged on back in the plane. It was a short documentary about how engineers handled the challenge of supplying millions of gallons of clean, filtered water for the dome's seven swimming pools and three hotels. On-screen, a bearded Frenchman explained how under the dome, giant water pumps drew seawater into tanks, where it underwent several desalination and purification treatments before being distributed all over the resort.

When he was finished talking, I paused the video. "We could use those. It's a lot of water, but not nearly enough to sink the resort or cause any major damage. If we're able to drain those tanks *into* the first floor, it will create the impression that the dome has been breached, even if the whole thing is actually harmless: there would only be a few inches of water, just enough to cause a panic and have security evacuate the resort. If Gerone hasn't tried to make his move by then, not only will the guests be safe, but it could force him to move the cannon, or even give up altogether."

Also it would be a while before anyone dared to vacation again at the Poseidon, but I didn't say that.

March was the last person I expected to comment on this plan, but he did—and never looked at me as he spoke. "Erwin dispatched seven agents in the resort, six of which are Delta ops, and he has a second team ready in Rangiroa. Supposing that we consider this option, they might be the most qualified to sabotage the water pumps."

"What about Stiles?" I asked. "Is there any news from him?"

He pretended to answer the wall behind me. "No. He hasn't reported yet. That could become a problem."

Dries waved a dismissive hand. "Forget about that clown; he's asking to be burned."

The idea that Stiles could have been captured—or worse, killed—even if he was the Canadian devil, that didn't sit well with me. "Is there any way we can access the dome's security cameras and see where he went? Just to be sure he's okay?" I asked.

"There's a control room," Dries said. "But I won't take you there. Now that March has warned the Board there's a situation developing inside the dome, it's probably a matter of hours before Guita discovers I'm here too. Let us not tempt fate."

Oh. That was a tiny detail I'd overlooked. Guita—that was the Queen's name, or the one she had given me and Dries anyway—was a charming lady with a lot of power in her hands, and she had sworn to kill Dries following the Lions' betrayal in the Cullinan affair. Long story short: Dries had tried to steal *her* diamond, and because these people evolved in a giant kindergarten playground, revenge was high on the list of her priorities. There was a fair chance that once Guita figured out that Dries was sitting right under her nose, she'd choke him with a swing chain.

March got up on his feet. "I'd like to know where he is too. Ilan, can you use your contacts and tell us if the French have agents in the dome, and if they've noticed anything out of the ordinary? Meanwhile, I'll try to negotiate access to the security recordings, and I'll also contact Erwin to see whether he might be willing to help us plunge the entire resort into chaos," he concluded, raising a haughty eyebrow at me.

Dries agreed with a nod. "Be quick."

As he was about to leave the suite, March paused in the doorway. "Island."

Well, well . . . not only did Mr. Clean see me after all, but he even remembered my name. Ignoring the tiny spark of hope crackling inside me, I crossed my arms and pretended to count the dust specks on the coffee table. "Yes?"

He turned to look at me, the poker face letting nothing through. "I know you said that you didn't want to talk. But I would very much like a word with you . . . in private."

I mimicked his blank expression. "Where?"

"You could come with me, and we'll talk on our way."

To be honest, it sounded too good to be true. I half expected him to knock me out and shove me into a helicopter back to the atoll just to win the war, but I decided to trust him. Love is very complicated, I guess. Dries watched us leave the suite with a scowl but contented himself with petting Sabina to soothe his ulcer.

I followed March to the elevator. I figured he'd eventually talk—I hoped he would anyway, because I was drained, fricking sad, and I had no idea where to start. He remained silent as the doors closed and trapped us between walls made of cool brushed steel. The car started going down. We went down one, two floors, and I saw his hand move. Without warning, he pressed the emergency stop button, and the elevator jolted to a stop. He was looking at me, so intensely I feared I'd drown in those hypnotic blue pools.

His tongue darted at his lips as if they were too dry. He swallowed. "Are you leaving me? I need to know."

It hadn't seemed so real when I had suggested it earlier. I'd spoken out of anger but also out of fear. And now my anger was gone, but the fear, the doubts still simmered in my chest. Now it was real. He'd said the words, and he expected an answer.

I couldn't voice one. My eyes felt hot, and my heart was about to burst out of my chest. I panted, in a desperate effort to compose myself. "I know you won't believe me, but I actually almost never cried until I met you. I didn't even cry when Mufasa dies. Well, maybe a little, but—"

"Island." March's face was a little blurry, and his voice sounded strangled. "I need to know."

On the elevator panel, a red light blinked and a series of bipping sounds announced the connection to a hotline. Without looking, March pressed a button to interrupt the call. Those damn tears wouldn't stop, but this time he was making no attempt to come closer, to dry them. He just waited, his features taut, like he was in pain.

I gasped several times and wrestled a string of mildly coherent words out of my throat. "I don't know. With you, it's like a roller coaster . . . the highs feel so good it's like I'm on drugs, and the lows . . . the lows are so, so bad, and it doesn't help that everything we touch blows up." I sniffed a few times, knowing I was seconds away from releasing a torrent of snot. "I'm so scared we can never learn to function with each other, that it's always going to be like that until I'm like . . . a chalk outline of myself."

Through the haze of my tears, I noticed he'd pulled out a tissue pack from his pocket. I reached for it blindly with my right hand.

He waited until I was through blowing my nose to ask again: "Does it mean you don't want to try?"

"And you, do you still want to try?" I said in a broken sob.

He drew a shaky breath. "I fired Phyllis. I have no idea what took over me." For the first time in hours, March touched me. His fingertips trailed down the synthetic sleeve covering the cast around my forearm, butterfly-like, as he forced the words out. "All I could think was that she'd brought you here, put you in danger, and I was . . . I wasn't thinking straight."

I nodded, wiping more tears. "Tell me about it . . . I'm *never* thinking straight around you."

Several seconds of silence followed, our mutual breathing the only sound in the still air. The alert button was still blinking steadily.

When March spoke, the words were so low, so tentative that I almost didn't hear them. "That's what it's like . . . when you're in love with someone."

Imagine munching a dozen Fisherman's Friends, and suddenly it's like there's an ice storm blowing inside you, clearing your sinuses, your head, your entire body, something so strong that you're coming apart and together over and over again right here, on the spot, like you're molecular food in liquid nitrogen. I'm aware that I'm not making any sense, but my point is that this is not even remotely close to how I felt in that elevator.

I wiped my nose with my sleeve. This time my vision was clear enough that I saw him wince. "Sorry about that." As soon I said this, the gravity of the moment hit me. March was waiting, his eyes wide, his mouth slightly parted. This was not about my snot. Or even clear sinuses. In the cradle of my ribs, my heart drummed fast.

"I love you."

I wasn't sure the voice was mine, and if it was, it was too brittle. I gave it another try. "I really, really love you. And I want to try to be with you. I'm so sorry I said . . ."

March brought me against him carefully, caressed my hair, my cheeks with his palms. They were so warm that I forgot what I wanted to say. Behind us, a series of bips announced another call. He punched the same button again to end this new attempt to rescue us. His mouth brushed mine, captured my upper lip. *God,* yes, the highs were . . . divine. It seemed almost absurd that something so simple as the mineral taste of saliva, the gliding of your tongue against a tongue you happen to love unconditionally, that those could be so powerful.

The lesson here is: pay attention to the guy's Cupid's bow next time you're on a date—once you're hooked, that tiny strip of skin will become the most important thing in your life.

March was slowly driving me against the elevator's wall, his body pressing into mine. My brain shut down, and so did March's, as evidenced by the LEGO piece poking me insistently through our respective clothes. He was doing that thing again where he suckled on my neck to leave a hickey there and make Dries suffer. I let out a long moan, which seemed to bring him back to reality.

"Biscuit . . . we can't do this in an elevator."

I gasped. "I know. And Gerone, the dome . . ."

"Exactly."

His hand slid away from my waist to fumble with the elevator's buttons. Time to go back to work. We pulled apart reluctantly, stealing one last kiss. The red button had stopped blinking, but the elevator still wasn't moving. March looked around, a faint frown replacing the blissful expression on his face.

You know, when I said that being with March was a roller coaster with horrible lows, I didn't mean it literally, of course. Except for the time we stood in an elevator, and a trapdoor opened underneath our feet.

THIRTY-THREE
THE LIFE AQUATIC

I couldn't take my eyes off of his sculpted abs and long, muscled tail as he circled around me in the water and asked, "Sir, do you know how fast you were swimming?"
"Um, no. Actually I'm new to this beach, and I had no idea—"
"Sir, I'm going to need you to take off your trunks."
—*Tuck Chingle*, **Pounded in the Butt by the Shark Cops**

I screamed when the floor opened beneath us. My stomach heaved with the sudden, horrifying sensation of free-falling. March was swallowed in a split second—right before I was—calling my name once in surprise. My first thought was that the elevator was falling, and I pictured us crashing several floors below in a tangle of gore and bones. It wasn't that, but I can't say my heart rate slowed down in any significant way when I realized we had simply been disposed of down some kind of slide.

I felt March's hand grab one of my legs as we tumbled in darkness. There were a few turns that shook my internal organs unpleasantly. I was trying to catch my breath, and I couldn't even manage to call for help. I caught a flash of blue before we were both plunged in cold, salty water. Pain cracked in my wrist, and incongruous thought flashed through my mind that I wasn't supposed to get my cast wet. Hindered by clothes, my body felt instantly heavy as I paddled desperately to keep my head out of the water. I held on to March when one of his arms circled my waist, and he helped me swim toward a tiled ledge.

Through the salt prickling my eyes, I glimpsed concrete. We had been thrown into a pool somewhere in the lowest level of the dome. That, I could deal with. But the fins . . .

Wait. Waitwaitwait. The fins?

The horrifying truth dawned on me, and with it, panic electrified my body. I howled for help and jerked helplessly against March as grayish fins circled us and *something* grazed my legs.

My fingers dug into the wet fabric of his jacket. "March! March, it's a shark pool! Oh my God! *Oh my God!*"

"Biscuit, it's going to be all right . . . Let me get you out of the water."

When a nose poked my butt, I shrieked so loud March probably lost some of his hearing that day. It was only when my voice broke from all that bawling that I registered the clicks and whistles echoing in the massive concrete vault housing the pool. Hold on. Sharks didn't do that.

Sweet Jesus, how *sick*, how *damaged* do you have to be to set up an elevator trap door that throws people in a pool full of fricking *dolphins*? They were swimming all around us, shoving us playfully, laughing, it seemed. I'm pretty sure those whistles must have meant something like, "Ha ha, she nearly crapped herself! Did you see that, guys?"

At last, I felt the ledge under my fingertips, the altar of my salvation. March helped me haul myself out of the water while the dolphins called us stupid twats with Ricky Gervais's voice, or so I feared. We were both lying on cold tiling, blinded by the fluorescent lights lining the ceiling, when across the room, a door slid open.

Heels clanked on the floor as March helped me up. I stood on shaky legs, watching a woman in her late forties walk around the pool toward us, flanked by a bunch of men in black suits. Her burgundy silk jumpsuit billowed with every step she took. It was the single pearl hanging from a golden chain around her neck that I recognized first. The black tresses falling onto her shoulders and framing the pearl were familiar too, as were the piercing brown eyes and honeyed skin.

The Queen had found us. Well, fished us, really.

Her light laugh ricocheted on the walls. "Dear March, it's not often that I catch a man like you off guard."

March greeted her with a slight bow. "I must admit I never expected to end in the pool. I'll be more careful next time."

"Then let us pray there *is* a next time." Her voice had cooled down a notch, and I started to fear the worst when she seemed to notice me. "How do you like the Poseidon, Island?"

I managed a trembling smile. "It's . . . nice."

She winked. "You haven't seen anything yet." She snapped her fingers. "Farouk."

As I prayed that the dolphins were the worst life-form we'd have to face in these walls, one of her bodyguards stepped forward. I hadn't paid attention to the fluffy black towels in his arms, but when he handed them to us, I could have hugged him. Or not, because the slicked-back-hair-and-sunglasses-inside vibe was a little scary.

Guita didn't wait for us to dry ourselves. She and her men started heading back toward the door they'd come from, visibly expecting us to follow. March and I tagged along, patting our faces dry. On the other side of the sliding door was another world. The long hall we stepped into was decorated in the purest Moorish style, its walls covered with intricate geometric tiling and elegant sculpted stone arches framing the doors and windows. It was like we'd jumped right into a spatiotemporal portal and been sent to Granada. I was willing to bet that half of that had been imported directly from Andalusia.

The only infidelity to historical detail was the breathtaking underwater view through the windows. A shoal of bright-yellow fish undulated past us. Fricking surreal.

Guita crossed the room to sit in an antique armchair that was basically wood and nacre lace. There were other chairs, and even a desk, but I gathered that here, in her lair, you were expected to stand before the Queen. So we gave the towels back to her guard and did just that. She crossed her legs and studied us, her head tilting in undisguised interest.

"I have to say, when I first received your message, March, I didn't believe it."

"It's a very daring attempt," March conceded.

"In fact," she said with a pout, "I still didn't fully believe it until we found this in a hallway on sublevel two twenty minutes ago." She reached for a black box sitting on a finely carved brass tray. She opened it and took out a plastic bag, which she threw for March to catch.

While he examined it, I leaned closer to him to check its contents. *Oh God.* There was a pair of glasses and a gun, both smeared with blood. My heart stopped when I recognized Stiles's magical Ray Bans. "I think they belong to one of Erwin's men. His name is Joshua Stiles. Do you know what happened to him?"

One of Guita's shoulders jerked in the semblance of a shrug. "We haven't found the rest of him yet."

I desperately wanted to believe that Alex wouldn't kill one of his former colleagues, but a nagging little voice inside me suggested otherwise. A chill cascaded down my spine, spread through my limbs. I wanted my Facebook friend back. March's hand clasped my shoulder, all the comfort he could provide as we stood before the Queen. I took a deep breath and stood straighter.

"I'll give your men a full ID. He came here with six other agents," March confirmed.

Guita curled her fingers and examined the carmine polish on her long, lacquered nails. "So, correct me if I'm wrong. At the moment, under my dome, I have at least one Lion, six to seven CIA agents, another rogue agent Erwin let loose, a few French operators thrown into the mix, an unspecified number of armed men, a disfigured madman, a weapon capable of destroying the entire resort . . . and you two."

March gave a curt nod. "That would be correct."

"You've been busy."

He responded with a tight smile. "Perhaps a little more than I wished to."

"How do we contain this situation?"

By then, I knew that peasants of my kind were discouraged to give any amount of attitude to the Queen—or to even address her at all—but I suppose the lack of sharks in her pool emboldened me: I stepped in. "We have a plan. Something that will allow you to evacuate the dome without making it look like you chickened."

Her eyes went wide, and she gave a snort of laughter. "That I . . . *chickened*?"

I wasn't sure it was a good sign, but I forced myself to look her in the eyes and went on. "You're supposed to gather those Towers people tonight, and Anies chose that meeting to attack you frontally. Common sense would dictate that you cancel, evacuate everyone—you included—and let the dome be destroyed if it can't be avoided. But then the Lions win this round, and that would undermine your authority over the Board. So you're counting on March and everyone else to catch Gerone in time."

She sobered. "And?"

My eyes darted to March; he responded with an imperceptible nod of encouragement. I stood taller. "We came up with a compromise."

"Which is?"

"Using the filtered water tanks to fake a structural breach and partially inundate the first floor. That will force everyone to evacuate for a good reason, and hopefully mess with Gerone's plans."

She rose from her improvised throne and paced in front of us. "How would you do it?"

A confident smile returned to March's lips, one I had sorely missed. "Erwin's Delta ops can sabotage the tanks, but their job will be even simpler and safer with the help of your engineers. The water level will never become threatening; it should rise only enough to, say, *motivate* your guests."

"And after that?"

"Best-case scenario, Gerone's plan is sufficiently derailed for us to neutralize his weapon. Worst-case scenario, he reacts fast and manages to launch an attack: we'll ensure minimum possible casualties by provoking the evacuation."

"In other words, you guarantee no results."

March answered in a matter-of-fact, unapologetic tone. "Even if we manage to smoke out Gerone and Morgan, I'm afraid we face a number of contingencies as long as we don't know where the weapon is."

She walked to a window and gazed at the seabed beyond. "I don't want to owe a favor to Erwin."

"No one does," I said. "But look at the bright side: he's way overdue for lung cancer."

A throaty chuckle escaped her. "People were already saying that when I met him, and that was twenty-five years ago."

I shuddered at the thought that the Caterpillar might be immortal on top of everything else. Meanwhile, Guita strolled back to her throne and let herself fall onto the embroidered silk cushions. "All right. Tell Erwin to send down his men to sublevel three."

I stifled a victorious *Yes!* and the little karate pose I mentally pictured myself performing along with it.

March's chin ducked in confirmation. "Understood."

Guita was no longer looking at us; I gathered that our meeting was reaching its end. It was a little risky, but I decided that this might be our last chance to address the elephant in the room. Or rather, the Lion. "What about Dries? He's working with us; if your men target him, it'll blow the whole operation."

Next to me, March stiffened. *Wrong move?*

Her right hand clasped around her left arm in what struck me as a typically emotional gesture and, therefore, a novelty for a woman I'd always seen in perfect control of herself and others around her. "I have no idea what he was thinking coming here," she said, sounding a little flustered. "But there won't be any favors. The moment we've ascertained the dome is safe, he can expect to be treated as he deserves."

My eyes darted left and right, at March, at her goons. Was I the only one in this room who noticed that she was in fact doing Dries a huge favor by postponing the hunt?

March wouldn't say anything. The question sizzled on the tip of my tongue, but I decided not to ask. I feared I'd uncover yet another ghastly record of Dries's egregious use of his magic shtick . . .

She clapped her hands twice. "Farouk."

That guy with the shiny slicked-back hair and the sunglasses took a step forward. "Find our guests something to wear. They're going to the opera tonight."

March bowed his head in silent thanks, and we were about to follow Farouk when Guita's voice stopped us. "Oh, and before I forget . . ."

We both waited for the rest, watching in mild concern as her smile returned and grew foxy.

"The elevator . . . what a show. Especially the ending." She turned to her bodyguards. "We really enjoyed the ending, didn't we?"

Unlike Ceraglass, my face had a regrettably high level of thermal conductivity, and it caught fire almost as soon as she was done talking. March, whose own thermal protection system rivaled that of a space shuttle's, contented himself with clearing his throat repeatedly, as if something was stuck in there that wouldn't go down.

Like the fact that the Queen and her goons had watched our emotional exchange and subsequent making-out like it was late-night Bravo trash.

At last, March found his voice. "We will be more cautious in the future."

"Yeah . . . um"—I fidgeted, unable to meet their gazes—"sorry."

She waved my apology off and locked eyes with March. "Cautious, indeed. I never knew you had such a wild side, but we wouldn't want it to get in the way of your duty."

March's poker face fell back in place, a mask of icy congeniality that mirrored hers. "It won't."

I'll start with the good part: sublevel four was damn cool. We were given a little privacy to shower and change, in a bedroom that boasted the same Moorish design as Guita's meeting room. I was pleased to find a hair dryer to blow-dry my cast after the dolphin attack, and—sweet Raptor Jesus—in the bathroom too, we had one of those crazy windows to watch the ocean while we bathed. Like I told March while rinsing my hair, "You should see this. I'm totally flashing that grouper, and it just stays there watching!" I suspected that March would have indeed wanted to see "this" and been the recipient of all that flashing instead, but we didn't have time for that, and certainly not in a place that might be riddled with more cameras!

Now on to the questionable stuff: Guita and her goons somehow figured that I would make fine bait for Anies's men, and that, to this end, I should be made visible from a distance. After I was through cleaning up and drying everything that needed to be dried, I stood in my underwear and gazed at the fire truck–red dress laid on the bed for me. Farouk—who wasn't so bad once you got to know him—had mentioned that the pearl-embroidered bustier was bulletproof, as was March's tux jacket. A delicate attention, but still . . .

"Is there a problem with the dress?" March asked, after he had shrugged on his jacket and adjusted his cuffs—the bowtie a maid had brought stayed in its box though. I made a note to ask him later why he never, ever put anything around his neck.

"No, I'm good. It's just all . . . very flashy."

Reading my mind, he went to stand behind me and massaged my shoulders in a soothing gesture. "I won't leave you for even a second."

I leaned into his touch and purred, "I know."

March helped me zip the dress's back—I can't even begin to list all the mundane tasks that suddenly take an epic quality when you can't bend your left wrist. There was an odd contrast between the bustier's tight and unusually thick material and the many layers of weightless red muslin cascading down all the way to my feet and caressing my legs. A length of veil attached to the bustier would conceal my cast nicely, and I was pleased to find flat red sandals to wear with the dress: thank you, Board, for understanding that you don't save the universe perched on four-inch heels, dammit!

Once I was done, March trailed a reverent hand down my hip. "You look beautiful."

I blushed.

"And also very red."

That made me dissolve into a welcome fit of giggles. Even standing in a giant glass bomb, we could still laugh at each other. That was something already. He handed me the crimson clutch completing the ensemble—Jesus, all we were missing was a traffic cone on my head. The bag felt a little heavy; I opened it. Inside rested a small black gun.

"Walther P99. I thought you'd like that."

I wasn't sure whether to grin or to be freaked out. James Bond's gun, yes, but still a gun nonetheless. I touched it gingerly.

"You have twelve rounds. The cocking switch is on top, and the safety is on the left side; do you need me to show you?"

"No, I think I've got the hang of it," I said, gripping the gun in my right hand and feeling a button click under my thumb. Uncocked. Locked.

"Good. Keep it with you, just in case."

"Okay."

March's hand rose to caress my cheek. "Island?"

"Yes?"

"I hate doing this. Once this is all over, I want us to go somewhere safe and quiet, just the two of us. And there won't be any missions or guns in your handbag."

I kissed his palm. "Agreed, Mr. November. By the way, did you call Phyllis?"

"Yes."

"And?"

His lips twisted in what looked suspiciously like a pout. "I apologized."

"And?" I insisted.

"She's back . . . but she renegotiated her Christmas bonus."
I patted his chest tenderly. "That bad?"
"Outrageous."

THIRTY-FOUR
PARENTAL GUIDANCE

"Since you won't give your heart to me, I will find the man you love, and I will castrate him, so no other can ever satisfy you, Rica!" Ramirez growled menacingly, his thick moustache inches from her face.

—*Kerry-Lee Storm*, The Cost of Rica III: Shackles of Lust

"*Bavaram nemishe*... fifteen years in the business, and this is the weirdest thing I've ever done." That's what Farouk told us in the elevator taking us away from sublevel four, after he'd given instructions for his colleagues to help Ilan and the Taco Delta ops sabotage the dome's filtered water tanks.

March's dimples creased his cheeks as the doors opened to a poorly lit level that seemed unfinished. "Until now. The night is still young."

Farouk shook his head in response, the sunglasses concealing whatever despair might have been brewing in his eyes. The three of us stepped out and into a long hall whose bare walls still awaited some paint. Scaffolding remained here and there, half concealed by transparent tarps. Red carpet rolls had been stacked against a wall, next to golden signs still wrapped in plastic sheets. *Orchestra level. Bar du Pacifique* . . . We must be near the concert hall. Backstage? No, more like right underneath.

"So you and the Queen, you're Iranian, right?" I asked, inspecting the dim fluorescent lights buzzing above our heads.

Farouk tucked his phone back inside his tux jacket, adjusted his sunglasses, and remained silent. I took that as a yes.

March offered him an apologetic shrug. "I'm afraid I didn't brief her on the etiquette."

The offended party considered me from behind his sunglasses. "It's all right. I won't kill her."

Goose bumps bloomed on my arms.

March winked at our host. "You know I wouldn't let you."

Farouk's face remained impassive for a few seconds. His thick black eyebrows lowered behind his glasses until he barked a dry laugh. "Ah! Weird, weird day . . ."

And it's about to get even weirder, I thought, when at the other end of the hall, a pair of security doors opened, letting in the two leads of tonight's drama. Night and day. Him, in a black tux very similar to March's save for the black bow tie, her, ethereal in a champagne sheath dress that was perfectly assorted to her new straight blond bob. I didn't miss the way Sabina clung to Dries's arm as the two of them walked toward us though: underneath the class act, she was probably terrified. Next to me, Farouk tensed visibly. As per his Queen's orders, however, he made no move to reach for his gun.

Dries gauged him with a smirk. "Here's a face I haven't seen in a while." His arm wrapped around Sabina's shoulders. "Farouk, this is Sabina, who's here to help us keep the dome in one piece, at least until dawn. Sabina, this is Farouk, my favorite lackey."

This time, Farouk's right hand jerked instinctively to reach inside his jacket, but March's hand was on his forearm in the same instant, acting as a safeguard. He turned to Dries and Sabina. "Are you two ready to go?"

She cast an uncertain look at Dries. "Yes. But you promised—"

"Don't worry. I'm a man of my word."

I refrained a grimace. "Um, what did you promise?"

Her face took on a pleading expression. "Dries said that if we can catch Lucca, he won't kill him. He has to be stopped, but he's . . . I think he's very ill. He doesn't realize, because he suffered so much—"

"And I said I wouldn't kill him." He gave her shoulder an almost paternal squeeze. "I already told you you have my word."

March and I exchanged a look. Dries wouldn't kill Gerone, indeed. Our mass-murdering emo was looking at a swift forty-five if he got caught. Seeing Sabina's frightened, hopeful eyes made even bigger by a copious amount of eyeliner, I felt uneasy. She saw something we didn't in Lucca Gerone: the man he had once been. She still retained a tiny drop of faith in him, even after all he'd done. Entrusting that drop in Dries's hands was a highway to heartbreak, but for now, we needed her to trust him. We couldn't afford for her to freak out.

I boxed my guilt in a small part of myself I knew would probably shatter when this was all over and offered her an encouraging smile. "It's gonna be okay. I can't believe I'm saying this, but I think you're safe with Dries."

A nervous laughter shook her frame, and she bobbed her head in agreement.

Farouk checked his watch and tilted his head toward the elevators. "It's time."

"Island and I will join you upstairs in two minutes," Dries said, letting go of Sabina.

March's brow furrowed. "Island? That's not what we planned."

I looked back and forth between him and Dries, dumbfounded. "Uh, I know. Dries, is there anything . . . ?"

Dries's jaw ticked in impatience. He waved a dismissive hand in March's general direction. "How come you're still here? Go. We need a moment."

I mouthed a silent *It's okay* to March and watched him, Farouk, and Sabina disappear in the elevator, his eyes never leaving me until the doors had closed.

When I turned around, Dries stood with his arms crossed, giving me what can best be described as the "dad eye," a narrowed stare that was at once concerned and judgmental. "So the two of you . . . patched things up?"

"Yes."

He gave me a leveled stare. "Surely it won't last."

I thought of March's words, right before Guita's dolphins had tried to eat us. Instantly, the glow returned, warming me from the inside. "I hope it lasts. For a very long time."

Dries's eyes screwed shut, like I'd stabbed him. "I see. Well"—he stroked his beard—"I suppose we're all entitled to our mistakes, even the gravest ones."

It was probably the closest thing to a blessing I'd receive. I smiled. "Thank you."

He pulled me to him for a loose hug, which I returned as best as I could with my right arm. "March gave me a P99, you know," I murmured in his chest.

"Good."

"If I you ever barge into our bedroom again, he won't shoot you. *I* will."

The moments my words registered, Dries broke our embrace to look me up and down. For the first time, in his eyes, I saw more than the pain and confusion of a man trying to pick up the pieces of his past. I saw pride, and perhaps even happiness. In his irises, the gold shone bright. "That's the spirit, little Island. That's the spirit."

In the elevator taking us to the concert hall on the first floor, Dries showed me how you could avoid ending up in the pool by placing your feet on each side of the trapdoor I now knew how to detect on the floor. I didn't think I'd ever need that again, but when I told him about the dolphins, he seemed surprised and made a passing comment that they were "something new." Upon my asking what other life-forms had previously been inhabiting the pool, he declined to comment. I gulped.

When the elevator's doors revealed the wide hall leading to the orchestra, March was there, waiting for us. He extended his arm for me to take, but Dries moved faster and barred the way. He wrapped a hand around the nape of March's neck, something that might have looked like an affectionate gesture to the external onlooker, not unlike a bro hug. I saw the way he tapped March's cheek mobster-style, though, and heard his gravelly hiss. "As jy haar swanger maak, ek sal jou piel plastinate." *If you get her pregnant, I plastinate your cock.*

March was smart enough not to answer, not even with a pledge to practice safe sex at all times: this was about an old Lion giving his daughter away to the favorite disciple with as little damage to his ego as possible. Satisfied with his performance, Dries moved to join Sabina, who stood behind March. At last, I was able to take his proffered hand, and we were engulfed by flashy cocktail dresses, elegant gowns, and a battalion of tuxedos.

In a moment of scathing irony, I came to realize that while my eyes kept darting around, anxiously checking the crystal chandeliers hanging above our heads or studying every single tux to guess if the owners were spies, the guests were in fact looking at *me*. Well, not me, I suppose, but that firetruck of a dress. Or maybe it was the cast around my arm, barely visible under the veil cascading down my shoulders, that had people wondering what sort of grim punishments were dished out in the intimacy of our hotel room. Whatever it was, it worked. If Gerone and Alex were hidden in that crowd, they couldn't possibly ignore my presence . . . or Sabina's.

Quite a few heads turned as she walked across the hall on Dries's arm. They pretended not to notice, taking the stairs to reach their box and get in position.

March's hand settled on the small of my back. "You're a sensation."

I shrank under the scrutiny of yet another woman. "I dunno. Maybe."

Like Dries and Sabina, we took the stairs all the way up to the fourth tier, where a box strategically placed on the side and across from Dries's would give us a perfect view of the concert hall. Everything, from the walls to the seats, was lined with burgundy velvet, like a wink to the rococo debauchery of times long gone. After we sat down, I scanned the rows of seats and the orchestra below us. The red curtain wasn't open yet. The musicians had started tuning their instruments, filling the space with an oddly soothing cacophony.

When I dared to look up, I was swallowed by the immensity of the dome. Fifty feet above our heads, gigantic incurved steel beams supported thousands of tons of Novensia's cursed Ceraglass. Beyond, in a cloudless night, billions of stars shone, nested in the mysterious fog of the Milky Way.

In another life, I wished we could have been there on an actual vacation, because, really, that dome was beautiful enough to make me cry, and although I was rapidly rethinking my rankings, the Magic Flute had always been my favorite opera. I used to sing the Queen of the Night's second aria in my bathroom as a child, because that's where artists of my caliber belong.

A hum reached me and soon turned into low vibrations that thrummed through my body and made the chandeliers hanging from each box's ceiling tinkle softly. I looked up at the stars moving away from us. No. *We* were moving. We were going down. Everywhere, the hubbub of the concertgoers stopped and was replaced by an explosion of cheers and applause. March's hand squeezed mine.

"They're locking the iris," I murmured, as the dome slowly sank until dark-blue waters engulfed two-thirds of the structure, leaving a disk of stars in the guise of a ceiling. I inched closer to March, unable to stop the tremors in my body when I noticed schools of fish roaming on the other side of the glass walls, glimmering like sapphires thanks to external lighting.

That was it. If we were unable to locate Gerone's cannon, all we could count on was our evacuation plan. The more I thought of it though, the less likely it seemed that the dome's personnel would manage to evacuate everyone in time. Maybe I'd made a terrible mistake.

"Breathe. It's going to be all right."

I looked up at March, perfectly composed as usual. I was amazed that he could withstand so much stress, and that, ultimately, I was the only one who could push his buttons to the point of no return. A kryptonite of sorts. The lights went off. I retrieved the pair of opera glasses Farouk had given me before leaving sublevel four, which I'd put in my red clutch next to the gun. Placing them before my eyes, I discovered we'd been given a different model than the rest of the audience: onstage, Tamino's infrared signature ventured into the Queen of the Night's mysterious kingdom.

We watched and listened as the first half of the opera unfolded. Scene after scene, the infrared picked nothing spherical or big enough to fit the description Sabina had given us. My neck was getting damp with sweat. Gerone was here, somewhere, and there was nothing, no fricking sign of him.

On the stage, princess Pamina fought the evil and ugly Monostatos trying to kiss her. The Queen of the Night appeared in a roll of thunder to chase that piece of shit Monostatos away, terrifying in her glimmering black gown. A trapdoor slid, from which giant black lotuses bloomed all around Pamina as the Queen's divine voice ordered her daughter to kill the kind magician Sarastro.

March and I saw it at the same time. His arm, which held the glasses, jerked as he tried to get a better look. In my visor, all I could see was the largest of the black lotuses. The only one emitting a faint heat signature, unlike its counterparts.

THIRTY-FIVE
DER HÖLLE RACHE

"Hell's vengeance seethes in my heart;
the flames of death and despair engulf me!"
Emanuel Schikaneder, Libretto of *The Magic Flute*

"March. This is it!"

How fitting, I thought, as the first angry notes of the Queen of the Night's aria filled the dome. A vengeful rant and a promise of death: I almost felt stupid for not having foreseen that Gerone would pick that particular scene for his grand finale.

March sprang from his seat and whispered into a tiny mic concealed under the lapel of his tux, sending a signal for Ilan and the Taco Delta team to go ahead and blow up the filtered water tanks.

He took my hand and practically hauled me up from my own seat. "Island, we're moving!"

Across the Poseidon Dome, the soprano's voice gradually rose, and those terrible, grandiose *F*'s tore the air. They rang in my skull as we ran down the stairs to the orchestra, sharp like the dagger the Queen wielded.

We reached the ground floor and raced toward the stage in the dark. A rush of adrenaline surged through my veins when cold wetness splashed my feet. The water. No one had noticed yet, and the soprano kept singing, each note higher than the previous, until the aria ended, and a round of applause thundered in the hall. On the stage, however, the singers looked down at the orchestra in confusion. It was a woman's ear-piercing shriek that started the commotion. The singers and musicians snapped out of their shocked daze and ran away, some back to the wings, others hurrying up to the doors without even taking their instruments.

The water was now rising fast, and the spectators panicked in their turn, scrambling up from their seats. I heard a child's cries. There was nothing I could do, and in that moment, I felt shitty that the whole thing was my idea, and that these people were experiencing what might turn out to be the biggest fear of their lives. March and I were less than twenty feet away from the stage, trudging ankle deep in a pool that shimmered and undulated across the orchestra's floor. We dodged countless tuxes and wet dresses; some bumped into my arm, and I hissed through the jolts of pain.

"Stay close." March took my hand and pulled me to him, shielding me from the last spectators running away.

All around us, lazy vibrations and metallic moans indicated that security had regained control of the elevation system. Waves crashed against the dome; we were rising back to the surface. Relief washed over me, so intense that my knees grew weak for a second. A strange peace fell onto the hall as we reached the orchestra pit. There too, instruments had been abandoned, and glitter from the stage decor floated across the water's surface.

March helped me up the stage, and I ran toward the giant black lotuses that had bloomed earlier around the Queen of the Night. The petals were made of velvet-lined plastic, and pleated golden tulle in their center made for a seedpod. I carefully lowered myself inside the biggest flower, and my feet met something hard.

"Help me; there's something inside," I said to March.

Shredded tulle flew in all directions as we uncovered what seemed to be a giant black sphere and heavy-duty four-hundred-ampere cables underneath we couldn't easily reach.

"I think it's the cannon, but I don't know how to cut the power. I can't see where the cables go."

I crawled closer to the sphere, battling the waves of pain shooting up my wrist. God, if this thing went off and fired high-intensity ultrasounds directly in my face, I'd probably be howling in agony and begging for the sweet kiss of death in seconds. That's the sort of LRAD they use against protesters who stand dozens of yards away from the device. Now imagine being nose-to-nose with it...

March helped me out of the flower.

I gestured to the deadly boom box we'd just uncovered. "We need to cut the power and disassemble it. And we need to do it fast. Gerone isn't stupid; the cannon might be connected to its own generator."

"All right, I'll warn Erwin's team."

As he reached for the tiny mic in his lapel, splashing sounds reached us, coming from the orchestra. We both looked down to see Sabina, whose silk sheath dress left little to the imagination now that it was half-drenched. She rolled frightened eyes at the lotuses onstage. "Is it there? The cannon?"

"Yes. We need to get away from here. Where is Dries?" March asked.

She wiped tears from her eyes with her forearm. "He went after a man."

Alex . . . ? I frowned. "Who? Did you see him?"

"No." She sniffed. "Dries said he's a little shitstain."

Yup. Alex all right.

March forced a smile on his lips. "Come on, Sabina. We can't stay here."

She extended her hand to him. "Yes . . . we need to find Dries."

I nodded. "Yeah, we—"

The ultrasound wave hit me like a freight train, the unbelievable power of the vibrations twisting me into knots. Over the agonizing pain in my skull and the nausea boiling at the back of my throat, I saw that March and Sabina had collapsed too in a similar fashion.

March called my name, reaching for me, hauling me up. I didn't answer. There was no time, and I could barely stand. I thought, *We need to see where he is. It's the only way*, and that's when I remembered the infrared glasses I'd put back in my clutch when leaving the box. The bag was a few feet away—I'd dropped it when climbing inside the lotus. I wrenched my hand away from March's and went to my knees, grabbing at the bag.

I struggled to bring the glasses to my eyes. Was I hallucinating those cracking sounds around us? I prayed I was. In the deserted concert hall, all it took was one look. High above us in the backstage scaffolding, a bright spot moved, the glowing heat of several bodies. I pointed the direction to March and screamed at the top of my lungs, "Up . . . there!"

Never had I been so glad to be dating a former hit man. I saw his arm rise, aiming at the shadows moving in the scaffolding. A series of shots cracked over the powerful hum filling the dome. I registered a muffled groan. Above us, something fell down, clanking repeatedly against the scaffolding's steel. And, blessed be Raptor Jesus who no doubt guided March's aim, the pain stopped. Footsteps shook the metal structure right before the bullets started raining.

"Island, stay down!"

March's command was superfluous—while Sabina threw herself to the ground with a scream, I curled into a ball behind the black lotuses, feeling in sadly familiar terrain. Yet, for the first time, I wasn't scared. I was under an unbelievable amount of stress, and enough adrenaline pumped in my veins to trigger a heart attack, but I wasn't paralyzed by the same sort of immediate fear of death I'd always experienced until now. Somewhere along the way, over the past six months, I had toughened up.

In between two rounds, I saw March run toward the scaffolding's stairs and find shelter a few yards away from it, behind one of the fake walls enclosing Princess Pamina's bedroom. In the dark, shapes moved, shooting in March's direction as they climbed down the stairs.

I figured my day wouldn't get much worse anyway—still hiding behind the biggest lotus, I pulled out my gun. Cocked, unlocked. Panting fast, I raised my arm and took a series of blind shots toward the bunch of shadows I assumed to be Gerone's men. I entertained no hope of hitting anyone, especially given how my arm shook each time I pressed the trigger. I just wanted to distract them long enough for March to get up those stairs and teach them why both Erwin and the Queen appreciated his services so much.

As expected, as soon as I as started emptying my magazine their way, loud shots strafed toward me. I covered my head reflexively when bullets crashed into the lotus I'd been shielding myself behind. Velvet and glittery shredded tulle flew all around me. If these idiots managed to ruin Gerone's cannon, we'd at least be able to call it a night. Someone smart shouted for the men to stop shooting at the lotus. Right afterward, a new pair of footsteps clanked on the boards of the scaffolding. March had managed to get up there.

I saw a guy wearing the Poseidon's teal uniform fall from the scaffolding and crash onto the stage in a pool of blood. I heard fighting and several rounds of automatic fire, before a second body fell down the stairs. I figured that for these guys, it must be like in those horror movies where some creepy space creature is waiting in the dark for an opportunity to snatch you and spit back a body part in front of the camera. I'm pretty sure that's how some of them must have felt as March progressed up the stairs . . .

I could no longer see him, but, crawling a couple of feet away from my hiding spot, I made out two bodies wearing black fatigues resting on the scaffolding's first story. I prayed he was still doing fine and eating people up there. My gaze locked on that thing I'd seen fall earlier, a small black device, a phone maybe, still resting on one of the steel boards—March had been perhaps a little too busy to pick it up. I tightened my grasp around the P99 and took a shaky breath. In the orchestra, Sabina still sat huddled between the first and second row, while up there, her crazy ex was getting ready to crush us all under an approximate seventeen thousand tons of water. Possibly with that very device . . .

When the gunshots paused, likely because each side needed to reload, I scuttled all the way to the stairs leading up the scaffolding. If March ever noticed me climbing over the renewed fire exchange, he didn't shout for me to get down like I feared he would, which would in turn give away my location. It was only when I reached the first floor and found myself shrouded in darkness and standing among dead bodies that around the P99's grip, my hand started shaking. I swallowed and steadied it.

The board I stood on couldn't be more than thirty feet long, and at the end, a blue hue filtered, coming from the night sky outside the dome. I glimpsed my goal, which rested a few feet away, on the edge of the board. I crouched down and listened, still as a sparrow. Metal clanked above my head, the noise barely perceptible. Whoever it was, they were at least two floors above me. I crept forward and struggled to grab the black object with my left hand—yep, that hurt, but I didn't want to let go of the gun I held in the right one.

The device did look like a phone, but the screen was fingerprint locked, so no way to find out if I could use it to at least call my dad. I tucked it in my bustier and made my way back to the stairs. The gunshots had stopped, but I didn't like this new silence. I needed to find March.

As I'd feared, on the second story, I found several dead bodies, some wearing the same teal polos as the Poseidon's personnel. I was about to proceed to the third and last level of the scaffolding, but I froze. Fifteen feet above my head, I caught the dangerous whisper of March's voice, speaking to someone.

"Have you ever met him? What can you tell me? Speak. Or die."

A chilling synthetic voice answered him. "You can't kill me. Pio already did."

Gerone. I climbed the first steps as silently as humanly possible. Around the gun's grip, my fingers were clammy.

"Maraì? Not a lab accident then?" March asked in that stony, remote tone I knew he reserved for clients.

When I was close enough to see him, March's fingers clenched, save for the index, which he shook slightly in a *no* gesture. Relief flowed through me as I realized he knew I was here. Had probably known all along, in fact. I stayed hidden. At his feet, bathed in the bluish hue coming from the glass, an indistinct mass rested, wearing a blood-soaked tuxedo. The man raised his head. I jerked in surprise when a human face appeared, framed by wavy gray hair. *Not Gerone?* No, it had to be a silicon mask, because nothing was moving on that ageless face, even as the robotic voice echoed again, ghostly.

"He knew what was in my report," Gerone said. "I showed him, told him. But it was always the money, the production costs, all against hypothetical risks. I taught him the difference between hypothetical and *zero*." He was shaken by a series of hiccups I realized were in fact uncontrollable laughter. "Surely now you understand that difference too."

"Are you saying he caused your accident?" March prodded.

A whizzing sound fought its way out of the mask. "He locked me in the test chamber." With a sigh, he seemed to calm down. "He didn't even have the courage to finish me. He ran away when security arrived, like a coward. How glad he must have been that I couldn't speak anymore, couldn't move for months."

"But you took the settlement money."

"That was his mistake. Without it, I would have never recovered." His chest heaved a few times. He was laughing again. "I would have never been able to convalesce in Pretoria."

March's spine straightened. "Where you met Anies."

"*Him*," Gerone corrected. "We don't say his name, and you shouldn't either. Although it doesn't matter much in your case."

"Why serve him?"

"Have you ever been near him?"

There was not a trace of admiration to be found in March's voice as he answered, "I have."

Gerone's body relaxed. "I met him at the clinic one night. He never even told me what he was there for. My mask wasn't working very well then, but he was interested in my work. We spoke for several hours." He paused. "It was like being near the sun."

Burning bright, attracting those around him, reducing them to ashes. Yes. Although I had never met Anies, I could imagine him as that sort of man. Solar, in the most dangerous way.

Gerone was breathing hard, but none of what he might possibly be feeling was conveyed by the computerized voice. "He brought me back to life. He gave me strength and purpose."

Strength and purpose. Why did that sound suspiciously like the kind of motto a Lion could have lived by? Alex's words back in Krvavica played in my head. *He's gonna fuck you up* . . . Maybe it wasn't just his accident. Maybe Anies had groomed Lucca Gerone and "fucked him up."

March knelt by Gerone's prone body and picked him up. "You'll tell that to my good friends at the CIA. I'm certain they'll understand."

Gerone panted. "You're wasting your time."

No, *he* was. Anyone who knew March would have been aware that he wasn't the kind of guy you stalled or derailed with words. He secured Gerone's body in his arms and turned around. At last our eyes met, and I managed a smile when I got visual confirmation that he was physically okay. The blood on his shirt wasn't his, and while the crease-free technology had been defeated by the events of the night, we would leave this place alive, and it was all that mattered to me at the moment.

I pointed at the phone in my bustier. "I wanted to get this."

"Thank you. Let's go. I want to get you and Sabina out of here. Then I'll look for Dries."

I nodded, my throat a little tight. No lecture on the risks, no demands that I never do that again. For the first time since we had met, March and I were equals. Just equals.

When we reached the stage, Sabina was waiting for us. No doubt having noticed the absence of gunfire, she'd gotten up from between the seats and ventured closer to the lotuses to examine Gerone's sound cannon too.

At first, she didn't react, fooled by the silicone mask. With a pair of sunglasses, he could have been anyone; maybe we'd even walked past him in the dome, totally unaware. The eyes though, they were wrong, like the eyelids didn't crease around the eyeballs in a natural way. That's what must have tipped her off.

She ran toward us, a sob breaking her voice. "Lucca!"

A pang of sadness squeezed my chest; she still wouldn't give up on him. She took a step toward us; her eyes were wide with distress. "Is he dead? Is he dead?"

"No," March said. "But he needs medical attention." He laid Gerone on the stage, checked something on his watch, and spoke a few words in the speaker hidden in his lapel, apparently asking Ilan and the Taco Deltas to join us and pick up Gerone.

For the first time, I was able to take a good look at the wound Gerone was clutching on his chest. It looked bad; blood oozed from the bullet hole, overflowing between his knuckles in dark rivulets. Sabina climbed on the stage and approached him with cautious steps.

She knelt by his side. "Sta andando tutto bene, Lucca." *It's going to be okay, Lucca.*

A whizzing sound came from under the mask, and his upper body shook quietly. He was crying, mourning, but no sound would come out. "Volevo a rimanere per sempre. Mi ferisci." *I wanted you to stay forever. You hurt me.*

She wiped tears from her eyes. "Lo so, ma ti ho perso. Mi ha ferito anche." *I know, but I lost you. It hurt me too.*

All of a sudden, Gerone started convulsing. Sabina pressed her hands on his wound with a desperate sob, and I too thought he was dying. I panicked, but when he kept going, I realized that this was in fact uncontrollable laughter.

The computerized voice rose. "Knock, knock."

Sabina looked down at him with a mixture of relief and confusion. "Knock, knock."

March's eyes narrowed, and my index curled around the P99's trigger, sticky with sweat. "Stop that, please. Save your strength for the police."

"Knock, knock."

None of us had the time to ask who's there. Two gunshots ricocheted in the concert hall. I crouched reflexively; March yelled for

Sabina and I to get down. But it was too late. Between her breasts, a large red rose was blooming already. She collapsed on Gerone with a gasp, her mouth working in vain.

Before I could even process that there was at least one shooter remaining in the concert hall, March had grabbed me and thrown us both off the stage and into the relative security of the orchestra pit. Pain shot in my wrist as I landed in cold water, surrounded by floating purses vomiting makeup, tissues, and opera tickets. He dragged me into a corner, gun in hand. I'd lost my own weapon in the fall, but it was not what worried me. Next to me, March's breathing sounded fast and ragged.

Two shots. One that killed Sabina, and . . .

I checked his tux jacket frantically. There was a dark hole on his side. My heart rammed against my ribs. The jacket was supposed to be bulletproof! What kind of ammo . . . ?

March clutched the wound and gasped. "Stay down, biscuit. Erwin's men are almost here. It's going to be all right."

No, this time, I wasn't sure it would be, because the blood spreading on his shirt . . . it was his.

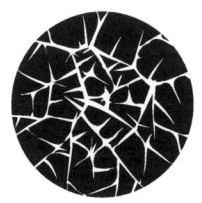

THIRTY-SIX
THE GOOD SUIT

"Help! Help! Otherwise I am lost! Selected as offering to the cunning snake."
Emanuel Schikaneder, Libretto of The Magic Flute

The shooting had stopped. Huddled in a corner of the orchestra pit, crouching in cold water, we could see shadows moving in the first and second tiers above us, curtains shivering as more shooters took position.

March breathed deeply through his nostrils. "Seven men at least. Probably more."

I moved closer to examine his wound. It seemed too low for his lung to be at risk, but the blood wouldn't stop, soaking his hand and his shirt, and I had no idea what to do.

"But they can't . . . we're in a blind spot, right?"

"No. Second tier, all the way to the right, in the last box. He's locked on us."

I craned my neck and spotted a dark shape hidden behind the box's balcony. All of a sudden, it was as if the water we were sitting in had turned icy. Goose bumps erupted all over my body.

"What's he waiting for?"

March glared in the direction of the hidden sniper. "A clear shot."

Because of me, I figured. They wanted to get rid of March, but they'd never dare to take the winning shot with Anies's "little princess" in the way. I scooted closer, embracing March, so close our foreheads touched. The blood felt warm and sticky between us, dampening my dress. We were looking in each other's eyes, and for a second, everything else blurred around me. Even that asshole waiting up there didn't matter so much.

I touched his cheek, the skin clammy under my fingertips. "They won't dare. They'll never dare."

In March's earpiece, someone spoke, and his eyes lit up. "Island. Erwin's men are moving; the Queen sent a team too. As soon as they enter the hall—"

"We run?"

"Yes. Be ready."

Second's ticked on the dial of March's watch. His brow was low, knotted, his eyes half closed as he pressed on his wound and waited. I couldn't stand to see him in pain like that.

"How long?" I whispered.

"Fifteen seconds."

As if on a cue, all around us, the lights died in the concert hall. We were in the dark, the eerie green glow of emergency lighting outlining the abandoned music stands and shimmering on the surface of the water.

Ask me to explain *Donnie Darko*'s plot, and it'd probably clearer than the two minutes that followed. The Taco Deltas announced themselves with two loud detonations and a burst of blinding light—grenades, very likely—followed by a tangle of red laser beams swiping in all directions.

Over the ringing in my ears, I heard March shout, "Island, *now!*" My legs jerked and moved automatically, scrambling in ice-cold water, even as the deafening rattle of automatic rifles echoed all around us. March's hand let go of his side and clamped painfully around my shoulder, sticky with blood. He pulled me across the orchestra pit and toward an alley between the seats. There were voices barking orders in the dark, several screams all forming a white noise in my head. I only focused on my legs, on March's hand, on running, in spite of the ache in my muscles and the fear squeezing my lungs.

At some point, we crashed through a small padded door, and there was light again. Chandeliers above our heads, librettos floating all round us on the water. We were in the hallway circling the orchestra. Behind us, gunshots still crackled, getting ominously louder. March collapsed to his knees with a groan, and the water around us turned pink. He swallowed hard, each intake of air a tremendous effort. "You need to keep going . . . Ilan is waiting for us at the helipad. I'll join you there."

"No! I'm not leaving you." I struggled to fling his left arm over my shoulders and help him back on his feet, my own pain an abstract, remote sensation. *Dammit*, I wished he was lighter. "Come on!"

March croaked. "That's not what we agreed—"

"Fuck the agreement!"

I was shaking, but I welcomed the weight of his body: as long as it meant he could keep walking, I'd do anything, cheat exhaustion until we were both safely away from that fricking dome. I'd worry later about what kind of additional damage to my wrist the purple cast concealed. For now, I trudged onward, completely drenched and in a near trancelike state.

There was a flight of stairs leading down to the mall; I led us to those because I didn't trust the elevators in this place. Against me, March's chest heaved with comforting regularity. He'd be okay. We could do this. The first tiki huts and palm trees came in sight and beyond them the water wall near which the promiscuous flutes had been arrested earlier. We'd be outside in a few minutes.

Halfway across the mall's first level, March stopped us. The fingers of his right hand tightened around his gun. "Wait."

I went perfectly still, listening to the silence, barely troubled by the sounds of water flowing and the distant hubbub of the last boats and helicopters evacuating.

March let go of me and stood straight with a grunt of effort. "Show yourself," he called, his voice rising and echoing over and over in the deserted mall.

I looked around in panic. Behind the water wall, a blurry silhouette appeared.

"What a night, Mr. November."

Alex. *Shit.* I should have guessed that if we hadn't found him, *he* would find us.

Without so much as a blink, March pushed me to the ground, steadied his arm and fired three shots at the water wall. Alex's shadow vanished instantly, leaving the bullets to crash into a glass balcony past the fountain.

New gunshots cracked in the air, which narrowly missed March. I crawled toward an information kiosk to find shelter behind its large stand. He crouched by a tiki hut, blood spilling on the floor's pale marble at his feet. I breathed through my nose and bit my lower lip hard not to cry. He couldn't go on much longer like this. We needed to get out of here, fast.

Alex's voice resounded somewhere to my right. "Baby, Mr. November isn't doing so great . . . Maybe it's time to negotiate."

In guise of a reply, March fired again. This time I registered movement behind a group of palm trees. Maybe if I could just distract him . . . "I spoke to Erwin," I said out loud. "He told me about Poppy."

March and I exchanged looks. Waiting. But there was only silence. I crawled a few feet away from my hiding spot, revealing myself. Panic registered on March's face, but I shook my head for him to wait. I was going to ferret Alex out, even if it killed me.

"Why did you lie to me about her?" I yelled again. "Is that how she lives on? In your bullsh—"

Boots slammed hard on the marble. I saw a flash of jeans and leather. Holy shit! I hadn't realized he was that close. From the corner of my eyes, I saw March move in the same moment that Alex lunged at me, way too fast. I tried to run past, but that asshole grabbed my leg and tripped me. I fell and screamed in pain when my left wrist hit the marble hard. "March!"

Alex's nails clawed at my calf, digging, drawing blood, before March hauled him back. There was a gunshot before a black semiautomatic spun away on the floor. March had disarmed him, but a powerful kick in his wounded side sent him flying backward before he could finish the job. This time, March too had lost his weapon, and when Alex jumped on him, I saw more blood smeared on the floor around him in a carmine pattern, like wide brush strokes. He could hardly breathe let alone stand up.

I tried to get back on my feet, but the unbearable pain in my arm stopped me. Long past my earlier efforts to be a superspy. I was spurred by the primal instinct to crawl toward March and stop Alex any way I could. But I wasn't fast enough, strong enough.

I saw Alex punch March repeatedly. I screamed hysterically for him to stop. Just as I was losing hope, heavy footsteps stomped past me. There were several suppressed gunshots, and almost instantly Alex's howl of pain tore through my eardrums. His jeans now covered in blood, he let go of March.

And the parent of the night award goes to . . . Dries, whose tux still looked impeccable, although a little damp, as he lowered his gun. Alex snarled, his features distorted by a mixture of pain and hate, but before he could move, Dries's hand clamped around his throat to drag him away from March's prone body.

"Look what I found; the only Morgan I haven't killed yet." Dries growled, bringing Alex's face inches from his.

Alex spit in his face in response. Dries remained still for an instant, stunned or perhaps further enraged. He tucked away his gun and instead, in his hand, a switchblade clicked. "If you survive this, you're going to carry a message for me."

Alex jerked helplessly in his grip. "Fuck you!"

"I want you to tell Anies that from now on"—he brought the blade close to Alex's face—"it's an eye for an eye."

I tried to get on my feet to stop him. "Dries, don't!"

He couldn't hear me, not through his rage, and my body had never been heavier as I screamed for him to stop and tried to get up using only my right hand for support.

From where I sat, it looked like nothing more than a nick. A single flick of the blade across Alex's face. But the sudden splatter of blood, the inhumane scream that came from Alex . . . they shattered my insides like glass.

He curled into a ball, holding his face, continuously moaning. Dries didn't say a word, and all I could do was watch, in a state of shock, as he moved away, his revenge accomplished. Alex went quiet. He lay on his side, still in a fetal position, the occasional tremors shaking his body the only sign he was in fact alive.

Next to him, March was still clutching the wound on his side, his breath a low hiss. There was no strength left in me, only fear and horror. I just broke and sobbed. "Dries, help him! Please help him!"

Dries knelt by his favorite disciple. He reached for a small plastic packet inside his jacket, which he tore with his teeth. A syringe. Without further ado, he stabbed the needle in March's thigh. A low groan rose from his throat, and after a few seconds, he found the strength to take Dries's proffered hand. Dries helped him up, a sad smile on his lips. "No time to laze around, boy."

I didn't even know how March's legs could still carry him, but they did. I figured it had something to with whatever Dries had injected in his leg. With a final effort, I too managed to get back on my feet and immediately went to support his left side while Dries supported the right one.

I buried my face in his chest. "You're gonna be okay; we're almost there."

His hand squeezed my arm weakly, and he murmured, "Thank you, biscuit . . . thank you."

"You'll thank her later, in ways I refuse to think about. Now hurry up. Erwin's men are done up there, and I want us gone quickly."

As we progressed toward the escalator leading back to the dome's entrance hall, something weighed in my chest that I couldn't contain.

"Sabina is dead. What took you so long? We could have used your help a little earlier."

He drew a heavy sigh. "Poor girl."

"Dries, what were you doing?"

"Chasing ghosts. I can't believe I didn't recognize that sneaky piece of shit back in Venice," he mumbled, seemingly to himself.

"In Venice?" March ground out.

"The Georgian," Dries spat. "You wouldn't know him. That was years before you."

Against me, I felt March stiffen. He looked at Dries, and I think he wanted to say something, but all of a sudden, a sharp sound ricocheted in the mall. Dries fell to his knees with a shout of pain, taking us with him. "Son of a . . ."—he turned to me, and I saw a bloody spot growing fast on his knee—"Island, run! *Now!*"

Adrenaline exploded in my veins, revving my heart, but my feet were stuck in place. I couldn't leave. I couldn't. March shoved me forward, Dries's mysterious drug in his system the spark he needed to burn through his final reserves of energy. The second after, I couldn't believe it, but I was running toward the escalator, and so was he, his hand crushing mine, never letting go.

I heard another crack behind us. A bullet had just missed us. I panicked at the idea that Dries might be dead, but true to his command, I kept running. My entire being was focused on March's hand around mine as the escalators took us to the nearest sea-level exit in the mall.

New gunshots echoed, louder, closer, until something sliced my forearm. I fell forward, taking March with me. I screamed as we both tumbled down the stairs while the escalator kept running downward. Renewed pain tore through my knees and wrist, but I didn't care: all I could see was the bloodstain on March's shirt, growing wider by the second.

He was still holding on to me, his voice a barely audible rasp. "Biscuit . . . stay down; we're almost there."

Under my knees, the metal stairs slid away. We'd reached the sea level. We crawled past a bunch of tiki shops and hid behind one of them. March managed to get up on one knee and raised his gun in the direction the shots were coming from. His eye set on the sights, he hesitated. I couldn't see anyone, and the only thing I was truly focused on was the sticky red trail on the milky marble floor. New gunshots tore the air, coming from above us; Dries must have managed to move and was trying to get rid of the sniper too.

I saw it—a movement, or maybe just a reflection, a shadow on the wall. March did too. He struggled to his feet with a growl and shot once. After the burst, there was silence—seconds ticking one after another. Then a single shot.

March gasped and staggered backward. I clambered to my feet. There was a sound, something building in my throat, that wouldn't come out. A second red stain was growing fast on his chest. He reached toward me, his lips moving in a silent plea I couldn't understand. His breath was coming in choked pants, and he looked surprised, desperate. His hands dropped the gun. I lunged for him. I tried so hard, even as I could see him fall to the floor. I called him, begged in vain. In that moment, he was the most important thing, the *only* thing in my world, and I wasn't strong enough to protect him. I tore a large strip of red muslin from my dress and pressed it on his chest, powerless as more hot blood flowed from the second wound.

His eyes were open. He lay still on a crimson bed, and he wouldn't give up. He was looking at me, his right hand jerking to reach me. No, to reach . . . *past me?* I looked over my shoulder and glimpsed an anthracite sleeve, a suppressed sniper rifle. I shielded myself with my arms reflexively, but it only made it easier for my attacker to grab them. My sandals skated uselessly on the bloody floor. My heart was beating so loud and so fast that I wasn't sure the screams echoing in the deserted mall were mine. They were. The agony as they ripped through my throat told me so. I felt something pricking my neck, plunging into a vein, and the physical pain stopped. Everything stopped, in fact. My voice, my limbs.

I could see, hear, but my body no longer responded.

Over the suffocating horror, the din in my brain, a disconnected part of me noted that it was the first time I'd seen Stiles wearing a well-cut suit. There was the usual softness in his eyes as he reached inside my bustier to take Gerone's phone. Baby blue, like they say. His lips moved, but I didn't understand the words. He picked me up carefully.

I didn't want to go. I couldn't leave March, but around me, the dome was spinning, and Stiles was taking me away. Past the doors, into the crisp night air. Everything tilted and rolled; water lapped at the hull of a speedboat. I couldn't close my eyes, so I watched as he pressed his thumb to a fingerprint scanner on Gerone's phone.

There were other boats, but to me, they were just blurry, glimmering shapes at the edge of my vision. Voices moaned, shrieked, witnessed in horror as the first cracks appeared on the surface of the bubble. I couldn't blink away the tears rolling on my face. In a thunder of exploding glass and roaring waves, the Poseidon Dome was slowly collapsing, swallowed back by the dark waters of the Pacific.

March. Help me. Wake up. Come back!

Stiles touched my face, closed my eyes. I was lost in the void, his soft drawl the only thread left to hold on to.

"It's going to be all right. Try to sleep now. He's waiting for you."

THE SPOTLESS SERIES WILL REACH ITS CONCLUSION WITH BOOK #4,

TO BE RELEASED ON 5/12/17

Other books in the Spotless Series:

SPOTLESS
(Book #1)

BEATING RUBY
(Book #2)

BUTTERFLY IN AMBER
(Book #4)

Acknowledgements

This book could never have been made without the help of my fantastic editors, Tiffany Yates Martin and Lindsey Nelson, who put up countless hours of work trying to shape my incoherent rambling into a palatable manuscript.

Again, I would also like to thank Benoît, my husband, for his unrelenting support of my deplorable literary efforts, and for allowing me to use his beard trimmer to draw a half-finished cross in his chest hair. It gives no sign of growing back, which is a considerable source of concern for both of us, but still, what fun!

And most of all, thank you, my readers, for putting up with me. Many of you wrote me, stressing the necessity for March to bang Island hard: by now I'm sure you've come to understand that I feed from your tears.

ABOUT THE AUTHOR

Camilla Monk is a French native who grew up in a Franco-American family. After finishing her studies, she taught English and French in Tokyo before returning to France to work in advertising.

Today, she's a managing partner in a small ad agency, where her job is to handle all things web-related and make silly drawings on the white board when no one is looking. Her writing credits include the English resumes and cover letters of a great many French friends, and some essays as well. She's also the critically acclaimed author of a few passive aggressive notes pasted in her building's elevator.

Visit camillamonk.com
for more (questionably useful) information.

Made in the USA
Middletown, DE
04 October 2018